Praise for *False Mermaid*

"Pinpoint plotting and sure sense of place make this tale a winner."

—*Kirkus Reviews* (starred review)

"Outstanding. Many readers will find this passionate, complex novel almost impossible to put down."

—*Publishers Weekly*

"In Erin Hart's much-welcome third mystery . . . Irish music, myth, and history are integral to setting, character, and even plot. The reader will find herself almost believing, along with Elizabeth and Tríona, in the ancient stories of the selkies, humans on land and seals in the sea."

—*BookPage*

"Erin Hart infuses her lyrical romantic mystery with the myth of the selkie . . . [to] elegantly weave the nineteenth-century story of the disappearance of a fisherman's wife in County Donegal with the twentieth-century murder of her main character's sister in Saint Paul, Minnesota."

—*Milwaukee Journal Sentinel*

"Chilling reading. Hart nimbly intermingles the Minneapolis scenes with the Ireland scenario, bringing it all together for a bittersweet finale."

—*Open Letters Monthly*

"A complex, beautifully written gem of a book with a very satisfying ending."

—ILoveAMystery.com

"Hart combines her page-turning storytelling skills and deep knowledge of Ireland and Irish myth with a Minnesota setting close to her heart."

—TheIrishBookClub.com

Also by Erin Hart

Lake of Sorrows
Haunted Ground

False Mermaid

ERIN HART

SCRIBNER
New York London Toronto Sydney

Scribner
A Division of Simon & Schuster, Inc.
1230 Avenue of the Americas
New York, NY 10020

This book is a work of fiction. Names, characters, places, and incidents either are products of the author's imagination or are used fictitiously. Any resemblance to actual events or locales or persons, living or dead, is entirely coincidental.

First Scribner trade paperback edition March 2011

Manufactured in the United States of America

1 3 5 7 9 10 8 6 4 2

Library of Congress Control Number: 2009037969

ISBN 978-1-4165-6376-1
ISBN 978-1-4165-6377-8 (pbk)
ISBN 978-1-4165-6384-6 (ebook)

To my siblings
Julie, Amy, and Jere
and their mates
Colin, Panayiotis, and Sheri

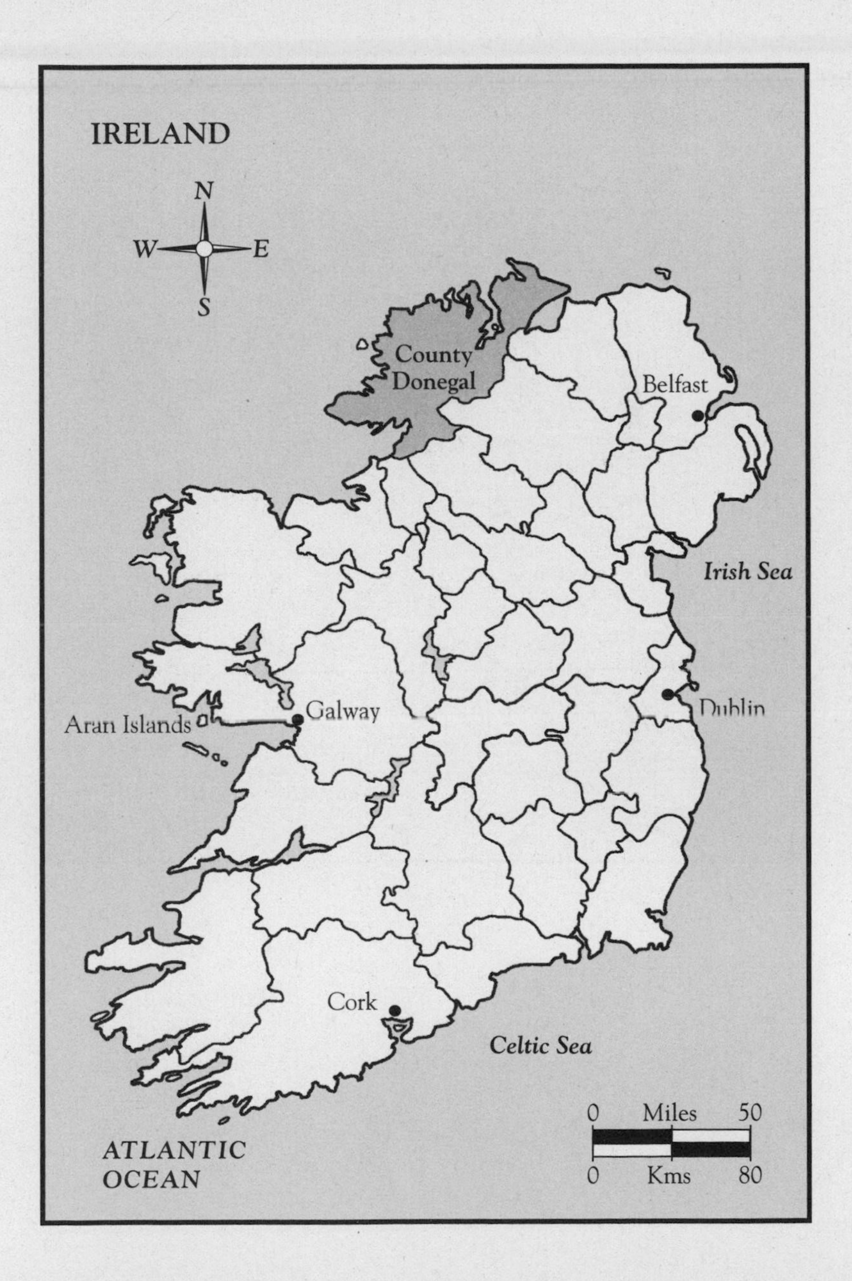

IRELAND
N
W
E
S
County
Donegal
Belfast
Irish Sea
Galway
Aran Islands
Dublin
Cork
Celtic Sea
0
Miles
50
0
Kms
80
ATLANTIC
OCEAN

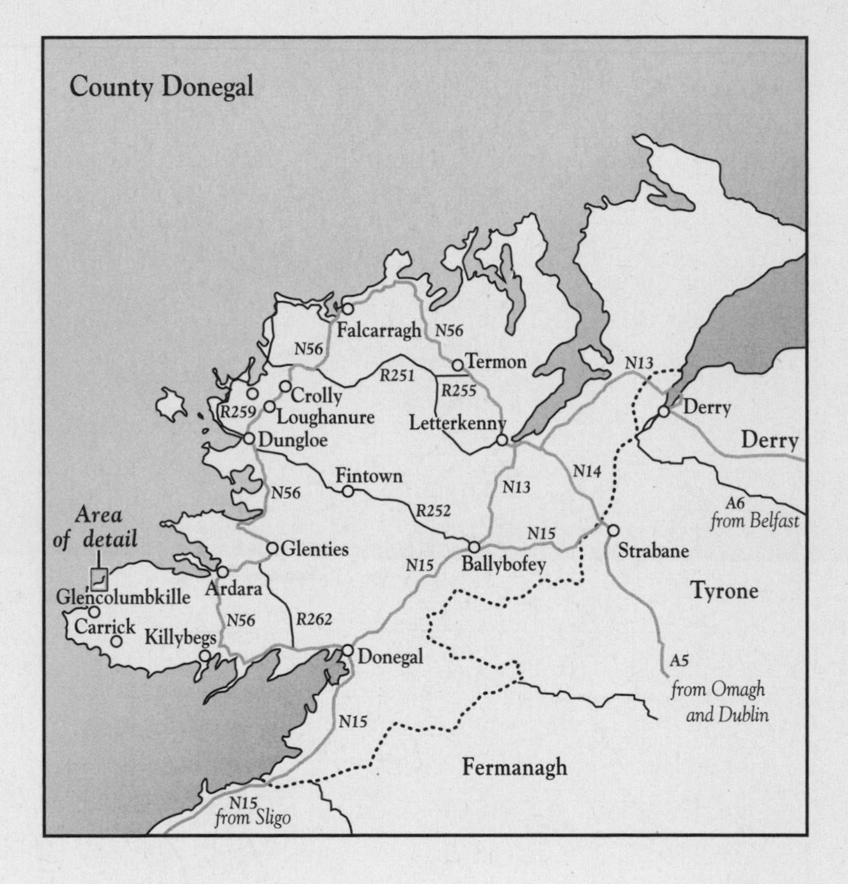
County Donegal
Falcarragh
N56
N56
Termon
R251
R255
Crolly
R259
Loughanure
Letterkenny
Dungloe
N13
Derry
Derry
N14
Fintown
N56
N13
A6
from Belfast
Area
of detail
R252
N15
Strabane
Glenties
N15
Ballybofey
Tyrone
Glencolumbkille
Ardara
Carrick
N56
R262
Killybegs
Donegal
A5
from Omagh
and Dublin
N15
Fermanagh
N15
from Sligo

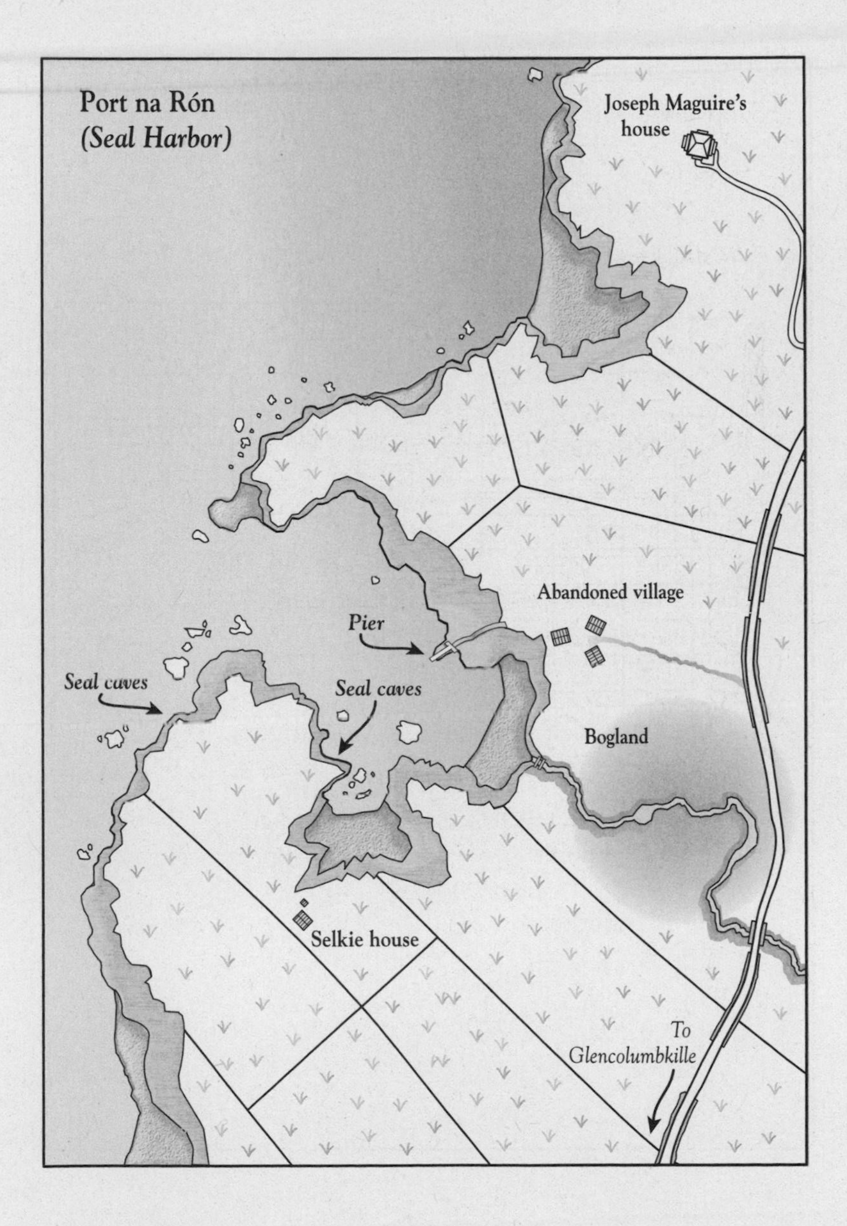
Port na Rón
(Seal Harbor)
Joseph Maguire's house
Abandoned village
Pier
Seal caves
Seal caves
Bogland
Selkie house
To Glencolumbkille

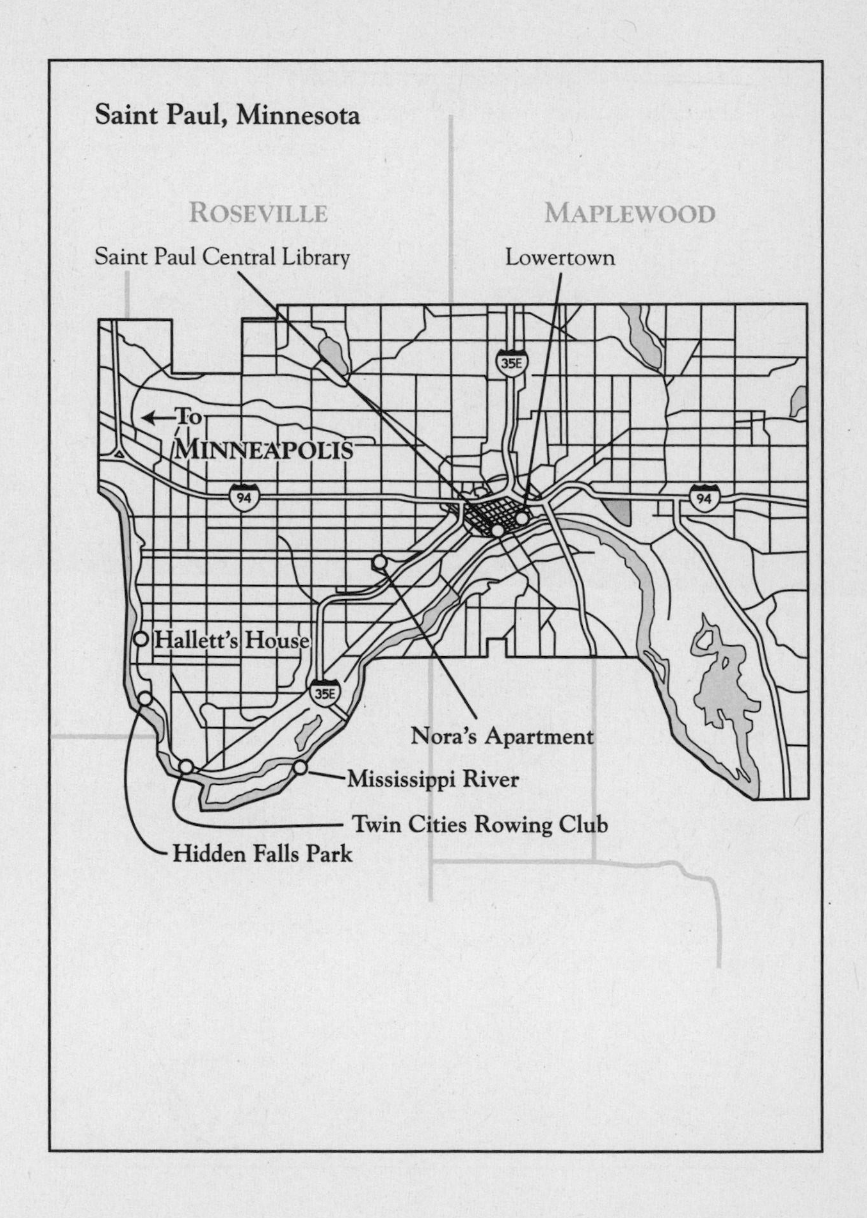
Saint Paul, Minnesota
ROSEVILLE
MAPLEWOOD
Saint Paul Central Library
Lowertown
35E
To
MINNEAPOLIS
94
94
Hallett's House
35E
Nora's Apartment
Mississippi River
Twin Cities Rowing Club
Hidden Falls Park

Tri rudan a thig gun iarraidh: an t-eagal, an t-euduch 's an gaol.
Three things come unbidden: fear, love, and jealousy.

—traditional Irish proverb

An Mhaighdean Mhara

Is cosúil gur mheath tú nó gur thréig tú an greann
Tá an sneachta go frasach fá bhéal na trá
Do chúl buí daite is do bhéilín sámh
Siúd chugaibh Mary hÉighnigh is í i ndiaidh an Éirne a shnámh.

"A mháithrín mhilis" dúirt Máire bhán
Fá bhruach an chladaigh is fá bhéal na trá
"Maighdean mhara mo mháithrín ard"
Siúd chugaibh Mary hÉighnigh is í i ndiaidh an Éirne a shnámh.

Tá mise tuirseach agus beidh go lá
Mo Mháire bhruinngheal is mo Phádraig bán
Ar bharr na dtonnta is fá bhéal na trá
Siúd chugaibh Mary hÉighnigh is í i ndiaidh an Éirne a shnámh.

Tá an oíche seo dorcha is tá an ghaoth i ndrochaird
Tá an tseisreach 'na seasamh isna spéarthaí go hard
Ach ar bharr na dtonnta is fá bhéal na trá
Siúd chugaibh Mary hÉighnigh is í i ndiaidh an Éirne a shnámh.

—amhrán traidisiúnta Gaeilge

The Mermaid

It seems you've faded away and abandoned the love of life
The snow is spread about at the mouth of the sea
Your yellow flowing hair and little gentle mouth
We give you Mary Heaney who has swum across the Erne.

"My faithful mother," said fair Mary
By the edge of the shore and the mouth of the sea
"A mermaid is my noble mother"
We give you Mary Heaney who has swum across the Erne.

I am tired and will be until dawn
My bright-breasted Mary and my blond Patrick
On top of the waves and by the mouth of the sea
We give you Mary Heaney who has swum across the Erne.

The night is dark and the wind is ill
The Plough can be seen high in the sky
But on top of the waves and by the mouth of the sea
We give you Mary Heaney who has swum across the Erne.

—traditional Irish song

Contents

Book One

MYSTERIOUS DISAPPEARANCE OF A YOUNG WOMAN

THE LAND OF THE BANSHEE AND THE POOKA

What would read as akin to the fairy romances of ancient times in Erin, is now the topic on all lips in the neighborhood of Ardara and Glencolumbkille. It appears that a young woman named Mary Heaney, wife of a local fisherman, living with her husband and two children in a fisherman's cottage in the townland of Port na Rón, disappeared on the evening of May the fourteenth, 1896, and has not since been heard of. Up to the present, notwithstanding the exertions of the police and numerous search parties, no account of her, live or dead, has been found.

One event did take place, which has produced all the sensation—the husband swore that the evening before his wife's disappearance he observed her speaking in a low voice to a wild creature—a seal—outside their cottage window.

There is a local superstition concerning seals who may change their skins at certain periods of their existence, sometimes coming ashore in human form. It is said amongst the local people that upon discovering the skin of such a creature, a 'selkie,' while it is in its human form, the person so doing becomes the master of that person or soul, until the creature may regain its own skin again. Of course at the evening firesides such wild stories of ghosts and fairies are devoured with an avidity that only a mysterious occurrence of this kind can produce. Possibly the appearance of the woman in the flesh, by-and-bye, may rob the case of all romance.

—*The Ballyshannon Herald,* 18 May, 1896

1

Death was close at hand, but the wounded creature leapt and twisted, desperate to escape. Seng Sotharith pulled his line taut and played the fish, sensing in the animal's erratic movements its furious refusal to give in. He would do the same, he thought—had done the same, when he was caught.

Sotharith sat on the crooked trunk of an enormous cottonwood that leaned out over the water and watched the river flow by. Sometimes as he sat here, suspended above the water, he whispered the words over and over again, intrigued by their strangeness on his tongue. *Minnesota. Mississippi.* He had been in America a long time—five years in California, and now nearly eight years with his cousin's family in Saint Paul, but still the music of the language eluded him.

High above on the bluffs, the noises of the city droned, but here he could shut them out. Sometimes on foggy mornings, he looked across the water and felt himself back in Cambodia. He saw houses on stilts, heard the shouts of his older brothers as they played and splashed in the river. The pictures never lasted long, dissipating quickly with the mist. Now the sun was rising behind him, gilding the leaves on the opposite bank. Soon he would have to scale the steep bluff and get to his job at the restaurant. All afternoon and evening, deaf to the shouts and noise of the kitchen, he would wash dishes, wrapped in his thoughts and in memories that billowed through his head like the clouds of steam that rose from the sinks.

He had once harbored a secret ambition to follow in his father's footsteps and become a doctor. Now, nearly forty years old, he knew it was far too late. But he was determined to learn English at least, to conquer its strange sounds and even stranger writing. It was the one way he could bring honor to his father's memory.

Sotharith concentrated on his fish, letting the creature run one last time before reeling it in. Coming here helped clear away the images from his dreams, the tangled arms and legs he stepped through every night, the expanse of skulls covering the ground like cobblestones.

When he first arrived in Saint Paul, his cousin had brought him to a doctor, a gray-haired woman with kind eyes. She asked him to speak about the bones, but he could not. No words would come. They all looked at him—his cousin, the interpreter, the doctor. She tried to tell him that he had nothing to worry about, that he was safe here in America. He repeated the English word inside his head: *safe*. No matter how many times he said it, the sound meant nothing to him. Sotharith only knew that he had to climb down to this riverbank as often as he could, to walk the woods and sandbars below the green canopy and hear the birds at first light.

His catch was finally tiring. Sotharith stood and edged his way down the cottonwood's broad trunk and landed the fish in the shallows beside its exposed and twisted roots. It was time to go. He gathered his sandals and the rest of his gear and headed to the place where he cleaned his fish, a pool in a marshy clearing just below the bluff.

When he reached the place, Sotharith took out his knife, giving the blade a few sharpening swipes against a small oval whetstone he kept in his pocket. The flash from the knife fell upon a bunch of red berries growing a few feet away. Sotharith set the knife aside and crawled toward the fruit that hung like tiny jewels, bright crimson against the dry leaves. He plucked one berry, biting into its sweet-and-bitter flesh, the taste of survival. Then he lifted the fish from the basket and cleaned it with a practiced hand, slitting open its pale belly and clearing the shiny, slippery viscera from between the ribs with one finger as he watched the light in its staring eyes go out.

The sun was barely up, but already the heat—and the smell—were almost overwhelming. They were being marched across a muddy field littered with bodies, and although he tried not to, he could not avoid stepping on them. The soldiers ahead stopped for some reason, and they heard voices raised in argument. Get down, *his father whispered suddenly.* Get down and be still. *He'd felt a hand pressing on his shoulder, and had done as his father commanded, slipping down between the still-warm bodies, and trying not to look into their unseeing eyes. He felt a cold, lifeless hand laid across his face, then heard the orders barked at his father and the others, and felt icy terror as they moved on without him. He did not make a sound. A few moments later he heard the soldiers call a halt. No shots followed, no shouting, just the distant, dull sound of blows and bodies falling, and a single faint cry, abruptly cut short. It hadn't taken long; by then the killing had become habit.*

Everything was less clear when he tried to remember what came after, how long he had lain among the dead, waiting for a chance to escape, or all the days and weeks he'd spent hiding in the jungle, catching rainwater as it fell from palm fronds, eating the fruit he could gather, insects and grubs he dug out of the ground, whatever he could find. Time lost all measure; it seemed that he had lived with the birds and the monkeys for years before the soldiers caught him and sent him to the camps. It had taken another kind of will to survive there.

Here in America, he had always felt the mark of death upon him, a stain where that cold hand had touched his face.

He washed the fish blood from his hands in the pool of spring water that rose up from the forest floor. After cleaning fish, he always took care to bury the entrails. He'd chosen this spot not just for the spring, but because the earth around it was soft—easy to dig. With one hand, he cleared away dead leaves; with the other, he picked up a broken branch to use as a tool. At first, the ground yielded easily, coming up in irregular clods. Then his makeshift hoe snagged on something. Rocking forward on his knees, he pulled harder, tugging the branch to one side and then the other, and felt the earth erupt beneath him as the object suddenly came loose. He tumbled backward, tasting a shower of rotting leaves and feeling dry branches snap under his weight. Sotharith raised himself on his elbows and looked down to see what he had unearthed.

On the ground between his feet rested a human skull, its cheekbones cracked and splintered, empty eyeholes staring. Sotharith could only stare back, not daring to breathe. Inside his chest, he felt a slow resurrection of the knowledge that he had carried within him for so long. There was no safe place, not even here. The killing fields were everywhere.

2

The elevator opened, and Nora Gavin peered out into a long, broad hallway. It was dimly lit, empty, and silent. She stepped off and felt the whoosh of closing doors behind her. No signs, nothing to tell her where to go. But this must be the place. Her footsteps sounded in hollow echoes against the tile, and she was acutely aware of passing through pools of light that fell from buzzing fluorescent fixtures.

Upon reaching the wide door at the end of the hall, she raised one hand to shade her eyes and peered through the window. In the glow of a single hanging light, a still, silent figure draped in white lay on a table in the middle of the room. A tangle of dark red hair fell from beneath the sheet. It was happening again. She backed away, pressing herself against the chilly tiles, unable to speak or move. The door began to swing open, and all at once a loud voice sounded close to her ear: "Ma'am, would you mind bringing your seat forward?"

She awakened with a start, still in the cold horror of the nightmare. It took her a moment to remember where she was—on a plane, headed from Ireland home to Saint Paul. She tried to take a breath, but her chest was still constricted with fear.

"Are you all right?" the flight attendant asked.

"Fine, thanks."

The woman's eyes held hers for a moment longer, until she felt obligated to say something more: "Bad dream."

The flight attendant nodded sympathetically and moved on. Nora sat up and pulled the blanket from her shoulders, raking both hands through her hair to make sure it wasn't sticking up in odd places. She must have been out for an hour or more. She had slept only fitfully the last few nights, probably the only reason she could nap on a plane—in broad daylight, too. It seemed like an age since she'd left her flat in Dublin, but that had only been the start of this strange, overlong day. Following the sun on its westward journey always felt like traveling back in time.

She scrubbed at her face with both hands, trying to erase the pictures that seemed to linger just behind her eyelids. Now that she was returning home, all the images she'd tried to push away these past three years were invading her waking thoughts and dreams once more. Strange—in all the times she'd had that awful dream, she had never made it inside the viewing room, never once lifted the sheet. And that was odd, because in real life, the nightmare hadn't stopped at the door.

She had not been alone. Flanked by two detectives, she had entered the viewing room sick with dread. A disembodied voice had asked: *Are you ready?* She remembered nodding once, knowing it was a lie. How could anyone be ready for what she was about to see?

When the morgue attendant pulled back the sheet she stood frozen, trying to make sense of the coil of red hair and the features so brutally disarranged. A strident chorus of denials echoed in her ears as the attendant gently lifted the body's right arm and turned the wrist to her, a reminder that she was here to check for identifying marks. What was the point, if this wasn't Tríona? It couldn't be.

Then she had seen it, a shape like a half-moon just below the wrist. There was no denying her sister had such a mark. The attendant moved down and lifted the sheet to reveal another small dark blot of pigment on the calf—yes, Tríona had something very like that as well, but still the voices shrilled—until he rounded the end of the table and gently turned up the sheet at the ankle to expose a small whitened zigzag scar. It was only then that the clamoring voices in her head were stilled. In the silence that followed, she reached out and placed one hand over the scar, remembering how she had been responsible for that particular distinguishing mark.

It had been a sweltering day in the heat of summer. Fifteen years old, and forced into a bike ride with her sister, she had deliberately taken a rough gravel path too difficult for ten-year-old Tríona to navigate. She remembered turning back at the sound of tires skidding in gravel, and how the oily bicycle chain had bitten so cruelly into her sister's ankle. How she'd gone into automatic mode, doing all the things she had learned in first-aid class—wrapping the wound, applying steady pressure—until the blood stopped. She remembered her satisfaction when her first aid worked. She had felt prepared for anything in that moment—anything, that is, except for the way Tríona looked at her. How could she have forgotten? That moment had altered everything, when she saw herself for the first time through her sister's eyes, and felt thoroughly ashamed.

Standing in the mortuary, she could feel that there was no pulse, no breath, no life at all beneath her hand, and still she could not let go.

Nora sat back and closed her eyes again. Today was five years to the day that Tríona had gone missing, nearly five years since her almost unrecognizable remains had turned up in an underground parking garage in the trunk of her own car. Nora knew she could not let herself be pulled back into the downward spiral that seemed to draw her in whenever she thought of Tríona's murder. Nightmares and flashbacks were not a good sign.

She reached into her pocket for the knot of green hazel Cormac Maguire had woven for her on their last evening together, at a place called Loughnabrone. Lake of Sorrows. A place where a number of people had died, where she had nearly lost her own life. She did not dwell on that thought. What she remembered most clearly from that awful day was the expression on Cormac's face when he saw her hands, her clothes covered in blood. And the relief that washed over his features when she said: *Not mine. It's not my blood.*

Swells of longing swept through her. It was just as she had feared that day out on the bog, that upon leaving Cormac she would start to see him everywhere. *Stop.* She was going to drive herself mad, thinking like this. And yet it was really because of him that she was on this plane, heading back home again. The time they'd spent together these last fourteen months made her question whether she'd done all she could for Tríona. Without Cormac, maybe she'd still be working away in Dublin, trying to avoid thinking about what had driven her there. But working beside him, she had been carried along into stories of people whose lives had ended in grief. They were all real to her, though she had become acquainted with them only in death. And most of all there was the red-haired girl, the *cailín rua,* that nameless, decapitated creature from the Irish boglands who had set everything back in motion. It was the *cailín rua* whose fierce and unending suit for justice had set Nora's own foot again on the path she never should have left. As deeply as she'd become involved in the stories of the bog people, whose stories she had helped to reconstruct, she had come to realize that they were all just stand-ins. Behind everything, it was Tríona's unfinished story that kept catching at her conscience, pulling her back into places she did not wish to go.

Cormac had not asked her to remain in Ireland. On the contrary, he said he understood why she had to make this trip—but how could he begin to understand, when there was so much she had deliberately kept from him? She had explained what happened to Tríona—the bare facts of the murder, at least—and confessed her suspicions about her brother-in-law, Peter Hallett. But the thought of spelling out all the rest of it—trying to find words to explain about the rift with her parents, about her young niece, Elizabeth, not to mention the harrowing dreams and doubts about her own grip on reality—all of that was more than she had been able to face in her evolving relationship with Cormac.

She must remember Elizabeth. How long would the innocence of childhood protect her, how long would it be before Elizabeth had to navigate the same minefields with her father that Tríona had tried to cross? No matter how many different ways Nora thought about the situation, it always came down to a final question: What was she prepared to sacrifice to see that tragedy did not repeat itself?

This time she would not fly away to Ireland when things got difficult—and they would get difficult; there was no point in deceiving herself. She felt the power of the jet engines only a few feet away, anticipating the dreadful roar they would make at touchdown, trying to reverse their own lethal momentum. She felt the last stomach-churning lift just before the huge wheels skidded onto the tarmac and understood that there was no reverse, no slowing down, no stopping now.

3

Rain was nothing new in Seattle. Usually it was just damp and misty, but today the clouds had begun to pile up in varying shades of black, letting down a hard rain all day long. Eleven-year-old Elizabeth Hallett slung her heavy backpack into the empty back seat in the yellow mini-bus, and sat down beside it, pushing the wet hair out of her face and watching the water streak against the windows, turned to shadowy mirrors by the strange mid-afternoon darkness. As she stared at her reflection—the high forehead, the sprinkling of freckles, the wavy red hair now plastered to her head and shoulders—she wondered what it was, exactly, that made people stare at her. To her own eyes, nothing stood out. But there must be something. She could see it in the way they looked at her. Maybe she should just learn to ignore it. Being different wasn't so terrible. It was just a fact, like having freckles or red hair.

It wasn't just the rainstorm that set this day apart. For the past week, she'd been going to day camp at the art museum downtown. Her dad's idea—probably just a way to keep her out from underfoot while he was busy. Today, her last day of camp, was also their last day in Seattle. Tomorrow she and her dad were moving back to Minnesota.

Elizabeth wasn't quite sure how she felt about that yet. The moving part might not be so bad—her grandparents lived in Saint Paul, and it was a long time since she'd seen them. It was the other part that made her feel strange, about her dad getting married again. Why did he have to get married? Weren't things all right as they were? When she thought about all that, it seemed like something was caught in her throat, and she couldn't seem to swallow. She should have known something was up when he started asking what she thought of Miranda. What was she supposed to say? She couldn't tell him the truth, so she just said something stupid about how pretty Miranda was. That wasn't a lie. But how could it not bother him when the look in Miranda's eyes didn't match her perfect, pasted-on smile? Elizabeth wondered why her dad didn't notice things like that. Maybe he couldn't see it.

Miranda was Uncle Marc's sister. Elizabeth had always thought of him as her uncle, even though they weren't really related—Marc was her dad's best friend. He would have been her uncle if he'd married Aunt Nora, but something had happened, grown-up stuff nobody would talk about. Now Marc was going to be her uncle anyway, sort of.

Miranda was already back at their old house in Saint Paul—working on the wedding trip, she said, like it was a real job or something. Miranda had a real job—an event planner, whatever that was—but she never seemed to work. She seemed to like hanging out at their house a lot more than working.

The ride out to the island took a while, and the rain had begun to diminish as the mini-bus wended its way through the island's curving roads and cul-de-sacs. When it pulled up beside their driveway, Elizabeth hopped out, hoping she could make it to the house before the rain started again. The driveway snaked from the main road along a crooked shoreline through spruce trees and white pines whose fallen needles made thick beds on either side of the road. Elizabeth felt the heavy backpack pounding against her as she tried to walk quickly.

A wild gust blew up and rain began to fall in sheets around her, pushing her forward, making it difficult to walk upright. She ducked under a pine tree to wait until the rain subsided. Among the books in her pack was one she had stolen from the public library two weeks ago. She had never stolen anything before and now felt pangs of conscience, remembering how her fingers had trembled as she removed the crinkly plastic jacket and substituted one of her own books instead. By the time the library figured it out, she would be gone. Of course they had library books in Saint Paul, but they might not have this one. She could not leave it behind.

She zipped open her backpack and took out the stolen book. *The Selkie's Child.* A picture book, really, meant for little kids. But she had come across it by accident in the returned book bin, and found the picture on the cover irresistible. The story told of a fisherman taking refuge on an island during a storm. The next morning, climbing on the rocks, he happened to catch sight of a beautiful fair-haired selkie as she was shedding her sealskin and taking human form. He fell in love with her, and made up his mind to steal her sealskin, which meant she could not return to the sea. He took her home with him, and for a while they were happy. They had a child, a boy named Dónal. As Dónal grew, he could see that his mother was troubled. For days on end, she would weep and stare out at the sea. Sometimes she would sing in a low voice, in a language he could not understand. He began to hear whispers in the village that his mother was one of the seal folk, and she wept because she was missing her own people in the Land Under Wave. One day Dónal found a bundle of sealskin in the rafters of their house, and showed it to his mother. He didn't understand the change that came over her. She snatched the bundle from his hands and disappeared over the sea rocks. When she didn't come home, Dónal and his father had bread and tea for their supper. His mother had been gone for a few weeks when Dónal thought he saw her, one stormy day, floating on the waves at the mouth of the sea. He could have sworn that she raised one hand, as if to wave good-bye, and then she disappeared. He called her name, and squinted against the wind, but no one was there. From that day until he was an old, old man, he swore he had seen his mother's bright head bobbing beyond the rocks at the edge of the sea.

Elizabeth closed the book and held it to her, aware of the new, slightly foreign tenderness of the skin beneath her clothes, wondering what it felt like to shed your outer shell and become something new. She didn't fully understand why she couldn't let go of this book; all she knew was that the words and pictures made her feel strange and sad, and that returning it to the library was out of the question.

From her refuge under the tree, she could see out into Useless Bay. Such sad names—Useless Bay, Deception Pass, Cape Disappointment—what were they looking for, the people who had put those names on the map? To her, this bay was anything but useless; at low tide, its beaches were studded with anemones, bright starfish, and sand dollars. She would miss the swirling patterns in the sand, the scuttling crabs and tiny freshwater streams and rivulets that trickled down from higher ground. She had studied the map of North America. Minnesota was as far from the ocean as you could get. Her dad said their house in Saint Paul was on the Mississippi River—but what good was that? A river wasn't at all the same.

Through a curtain of mist, she could see a small shape moving far out in the bay—a seal, floating on its back, tasting the raindrops. The same one that came nearly every day, watching from a distance as she walked the beachfront. Sometimes she waved, and the seal would raise a flipper or dip its head in greeting. At least that was how it seemed. Mostly they just looked at each other. She knew it was the same seal from the mark on its face, an irregular dark spot like a star that covered its missing eye. Once she had even waded out into the water, and the seal had come right up to her. But when she reached out her hand, it had turned and backed away. She liked to imagine there was a communication between them, the understanding of two silent creatures, alone together. She had resisted the urge to give it any sort of a name, preferring to think that it already had one—something strange and beautiful in its own language. Seals did have their own language; Elizabeth had heard them calling to each other. An ordinary human name might be a bit insulting. As the seal ducked under the water's surface, she felt an uncomfortable tightness in her throat. And suddenly her face felt hot, as she remembered an incident from earlier in the day. Normally she would have taken her lunch outside, but they'd been forced to stay inside the museum because of the rain. She was sitting alone—reading, as usual—when a group of girls walked by. Shelby Cooper and Nicole Buckley and some others. Girls like Shelby and Nicole and all their Crombie Zombie friends usually made a point of avoiding her, but today they'd been staring and whispering behind their hands. She had heard Shelby's hushed voice as they passed by: "No, it's true—I swear to God. Her mother is—"

The last word dropped to an inaudible whisper, and the girls moved closer together, covering their mouths and laughing nervously.

Nicole said: "If you don't believe us, we'll show you. It's all on the Internet."

Elizabeth knew her mother had been killed in a car accident when she was six. Why should that be some big secret? She felt a little sick, suddenly realizing that she didn't know anything about the accident. Nobody ever came right out and told her what had happened. All she remembered was a series of strange, endless days where conversation seemed to be taking place far above her head, hushed voices stopping abruptly whenever she came near. At one point, she overheard something about a car. If she asked when her mother was coming home, her father would just look pained and turn away. One thing she did remember distinctly was Aunt Nora taking her aside one day, asking if she understood that her mother was not coming home. If she knew what it meant when someone died. Elizabeth thought about the baby bird she and Nora had found on the sidewalk once. She asked whether it was like that, and Nora said it was. Elizabeth had nodded then, and said she did understand, but it was a lie. She hadn't understood anything at all. Any tears she had shed that day had been for the bird. She could still remember the downy softness of its breast, the wrinkled lids on the tiny eyes.

She couldn't even remember her mother's face anymore. In five years, the picture in her head had faded away until it was only a hazy impression, a shape without features. She did remember a few things: hiding in a closet, face pressed into clothes of rough wool and soft fur, the thrill of being discovered, gathered up and rocked by someone with a low voice, humming a tune that traveled through her bones. She remembered letting her fingers slide through long, smooth hair that smelled faintly of soap, drifting to sleep on whispered stories about fantastic creatures, half animal, half human. The stories themselves had mostly slipped away, but sometimes an unfamiliar word or the ghost of a scent could conjure up that strange mixture of sadness and contentment she had felt lying in bed and listening, fighting to stay awake.

Sometimes she could see her mother's face, but only when she was dreaming. One particular dream came over and over again. A bell would ring, and she would answer the door to find a red-haired stranger on the front steps of their house. Even though the face was unfamiliar, somehow she knew this smiling visitor was her mother. That's the way dreams were. Her mother would take her hand and walk with her down to a rocky beach, where they stepped into the water, wading out deeper and deeper, past floating seaweed and foam until the ground disappeared from under their feet and the waves pulled them under. Then came the big surprise: in dreams she could breathe as easily underwater as in the air above. It wasn't even cold. Of course she knew it was only a dream. But upon waking she felt half sick with longing, wishing it could be true.

Elizabeth stared out at the rain, filled with a slowly expanding anxiety about all the things she didn't understand. She had always felt as if other people saw and understood more than she did. They expected her to grasp things she hadn't quite figured out. And at that moment, a notion—vague and indistinct at first—began to open up and spread out inside her. What if everyone had been lying? What if there had been no car crash, and her mother had just gone away? That happened sometimes. Her mother might even have another family by now, a new family she liked better than the old one. Elizabeth lifted the edge of a scab on her knee and watched as a few bright drops of blood began to ooze from the exposed wound. It hurt a bit, but she couldn't seem to stop until she had removed the whole scab, exposing a patch of brand-new, bright pink skin beneath.

The violent cloudburst was over. She stood up and scanned the expanse of gray water in the bay, hoping for one last glimpse of her friend, but there was no sign of the dark, familiar shape. It was time to go.

4

It was late afternoon when Nora's rental car pulled up in front of an Edwardian foursquare on a crooked side street off Summit Avenue in Saint Paul. Before leaving Ireland, she'd found a furnished apartment to rent here, a former chauffeur's quarters tucked above a carriage house. The neighborhood was a maze of tree-lined boulevards atop the river bluffs, where nineteenth-century lumber barons and steamship magnates had spent their fortunes on extravagant homes. The carriage house happened to be only a few blocks from where her parents lived on Crocus Hill—easy walking distance. If only the breach between them could be bridged as easily as that.

Nora found the key hidden under a window box beside the carriage house door—exactly where the owner had said it would be. She unlocked the apartment door, venturing upstairs to look around before lugging in her bags. Standing on tiptoe, she could just glimpse the Mississippi river bluffs from the kitchen window. Wherever she went today, the river seemed to follow, lurking at the edge of her vision, never letting her forget its presence. Somewhere along that river was the place her sister had been murdered.

Tríona's body had been found in the trunk of her car in an underground parking garage downtown, but seeds and leaves combed from her hair at the postmortem said she'd most likely been attacked and killed in an area of black ash seepage swamp. The trouble was, there were hundreds of miles of black ash swamps along the Mississippi corridor. They'd never found the primary crime scene.

Sweat was trickling down Nora's back by the time she'd hauled everything up the winding stairs to the second-floor apartment. She flipped the switch on the ancient window air conditioner and heard it hum to life as she changed out of her travel clothes into a pair of shorts and a tank top. Three years in Ireland, and she'd forgotten how the Midwest summer felt against bare skin. She caught a glimpse of herself in the full-length mirror that stood in the corner and ventured closer to make an assessment. Although she was usually oblivious to her many flaws, they were now all she could see: the short, dark hair flattened from sleeping on the plane, eyes too large in the pale face scattered with freckles, mouth set in grim determination. She'd lost weight in the past few weeks. The pallor of her limbs was suited to the Irish climate but looked positively unhealthy here. Nora examined her face in the mirror. *I wasn't always like this.* Where was the person she had been before, the one who could think straight, who could laugh and feel joy—could feel something, anything, besides this terrible hollowness? She spoke silently to the strange, melancholy creature who stared out at her from the mirror. *Where is she? What the hell have you done with her?* She had to fight a sudden urge to smash the glass. Not a mirror's fault what it reflected.

She turned away and started to survey her new surroundings: windows on three sides of the sitting room, including a deep window seat on either side and an arched triptych of leaded glass at the gable. The sitting-room furniture was a hodgepodge of different styles, definitely secondhand, but comfortable enough: there was a full-sized spindle bed covered in a handmade quilt, a cane rocking chair and upholstered love seat, a small oak desk. The sloping walls were covered in ornately patterned wallpaper, the kind that might play tricks on you in the dark. The place was certainly sufficient; she wasn't here for luxury. But it was time to rearrange. If she was going to act the detective, she might as well let this space play its corresponding role as incident room. She pulled the bed away from the center wall, repositioning it under the eaves. Then she returned to the wall and ran a hand over the smooth, papered surface. It would do as a bulletin board—any damage could be dealt with later.

Her second suitcase still stood in the middle of the floor. Inside were the files and papers she'd collected for the past five years, all the evidence and leads in the case, all the abandoned theories and blind alleys she had traveled down. The contents of the suitcase must have shifted in transit; as she began to unzip it, an avalanche of paper spilled across the floor. Sifting through the mixed-up files—autopsy reports, notes on physical evidence, search inventories, photographs, interview notes—she thought about the wasted effort these files represented. For two years after the murder, she'd spent nearly every waking hour trying to find enough evidence to put Tríona's killer away. And she had failed. Seeing all the familiar, dog-eared corners, feeling the well-worn softness of every file, she was nearly overcome with despair, knowing there was nothing new inside them, nothing to tip the scales one way or the other. Every index card, every photograph, every scrap of paper had a dozen or more holes in it from being tacked up to walls, first here, and then in Ireland. It occurred to her, and not for the first time, that she had just been rearranging the pieces, trying different configurations, hoping that a recognizable pattern might begin to emerge. But if some major piece of the puzzle was missing, she could rearrange these things all she liked and the picture would never come clear. From the edge of the pile, she unearthed the ragged, taped-together city map she had carried to Ireland and back, tacking it up on the wall and once again marking important locations with red pushpins: Peter and Tríona's house along the River Road, her parents' place on Crocus Hill, the house she had shared with Marc Staunton across the river in Mendota, the sites she had scoured for evidence along the river, the library where Tríona had been spotted in the hours before the murder, and finally, the parking garage in Lowertown, where her sister's body had been discovered.

She fished out and unrolled the timeline she'd begun five years ago, marking out the days and hours between the established facts, the documented events in the final week of Tríona's life. Some of the handwriting was hardly recognizable as her own. As she glanced at the place where the solid red line representing her sister's earthly existence came to an abrupt end, Nora realized she could never look at this piece of paper again without being reminded that her own life, similarly represented, would reach the edge of the paper and beyond. What exactly did she have to show for her continued survival? Since Tríona's death, so much in her life had spiraled downward and ended in failure: her once-bright teaching career, her relationship with Marc Staunton, even the closeness she'd always had with her parents—all gone. She'd been away from Ireland less than twenty-four hours, and already her whole life there seemed like a distant dream. How had she let herself believe that time with Cormac had been real? It seemed such a long time ago now, though it had been barely three days since she'd awakened beside him. She stooped to pick up a bundle of photographs that had fallen on the floor. Ireland had been a temporary respite, and now it was over. Time to wake up, get back to reality.

She took apart the bundle of photos and began tacking images of Tríona to the wall: first, the close-up of a toddler with red corkscrew curls, dressed in overalls and a pair of homemade fairy wings, then a gawky ten-year-old straddling a bike and squinting into the sun—and, finally, the grown-up Tríona, in profile against the rocks and trees of Lake Superior's North Shore. She kept these pictures together because they came the closest to capturing that rare quality her sister always had—she remembered looking into those eyes, even before Tríona could speak, and grasping the fact that there was a fully developed consciousness in there.

That Tríona had actually loved Peter Hallett, Nora had no doubt. He'd probably never deserved it. But what would the world be if people loved only those who were deserving? She often wondered what had been set in motion the first time Peter Hallett laid eyes on her sister. People talked about chemistry, and some of what people considered chemistry was actually measurable—pheromone levels, synaptic activity, pupil size. But those were just the observable responses surrounding the original glimmer of attraction, just as the songs and poems that tried to delimit love were not the thing itself. And what of the end of love? Sometimes it seemed to reverse itself in an instant. Perhaps it was not chemistry after all, but more akin to a magnetic charge, a force of nature that could bring people together and just as strongly repel them. Was that what had happened with Peter and Tríona?

The very next picture in Nora's bundle was of Peter Hallett himself. Every detail of his appearance was exquisite: the thick, wavy black hair, full lips so prominent in the lean face, the eyes that could vary from deep aquamarine to cobalt, depending on the light. For some reason, it was always the word "beautiful" rather than "handsome" that sprang to mind when she looked at him. Always something subtly ambiguous about his sexuality, which somehow seemed to magnify its power. His gaze conveyed a blend of sensuality and self-assurance, tempered perhaps with a touch of wariness, a hint of vulnerability. There was something restless and impulsive about him, something dangerous and mysterious and mercurial—all qualities not unlike those of the theater directors and other creative types to whom Tríona had ever been drawn. One glance from those blue eyes could make you feel extraordinary, adored. Without warning, Nora was jolted back to the day she'd met Peter Hallett.

It was only about six months after she'd started seeing Marc Staunton, a fellow med student. Marc had been in excellent spirits that evening, pouring them each a glass of wine before they were off to dinner and then to the opening night of *The Winter's Tale*. Tríona was starting to show real promise as a professional actress. She'd caught some critical attention for roles at smaller theater companies, and had just been cast as Hermione, her first major Shakespearean lead at the flagship regional house. It was a very big deal. Nora remembered feeling jittery with anticipation. Marc said: "You'll never guess who called me today, out of the blue—my old college roommate. He's just back from living in Europe, thinking of setting up shop here as an architect. I told him we might be able to swing an extra ticket tonight, introduce him around a bit. I hope you don't mind."

"Why should I mind? I'm sure we can finagle something. What's he like?"

"All right, I suppose—if you go in for charming, talented, unbelievably good-looking people. He's always been like that—a little *too* extraordinary. You want to hate him, but it's not possible." Marc hesitated. "You know, on second thought, maybe I should call the whole thing off, tell him I couldn't score the extra ticket."

"Relax—he's probably fat and bald by now."

Marc shook his head. "Nora, Nora, Nora. You don't seem to comprehend the sort of person we're talking about. It's all right—you'll understand when you meet him."

Even with that forewarning, she was not prepared for the dazzling, dark-haired stranger who approached her in the theater lobby. He took her hand with a flourish, and pressed it to his lips.

"Nora—Marc's description didn't do you justice." He must have seen them come in together.

She was genuinely flustered, not only by the suddenness of Peter Hallett's approach and the oddly antiquated gesture, but also by the intense blue eyes that locked onto hers with a mixture of curiosity, playfulness, and frank sexual appraisal. The memory of that first encounter made her blush, even now.

"Unhand her, you rotten bastard," Marc said, approaching from behind and clapping his friend on the back. "God, you haven't changed a bit. I turn my head for half a second, and there you are, worming your way into my place—" In that fraction of a second, Nora wondered what the little exchange revealed about their relationship as roommates. Despite the mock jealousy, it was clear that Marc was enjoying himself.

But as soon as the curtain rose and Peter Hallett set eyes on her sister, all idle flirtation with Nora and anyone else abruptly ceased. How perfectly still Tríona had stood in that shaft of light at the play's closing scene. How strange and magical she had seemed—the wronged wife turned by her grief into stone. Nora had often found herself wondering whether Peter Hallett had been attracted to the flesh-and-blood Tríona that night or to her character, Hermione. Whatever the answer to that question, his pursuit of Tríona had been relentless, full press from the beginning, and he had not stopped until he possessed her. His campaign had begun at the opening-night party after the show, when he stole a bottle of champagne from the servers and followed Tríona around all night, ready whenever her glass was low.

Later, as they stood at the mirror in the ladies' room, Nora had ventured an aside: "I think Marc's friend likes you."

Tríona stared absently at her own reflection. "Who are you talking about?"

"The guy who's been following you around all night—Marc's friend, Peter Hallett."

"Oh—right." Tríona concentrated on something in the corner of her eye. "The stalker."

"Something wrong with him?"

"I really can't say, Nora. I only just met the man. He's a little *too* good-looking, don't you think?"

Was it tragic, or merely ironic, to be written off as too good-looking by someone whose own appearance had made passersby walk into doors and lampposts? Nora had actually witnessed such occurrences, sad to say, on more than one occasion. To her credit, Tríona never had any idea about how her exterior affected people. Perhaps it was growing into beauty after an ugly-duckling childhood that made her so infuriatingly oblivious. And maybe it was that very indifference that piqued Peter Hallett's interest; maybe he couldn't resist a challenge. He could have simply toyed with Tríona and cast her aside—but it didn't happen that way. He was the one who pressed for marriage, for children. Tríona had always expressed ambivalence about both, but for some reason she went along with Peter Hallett. Eventually, every one of them had fallen under his spell. Some were caught in it still.

Nora told herself she shouldn't have been so surprised when her parents stood by him after Tríona's murder. They were quintessentially decent people, and Peter knew exactly how to play that against them. Her father, especially, had always been uncomfortable outside the realm of fact; he was mistrustful of secondhand information, of shadowy suspicions and feelings. Tom Gavin was a scientist, after all, someone who lived in a world shaped and defined by demonstrable proof, so how could he possibly condemn anyone without hard evidence? He had no choice but to believe that Tríona's death was a random crime. Nora had seen flashes of doubt in her mother's eyes, but Eleanor Gavin was possessed of an inborn pragmatism that would not let her risk alienating the one person who controlled access to her only grandchild. It was impossible to fault them, and impossible not to. Nora and her parents had lived the past five years in a state of artificial suspension, never speaking about Peter, never speaking about Tríona—barely speaking at all.

It wasn't that she hadn't tried. She had gone to them right after Tríona was killed, trying desperately to convince them that Peter was responsible. They had refused to believe her. And they weren't alone—everyone who knew Peter Hallett thought she was certifiable. After all, what had she seen, exactly? Nothing obvious. Only tiny nuances, accumulations of behavior: a certain glint in Peter's eye when he looked at Tríona, the faintly proprietary way he touched her. But whenever Nora tried to describe the things she'd witnessed, all those formless, nagging suspicions seemed to scatter, like so many slithering spheres of mercury. So she tried to ignore them, push them away. How could anyone fathom the intimate connection between two people from the outside? Again and again, she had to convince herself that whatever went on in Tríona's marriage, it was none of her business. Until that night—

Nora stared at the picture in her hand, carried back once more, this time to a splendid May evening, the first warm night of burgeoning spring just five years ago. The trees along the river were beginning to leaf out in earnest, branches decked in shades of pale green. She had arrived at Peter and Tríona's house just after five, to stay with her niece while they were off to the gala opening of his latest triumph, a gleaming new modern art museum in downtown Minneapolis. Elizabeth was supposed to go along, but she'd come down with a fever. Tríona had wavered about going out at all, but the museum was an important milestone for Peter's firm, and he'd insisted on having his muse beside him. No excuses. A car would be arriving for them at six.

Tríona answered the door a little out of breath. "Oh good, you're early. Sorry the house is such a disaster. I'm late for my half-hour call, as usual." Tríona waved a hand as she bolted down the hall. "Why don't you go in and talk to Lizzabet while I finish getting ready?" She seemed a little more distracted than usual, clasping a silky robe around her, trying to tidy up toys and clothes that were strewn about. The place wasn't usually such a mess. Nora thought she detected an extra glassiness in Tríona's eyes, almost as if she'd been drinking.

Despite her fever, Elizabeth had Nora deep into negotiations about snacks and bedtime stories when Tríona came in to say good-bye. Though less than forty minutes had passed, her transformation from harried young mother to goddess was complete. Tríona had never looked more radiant. Her long red hair hung loose as she whirled before them in clingy, beaded silk that shifted from pale sea green at the shoulders to deepest indigo about her feet. At her throat hung a stunning mother-of-pearl pendant, set off by a wrap of some translucent fiber that seemed to have been spun from water and air. Her eyes glittered more intensely than before, and her limbs seemed to float. Elizabeth sat up in bed, wide-eyed and bright with excitement on top of fever. "Oh, Mama—you're like the queen of the sea!"

They'd all laughed as Tríona spun around once more, careful not to lose her balance.

Peter's voice carried from downstairs: "It's time to go."

"You can have a little ginger ale, and if you're very good, maybe Nora will make some popcorn. I'm sorry to leave you—" She leaned down to kiss the top of Elizabeth's head. "Wish me luck."

They listened to the wonderful silk dress rustling all the way down the hall.

Nora had thought nothing at all of Tríona's last remark. But a few minutes later, after venturing down to the kitchen to microwave some popcorn, she heard strange sounds coming through the intercom beside the front door. Ragged breathing, almost like a violent struggle—what was happening? Pressing an eye to the peephole, she saw Tríona pressed against the wall outside, back arched and eyes closed, fingers twined through Peter's dark hair. Her bare legs cinched his waist as he thrust himself again and again into the billow of beaded silk that rode around her hips. Was he hurting her? When a car pulled into the driveway, it was Tríona who held tight, panting, "No—don't stop! Don't you fucking dare stop now."

Nora had clapped both hands over the peephole, rigid with shock as the ragged breathing on the other side of the door continued just a few seconds longer. Then the intercom speaker suddenly went dead, and in the same instant, the smoke alarm in the kitchen began sounding a piercing protest. The microwave was filled with smoke that burned her eyes and throat as she opened the door. She felt her way to the switch for the exhaust, and eventually managed to stop the shrieking alarm by flapping a towel beneath it. Once the noise was quelled, she emptied the scorched popcorn into a glass bowl, trying to regain her composure, when a small voice sounded from the doorway behind her.

"Nora? Where did you go?"

She spun around, startled, watching the bowl as it flew in slow motion. Clear glass and burnt popcorn seemed to explode everywhere, and in the brief, dead silence that followed, Elizabeth covered her ears and began to whimper.

"It's all right, love, stay right where you are. It wasn't your fault—I was just clumsy. Everything's going to be all right."

She never told anyone what she had witnessed that night. Not the police, and certainly not her parents. Looking back now, the paranoid part of her couldn't be sure that Peter hadn't staged the whole thing for her benefit. She pushed the thought away, telling herself it was a crazy idea. He couldn't possibly have known she was there, on the other side of the door. He couldn't have made Tríona behave that way—could he? And yet she was positive about one tiny detail—the hand she had seen pressed against the intercom definitely belonged to Peter Hallett.

The next troubling tilt of the seesaw came only a few weeks later, with Tríona's final phone call. Nora had relived every word of their conversation, heard it in her head every day for the past five years.

"Nora—I'm sorry to wake you."

"It's all right, Tríona, I'm awake." She sat up and looked over at the numbers glowing from the bedside table: 10:23 P.M.

"Is Marc there?"

"No, he's on call—down at the hospital. What's happening, Tríona?" Fear rose in her throat. "Is Elizabeth all right?"

"I sent her off for the weekend with Mammy and Daddy. I'm at their house now."

"Something's happened—what is it?" There was silence on the other end. "Tríona?"

"I'm leaving, Nora. I've got a bag packed. Can you meet me? Not your house, someplace else. You can't tell anyone where I am—promise me."

"I promise." Still groggy from sleep, Nora seized upon the first place that came to mind. "What about l'Étoile?" The grand old hotel was a Saint Paul landmark. "I can be there in twenty minutes."

"I need more time. There's something I have to do first. There are things you don't know, Nora. About Peter, about me—"

"Tríona, what are you talking about?"

"It seemed harmless at first, but now—I let everything go too far. It's like he gets a strange sort of pleasure from hurting me. I couldn't tell anyone, I was too ashamed. Because I've done things, too. You don't know—unspeakable things. I've lied and deceived everyone. I don't even know myself anymore—"

"If he's hurt you, Tríona—"

"I can't even tell what's real anymore and what isn't—I feel like I'm going crazy."

"You're not crazy, Tríona—you're not. Listen to me—whatever it is, I will help you. We'll get through this together, all right? Do you hear me?"

"I can't talk anymore. I've got to find the truth."

In the brief pause that followed, Nora heard her sister breathing at the other end of the connection. "Tríona, are you still there? Talk to me."

When Tríona did speak, her voice was a hoarse whisper. "Isn't it shocking, what you'll do when you love someone?"

How many times in the last five years had she relived that fatal night? Pacing up and down the hotel lobby under the watchful eye of the night desk clerk. She had tried calling Tríona's cell phone, but was diverted each time into voice mail. Two hours went by, then three, then four. At first light, Tríona had still not appeared. Unable to wait any longer, she had driven to the house along the river. Peter had looked genuinely surprised when he answered the door. It was just after eight on a Saturday morning, and he'd already been for a run, showered, and dressed. His hair was unusually wet, dripping onto the collar of his shirt—for some reason, that point had stuck. So had the fact that he stood blocking the door so she couldn't see into the foyer.

"Where's Tríona?" she had asked. "What have you done with her?"

He drew back slightly. "What have I done with her?"

"Is she here?"

"No, she said something yesterday about going for a massage—"

"At this hour?"

"Why not? I assumed she left while I was out for a run. You're acting strange, Nora. Is something wrong?"

"I don't know, Peter. You tell me."

It was impossible to explain what she had seen in his eyes at that instant. No worry, no puzzlement. He was an island of calm and self-possession in the eye of a storm. He said: "I'll leave a note, ask her to call when she gets home."

Nora had often relived that conversation, imagining Tríona's packed bag just out of sight in the front hall, the ghost of her scent still in the air, and somewhere deeper, behind closed doors, a swirl of pink-tinged water sluicing down a shower drain.

The whispering campaign had started almost immediately. A very efficient apparatus, the rumor mill, to anyone who knew how to operate its machinery. And Peter Hallett knew exactly how. In the days after Tríona's death, people who'd been at the museum opening a few weeks earlier began to talk about her steady consumption of champagne. Nora realized she hadn't been alone in her assessment. Something about Tríona had clearly been off that night; she hadn't been herself. The glittering eyes, that strange note in her voice over the intercom. When the police found a bottle of liquid ecstasy in Tríona's purse after her death, and as additional bottles of the stuff turned up hidden around the Halletts' house, even uglier rumors began to surface. Some people were no doubt relieved to find the perfect couple were not so perfect after all. Everyone—including people who didn't know Tríona—had pet theories about what had gone wrong in the marriage and who was to blame. A kind of protective wall had sprung up around the grieving widower.

Of course Nora told the police about Tríona's final phone call. But in the end it came down to her word against Peter's. It wasn't as if the police didn't want to believe her; the truth of the matter was that they had no other viable suspects. But without Tríona to back her up, without physical evidence, that last phone conversation had been rendered useless, reduced to hearsay. All Peter had to do was deny, which he had done, quite convincingly. And so the case had remained in limbo, with no new leads, for five long years. To those who only knew Peter Hallett's public side, the notion that he was even capable of such a brutal murder seemed ludicrous. How easy it was to deny a shadow that came to life only in private, in that secret, intimate space between two people. Nora looked down at the photograph in her hand. He must have made some mistake. There must be something she could do or say to trap that warped creature who lived inside him. Perhaps the worst of it was that he actually enjoyed the cat-and-mouse aspect of his ghastly game. What would happen if she refused to play the mouse any longer? Holding the snapshot against the wall, she reached for a red pushpin and stuck the sharp point through Peter Hallett's handsome forehead.

5

Elizabeth let herself into the house and ran straight up to her room to stow her backpack. She peeled off her wet clothes and put on a dry pair of jeans and her favorite shirt. No sign of the movers—maybe she had it wrong and the moving men weren't coming until tomorrow. It wasn't like they really needed movers anyway. The house in Saint Paul still had all the old things inside—everything they would need, her dad said. She could just move back into her old room. It felt a little weird, to know the old house had been there all this time, waiting for them to come back.

As she toweled the rain from her hair, Elizabeth's eyes flickered across the broad flat glass of her fish tank. She felt reassured by the familiar and silent presence of the fish, swimming in their underwater world. What would happen to them during the move? Maybe the moving company had a special way to transport fish. Her dad had told her not to worry about them, but she couldn't help it. She sprinkled a few flakes onto the water and stood watching them nibble at their food, darting to the surface, then back to the bottom again.

She was almost all the way downstairs before she sensed the stillness in the house. Her dad should be here. Something wasn't right. She jumped down the last few stairs and pushed open the kitchen door.

"Daddy?" No answer. Elizabeth crossed to the phone and began dialing her father's cell number. Then she hesitated. There was no real emergency. She was old enough to be on her own awhile. She set the phone down, and looked around the kitchen. The cabinets and stainless appliances gleamed dully in the late-afternoon gloom. Despite the recent storm, the sky was growing blacker. And at that instant, a notion began to twine around her brain.

Why couldn't she just find her mother on the Internet, like Shelby and Nicole had done? The thought hadn't occurred to her before. She didn't exactly live on the computer like most kids. Wasn't even allowed to use the Internet without her dad looking over her shoulder. Too many weirdos out there, he said.

She climbed the stairs and crept down the long hallway to her father's office. Her legs felt cold and heavy, and her heart thudded against her ribs. The office had a glass wall facing into the trees, a computer desk, and a drawing table with its grid of cubbyholes underneath. Switching on the laptop, she sank into her father's chair as the screen glowed to life. A sudden desire to know grappled with a never far-distant fear. Maybe no one had lied to her; maybe they hadn't had to lie, because she had never asked.

Elizabeth steered the pointer toward a small box and typed in "Tríona Hallett." There wasn't much time—her dad might be back any minute. She had read about Pandora, and knew that hitting the button might be like opening that magic box. It could change everything. Her insides felt queasy and uncertain. Her mother's name—a few small black shapes on a white background—hung before her. She remembered the whispers and stares, and realized she had never wanted to step across this threshold. All these years she'd been covering her ears, trying to stop the voices that were telling her what really happened. Now the knowledge lay before her, just within reach, and she felt herself unable to resist. She pressed the button, and in the space of a single heartbeat more than a hundred results turned up on the screen before her. Halfway down, one headline stood out:

> **POLICE HAVE DOUBTS IN HALLETT SLAYING**
> Two years after the high-profile murder of Tríona Hallett, Saint Paul homicide investigators are concerned that they may never solve the case—despite the fact that the victim's husband remains the primary person of interest. But insufficient evidence linking Peter Hallett to the crime has police worried that they may never crack the case.

Elizabeth felt the world around her begin to dissolve. The wind stirred leaves outside the window as she sat dry-eyed at her father's desk, opening window after glowing window like the pages of a forbidden book. The letters seemed to shimmer on the page, turning from black to silver, and back again. Each word was a sharp hook, dragging her deeper against her will, but she could not look away. There had been a car, but what happened to her mother was no accident. She began to hear a noise inside her head, a sound like someone crying. She sank deeper into the chair and began to rock slowly, covering her mouth with both hands.

She had asked her dad once why Nora never came to visit. They lived far away now, he said, and Nora was busy with her own work—too busy to visit them, he seemed to be saying. Even at the time, she had known it wasn't true. Now she understood—it was because Nora knew. She knew about all the things that came swimming back to Elizabeth now from dim, distant memory. Why Mama sat and cried sometimes when she thought no one was around. How she slept and slept and wouldn't wake up. A hazy memory of Mama sitting on the couch, the round globe of a wineglass in her hand, dark red liquid sloshing dangerously close to the rim. Elizabeth remembered feeling a terrible, rising dread in case Mama would let the glass tip too far and spill on the white carpet.

A sudden noise sounded down the hall, and her father's voice came booming up the stairs. "Elizabeth—are you home?"

Elizabeth heard her own heart pumping noisily in her ears. She abruptly switched off the computer, and in her haste knocked over a pencil cup, feeling clumsy as she tried to gather up rolling pens and pencils. Her father liked everything a certain way—were the points supposed to go up or down? No time to think. She shoved the whole handful into the cup, points upward, hoping her memory was right. He couldn't know she had been here.

She tiptoed to the office door and peered out into the hallway. Hearing water running in the kitchen, she knew it was her chance to scurry down the hall. Once inside her own room, she pressed her back against the wall and tried to breathe. Beneath the panic, she felt something at the center of her chest squeezing to a cinder, shrinking smaller and smaller until it was no more than a dark, glinting lump of stone.

6

Cormac kept his foot on the accelerator, determined to make it to his evening lookout before the light was gone. The road up to the cliffs at Bunglas seemed harmless enough at the park entrance, just a cattle grid and a gate across the road outside Teelin. But here, only a quarter mile farther along, the incline was so steep that at times the car seemed to be climbing into empty space. This was his third visit in three days. If anyone had asked why he felt compelled to come here every evening, to sit on the cliffs and stare out over the North Atlantic, he could not have put the reason into words. It was just as well that no one asked.

He pulled into the car park and switched off the engine. Not many visitors stayed into the evening. Beside him, a narrow gravel path led up to One Man's Pass, a treacherous trackway above the highest sea cliffs in Europe. Slieve League, the maps named this place. But the locals called it Bunglas—green bottom in Irish—maybe for the grass that grew on its almost vertical slopes. He could see two tiny figures at the top of the ridge, nearly two thousand feet above the sea. What were they thinking, hiking all the way up there at this time of day? The light would soon be gone, and it wouldn't be safe. They must be mad, people who went climbing here for pleasure. Letting his gaze travel down the sloping cliff face, he stepped to the edge and stopped for a moment to watch the blue-green tide boiling around the Devil's Chair and Writing Desk, a couple of rough crags hundreds of feet below. The person who had bestowed the name had no doubt taken one look at the dizzying height and felt a need to invoke the most extreme fall from grace.

The wind was fresh out of the west, and the sun loomed orange behind a bank of clouds at the horizon. He set off the opposite way from One Man's Pass, in the direction of a tower that looked out over the small bay's southern cusp. Above him, their nesting grounds disturbed by the hikers, gray fulmars and red-billed choughs rode the wind in great wide circles. Below, in the sun-gilded waves, several seals made their way to shore for the night.

The dilemma he faced nagged at him again this evening, as it had done every minute since he'd arrived in Donegal. He'd been here three full days now, and still hadn't managed to tell Nora what was really going on—with his father, with himself. They'd spoken on the phone as recently as yesterday evening while she was still in Dublin, and he'd passed up several opportunities to explain, not knowing how she would respond. And now he was stuck. He glanced at his watch. She was probably safely landed in the States by now.

Should he try ringing, and hope that her Irish mobile was working in America? She hadn't offered an alternate way for them to keep in touch, and he had to wonder whether that had been a conscious choice. There was e-mail, of course, but it seemed woefully inadequate. How could any electronic device capture what he wanted to say?

He wanted to tell her how he had pulled into the gravel driveway at his father's house three nights ago, expecting to find quiet and darkness. Instead, he'd found a strange car parked beside the house, lights blazing brightly inside. He could hear music and laughter; animated conversation floated out through the open door. The ground-floor windows were wide open as well, and music played in the background, a jazz piece he vaguely recognized but could not name. Then Cormac had heard his father's voice. Decades away from this place, and the Donegal accent had not faded; it had a milder northern edge than Belfast or Derry, but the same narrow-throated vowels. The laughter that seemed to follow Joseph Maguire's every utterance was undeniably female.

Not Mrs. Foyle, surely. Recalling a few conversations with his father's neighbor, he couldn't believe the woman ever laughed. He had stood listening to the two voices as a person might hearken to birdsong. No, definitely not Mrs. Foyle.

She'd been very specific on the phone: His father had suffered a stroke, and needed looking after—more looking after than a mere concerned neighbor such as herself could offer, was the implication. But from the sound of things, his father wasn't at all unwell. There must have been some mistake. Cormac walked to the open doorway feeling confused, relieved, guilty. Just what did Geraldine Foyle think she was playing at here?

"Hang on now," his father was saying. "Hang on. We've gone past it now. This is the part I especially wanted you to hear." Joseph stood to lift the needle from a spinning 78 rpm disc on the gramophone, and carefully placed it back to an earlier point in the groove. "Would you listen to that—" He paused to let the instruments speak, raising a hand to indicate a particular passage. "Pure genius, don't you think?"

The woman in the easy chair opposite swirled and sipped from her glass of red wine as she listened to the music. Cormac was startled to discover that his father's guest was someone he knew—Roz Byrne, one of his university colleagues from Dublin. They'd been hired on at the same time, and sat together on a few faculty committees. They'd always got on very well. Roz was a folklorist, a good-natured woman with a great hearty laugh, lively green eyes, and an unruly tumble of gingery hair. As neither of the room's occupants seemed to mark his presence, he raised a hand and rapped lightly on the door frame. Roz put a hand to her throat. "Jaysus Christ, Cormac Maguire—you nearly put the heart across me. What in God's name are you doing here?"

"Hello, Roz. I was about to ask you the same thing."

Joseph Maguire looked from one to the other, slightly befuddled. "Don't tell me you know each other?"

"We've only worked together these last twenty years," Roz said. "What's your connection?"

Cormac felt his color rising. He'd let the world believe his father was dead. Perhaps it was petty, but the first thought that leapt to mind was now that Roz knew his father was alive, everyone else at the university would soon know it as well.

"Ah," she said, evidently experiencing a sudden flash of comprehension. "Maguire—you're related."

"Father and son," Joseph said.

"I always had you down as a Clareman," Roz said to Cormac.

"I am," he said. "It's—complicated."

Joseph rubbed his hands together. "Now we've got all that rubbish out of the way, Roz, shall we offer my poor starving issue some of your marvelous fish stew?"

At that point it hadn't seemed politic to bring up Geraldine Foyle. Cormac had to admit he was ravenous, and saw no other option than to sit down to a bit of supper and listen to the tale of how his father and Roz had met.

"I've been here a few weeks, digging into research for a book—" Roz began. "It started out as a collection of selkie stories from Donegal, but it's morphed into something quite different. Anyway, I tried to find a little house to let for the summer, but you wouldn't believe how tight things are at the moment. I had a research grant, but the money was literally being hoovered out of my pockets by an unscrupulous landlady all the way up in Portnoo. Bloody atrocious place, but all I could find. I happened to be walking the beach just over the headland here one evening—it must have been about three weeks ago—trying to work out whether to stay or to go. For some reason, I picked up a stone and pegged it into the sea—letting off steam, I suppose—"

"And I happened to be out for my constitutional. What can I say? I praised the ferocity of her stone-throwing, and we struck up a conversation—"

Roz said: "Of course I started whinging about the grant that was supposed to last all summer, when Joe had a sudden brainwave and offered to let me stay here. I'm making great headway now. And I have to say, it's wonderful to have someone to bore with all my new discoveries at the end of a long day."

She turned to cast a warm smile at "Joe." Cormac added the cozy scene into which he'd just stumbled to Mrs. Foyle's taut urgency on the phone. It was all beginning to make sense.

The old man said, "Well, scholarship is important, and sure, it's not like I haven't the room. Tell Cormac a bit about your project, Roz—it's fascinating stuff."

Roz said: "Shape-shifting and fairy-bride archetypes have always been my bread and butter as a folklorist. There's a famous Donegal song, '*An Mhaighdean Mhara*'—maybe you've heard it—about a sea maid tricked into marriage with a human, who eventually leaves her family and returns to the sea. I've been fascinated by that song for as long as I can remember. What's left of it is only a fragment, only four short verses, so that's automatically intriguing. There were loads of stories about mermaids and selkies collected in this part of the world, but there's one detail that makes '*An Mhaighdean Mhara*' stand out. The sea maid has a Christian name and a surname—"

Cormac wasn't sure he understood. "You're not saying the woman in the song was a real person?"

"Why not? All sorts of songs were written about actual people, historical events."

"Yes, but a mermaid as historical figure?" Cormac couldn't contain his skepticism.

"There are several old families in Ireland—the O'Flahertys and the O'Sullivans, the MacNamaras, the Conneelys, and several famous old Scottish and Welsh families as well—who all claim to be descended from seal folk. I'm not saying it's literally true, but such things were believed at one time—taken as fact. We can argue about that later, if you like. In any case, the woman in the song was called Mary Heaney, so I started to search the historical record for people with that name. To be honest, I didn't expect to find anything useful. The song was originally collected in Gweedore in the fifties, and the singer, Síle Mhicí Uí Ghallchóir, referred to it as '*Amhrán Thoraí,*' which means it probably came from Tory Island, way up north. I found similar versions collected in the Hebrides and Shetland—not at all surprising if you know anything about the cultural connections between Donegal and Scotland. I began with census rolls, starting from the sixteenth century, and a rake of Mary Heaneys—it isn't an unusual surname in this area, and Mary—well, you couldn't find a more common Christian name in Ireland, in any century up until the present. There were birth, marriage, death records for dozens of women called Mary Heaney, but none seemed to fit the particular circumstances of the woman in the song. I was about to give up. Finally, in local parish census records from 1901, I stumbled across a fisherman called P. J. Heaney, listed in the rolls with his two children—a daughter Mary, and a son Patrick—those were the names of the children mentioned in the song. They were living at Port na Rón—the place I met your father, just over the headland from here. There was no record of the children's mother."

"Perhaps she died," Cormac offered.

"Certainly possible. But everyone else on the rolls seemed to be accorded a status—'married,' 'unmarried,' 'widowed.' No such designation for P. J. Heaney, even though he had children. It was odd, so I started asking around. Turns out Heaney never married, but he did have a common-law wife, who disappeared under rather mysterious circumstances in 1896. She was called Mary."

"It all started to come out then," Joseph said. "People said Heaney's wife was a selkie. They remembered hearing their grandparents speak about her."

Roz was really warming to her subject now. "I started digging out all the newspaper articles I could find about the disappearance. And I started thinking, even if the song is old, this woman may have been inserted into it because she fit the story. She was a foundling, you see—just appeared one day with Heaney on his fishing boat. He never explained where she came from, so of course that gave rise to all sorts of wild speculation. Some said he caught her in his net. Others swore he found her washed up on the beach—naked, some said, or wrapped in seaweed. Of course no one ever knew for certain, because Heaney was alone in the boat when he found her, and he was beyond taciturn. Never spoke more than two words to anyone. No one ever knew her real name. They said she spoke no Irish, and no English either, for the first several years that she lived here."

"But why would they leap to the conclusion that she was a selkie?" Cormac asked.

"People had heard stories from childhood about the mysterious merging of humans and seals. It's something deeply embedded in their consciousness. The way it usually happened was that a fisherman would come upon a selkie who had shed her skin, a beautiful young woman bathing naked in the sea. Of course, she was no ordinary female, but a selkie who had slipped from her sealskin and left it on the rocks. The fisherman would capture her by stealing her skin—without it, she had to remain in human form. Belief in the otherworld was still very strong a hundred years ago—if you look carefully it's there still, under the surface."

"But surely there was some logical explanation for this mysterious woman's appearance. She could have washed up from a shipwreck—"

"I checked all the shipping records I could find for 1889—that would have been the year she arrived in Port na Rón. Nothing—no reported distress signals, no debris or other evidence pointing to a shipwreck in the locality. I suppose she could have gone overboard from an immigrant ship—God knows there were plenty of people sailing to America at that time. People said she was always staring out to sea. Some even claimed to have heard her singing in a foreign language. From the descriptions of her, and the way they described her language, I have a suspicion she may have been from the Faroe Islands, or somewhere in Scandinavia. You know how stories begin to circulate and grow."

"What happened when she disappeared?"

"Her husband never reported her missing. According to the newspapers, she was gone at least four days before someone finally remarked on her absence. Heaney was questioned, but he told the police she'd run off. There were no witnesses, no evidence against him; she simply vanished. Her body was never found, so they let him go."

"And you think people really believed she'd gone back to the sea?"

"It's probably what most preferred to believe. If they could claim to have seen her, they wouldn't have to admit what really happened. I've come to believe that she was murdered—most likely by her husband. A lot more plausible, unfortunately, than any other explanation. As a folklorist, I'm interested in the song, of course, and how it was handed down. But I'm also interested in the broader context of communal beliefs—what the song says about the attitudes and mores about female roles. The late nineteenth century was a period of upheaval in gender politics. Women were beginning to claim a bit more independence, economically and socially, and some people—some men, especially—felt that as a threat." Roz was suddenly self-conscious. "There now, I've rattled on far too long!" She started gathering up the items on the table. "I've a whole day's worth of interviews to transcribe, and I'm sure you two have plenty to talk about."

Cormac half rose from his seat. "Let me give you a hand, Roz—"

"Don't stir yourself. I'm just going to peg these into the sink—you and Joe can take care of them later." She backed through the kitchen door, arms full of crockery.

"Don't worry, you'll get your chance," Joseph said. "That's the one thing I've learned in living so long—the washing up never ends." He looked thoughtfully after Roz as she retreated into the scullery. "Well now, Cormac, I can't imagine what brings you all the way up here. Delighted to see you, of course—"

Cormac leaned forward slightly and lowered his voice: "Actually, I'm here because Mrs. Foyle phoned and told me you'd had a stroke."

"Bloody woman!" The old man looked like he was on the verge of apoplexy, but he spread both hands on the table in front of him, trying to stay calm. "I was going to tell you in my own time. A few days ago, I had what you might call a spell—not serious, a bit of dizziness—Roz drove me to Casualty over at Killybegs. A mini-stroke, they said—transient ischemic attack, if you want to get technical. They put me on blood thinners, advised plenty of rest. I've done everything they told me, and I've been right as rain since then, I swear. Don't know how Geraldine Foyle managed to get hold of that intelligence. Foostering auld magpie—it's she who'll give me a stroke with all her meddling. The curse of fuckin' Jaysus on her!"

Cormac felt slightly alarmed. "I'm sorry if I've been the cause of any of this. When you first came here, she offered to look in, see if you needed anything, and I'm afraid I didn't dissuade her—"

"Ah, no, no, I didn't mind, when I was first here it was grand, you know. She'd pop over—neighborly enough. That was fine. But here's what happened lately—come here till I tell you." He gestured for Cormac to lean in, and spoke under his breath. "Didn't she happen to see Roz coming out of the house one morning about two weeks ago, and decided on the spot she'd call in? To see how was I getting on, she said. But what was she doing, only sniffing around the place, jumping to all sorts of preposterous conclusions! 'At your age,' says she, 'you ought to be ashamed.' I told her there was no need for me to feel shame, since she obviously fetched up enough for the whole parish. You should have heard her, the sanctimonious, Holy Mary carry-on. Wages of sin, all that auld shite. When you think of the suffering it's caused in the world—" He stopped himself, but only momentarily. "Not to mention the sheer bloody hypocrisy of it—Roz may have neglected to mention it, but that flahoola of a landlady above in Portnoo happened to be Geraldine Foyle's first cousin. At any rate, a few more words were exchanged." He waved a hand. "I may have passed some intemperate remarks about the late Mr. Foyle's untimely exit." Cormac could see the old man was still feeling less than apologetic; on the contrary, he seemed rather pleased with himself. "She hasn't put her beak in since."

"Why drag me all the way up here over nothing?"

"Well, Geraldine Bloody Foyle wasn't getting satisfaction from me, obviously. She had to create some pretext so that you'd come rushing up here to break up the love nest. Ah, don't ask me how her mind works—the woman is sick."

Cormac considered for a moment. "I hope you'll forgive an indelicate question, but is there anything for me to break up?"

Joseph's eyes flickered over to the kitchen door, beyond which they could hear Roz humming absently. His demeanor softened. "Are you serious? Roz Byrne may be a kindhearted woman, but she's not completely daft."

In the end, they'd agreed Cormac should stay on another few days, to spare him the long drive back to Dublin after he'd just arrived, and to be doubly certain that his father was suffering no ill effects from the "spell."

As he looked out over the silent waves below Slieve League, Cormac realized that the time had come to make a decision: head back to Dublin in the morning, or catch a plane to the States. He had felt Nora deliberately keeping her distance when they'd last spoken on the phone, but was it because they were finished, or because she didn't want to burden him with troubles that were not his own? Either answer, he realized, was unsatisfactory. He looked at his watch. Just after nine Irish time; she must have arrived at her parents' place in Saint Paul by now. At least he'd assumed that's where she would be staying; she'd offered no confirmation.

The setting sun slid down below a bank of gray clouds, a solid orange mass defying him not to stare. Out here on the headlands, each day mirrored the cycle of life. That was the way the ancients had seen it. Every new day was a resurrection, every nightfall a little death. How many more times must the mighty chariot driver perish in the sea before he stopped his dithering and actually did something?

He had simply appeared on Nora's doorstep once before, fourteen months ago, and everything had worked out then. Beyond all expectations, really. He could make it to Saint Paul in a day or two, if he could only convince himself that she would welcome him. It was obvious that she wasn't going to ask for help, but she couldn't refuse it either—could she? He'd been going back and forth like this for days, trying to read into her words what perhaps wasn't there. He didn't even know how he could help her, only that he felt an overwhelming desire to try. Climbing to his feet from the damp, rocky ground, Cormac looked out over the choppy waves and considered everything he'd given up to be here, all because of Geraldine Foyle's priggish puritanical streak. The curse of fuckin' Jaysus on her, indeed.

Standing at the edge of the precipice, looking down hundreds of feet to the dark sea below, he knew he'd already flung himself from that place of safety, metaphorically speaking. He would go to America, just as soon as he could book a flight.

Cormac wondered whether he ought to tell Nora of his plan. Words—and e-mail most especially—seemed altogether too puny for his purpose. At that moment, the first notes of a sinuous melody began to snake through his brain, beginning long and low, then rocking back and forth, then surging forward with a wild abandon. That was it—he would send her a tune. The idea was beautifully simple—just attach an audio file to an e-mail message. How was it this notion had never occurred to him before?

The sudden stroke of inspiration absorbed his thoughts the whole way back to the house at Ardcrinn. He wasn't even aware of the jarring ride along the narrow, crumbling road that went up the mouth of the glen from Teelin. In his head he was already holding the wooden flute, feeling its familiar heft, and thinking how strange it was that a man might pour the breath of his body into a hollow tube, and through a kind of wizardry that breath could be captured—bottled, in a way—and transmitted over vast miles, to any spot on the face of the planet. He tried to imagine where Nora was at this very moment, and how she might react to such a cryptic message. If she listened closely—even if she was unfamiliar with the tune, even if its title was obscure to her—surely she would hear and understand everything he was trying to say.

7

Nora pushed aside a teetering stack of manila file folders and checked her watch. A quarter to ten. She had only meant to unpack, but had been pulled again into the mystery of Tríona's death. She'd been going through files for four solid hours. Dusk had come and gone, and the room was illuminated only by the bedside lamp and a shaft of light from the kitchen. She switched on the overhead fixture and studied the wall, now covered with maps and photographs, newspaper clippings, and dozens of index cards, each one enumerating a scrap of physical evidence, a witness, a lead. She had envisioned this wall like an incident room—thinking perhaps that seeing everything laid out would trigger some connection, some logical leap she might have overlooked. It looked more like one of those crazy collages put together by a deranged stalker.

She had already begun to go back over leads, looking for any loose threads that might begin an unraveling. There were a few facts she had never told anyone—not Cormac, and certainly not her parents. Forensic details that simply didn't fit. The liquid ecstasy in Tríona's purse was one. That glazed look in her eyes the night of the museum opening was another. What if pulling on any of these loose threads began to destroy her parents' idealized picture of Tríona? Wouldn't that be like killing her all over again? How willing was she to risk putting her mother and father through a second wrenching loss? She tried to summon the resolve she had felt on the plane this afternoon. No stopping this time. No going back.

A heavy fatigue had begun to settle in her limbs—apart from a nap on the plane, she hadn't slept in almost thirty-six hours. It wasn't too late to call her parents or Frank Cordova. What was she waiting for? Digging a small address book out of her bag, she looked up Frank's home number, but hesitated before dialing.

He'd been the lead investigator, the person who had pulled her away from Tríona's body in the mortuary. Two days ago, she had phoned Frank from Dublin to let him know she was coming home, and was relieved when the call went straight into his voice mail. She had left a rambling message, promising to call when she got in. He'd rung back the same day, but the conversation had been awkward. Frank Cordova had not forgiven her for running away.

For three years she'd tried hard not to think about the last time she'd seen him. They'd both been working around the clock, barely eating or sleeping, getting nowhere on the case. It wasn't that Frank had ever taken advantage—if anything, it had been exactly the other way around. She remembered the desperate craving she had felt for a human touch, something to ease the pain. What she'd needed most that night was a respite from betrayal and brutality, a few hours not spent thinking about death. Not thinking at all. Of course, like all cravings, her need was short-lived. By the time the sun rose the next morning, she knew that her one night with Frank Cordova had been an admission of failure, a leave-taking of sorts. Frank had surely felt it too.

But whatever had possessed them that night was history now. So much had changed in the three years she'd been away, for her, and no doubt for him. She felt an involuntary twinge, imagining him with someone else—he could be married, maybe even a father by now. He'd said nothing about his personal life in their recent phone conversation, and neither had she. Better to call him at work in the morning, make it official.

That left her parents. She imagined the stony set of her father's jaw, her mother's gentler mien—they had always made a perfect pair of foils. But she ought to prepare for a shock upon seeing them. After three years, they would almost certainly seem older than she remembered. After pressing their number into the phone, she sat staring at the familiar string of digits, unsure what to say. She had told them she was coming home, of course, but hadn't mentioned exactly when or for how long. The truth was that she didn't want them meeting her at the airport, as if this were an ordinary homecoming like any other. All at once she was overtaken by a strong need to see them, to sit in the same room and breathe the same air, even if nothing in her childhood home could ever be what it had been before Tríona's death. She snapped the phone closed and headed downstairs.

She had grown used to late midsummer sunsets in Ireland, and found it surprisingly dark outside. The wall of humidity also came as a shock after the air-conditioned apartment, but within a few minutes her body adjusted, settling into the dewy atmosphere. She had nearly forgotten the sheer physical pleasures of a summer night, with a warm breeze stirring the trees, the brightest stars and the planets visible. She cut down the hill to Grand Avenue, then crossed over and followed the curved sidewalks into Crocus Hill, the tiny pocket of a neighborhood that looked out over the river flats to the bluffs on the opposite shore. The broad streets here, even the shapes of the houses, seemed strange after three years away. Perhaps it was only the darkness. Pools of shadow seemed about to swallow up the pin oaks and lindens; the trees themselves were devoid of color, recognizable only by their silhouettes, the peculiar rustlings they made in the night air.

Nora slowed as she approached her parents' home. She heard the music first, an Elgar cello concerto—her father's favorite. She stopped to listen as the instrument's deep vibrato, sonorous and sweet, spilled into the night. The broad screen porch at the side of the house was illuminated by a single reading lamp, and she could see her mother's head bent in concentration over the crossword, a daily passion. Her father's lanky frame was stretched on the daybed along the wall. He lay with his eyes closed, and fingers steepled over his chest as he listened to the music. Her parents had been like this always, Nora thought: two planets, each in its separate orbit. She remembered wishing once, when she was about thirteen, that her parents would shout or curse or throw things—display some feeling, anything at all. But the world around them was always calm and laid out according to scientific principles. Reason was the highest good. Nothing ever broke that peace.

When the music ended, her father sat up and leaned over to lift the LP from the turntable and slid it gently into the sleeve. He had never caught up with the world of CD recordings. Nora's heart suddenly squeezed tight, remembering how he had played that same recording incessantly in the weeks and months after Tríona's death. Some people reached out to others for comfort, but her father's grief had driven him ever more inward. After five years, this nightly dose of Elgar still seemed his only consolation.

Eleanor Gavin set aside the folded newspaper and removed her glasses, rubbing her eyes as if plagued by a dull headache. Nora heard her father's voice: "Are you all right, Eleanor?"

"I'm worried about Nora. I should have told her about Miranda. I just didn't have the heart to do it over the phone."

"She'll find out soon enough."

Nora stood in the shadows, wondering if she'd heard right. The only Miranda she knew was Marc Staunton's younger sister. Had something happened to her?

"I'm sure she'd want to know, Tom. I should have said something. Peter said they were leaving on Saturday. Dublin's not a large city. What if she were to run into them?"

"Have you tried the flat again?"

"No answer. Her office at Trinity will only say that she's on break, and I can't raise her on the cell phone."

"Wait until she gets home, love. It's all we can do. She's probably on her way now."

Nora stood in the darkness, a strange feeling settling in the pit of her stomach. What was it her parents had to tell her about Miranda Staunton?

And then she knew. Peter Hallett wasn't returning to Saint Paul with some anonymous, clueless female he'd picked up in Seattle. He was coming back to marry Miranda Staunton, his best friend's sister. And he was taking his new bride on a wedding trip to Ireland, where he and Tríona had spent their honeymoon. Was it some sort of deliberate taunt, a demonstration that he could do exactly as he pleased, and no one could stop him?

Nora wanted desperately to speak, but she couldn't make a sound. It had been a mistake, coming here. The crickets' thrumming suddenly turned unbearably loud and harsh. She turned and started back to the apartment, first walking, then running blindly, gulping air and trying to fight off the angry tears that stung her eyes. After two blocks, she slowed to a walk, suddenly so exhausted that she could hardly put one foot in front of the other.

Turning in at the carriage house sidewalk, she caught sight of a figure standing in silhouette at the side door to the garage. The door to her apartment. Her heart lurched as she jumped back out of view, perhaps too late. When there was no audible reaction, she leaned forward and peered around the corner again, slowly this time. A man stood in the shadows—not tall, but solid and powerfully built. He seemed to hesitate, outstretched thumb poised over the bell. Then he tipped forward, slowly banging his forehead against the door. "Press the button," he muttered to himself. "Just press the fucking button and get it over with."

She recognized the voice. "Frank—is that you?"

Cordova's head shot up and he stepped back, one hand reaching instinctively for his holster. "Goddamn it, Nora, don't ever sneak up on somebody like that. Especially not a cop."

He'd kept his jacket on despite the heat, but his tie was loose and slightly askew. The street light in the alley threw most of his body into shadow, but Nora could see the crown of straight black hair, the sharp angles of the clean-shaven face, cheekbones that offered proof of Mayan ancestors. Cordova looked a little unsteady on his feet, and she realized that her sudden appearance wasn't the only thing putting him off balance. He was holding onto the door frame for support. Something was a little off.

"I'm just surprised to see you here, Frank. How did you find me?"

"Give me a little credit. Carriage house, you said. Arundel Court." He leaned forward and whispered: "I don't know if you noticed, but there's no other carriage house on this street."

Each word was carefully formed—a little too carefully. Something was definitely off. She ventured closer. "Are you okay, Frank?"

"Perfect."

She was finally close enough to catch a whiff of alcohol. Not beer—something stronger. "You've had a few."

He looked wounded. "Maybe I had reason. You know, ever since you called, I keep seeing that bastard's face." He spat the name: "Hallett. Thinks he got away with it. I've seen guys like him, and they don't stop. They never stop. He's been laughing at us for five *fucking* years. Can't you feel it?" The anguish in his voice tore at her. "You and I both know what he did. He knows we know. And that's how he gets off, rubbing our noses in it, loving the fact that we can't touch him. But we're the same, you and me. Can't let go." His voice softened. "But we can nail him this time. I know we can." Cordova pointed an unsteady finger at her. "He doesn't know we found the other one."

"Frank, what are you talking about?"

"The other girl, the one from Hidden Falls. You don't know about her either. Nobody does. He thinks we're stupid, can't add two and two."

"Who is this other girl? What's she got to do with Tríona?"

Cordova squeezed his eyes tight. "You know, just forget about it. I shouldn't have said anything. Jesus. I don't know who she is, or if she's got anything to do with anything." He rubbed his head as if it pained him. "I don't know why I told you. I'm not thinking straight—"

He suddenly lost his balance and lurched forward, forcing her to reach out and place one hand against his chest. The liquor on his breath mingled with a faint, not unpleasant musk of perspiration and the barest whiff of cologne. That volatile mixture had done her in once before. If she wasn't very careful, it could complicate matters again in a way that neither of them needed right now. Frank Cordova wasn't in any shape to think things through tonight. Nora pushed against his chest with both hands, trying to set him upright. "We'll figure it out, but not right now, not tonight. It's late, and I'm completely wrecked—"

He resisted her efforts and leaned in harder, pressing against her, his warm breath brushing her ear. "What's the matter? You think if you let me in, we'd end up where we were before? Is it the worst that could happen?" As he spoke, his hands came up, the right around her waist, the left grasping her wrist as though they were dancing. Hot blood flushed her face and throat, a fierce flood of desire. She felt his eyes seeking hers in the humid darkness, and turned away, half afraid that he would find what he was looking for. Even standing with two feet on solid ground, she felt the heady, dangerous pull of that precipice. It would be so easy to go over, to forget about Cormac and all that had happened these past three years. Frank Cordova knew everything. He'd seen her at her absolute lowest point. As if he had read her thoughts, he said: "Don't be afraid. I'll catch you."

He stepped closer, and all at once she felt a sharp jab as Cormac's hazel knot poked into her hip. It was as if the pain pricked her awake. "Come on, Frank—I haven't slept for three days. What we both need is a good night's rest. Where's your car?"

His face was still pressed into her hair. "Don't ask me about the car. Fuck the car. God, you smell good."

She tried to pull free of his grasp, but he held on. She said: "Okay, we'll forget about the car. Why don't I call you a cab?"

At that, he drew back and looked at her, wounded and groggy. "You think I'm being a prick."

"Frank, stop it—you know that's not what I think."

"You do. You think I'm an inconsiderate, selfish prick. Maybe you're right." He put his head down and bulled forward, accidentally brushing against her as he made his way out the narrow sidewalk to the street. She held her breath as he lowered himself rather unsteadily to the curbstone and finally rested his head against crossed arms, like a wretched child.

He was going to feel like hell in the morning, and there was nothing she could do about that either. She studied the back of his bowed head, trying to imagine spending day after day as he did, raking through the deliberate harm people did to one another. After a while, maybe even your own fundamental decency wasn't enough protection. She reached for her phone to call a taxi, then headed out to join him at the curb.

It was nearly eleven, and in the gradually cooling night, the damp air had begun to cling like mist, making a halo around the light of the single street lamp. The roar of freeway noise below them was overlaid with a sharp, constant chorus of crickets.

"Get some sleep, Frank. We can talk in the morning."

"In the morning. Sure." He inhaled deeply, as if suddenly exhausted, unable to say any more. It wasn't only her own life she was disrupting by coming home. Nora found herself wondering what time Frank had been hauled out of bed this morning, how many other cases he was juggling. She could have asked how things were going, but from his appearance here tonight, she could venture a pretty good guess.

When the cab arrived, Frank didn't say even good night. He climbed into the backseat and gave the driver his address on the West Side. Nora watched the taxi pull away with his head slumped low in the back window.

8

As soon as the cab rounded the corner, Nora unlocked the carriage house door and began to climb the stairs, feeling as though she was moving in slow motion. Another eternity passed as she dragged out her laptop, and finally logged on to the archives at the local newspaper, the *Pioneer Press*. Another girl, Frank had said, at Hidden Falls. They had never found the exact spot where Tríona was killed. The words from the police report echoed in her ears: *Because the body was moved, the location of the primary crime scene remains unknown.* All they knew from trace evidence was that Tríona had been attacked in a wooded area, most likely along the Mississippi River. Maybe Hidden Falls. It was just one of many pockets of parkland along the river known as places to drink and get high, where people sometimes shed their clothes along with their inhibitions. Peter Hallett wanted everyone to believe that was what Tríona had done.

Sleep now seemed impossible. Nora typed "unidentified female" and "homicide" into the paper's search box, bringing up dozens of hits. She added "Hidden Falls." Still too many, all old cases. Had Frank mentioned a time frame? They'd spoken on the telephone a few days ago, and he hadn't said anything then about another victim. She felt the wheels in her brain turning like rusty gears, not even engaged, just spinning furiously in neutral.

Maybe the Hidden Falls case was too recent to have made the papers. Then again, maybe it was just the booze talking, and there was no other victim except in Frank's feverish imagination. He wasn't usually like that. She'd never seen him drunk before, even when things were really bad. Maybe she had made a mistake in letting him go home instead of bringing him in, trying to sober him up. No, in the state he was in just now, that would have led to more complications. She would call him at the station first thing in the morning, get the whole story. Never mind the prospect that stretched before her, a long night of trying to force a second specter from her mind.

Nora was just about to switch off the laptop when her inbox suddenly flickered with half a dozen new messages. Her heart lifted at the sight of Cormac's name, but it was a pleasure immediately dampened beneath a wave of remorse. She had promised to get in touch as soon as she arrived, and had completely forgotten. The message had been posted just after midnight Irish time. He must have sent it off before going to bed. She checked her watch. Just after daybreak in Ireland now, not a decent hour to call.

The subject read: *Tune.* No message, only an audio attachment. Opening it, she recognized Cormac's flute instantly, hearing his breath in the low register that seemed to scour up dusky earth, and in soaring high notes that rang with the freshness of spring water and clear air. The music brought back that astonishing moment out on the bog only a few days ago when she knew all the way through to the center of her being that she loved him.

She hadn't been sure for the longest time, and then suddenly it was a fact, a binary value that switched from zero to one in the space of a single heartbeat. The sound of the flute filled her ears, playing out all the fierce, secret relief she had felt at the sight of him that day on the bog. He would have come along on this journey, she was certain, had she given him the slightest encouragement. But for some reason she had resisted. She couldn't ask him to follow her, not here, to this terrible place. At least he had not asked for an explanation. She wouldn't have known how to answer, except to say that since Tríona's death, things like honesty and integrity and decency seemed strange to her—suspect, almost. After all, there had been a time when she had believed that Peter Hallett possessed all those qualities. Sometimes it felt as if she'd lost the ability to distinguish truth from falsehood. The whole world seemed skewed off-center, and try as she might, she couldn't manage to get it righted.

Cormac's tune began again, and she let it play. *You're not a person who gives up,* he had said. *But neither am I.* There was no doubt about the first part, much good it had done her so far. All she could do was to hold out hope that the second bit was true as well. Still, she could never blame Cormac for finding someone else, if he did. Someone who fit his life much better than she ever would. No promises, they'd agreed. Cormac had troubles of his own, without getting sandbagged by hers.

An instant message suddenly appeared on her screen:

—Are you there, Nora?

She could hear his voice in the words, and her heart jumped again. She turned down the music and picked up her mobile. He answered on the first ring.

"Cormac, I meant to call. I'm so sorry—"

"Everything all right?"

How could she tell him the truth? "Everything's fine. You're up early."

"I was going out for a row. Just thought I'd see if you were around."

"How's your father?"

"Actually doing what he's told—for once."

"I'm glad. Where is his home place, exactly?"

"Just up the road from Glencolumbkille. A very remote spot. Hard to believe, really. I didn't know places like this still existed."

"Sounds lonely."

He hesitated. "I actually like it—the wind and the waves. You know me—the wilder the better."

"Speaking of which, thanks for the tune. I was having a listen when I got your message just now."

"So it came through?"

"Like you were right here beside me."

She could hear the smile in his voice. "That was the general idea."

"What do you call it?"

There was a slight pause, and she imagined him looking up at her from beneath dark brows—nervous, hesitant, unused to rituals of self-revelation. "What if I tell you the next time we meet?"

"So mysterious. What was it that ancient Greek said about the Celts?"

" 'They speak in riddles, hinting at things, leaving much to be understood.' "

"Some things never change, apparently."

His voice turned serious. "Still got your hazel knot?"

She felt for it in her pocket. "Right here."

"Good—hang on to it. I feel bloody useless over here."

"Cormac, please don't—"

"Nora—" He was on the verge of saying something more but demurred. "You're probably knackered. I'll let you get some sleep. Mind yourself now—and sleep well."

"Good night, Cormac. Thanks again for the tune."

She hung up, and placed one hand over his picture on the screen. To her surprise, an instant message popped up beneath her fingers:

—*Oiche mhaith.*

Followed almost immediately by another:

—P.S. I like hearing you say my name.

She recalled the first time she'd spoken it aloud, in the conservation lab at Collins Barracks in Dublin. They were standing over an exam table, discussing the fate of the red-haired girl from the bog, and in her agitation she had touched his hand, addressed him by name for the very first time. "Cormac," she said aloud into the darkness.

They were both treading across no-man's-land, unsure where to put a foot down. She reached into her pocket for the hazel knot, studying the faint wrinkles in the greenish bark, the dark brown marrow of its angled ends. A charm against mischief, he had said. A protection. She couldn't tell him how it had rescued her from danger this very night. Nor could she ask the host of questions that tumbled around inside her brain—how long did the charm's peculiar powers last, and just how far did they extend? What if she wasn't the one who needed protecting?

9

Cormac leaned forward, pulling hard on the oars, pushing against the aft seat with his legs. Another twenty minutes and he'd be completely spent. It was just after seven o'clock, but the sun had been up for nearly three hours, and glorious light fell against the wall of black clouds that obscured the western horizon.

The conversation with Nora had unsettled him, but at least she seemed pleased with the tune. He should have told her the name—what had stopped him? He poured his frustration into the rowing, pushing himself against the limits of his own strength, feeling the strain in his shoulders and thighs. The distance between him and Nora seemed to grow in that brief conversation, and for the first time he understood that it might be a span he couldn't leap. But he'd made the decision, booked the ticket. It was too late now to turn back. With each oar stroke, he tried to wipe away his fears of the future, to concentrate on the task at hand.

The water was relatively calm today. Of course this wasn't the smooth river sculling he had grown accustomed to in Dublin, more like the rough seas he'd plowed back home in Clare. But the motion was the same, tucking one oar handle under the other in a thoughtless, rhythmic repetition he found calming. It cleared his mind, helped him to see things outside the clutter and noise of everyday life. The first morning up here, he'd inquired at the local post office at Glencolumbkille, asking if there was a local rowing club, or anyone who might let him take a skiff out for an hour or so. He'd headed off to Teelin harbor this morning before anyone at the house was up, hoping to get in a good workout before going back to tell his father that he was leaving, booked on a plane that took off from Shannon tomorrow morning.

As he rowed below Sail Rock, a group of seals pushed up alongside him, heads poking out of the water. The frank curiosity in the dark, liquid eyes made it easy to see the connection people felt with them. There was something almost human in their aspect. What else could have fueled the long-held suspicions that they could slip from their skins and walk about on land, even bear human children? How amazing it must have been to live in an age where gods and men, animals and spirits mixed together freely, where shape-shifters and hybrid creatures were taken for granted. Or perhaps the old beliefs masked a darker reality. If what Roz was discovering was true, the story of Mary Heaney's disappearance might implicate a whole community in her violent death. How much better if the villagers of Port na Rón could somehow convince themselves that she was a mysterious changeling who had simply returned to the sea?

Cormac looked into a pair of heavy-lashed, dark eyes that followed him silently from the water's surface. People said seals were fond of music, that you could call them just by singing or playing an instrument. He watched the animal's nostrils flare, trying to catch the scent of food, its flipper raised in unmistakable salutation. For one moment, it seemed possible that these creatures might carry knowledge of a young woman's strange disappearance. The seal beside him opened its mouth to sing in a strange, vowelish language, and others in the group responded. At last the whole pod, evidently concluding that he had nothing to offer, dived deep and abandoned him. If they did know anything about Mary Heaney, they weren't telling.

He'd almost completed his circuit out from Teelin, and now started to row back to the harbor. He stayed as far as possible from the base of the sheer drop, where, no matter what the weather, the sea boiled and churned around the rocks below. The Devil's Chair was barely visible here at sea level, proving once again that point of view was all. In only a few days, he had developed a fierce attachment to this stretch of rough coastline, to its seals and seabirds, the beaches and tiny harbors tucked up beneath the soaring cliffs. And yet he felt himself already halfway across the ocean, already parted from this place before he had even left.

Despite the relative calm, the western wind off the Atlantic was never indifferent, and it took all his strength to keep from drifting too close to the rocks at the cliff base. Although it was July, and he was rowing flat out, the chill would have cut through him entirely if he hadn't thrown on a windcheater over his fleece. He turned his rowboat toward the harbor and was tying it to a ring on the concrete jetty just as the dark clouds now settled overhead let loose their first few drops of rain. Time to head back and face the old man.

The house was dark when he arrived. He tried the switch inside the front door, but the wind had evidently knocked out the power—the second time in as many days. As he made his way through the darkened sitting room, he heard a slow creak from the back of the house. Someone else was up early. His father had been sleeping until at least half-nine every morning—following his doctors' advice. The same creaking sounded again, followed by a sudden crash.

Cormac followed the noises to his father's bedroom at the back corner of the house. The door was ajar, and in the half light, he could see Roz kneeling on the floor next to the old man, holding his hand, calling his name. He pushed the door open.

"Roz, what's happened?"

"I don't know—he just collapsed. We've got to call for an ambulance—quickly."

Cormac felt himself moving automatically, fishing the phone from his pocket, pressing in the number for emergency services, and holding the phone fast to his ear, hoping to God that his father wasn't going to die right here, right now. If Roz hadn't been in the house, if he'd gone rowing just a few minutes later or hadn't turned around exactly when he did—

"Yes, we need an ambulance—" He heard his own voice, calmly answering the operator's questions, while his eyes got used to the half darkness. On the floor before him lay his father, naked but for a flannel dressing gown open to the waist. Joseph Maguire's eyes were open but unblinking. That this could be the same man who had spoken so blithely about his "spell" the other night was inconceivable.

"They're on their way," he said to Roz. "They said to keep him warm."

As his eyes grew more accustomed to the darkness in the room, he suddenly realized that the duvet from the bed was wrapped around Roz. Her shoulders were bare, her loose hair in disarray. Conscious of his gaze, she reached for a bathrobe that lay on the floor and pulled it about her.

"Cormac, I know how this must look—we'll have to talk about it later. Help me." She took the duvet and began tucking it around his father, speaking in a low voice: "Everything's going to be all right, Joe—an ambulance is on the way. Can you hear me? Please don't leave us."

At the hospital, Roz sat beside Cormac in the waiting area at Casualty and handed him a plastic cup of weak tea, purchased from a woman pushing a food trolley through the wards. She took a deep breath. "Cormac, I know how things looked this morning, but it's not what you might think—"

"You don't have to explain yourself to me, Roz—"

"No, I do. He's your father—"

"The man walked out when I was a child, Roz. I didn't see him again for ten years. We're barely acquainted, if you want to know the truth."

"I know. He told me everything. About leaving Ireland, about his work in South America, all the people he knew who just disappeared. He told me about your mother—and you."

"Me? He doesn't know the first thing about me."

"He does. And he cares about you, Cormac, more than you know."

"He's certainly had a very odd way of showing it."

"You say he doesn't know you, but what do you know about him? He's such a remarkable man, Cormac. Do you know anything about his work in Chile all those years, the thousands of people he treated with no concern for his own safety—all the lives he saved? Did you know how many times he was arrested and tortured? And in spite of all that, I've never met anyone so . . ." She searched for the words. "I don't know—so completely engaged with the world, so alive."

"Why is it every person who tries to convince me what a great humanitarian my father is, just happens to be someone he's shagging?"

Roz looked as though she'd been slapped.

"Please forgive me, Roz. That was a rotten thing to say. I'm so sorry."

She was quiet for a moment. "We're both upset." A tear escaped and trickled down her face. She brushed it away, and then smiled. "Do you know what's funny? We haven't actually—I'd only moved my things down to his room on that day you arrived. He wanted to send me packing back upstairs, but I told him he was being ridiculous. For God's sake, I said, we're all adults. He kept insisting that he didn't want to be unfair to me. Almost as if he knew—" She buried her face in her hands. Cormac moved closer and put his arm around her.

"As long as we're offering true confessions," he said, "I'm booked on a flight to America first thing tomorrow morning. "

Roz looked up at him. "Who or what's in America?"

"Someone I don't want to lose."

She squeezed his arm, and shook her head in sympathy. "We are a pair, aren't we? You know I'll do everything I can to help."

"Start of term is only a few weeks away, Roz. Nobody expects you to stay on here. I might be able to request some emergency leave. We'll just have to wait and see what happens."

He stood and walked to the end of the corridor, where he could see the nurses still hovering over his father and hear the quiet murmurs, the squeaking of their shoes on the polished tile floor. One of his father's bare feet poked out from under the blanket, and Cormac felt an unfamiliar surge of protective instinct. One of the nurses finally noticed as well, and tucked the blanket more securely around the old man.

Part of him couldn't consider abandoning his father now, despite anything that had happened in the past. The man had left whatever life he'd made for himself in Chile to return home and care for his wife in her last days. Éilis—Cormac's mother—was still his wife. And still loved him, all those years later. Maybe that should count for something.

The fantasy he'd had of landing once again on Nora's doorstep was rapidly evaporating, and he could feel her slipping further away from him. Why had he not gone with her? Fear of crowding her, perhaps. But if she was going to reject him eventually, wasn't it best to give her a clear opportunity? She must know how he felt, that he'd never felt the same about anyone else. But their lives were not yet intertwined, and maybe they never would be. He'd always been so separate, unto himself. Could he change—was it possible, at this late date?

He looked in at his father, and decided it was no mystery why the ancient gods had been so often imagined as moody, capricious parents. Something buried deep within the life-giving force bestowed a kind of extraordinary, mythic stature. How strange it was to see the person he had once imagined as a divine being, a colossus, reduced to mere mortal once again. Cormac turned away from that unsettling sight and stared down at the pale, bitter tea in his cup, now gone cold.

Book Two

It was delightful and refreshing to see them disporting themselves in their native element. And their eyes! Such eyes! they were simply the loveliest I ever saw in any creature—large, dark, liquid, and lustrous, with a wistful, pleading, melancholy expression that went far to justify the local legend which represents them as a certain class of fallen spirits in metempsychosis, enduring a mitigated punishment for their sins. The seal has a way of looking right into your eyes, as though asking for sympathy and kind treatment. It makes one feel pitiful towards them, and I wonder exceedingly how the sailors who prosecute "seal-fishing" in the polar regions can have the heart to knock them on the head with a bludgeon.

—*The Home of a Naturalist,* by the Reverend Biot Edmondston and his sister, Jessie M. E. Saxby, 1890

1

The light was all that Nora could register, because her whole body was on fire. Strong hands held her wrists while soft, slow kisses found her most sensitive places. When her phantom lover raised his head, the face belonged not to Cormac but to Frank Cordova. Caught in his grip, she watched his lips move in slow motion: *Don't be afraid. I'll catch you.* When she tried to pull away, the face altered again, and this time the eyes looking into hers belonged to Peter Hallett. She struggled harder. How could this be happening? It wasn't real. She jerked awake and threw off the tangled sheets, shot through with cold fear and disoriented by the half light in the unfamiliar room. Heart still racing, she checked the locks on the doors and windows. Everything was secure; it was just a terrible dream. She didn't dare try to sleep again.

When the doorbell buzzed at a quarter-past eight, she had been awake and dressed and going through the case files for nearly two hours. She tried to look out and see who was downstairs, without success. Who besides Frank Cordova even knew she was here? After the bell sounded a second time, she ventured down the narrow stairs and peered through the peephole to see Frank standing outside, freshly showered and shaved, looking not much the worse for wear after last night.

"I figured with the jet lag, you wouldn't be able to sleep in," he said, when she opened the door. "I'm really sorry about last night." He was staring down at the threshold between them. "I shouldn't drink. I was way out of line. Sorry."

"I was nervous about seeing you, too." The memory of his looming countenance in the dream this morning made her flush, but he didn't seem to notice.

"So we're okay?"

"Yeah, we're okay. You want to come in?"

Relief broke over his face. "Yeah, sure." He followed her upstairs into the small kitchen.

"Are you hungry? I don't have much—"

He waved a hand, looking a little queasy at the prospect of solid food. "No—just coffee, if it's handy." He took a seat at the table, looking uncomfortable. He wasn't tall, barely six feet, but he had the sort of masculine bulk that made the kitchen furniture seem almost child-sized. Nora kept the door to the sitting room closed. For some reason, she didn't want him to see her makeshift incident room with files still spread across the floor.

She poured two cups of coffee, while he cast an appraising glance.

"Seems like Ireland agrees with you."

Nora felt the blood rising to her face again, and this time, Frank seemed to take note.

"It was good to get some distance," she said. "From everything. I think going away was the only thing that saved my sanity. You remember what it was like."

The downcast look said he remembered all of it—the late nights, the media circus, the grueling emotional roller coaster of leads that evaporated almost as quickly as they appeared. And the frustration and despair that had driven them together for one reckless night. It had been a mistake. But clearly she'd been wrong in thinking he perceived it that way as well.

"How have things been with you, Frank?"

Cordova shifted in his seat and looked away, and she could almost hear the sound of a door creaking shut. Not going to happen. Not in broad daylight, and certainly not when he was sober. He gave her a weary smile. "The usual. Not enough hours in a day. That's what they'll carve on my tombstone."

"Frank, last night—"

"Last night was not exactly the usual, if that's what you're worried about." His left thumb absently traced the groove around the rim of his mug. "I suppose you know about Miranda Staunton. You think her brother fixed her up with Hallett?"

Nora heard a note of antipathy in Frank's voice that said he hadn't forgotten or forgiven the way Marc Staunton had treated her. The way Marc had taken Peter Hallett's word over hers. The way he'd walked out when she wouldn't desist in unmasking his old friend. It was a little unsettling to admit how good Frank's lingering resentment made her feel. She took a sip of coffee, but found its taste bitter on her tongue. "To tell you the truth, just hearing that Peter planned to marry again convinced me to come back. I didn't find out that Miranda was the bride-to-be until last night. I can't let go of this crazy idea that we might be able to stop him."

"I hope it's not crazy—I've been thinking the same thing."

"Here's something you might not know. He's leaving the country on Saturday—taking Miranda to Ireland, the same place he took Tríona on their honeymoon. That was something I only discovered last night as well." She watched the news work its way across Cordova's features.

"So we have what—four days—to crack a case that's hung us out to dry for five years? Even if we had something, it takes time to build a case." Nora realized that he was probably swamped at work, and couldn't just drop everything for a cold case, even this one. They sat in awkward silence for a moment. "Four days. I thought we'd have a little more time."

"Frank, you said something last night, about another girl at Hidden Falls—"

His eyes narrowed. "What did I say?"

"That Peter didn't know you'd found her. You said you weren't sure it was anything to do with Tríona."

Cordova took a deep breath. "A Jane Doe turned up down at the river three days ago. A fisherman came across the body, in a patch of swampland down at Hidden Falls—you know yourself, sometimes it's just a feeling."

Nora felt the beginning of a vibration, as if someone had touched a tuning fork to her solar plexus. "Where was this patch of swamp exactly?"

"Up under the bluffs north of the falls."

Nora knew the place—one of a dozen sites the police had searched along the river five years ago, looking for evidence to pinpoint a primary crime scene, the place where Tríona had been attacked. There was nothing to say that this was the same wooded area—nothing, that is, except another body. Cordova's eyes met hers, and the same frisson passed through her again.

"How long had she been there?"

"Hard to say exactly. The ME said he's never seen anything like it. Half the body was reduced to bone, but the side buried deeper in the swamp was—"

"What?"

"Mummified, I guess—I don't know what else to call it. The doc said it was probably something to do with the wet ground. He was guessing she'd been there three or four years, maybe longer."

"And the cause of death?" Somehow she knew what Frank was going to say even before he opened his mouth.

"Somebody smashed her face in. I'm stopping over to pick up the final autopsy report this morning—"

"Take me with you."

"What?"

"I need to see her, Frank. If the ME has a problem with me being there, you can say I'm a specialist on preserved human remains."

His eyes narrowed. "Is that true?"

"It's part of what I've been doing in Ireland, studying Iron Age remains recovered from peat bogs."

Cordova smiled faintly and shook his head, as though it was difficult to process this new information. He stood and gestured for her to lead the way. "Okay, Dr. Gavin, let's go."

2

The Ramsey County medical examiner worked out of a low, nondescript building adjacent to the regional medical center in downtown Saint Paul. Nora hadn't been to the building since she'd identified Tríona's body. She tried to steel herself as Cordova parked in the small lot in front of the building.

Buck Callaway, the former ME, had been a colleague at the university, and a good friend who'd seen her through some rough times. They had kept in touch. Since his retirement, Buck and his wife had set off traveling the world. Nora was never surprised to receive their postcards from far-flung locales—the Peruvian Andes, Greenland, or the steppes of Mongolia. Buck's travel had a serious purpose; in his retirement, he was compiling an epidemiological library of the ancient world. It was Buck Callaway who'd first urged her to take up the study of ancient bog remains in Ireland. She had yet to meet his replacement.

"What's the new guy like?" she asked Frank.

"Solomon's good," Cordova said. "Very enthusiastic. Although that pretty much goes without saying for you pathology types."

They signed in at reception, and Cordova led the way down the hall and through the wide double doors leading into the autopsy room. Not much had changed since she'd last been here; the place still had the look of a combination laboratory and operating room, albeit with some rather unorthodox surgical instruments. Three of the five stainless-steel tables were occupied. At the first two, the mortuary technicians were washing a pair of pale corpses, preparing them for the next step. On the last table was an articulated skeleton belonging to the county's latest Jane Doe.

Nora's first thought was that she might be back in Dublin, looking at one of the National Museum's ancient specimens. The skull had been reduced to bone, along with one side of the body, just as Frank had described. Moving closer, she saw that the right side was mostly intact, from the shoulder down to the slightly darkened toenails and the sole of the foot. Taken as a whole, the image was grisly and surreal: a grinning, gap-toothed skeleton half veiled in tattered flesh.

Cordova said: "Something else, isn't it?"

Nora let her gaze travel slowly across the face—what was left of it. The nasal bones had all but disappeared, and the exposed frontal bone bore evidence of several shallow, dishlike compression fractures. The maxilla was badly broken and a handful of teeth lay loose on the table. Whoever this young woman was, her face had been destroyed, exactly as Tríona's had been. Nora reached out to grasp the edge of the stainless-steel table and felt Frank Cordova move incrementally closer behind her. He was about to speak when a voice sounded behind them.

"Hey, Frank. I've got that report for you, and personal effects are here somewhere—"

Nora turned to see a stocky, bearded figure in blue scrubs. She had to concentrate on putting on a professional face as Frank introduced her.

"Steve Solomon," the newcomer said, extending his hand. "Buck Callaway has mentioned your name. And he told me a little about your work—in Ireland, right?" He turned his attention to the body on the table. "I'm glad to have you here. To be honest, I haven't really seen much of this sort of thing, so I'm happy to have an expert—"

"Not exactly an expert," Nora demurred. "Just trying to understand bog preservation a little better."

Solomon said: "I do have a little experience with wet burials—did my residency at Tulane, and my first job was with the Orleans Parish coroner. But I never encountered anything quite like this. So how does our Jane Doe compare to what you've seen?"

"Most of the bodies I've examined were much older—about two thousand years older, actually. But there was one case recently, a young man who'd been buried in peat for only about twenty-five years." *Danny Brazil,* whispered the small voice in her head. *His name was Danny Brazil and he kept bees.* Aloud she said: "Even after that short exposure to the bog environment, the similarity to ancient remains was pretty amazing."

Nora turned back to the body and studied the edges of the flesh where the right leg must have been submerged in water; the visible tendons and ligaments looked frayed, and she could see a layer of adipocere beneath the skin—ordinary body fat transformed into a yellowish, waxy material—a common feature of preserved remains. "The darkening of the skin is just a basic Maillard reaction. It starts quickly, but takes a long time to become really well established. There's some recent research from Canada, studies of fetal pigs buried in peat for different intervals, and some of them showed a slight change in coloration after only a few years. Sometimes it depends on the age of the individual, and the quality of their skin—how receptive it was to the chemical changes. Frank said you thought she might have been in the ground three or four years at least. From the degree of coloration, I'd probably agree with that."

Nora could feel Frank checking her expression, gauging her reaction to the body.

She asked: "No evidence that animals had disturbed the site?"

Solomon shook his head.

"At first I thought that was strange, since people run dogs down there all the time. But it's a floodplain—things shift around in high water. There's quite a lot of debris, and very little undergrowth in the area where she was found, and I wondered if the body might have been buried deeper by sediment and floodwater. Might be a contributing factor to the state of preservation—and it could be one reason she didn't turn up before now."

"The gravesite itself—the surrounding material—what was that like?"

"Primarily organic," Solomon said. "Lots of peat. The crime scene folks took plenty of samples. It seemed very wet for this late in the year—the ground all around her was completely sodden."

"Probably a spring or a seepage area nearby. There are spots like that all over at Hidden Falls. It makes a huge difference in preservation, the water levels and temperature. Do you mind if I take a closer look?"

Solomon pulled the lighted magnifying glass into position for her. "Be my guest."

Nora studied the broken edges of bone through the plate-sized lens, gently probing with gloved fingers and noting the angle of the breaks—the inward slope suggested impact from a convex shape, a rounded weapon. A fleeting impression flashed through the synapses in her brain: a raised hand, a heavy weight delivering a crushing blow. And not just once, but over and over again. Asking the next question meant straying from her consultant role. "Frank said you were thinking blunt force as the cause of death?"

"Looks that way," Solomon said. "From the uniform weathering, it looks like the fractures occurred perimortem."

"What about defensive wounds?"

"No marks indicating use of a sharp weapon, no trauma to the hands or forearms that would indicate defense against blunt force. Chances are the first blow was fatal and everything after that was unnecessary. Overkill."

Overkill. The same word Buck Callaway had used about Tríona.

Nora asked: "How long will it take to find out who she is?"

"We've got eight missing women still on the books," Cordova said. "Most don't fit her description, so that helps narrow it down."

"It helps that she took good care of her teeth," Solomon said. "The incisors have come loose, but we recovered all of her teeth from the site. Just one filling. The forensic odontologist was here yesterday. She's comparing dental records from missing persons right now. And this particular consultant is also an expert on facial trauma, so she should be able to provide information on the degree of force, maybe even the sort of weapon used. I'm guessing she'll have an answer for us today or tomorrow."

"You said you had clothing and personal effects?" Cordova asked.

"Right here," Solomon said, reaching behind him for the marked evidence bags, which he handed over. "Running clothes, shoes and socks, a watch. No ID. Everything's there."

Solomon's glance tracked over Cordova's shoulder to the doorway, where the receptionist was signaling a call for him. "Sorry, that may be the odontologist. I asked them to track me down if she called."

After he left the room, Nora spoke under her breath: "These injuries, Frank, they're identical—exactly the same as Tríona's. And the location—a black ash swamp—it can't just be coincidence."

"As soon as we figure out who she is—"

Solomon came back through the door, looking satisfied. "Looks like you won't have to wait. The odontologist is faxing over her report right now. The dental chart matched one of your missing persons, a twenty-two-year-old female—"

Frank Cordova finished the sentence for him: "Natalie Russo. I've been going through the missing persons files, too. Natalie disappeared the third of June—five years ago."

The words sent a cold knife down Nora's spine. She had often been gripped by the paralyzing notion that her sister would not be Peter Hallett's final victim. But for some reason it had never occurred to her that Tríona might not have been the first.

3

Cormac stood at the window of the hospital room, looking in at his father. No one had ever been able to explain what had prompted Joseph Maguire to leave Ireland. Perhaps he didn't fully understand the reasons himself. Now he lay in a hospital bed on the other side of the glass, breathing steadily with the help of a ventilator, as the nurse checked intravenous lines, his pulse, his oxygen level.

An insult to the brain, the doctors kept calling it, as if mere effrontery could trigger physical disaster. But his father was in no immediate danger, they said, and could leave the hospital once he could breathe on his own, provided he had adequate care at home. Adequate care. The blithe assumption in those words struck him, and Cormac suddenly felt short of breath. He turned and made his way to the ward entrance, past the nurse's station and the visitors' lounge, the canteen area with vending machines for tea and biscuits. He pushed open the lobby door and felt the cool, damp air hit him in the face. The flight from Shannon to New York left in less than twelve hours. He could leave now, not tell anyone where he was going; he could still make it—

A voice at his elbow brought him back to reality: "I thought I saw you headed out here," the nurse said, the same one who'd been taking his father's temperature. "You can go in to him if you like. Just for a few minutes. Some say it doesn't help, but I think they know you're there, even if they can't say. Go on, speak to him. You've nothing to lose."

Gazing into the woman's kind brown eyes, Cormac felt his prospect of escape collapse like a sail suddenly robbed of wind. He walked slowly back to the ward and slid into the chair beside his father's bed. Speak to him? He hadn't even figured out how to address the man. Calling him "Da," or "Father"—anything remotely along those lines—seemed ridiculous at this stage. And using his given name seemed even more preposterous. Easier just to sidestep the whole issue. Call him nothing at all.

Cormac had long ago realized that the word *father,* whatever it conjured up for other people, held no association at all for him, unless it was a void, an absence. As a child, he had built a sturdy box around that void and buried it, tried to concentrate on filling his life with other things. But absence was something he understood, at least. It was his father's sudden presence that was so bewildering. Cormac let his gaze wander across the man in the bed: the ropelike veins in the backs of the hands, the broken blood vessels visible through the papery skin at the temples, the unruly shock of white hair. This man looked so small, so insignificant, Cormac thought, for someone who had cast such a looming shadow. In dreams, Joseph Maguire had taken up a great deal more space.

He had no recollection of his father leaving, but they must have been living in Dublin at the time. There was only a vague memory of arriving in Clare, first to stay with his grandparents, then eventually settling, just himself and his mother, in the house along the sea road. No one ever talked about his father in those days—not to him at least. Over the next ten years, all he'd ever learned had to be gleaned from the few bits of conversation he might overhear after a letter arrived in the post. They came only sporadically—once, sometimes twice a year—but he'd felt the eyes of the village upon him for days after each delivery. In a small place like Kilgarvan, his family's circumstances accounted for at least half the local scandal. Once the postmistress spotted a foreign stamp, the news spread, passed along in whispers and glances, and everyone in the town would know about his father's letter before it ever arrived at their house. Cormac had felt the excitement each letter generated in the air around him—a volatile compound of curiosity, pity, and envy. At first he'd been unable to fathom the envy, but gradually realized that most of it came from schoolmates whose fathers were all too present, loading them with work, and ready with the strap if they dared shirk or disobey. Because his father was absent, they no doubt imagined him as free from all that—free to be coddled and cosseted by his mammy, with no manly interference.

He remembered watching the subtle change in his mother's face when the post came bearing one of those striped air mail envelopes. She would retreat to her room, appearing still and composed when she emerged an hour or so later, but her eyes were always red. No one said the letters were from his father, but they didn't have to—he knew. There was never a separate note for him, no word of greeting or even a postscript. After the third or fourth one, he had tried very hard not to care. At one point, he'd tried hating his father, focusing all his energy steadily on that one thing for a few weeks. But he found that loathing required a certain depth of feeling, which he had difficulty mustering against someone who barely existed. Eventually, he began to let people believe that his father was dead. It seemed true enough.

The old man's first resurrection had come unexpectedly, when he was away at university. It might never have happened, if his mother had not fallen ill. Returning home one weekend to help care for her, he had found his place occupied by a white-haired man claiming to be his father. His parents had decided—without consulting him—that he should stay at his studies. But he had refused to go back to Dublin. He'd taken off the rest of the term, and they had all lived together for a few weeks in the house on the sea road, maintaining a veneer of civility for his mother's sake. When she died, the charade had abruptly ended. Rejecting his father's offer to stay on in Ireland, Cormac had returned to his studies an orphan, and Joseph Maguire, who had presumably gone back to Chile, returned to being dead.

The second resurrection had been as unexpected as the first. Cormac slipped a letter from his pocket, a small pale blue envelope that had arrived through his mail slot in Dublin more than three years ago. The return address had meant nothing then: J. Maguire, Glencolumbkille Post Office, County Donegal. The handwriting was small and compact, the old-fashioned Gaelic script taught in National Schools when the country was new. He occasionally received similar letters from amateur archaeologists, and expected this dispatch to contain an earnest account of a previously undocumented ringfort or souterrain. His expectation was immediately dashed at the salutation. "My dear Cormac," it began:

I hope you might forgive me for addressing you in such familiar fashion, since we have never met. My name is Julia Maguire; I am your great-aunt, and I am writing today to convey what I hope may be welcome information.

I am an old woman, and you and your father are the only family I have left. Recently, I wrote to your father to let him know that upon my death, the house at Ardcrinn and all its contents will belong to him. He replied promptly, saying that he intended to return to Donegal before the end of March. He has not said whether it will be a brief visit, or whether he plans to stay. Given my current state of health, I can't be certain that I will be drawing breath when he arrives, and have told him so. I am not at all sentimental about dying; I have lived longer than most reasonable people might wish. I have taken writing this letter to you as my last imperative.

I know you have not seen your father for many years, and I cannot tell you what possessed him to leave Ireland, nor how he chose the path that he has taken. For all I know, you may have no wish to see him ever again. No one would blame you, I daresay. I can only tell you that there has always been a streak of the Wild Geese in Joseph since he was a boy, and no denying it. But one important thing I have learned in living so long is that anger does not diminish love; it has been my experience that the two may live together, side by side, for a very long time.

It's a great pity that we've never had a chance to meet. I have followed your accomplishments from afar all these years with great interest, and I should like to have known you better. We'll say no more about that. But I didn't want to make my exit from this world without leaving a small passage open to you. As you well know from your work, the door to the past and the door to the future are often one and the same.

I realize these words may have little effect, coming as they do from a stranger, but they are things that wanted saying, nonetheless. If you should decide to visit Donegal, just ask at the post office in Glencolumbkille and they will direct you to this house. That's all for now, dear Cormac. I wish you well.

The letter was signed, "Highest regards, Julia Maguire." The signature was larger and steadier than the rest of the script, as if accomplished in a last burst of strength. The pages had laid on his desk for several days as he tried to work out how to respond. But as it turned out, writing the letter and seeing it posted were quite literally the last things his great-aunt Julia had done.

Gazing at the motionless figure in the bed, Cormac felt the past spilling over him, a torrent of images and sensations that felt as if it might overwhelm and drown him: he saw a solitary boy walking along the sea road, repelling all disapproving or pitying looks with his invisible shield; he saw the row of syringes lined up on a metal tray, and the worn chaise where his mother rested, wrapped in her paisley shawl; he felt in his bones all those years of digging, searching for answers in the distant past; and through all of it, the urge to flee so strong again now that he could taste it in the back of his throat. He bowed his head and grasped the edge of the bed for support.

It would be a simple act, getting up from the chair and heading down the hallway, out the front door again. He closed his eyes and saw himself crossing the threshold in the hospital's modern glass foyer, not stopping, not looking back, just walking until he disappeared down the road. Toward the airport. To Nora.

When he opened his eyes, Cormac discovered that his father's hand had slid down the bedclothes and come to rest against his own. The old man's flesh felt warm against his, and he realized it was their first physical contact in nearly thirty years. For some reason, he could not bear to pull his hand away. Perhaps one day the words might come. For now, all he had was the faint hope of yet another resurrection.

4

Frank Cordova stood next to his car in the parking lot of the medical examiner's office. Nora Gavin's eyes seemed to drill into him. "Who is Natalie Russo, Frank? You know something about her—please tell me."

"I'll let you have a look for yourself," he said. He opened his car trunk and pulled a slender file from the carton of missing persons reports he'd been hauling around the past three days. He remembered his own first sight of Natalie, down at the river three days ago, and how he'd felt that distinctive cold trace down his neck, wondering if this girl's death was somehow related to Tríona Hallett's. Nora took the file and climbed into the passenger seat. He knew what she was looking for, because he'd searched for it himself: an overlapping circumstance, a possible proximity, some person or place that would connect the dead girl and Peter Hallett. But there was nothing like that in the file.

Natalie Russo had been a recent transplant to Saint Paul when she disappeared five years ago. She had a job as a bike messenger for a company whose regular client list included law firms, graphic designers, people whose incomes depended on speed. But she worked only part-time, to leave plenty of hours in the day for training. Rowing was definitely her priority. The emergency contact on her employment application was a coach from the Twin Cities Rowing Club, Sarah Cates. Nothing out of the ordinary the week she disappeared: pickups and deliveries for the usual clients, rowing practice, her morning run along the paths at Hidden Falls. On Friday, she didn't show up for work or rowing practice, but no one realized anything was wrong until her bike was spotted in its customary place outside the rowing club. Her teammates had turned out to help with a foot search, but they found nothing. She was just gone.

Frank's cell phone began to vibrate, and he glanced at the number. His partner, Karin Bledsoe. She had already called twice this morning, probably wondering where the hell he was. He shoved the phone back in his pocket. She would have her answer soon enough.

He glanced over at Nora, watching the way she flipped through the pages in the file, the way her thumbnail absently brushed against her lower lip as she read. He felt suddenly unnerved by that gesture, and all the thousand other things he'd tried so hard to forget. It was stupid, thinking he could handle being with her again, any better than he'd handled it the last time.

Last night had started out innocently enough. It was sickening, wondering what he'd said and done. There was no car parked in front of the carriage house the first time he drove past in the afternoon. Never mind that the apartment was on a narrow, one-way street where nobody just happened to drive by. He could have turned around then, gone home. Instead he'd gone to a bar down on Grand Avenue to grab some dinner. Then he'd started ordering tequila shots, trying to talk himself out of going past the carriage house again on his way home. By the time he went back, there was a rental car out front. If she'd only been inside the apartment, he'd have been spared any humiliation. If memory served, he hadn't even managed to ring the bell. Just his luck that she'd been out, and found him on the doorstep as she came home. There was one small mercy—at least he hadn't tried to drive.

He'd awakened this morning just as he had three years ago—with a sore head, and a curious, buoyant feeling that lasted only until he'd turned over to find himself alone. Three years ago, after their one night together, Nora had managed to avoid him, and then left the country without a word. Not even a phone message or a note to say she was going away, that what had happened had been a mistake. That part he'd had to figure out all on his own. He'd been present when the need took her, but now it seemed he was nothing but a momentary lapse in judgment, a slightly embarrassing memory. Strange—even knowing all that didn't seem to change the way he felt. Something had taken hold of him that night, and he had never been able to shake it off.

Nora finally spoke. "There's nothing here, Frank. Nothing to connect her to Peter—except the river. He used to run down at Hidden Falls. That's probably where he was the morning after Tríona disappeared. And the blows to the face—"

In addition to the dental match, the forensic odontologist had determined from the fractures that the injuries to Natalie Russo's face had been made by someone with remarkable upper-body strength, most likely using a heavy, rounded object about the size and shape of a small grapefruit. Frank knew that Nora was thinking about the profiler they'd consulted at the time of Tríona's murder. Injuries to the face—like those sustained by Tríona, and now Natalie Russo as well—that sort of an attack was usually personal. Much more likely to occur, according to the profiler, when the killer and the victim were involved in an intimate relationship. As if murder itself wasn't enough, whoever had destroyed these women's faces had taken a step beyond and tried to rub them out, deny their very existence. A strange sound floated through his head, an old man's voice, like the buzzing of a fly: *Susto, susto.* He felt a tightening inside, a queasiness that hadn't gone away since last night. He never should have started drinking tequila.

Nora said, "Have you checked through the evidence from Hidden Falls? If we could line up the two crime scenes, or find something that would link Peter to Natalie Russo—"

"The crime scene unit just finished processing, but we've got some of the stuff logged in down at evidence storage."

"If they found something of Tríona's at that site—"

When they arrived at police headquarters a few minutes later, Nora followed Cordova down a chilly stairwell, listening to their footsteps reverberate against concrete. The few people they passed greeted Frank by name, and she felt their eyes surreptitiously checking the name on her visitor's pass. Some of them would remember the trouble she'd stirred up five years ago—and no doubt pity Frank, having to deal with her again. When they reached the basement, he led her to property and evidence storage, a vast expanse of shelving behind a glass window, home to thousands of cardboard file boxes. And this wasn't even a tenth of it—there was another whole warehouse somewhere close by, filled with thousands more sealed cartons. Somewhere in this place they could also find Tríona's blood-soaked clothing, all the physical details that painted the gruesome picture of her last moments. As many times as Nora had been here, for some reason it had never struck her before in the same way, this vast system of enumerated transgressions. This library of crime reduced every offense, even the most horrific, to office work. Perhaps boxing up and storing away all the disturbing details of robbery and rape and murder was a way to feel as though you could contain them somehow.

She hung back while Frank signed out the evidence files. He took the first two boxes from the property officer; they'd have to wait while the others were retrieved.

In the meantime, Frank led her into an evidence exam room and shut the door behind them. He set his boxes on the table. "Like I said, there's probably more on the way, but we can go through what's been collected—" He suddenly winced and tilted forward, pressing two fingers to his chest.

Nora felt stabbing fear. "Frank, are you all right?"

He waved her away. "It's nothing—I'm okay." He fumbled in his pocket and quickly popped two antacids.

"How often are you taking those?"

"I don't know—a couple of times a day." Cordova straightened, but his face was ashy. He let out a slow breath. "It comes and goes. I'm fine."

"Have you seen a doctor? It could be more than heartburn."

He turned on her. "Jesus Christ, Nora—will you stop mothering me?"

She took a step back, shocked by his sudden flash of anger. "I'm just worried about you, Frank."

"Well, do me a favor and stop worrying." He kept his face turned away, shielded his eyes with one hand. "For three years, I've been trying to tell myself that what happened with us was a mistake. Unprofessional on my part, a slip-up. But every time I try to get that night out of my head, it won't seem to shake loose. I'm not sorry it happened."

"But it wasn't real, Frank—"

"How do you know that? You never gave us a chance to find out. For Chrissake, Nora, we never even talked about what happened. Can you honestly tell me you don't feel anything—"

"Of course not—it wouldn't be true. But things happen, Frank, things outside our control—"

His eyes narrowed. "You met someone. Over there."

"It's got nothing to do with you and me, with what happened—"

He let go a bitter laugh. "Christ, some detective I am. It was staring me right in the face. Here's an idea—why don't I stand here and make a fool of myself just once more, and you can stand there, laughing—"

Nora had never seen him like this; the change was bewildering. "Do you see me laughing? I care about you, Frank, and God knows I'm indebted—" She winced, regretting the choice of words.

His voice became deadly quiet: "So that's what you were doing with me that night—paying off a debt?"

The heavy metal door banged open suddenly, and a handcart piled high with file boxes seemed to roll on its own into the room. A uniformed officer, a wiry terrier of a man in his mid-fifties, cocked an eye at them above the boxes. "Where do you want these, Frank?"

Cordova shaded his face with one hand. "Just stack them up along the wall, I guess, Charlie. That's not everything, is it?"

"Hell, no—I got another half dozen in the lockup." He glanced sideways at Nora as he unloaded the cart. "You might need a bigger room." When the boxes were unloaded, he spun the empty dolly with a dancer's finesse, whistling as he steered it out the door and back down the hall.

Nora waited until the door was shut to speak: "Frank, please—you know very well that's not what I meant."

"Just tell me if you met someone. Yes or no."

Nora felt her throat tighten. "Yes."

"Is it serious?"

"I think so—yes."

Cordova's head had dropped forward. He stared at the floor for a moment, then took a deep breath.

Nora felt a sudden urge to reach out to him, but resisted. "I was confused. You were the only person I could really trust. In the morning, I was afraid I'd completely messed things up between us, and I didn't want to do that. I see now that going away wasn't right, it wasn't fair—I'm so sorry, Frank."

He looked up at her again, but he wasn't listening. His eyes had gone flat, and he seemed to be looking straight through her. "I should give Charlie a hand with the rest of those boxes."

When he had gone, Nora sat down at the table and buried her head in her arms. She had known since last night that this conversation was in the cards. But could it possibly have gone any worse?

A few seconds later, the door swung open, and Nora turned to see an athletic-looking woman about her own age, with pale blue eyes and a summer tan set off by short-cropped, naturally white-blond hair. She was dressed in a neat brown suit and a white blouse open at the throat. The ID on the lanyard around her neck said "Detective" in bold letters.

Frank Cordova, standing beside her with a couple of file boxes in his arms, looked thoroughly put out. He said, "Nora, I don't think you've ever met my partner—"

The woman smiled and put out her hand in greeting. "Karin Bledsoe. I've certainly heard your name, Dr. Gavin."

Taking in the polite but slightly frozen smile, Nora could only presume what else Frank's partner had heard. No time to worry about that now. Charlie was back with the next load of files, wheeling his cart past them into the room.

"So, what are you two doing down here?" Karin Bledsoe asked, managing with her tone to make the meeting seem slightly illicit. "I thought you were working that Jane Doe case today, Frank."

"I am. We just got an ID—Natalie Russo, one of our missing persons. I wanted Dr. Gavin to have a look at the evidence from the scene because it may have a bearing on her own case—her sister's case, I mean." Frank seemed inordinately uncomfortable, even considering what had just passed a few minutes before in this room. For a moment Nora couldn't grasp the reason, until at last she felt an unexpected jolt—it wasn't just happenstance or professional curiosity that had carried Frank's partner all the way down here to the basement. Despite the conspicuous wedding band on Karin Bledsoe's left hand, Nora suddenly knew that this woman was more than Frank Cordova's work partner. And if her intuition was true, it put a whole different spin on the conversation she'd just had with him, not to mention his appearance on her doorstep last night.

Karin Bledsoe turned to Frank. "I would love to give you a hand, but I've got court today. That's why I was trying to call you, Frank. Just in case you forgot. The duty officer said he saw you headed down here, so I thought I'd deliver the message in person." She turned to give Nora a last look and another frosty smile. "So nice to meet you at last, Dr. Gavin."

After Karin Bledsoe left, Frank wouldn't make eye contact. He turned away to open the first evidence box, and began checking its contents against the inventory list.

"Have you and Karin been partners long?" Nora could hear the brittle note in her voice.

Frank didn't look up. "Two years." From his tone, she knew he wasn't in the mood to talk about Karin Bledsoe—or anything else.

She decided not to push. Maybe after that disastrous conversation a few minutes ago, she ought to count herself lucky that Frank was willing to stay here and work with her. That his need for justice was stronger than his pride.

They worked for a long time in silence, Frank removing bagged items one by one from each box and handing them to Nora. They both knew exactly what they were looking for: when Tríona's body was discovered, her right shoe was missing, presumably lost at the crime scene or somewhere along the way to the parking garage. Her purse had been found in the car trunk with the body, but her cell phone—the same one Nora had tried calling from the hotel lobby—had never turned up.

The evidence collected from Natalie Russo's grave site at Hidden Falls was mostly an odd assortment of litter. Nora counted at least a dozen cigarette butts, a couple of flattened beer cans, six sodden matchbooks, innumerable food wrappers, two used condoms, an empty spray paint can. How was it possible to focus on what was important? She watched Frank linger over a prescription pill bottle, trying to read the faded label, as she peered through evidence bags at a stone arrowhead; an ancient, corroded pocket watch; a rusty penknife. The next box contained a handful of mildewed pages that looked as though they'd been ripped from a book of poems. Nora watched as Frank flipped through the curled, black-smudged pages, looking for writing in the margin, underlined words, anything that might tell more. How was it possible to know which stories might be connected? Maybe the pill bottle and the cigarette butts were part of the same story—or perhaps the penknife and the poetry? It was also possible that these fragments were all from completely disconnected tales that overlapped only in the physical world, rubbing together in the layers of detritus left by different generations. Two hours later, they were getting near the end of their search through the evidence, with no sign of a shoe or a cell phone.

"There might be more on the way," Frank said. "The state crime lab is still processing the rest."

"What's that?" Nora pointed to a manila envelope, the last item in the box.

Frank checked the label. "'Soil and plant material.'" He used his penknife to slit open the initialed seal and shook out a heap of dirt and organic material onto a large plastic tray.

Nora began to poke at the pile with a pencil. Some of the leaves were easily recognizable: cottonwood, ash and elm, buckthorn, along with loamy soil studded with many different kinds of seeds. She didn't look up. "Frank, do you remember the stuff Buck Callaway combed from Tríona's hair?"

"Sure—that's how we knew her body had been moved."

"If we compared these leaves and seeds—"

"What could that tell us? We already know Tríona was probably killed somewhere along the river."

Nora spoke slowly: "Yes, but if Tríona was attacked near the spot where Natalie Russo was buried, she might have carried away something very specific to that site. We never had anything to compare to the material from Tríona's hair. I'm just thinking—the leaves and seeds from a single parent plant carry the same genetic fingerprint."

"But DNA testing takes weeks, months, you know that. The state crime lab is always backed up—"

Nora waved a hand to stop him. "The testing wouldn't have to be done at the state lab. Do you remember Holly Blume, my friend at the University Herbarium? The forensic botanist who identified the seeds from Tríona's hair. Her specialty is population genetics—she runs DNA profiles on plants all the time. We could ask Holly to compare the samples from the two cases, see if we can't come up with a match on the crime scenes that way. It may be a long shot, but it's at least worth a try."

5

Thirty minutes later, Nora led Frank Cordova down an air-conditioned corridor on the eighth floor of the Biological Sciences Building on the University of Minnesota's Saint Paul campus. She knocked on an office door, and a small, dark-haired woman answered. Holly Blume's face brightened at the sight of her two unexpected visitors, but Nora was unprepared for her friend's fierce embrace.

"Nora Gavin! What happened to you? You dropped off the face of the earth. We were all so worried about you—"

Nora had gone away believing that she'd lost everything, but perhaps she'd been mistaken in thinking she had lost all her friends. As Holly drew back to study her, Nora had to fight to keep her emotions in check. "I'm fine, Holly. I've been abroad for a while."

"But nobody knew how to get in touch. You should have told someone where you were. I got married, Nora, had a baby." Holly's expression softened. "I shouldn't scold you. I know you had good reasons for going away. Just want you to know you've been sorely missed." She glanced at Frank. "Why do I get the feeling this isn't just a social call?"

"Holly, you remember Frank Cordova—"

"Yes, of course. How are you, Detective? It's a pity we only meet under professional circumstances. I'd ask you in to sit, but it's a bit cramped in here—let's go across to the Herbarium."

Despite its impressive Latin name, the Herbarium was nothing more than a climate-controlled room full of metal cabinets, each containing specimens of pressed plants from Minnesota and all around the world. No one could enter without comprehending just how antiquarian the field of plant biology remained. Color-coded maps of county biological surveys hung on the wall. The images might be computer-generated nowadays, and the ranges of various plants tracked with GPS coordinates, but the data were still collected by human beings traveling on foot, taking samples from fields and forests and ditches. Holly gestured for them to sit at the battered lab table at the center of the room, and sat forward herself, fingers laced together expectantly.

"What we've got are samples of plant material from two crime scenes," Nora said.

Frank held up two evidence envelopes. "We think both samples may have originated from the same site at Hidden Falls Park, but we need to know whether it's possible to prove that—beyond a reasonable doubt."

Holly eyed the bulging envelopes. "I'm not going to promise anything, but I can certainly have a look."

Nora asked, "Do you remember the seeds you identified from my sister's hair?"

"Sure," Holly said. "There were lots of different species, as I recall, pretty typical of seepage swamp: black ash and cottonwood, buckthorn, marsh marigold, Virginia creeper, touch-me-not, wood nettle. They're all pretty common. But there was one unusual find as well, seeds from a plant called false mermaid. It's only been documented a couple of places in Minnesota, and only outside the Twin Cities. I was sorry we couldn't pinpoint where the seeds came from—it would have helped your case, I know."

"We might have another chance," Nora said. "I remember that name, false mermaid. Something to do with mythology?"

"I'm astonished that you remember," Holly said. She pointed to a poster on the wall, photographs of a wispy-looking green plant. A corner inset showed a close-up of three wrinkled seeds. "There it is—the Latin name is *Floerkea proserpinacoides*: The genus, *Floerkea,* after the famous German botanist Gustav Heinrich Flörke, and the epithet, *proserpinacoides,* which means 'like *Proserpinaca.*' *Proserpinaca* is a semiaquatic plant, also called 'mermaid weed.' The fellow who named false mermaid thought its leaves bore a strong resemblance to *Proserpinaca*. As it turns out, they aren't genetically related, but the name stuck anyway."

"But that's the mythological connection," Nora said.

Holly smiled. "Wow—no flies on you! Proserpina was the daughter of Ceres—"

"Goddess of agriculture."

"That's right. When Proserpina was carried off by Pluto, god of the underworld, her mother spent ages searching for her. When she was found, Ceres interceded with Jupiter, who said Proserpina could return to earth, as long as she'd taken no food or drink during her stay in the underworld."

Nora felt her memory trickling back. "But Pluto had offered her a piece of fruit when she arrived, and she had eaten the pulp of a single pomegranate seed."

Holly threw a wry look at Frank. "And here's me, imagining myself the lone mythology geek in the room. Jupiter suggested a compromise; Proserpina got to spend half the year above ground with her mother, and half the year in the underworld with her husband-slash-captor. Now, here's the connection to the plant world: *Proserpinaca,* as I mentioned, is semiaquatic. That means the lower part grows underwater, the upper part grows in the air. That's how it ended up with the name mermaid weed. *Floerkea,* on the other hand, grows in seeps and marshes and other wet places, but it isn't even semiaquatic, so that's where the 'false' part comes in—sorry, I'm sure all this is *way* more than you needed to know. Back to the samples. What exactly are you looking for?"

Frank said: "We're trying to establish a connection between two crime scenes, and what we need are a few hard facts."

Nora jumped in: "I know you're involved in population genetics, and I wondered if there's any way to tell whether any of the leaves or seeds from these two samples came from the same parent plant. I know it's a lot to ask—"

Holly considered for a moment. "In order to have any statistical credibility, you need enough material to establish allele frequencies, to say definitively that the plants in your two samples are related. I'd have to go down to the site myself to collect more samples—thirty is usually the magic number."

Frank said: "The crime scene crews are finished up down there, but I'll talk to the supervisor, let them know what you'll need. They can give you a hand, if they know what to look for."

"Even after I get the samples, you realize DNA results are going to take a few days."

Frank said: "Unfortunately, time is the one thing we haven't got. Our suspect is leaving the country Saturday. If we could find something before then—"

Holly stood and held up a hand. "Say no more—the sooner you two are on your way, the sooner I can get cracking."

They were halfway down the hall when Holly stuck her head out the lab door and called after them. "I nearly forgot to say—you'll also want to double check any clothing you might have in evidence for seeds and pollen grains. Plants are clever stowaways. They're all about survival."

6

After dropping Nora back at her apartment, Frank Cordova sat at the corner, waiting to turn east onto Summit Avenue. He happened to glance into the rearview mirror, and instead of seeing Nora, he saw a small, dark-eyed child standing in the car's backseat. Suddenly he was that child, feeling hot vinyl upholstery burning the backs of his arms and legs, the soles of his feet as he stood looking into a pair of dark eyes that glared at him from the rearview mirror. There was no story, no context for the image, just terrible, crushing dread. And then the vision was gone; another random fragment of the past that floated briefly to the surface only to become submerged again. Frank put it out of his head. He had interviews to conduct, evidence to compare; there was no time for chasing phantoms.

But another memory surfaced: that girl's body laid out on the table this morning, and he felt an almost electrical surge, then another. The vague fear that usually lived deep in his gut began to rise, and with it came the smell of dust, and the air of a closed-up space. He felt the unwelcome heat of someone close beside him, heard the rough breathing, the loud whisper that kept asking, *Paco, what's the matter? Why is Papi yelling?* Stopping the questions took two hands. It also left his own ears open, but he had no choice. No one was supposed to know where they were. He cradled the back of his brother's head with his left hand and clamped the other tight over Chago's slobbery mouth, still mumbling beneath his fingers. He began to rock back and forth, hunching his shoulders, as if that might block his ears. He tried to drown out the noises in the next room by filling his head with a constant torrent of words: *Please oh please oh please oh please—Díos te salve, María, llena eres de gracia, el Señor es contigo, bendita tú eres entre todas las mujeres, y bendito es el fruto de tu vientre, Jesús. Santa María, Madre de Dios, ruega por nosotros pecadores, ahora y en la hora de nuestra muerte. Amén. Please oh please oh please oh please oh please oh please*—hoping somehow his hundreds of unvoiced prayers would help speed the merciful silence that always followed.

The noise of squealing tires suddenly roused him, as if from a trance. He swerved instinctively to avoid the car that came careening toward him, and jammed on the brakes. The other driver pulled up just short of a collision, his shocked face visible through the windshield. Cordova felt his heart pumping; he suddenly felt woozy and light-headed. The other car had come to a full stop just inches from his driver's side door in the middle of the intersection. The cathedral was directly in front of him, and all at once he knew what had happened—he'd run the red light. The other driver pulled alongside and lowered his passenger window to let go a string of curses. Frank could see the man's lips moving, but the words didn't register. It occurred to him, in some faraway part of his brain, that he must be in shock. The other driver eventually gave up and sped off, raising his middle finger in the rearview mirror as a parting salute. Cordova stared down at his own hands, still gripping the steering wheel. He remembered dropping Nora, and the next thing he recalled was the sound of squealing tires. The time in between was blank. His hands were clammy and his mouth felt dry. He finally shifted his foot from the brake and pulled away from the intersection. Behind him, the normal flow of traffic resumed.

He drove the rest of the way to the station on hyperalert, conscious of every turn and traffic signal. It wasn't the first time he'd suddenly awakened from a reverie in the middle of traffic, sometimes miles from where he'd last been paying attention.

The usual culprits joined the lineup in his head: overwork, lack of sleep, lousy food, too much to drink last night. He hadn't been to the gym in months; there was never any time. The way things were going, he wouldn't pass his next fitness test. He'd seen it happen often enough to recognize the signs. This was the way it came, the beginning of the end.

Pulling into his parking space, he lifted his hands from the steering wheel to find they were still shaking. He reached up to the rearview mirror and, tilting it downward, found himself staring into an unfamiliar pair of dark eyes. Suddenly disconcerted, he flipped the mirror back, but could still feel that baleful gaze upon him, burned into memory like something from a bad dream.

7

Thirty minutes after Frank Cordova dropped her at the curb, Nora was in her rental car and on her way to Hidden Falls Park. Holly Blume's parting words had only added to the creeping horror that had settled on her in the morgue this morning. Natalie Russo's death had something to do with Tríona, she was sure of it. But dead certainty was not the same as proof.

After Tríona's body was discovered in her car trunk, forensic details had come out only gradually. Buck Callaway estimated that death had occurred in the early hours of Saturday morning, probably sometime between midnight and 4 A.M. The seeds and leaves Holly Blume had identified from Tríona's hair pointed to a seepage swamp—a place just like the boggy spot where Natalie Russo's body had been buried.

On the map, the Mississippi meandered gracefully through the city of Saint Paul, from the leafy gorge on its western edge, to the railheads and stockyards of the east. Hidden Falls was just over four miles directly southwest of Crocus Hill, and it was a span Nora could have driven blindfolded. She headed west on Saint Clair, and turned south onto the river road. Just past the sprawling Ford plant, she made a soft right into the entrance of Hidden Falls Park. The parklands traced the southern edge of the only natural gorge along the Mississippi. The road plunged down a steep ravine, coming to an end at parking lots for the picnic grounds and boat landing along the river bottom. Nora knew the place well. The river was one of the few wild spots within city limits, and she had spent a lot of time here at Hidden Falls as an adolescent, collecting specimens, drawing interesting plants and insects, amazed at all the life-and-death drama in miniature going on below most human radar.

Parking in the lot next to the picnic shelter, she cast a glance in the direction of the river. Still high for this time of year. In midsummer, depending on the rains, the river sometimes had no visible current, but the water moved along under the surface all the same—she used to imagine the endless flow stirring the whiskers of huge carp that lurked along the muddy riverbed.

Because of the gorge, this stretch of river had long been a no-man's-land, a strip of wildness and disorder cutting through the heart of civilization. Sometimes the park seemed perfectly harmless, with families picnicking, people walking their dogs; at other times it seemed forbidden and even dangerous, the sort of place where female joggers would be discouraged from running alone. It was common knowledge that high school kids ran keg parties on the sandbar below the veterans' home; a mile or two in either direction were a couple of notorious gay cruising spots. For years, rumors of drinking and drugs and anonymous sex at the river's edge had floated above into the real world. People came here to be someone else, to indulge appetites and fantasies they wouldn't dream of admitting. Most understood that they were courting danger; no doubt for some of them, it was part of the attraction. Nora began to feel a vague unease, knowing what lay ahead among the chest-high undergrowth and layers of dead leaves underfoot. The fallen leaves and tangled branches of the forest floor suddenly seemed sinister, part of a teeming underworld of decay and corruption.

A few yards away, a man sat alone in a green pickup. Nora felt his eyes upon her as she walked past, but when she glanced up, he was staring at the river. She knew Frank wouldn't approve of her coming down here alone, but it was broad daylight, and she couldn't expect him to be her minder. He had enough to do. And she had to see it for herself, the place where Natalie Russo had been found. Slinging her backpack onto one shoulder, she locked the car and started on foot in the direction of the falls, glancing behind to make sure no one was following.

She'd always been drawn to Hidden Falls, as much for the mysterious name as for its wild, otherworldly aspect. A faint sound of falling water came from the ravine to her right. She stopped to listen. At the turn of the previous century, tourists had come from all over the city to see the falls, where water seeped through the rock face at the top of the bluff, spreading like a thin veil across a limestone ledge before spilling into the catch pool below. A hundred years later, the area was a little shabby, making it a perfect hangout for kids seeking adventure and danger.

She turned away from the falls and plunged almost immediately into one of the park's more primitive portions, where narrow footpaths wound over and around the corpses of fallen trees. Marshy areas filled the low spots, and the limestone bluff rose up sixty feet or more to her right, its lower surfaces marked with spray paint and scarred with crudely carved initials. The river wasn't even visible in this part of the woods, yet it was almost impossible not to feel the water's ominous presence. Earthen ridges, some eight and ten feet high, marked the river's variable path, and in the many low spots, drowned grass and broken branches aligned in one direction, combed out by floodwaters that had receded weeks ago. Nora felt a chill, and rubbed her bare arms as she walked along. She couldn't help thinking of all the evidence that must have been swept away and carried along in the river's current, swirled for miles in dirty water until it all piled up in that thick gumbo of silt and crawfish and chemicals that formed the delta more than a thousand miles downstream. This river had once been an artery, a channel that carried the lifeblood of a whole continent; in less than a hundred and fifty years, civilization reduced it to hardly more than a sewer and dumping ground.

She spied a few scraps of crime scene tape still wound around trees in a low-lying area a few yards ahead, and knew that she had arrived at the spot where Natalie Russo's body had lain. No one was about. The slope beside the path was steep, and Nora held on to a sapling to keep from sliding on the thick bed of leaves underfoot. Inching sideways, down to the area of disturbed earth, she thought of the other damp burials she had helped uncover in the past year, remembering all that a grave could reveal. Like the others she had seen, this was no careful inhumation, but the hurried concealment of a crime. There was a deep gash in the earth, and the ground was covered in clods of earth and peat, trampled by the boots of those who had removed the remains, searchers who had combed the scene for evidence. She crouched down and peered into the depression, amazed to find that Natalie Russo's burial place still bore the recognizable impression of a pair of shoes, soles outlined in a random maze of tiny whitened roots. Reaching out to trace the outline of the void, she was struck by the fact that even while she was viewing the body in the morgue, her thoughts about Natalie Russo had focused on whatever she might tell them about Tríona. The empty space before her now conjured a distinct human being. A person whose absence was no doubt still mourned by someone.

Sinking to her knees again, Nora picked up a handful of debris from the forest floor, staring down at the crumpled leaf skeletons and strange seeds, nearly overpowered by their damp smell. What would Holly look for when she came here to collect her thirty samples? What were the chances that the mystery of Tríona's death would finally be unraveled by codes hidden inside these cells?

Her ears picked up a sudden noise from deeper in the woods, like someone scuffling through leaves. Rising awkwardly from her crouch, Nora lost her balance and stepped forward into the marshy depression, sinking quickly in the saturated ground. If working on bogs had taught her anything at all, it was that instinct could not be trusted in a place like this. She knew that the more she struggled, the deeper her foot would go. The key was to spread out. She sat down on the ground, feeling cold wetness seep uncomfortably through her thin summer clothes, leaning back on her elbows and hoping the spot was too damp to support poison ivy. That was all she needed. But her foot was well and truly stuck. She pressed her back into the earth, trying to relax, studying the undersides of the leaves all around her, amazed once more at the tiny flowers and fruits that grew so close to the ground.

She sat up at the noise of twigs snapping underfoot, the random sounds of someone rummaging through the tangled vines and branches that littered the forest floor. Had someone followed her? It sounded like more than one person. She tried twisting around to see who was coming, but with her leg still buried nearly up to the calf, there was no way to escape. She pressed her back to the ground again, watching and waiting for the trespassers to come into view. When they did, the two pairs of plaintive, dark eyes observing her did not belong to anything human, but to a white-tailed doe and her fawn. The young deer, not yet grown out of his spots, had a twist of vine caught on his slender hind leg. The noise she'd heard was the crashing of his hobble through the underbrush. As they passed in front of her, the mother looked straight at her. Nora didn't dare blink or breathe. The doe stood still, too, sniffing the air as her offspring flailed his leg in an effort to break free. Finally the vine came loose, and they bounded off together, disappearing silently into the undergrowth.

Relieved to be alone again, she tried pulling her foot from the ground, slow and steady, until at last it came free. She started to climb to her feet, considering that if she hadn't been out on all those Irish bogs she wouldn't have known what to do—and no doubt would have lost the shoe.

All at once, a slow, horrible knowledge, a formless cloud of recognition began moving through her, thinking about Tríona's missing shoe. No one had ever thought to dig for it.

She fell to her knees and began to claw at the earth, not thinking, just scrabbling at the soft peat. She stopped suddenly, holding out her hands to find the nails completely blackened, just as Tríona's had been. Closing her eyes, she saw her sister being chased through these woods, scrambling and falling through brambles and stinging nettles, finally caught and pinned down—

Nora tried to force the images from her head, but they would not leave. She raised her eyes to take in all the loamy ridges and areas of disturbed earth. At least half a dozen within sight, and many more scattered all through the woods. Every one a perfect place to conceal a body. All those missing women in Frank's files—how many more might be buried here? Tríona's words came back: *There are things you don't know . . . about Peter, about me. I've done things, too. You don't know—unspeakable things—*

Nora felt a wave of panic beginning to gather inside her. She began to run, but stumbled forward and fell, waiting to be swallowed up.

8

Nora lay on the damp ground, letting the terrible knowledge rise up out of the earth and seep into her. If Tríona had been here, and if she'd been digging, it could mean that she knew where Natalie Russo's body was buried—

Isn't it shocking, what you'll do when you love someone?

To think of all the times she had listened to those words repeating over and over inside her head, never understanding what they could mean.

All at once there was a commotion a short distance away. Without stopping to think, Nora made a lunge for the fallen tree beside the path, leaping behind it just as two figures, male and female, came into view.

The woman spoke first: "Here it is, Rog. Let's get set up here—and make sure you get that crime scene tape in the shot."

Nora recognized the voice—Janelle Joyner, one of the local television reporters who had covered Tríona's murder. Janelle had boasted to more than a few people that Tríona Hallett was going to be her ticket out of the Twin Cities, maybe even her springboard to national cable news. Evidently not everything had gone according to plan.

Janelle must have come here to tape one of her awful teasers for the evening news. Nora couldn't bear to listen. She looked down the length of the massive tree trunk, hoping to find a way to escape without being seen, and found herself staring into a pair of dark eyes about ten feet away. A slender Asian man of indeterminate age had concealed himself behind the twisted roots of the same fallen tree. He eyed her warily, no doubt hoping that she wouldn't raise an alarm. He had a basket slung around him, and a fishing pole in his left hand—could this be the fisherman who'd found Natalie Russo?

Nora raised herself to peer over the log, watching Janelle check her makeup in a compact. When the shot was set, the cameraman gave the signal to go, and Janelle's face was suddenly transformed. If Nora hadn't watched her put it on, the look of concern might have seemed real.

Janelle was in top form. "A young woman's skeletal remains were found in a shallow grave here at Hidden Falls three days ago. Her identity is unknown, but she could be one of several women still listed as missing. Police are comparing details from this case with several other unsolved murders. Should local residents be concerned about a serial killer on the loose? We'll have the full story at ten."

The full story. Hacks like Janelle Joyner never had the full story on anything. They weren't even above dragging a victim's reputation through the mud if it could get them into a bigger television market.

Janelle seemed pleased with the take. "Got that, Rog? Okay, let's pack it up—we've still got to get that two-shot with the head of regional parks. People want to know if it's safe to bring their kids down here."

The cameraman muttered something inaudible, and Janelle turned on him: "Hey, I wouldn't go bad-mouthing the brand if I were you. Channel Eight's all about news you can use."

Still hiding behind her fallen tree, Nora glanced over to see if the fisherman had taken in the whole Janelle Joyner spectacle too, but he had vanished. For a split second, she wondered whether she'd seen him at all.

Heading north on the river road from Hidden Falls, Nora only meant to drive past Peter Hallett's house, but found her foot shifting to the brake almost automatically. She had stopped in this same spot more than once, taking advantage of its shielded view of the driveway and front door, as well as the adjoining terrace. The house stood well back from the road, across a deep wooded ravine. Peter had designed the place himself; with his signature modern style favoring strong horizontal lines and lots of glass, he had made sure his creation stood out from the neighboring houses, with their staid neo-Georgian brick faces and fan windows. Transparent walls had always seemed to Nora a somewhat paradoxical predilection for someone who led a double life. He'd left the house with furnishings, artwork, everything intact when he moved to Seattle—as if he knew he'd be coming back.

A sudden flash in the rearview mirror signaled a silver-blue Mercedes convertible rounding the curve behind her. Nora watched the car turn up the driveway, then flipped open her glove compartment and reached for the camera she'd stashed there. She focused the high-powered lens on Miranda Staunton climbing out on the driver's side—Marc's younger sister was in her mid-twenties now, with thin bronze arms, blonde hair perfectly cut and coiffed, eyes hidden behind a pair of stylish sunglasses. Nora zoomed the camera in closer, and braced for the jolt of seeing Peter Hallett again.

He was, as expected, still shockingly handsome, with a vital energy that she could feel, even across the distance that separated them. She watched as he turned and flashed his megawatt smile at Miranda, who reached out and led him up the steps and through the front door. Nora felt her body go cold. Beyond the chill there was something else—after five years of chaos and frustration, she sensed that things were beginning to align in some new and fateful way. There was the discovery of Natalie Russo's body—and her own arrival here, at the very moment Peter returned from Seattle. It was as if the last piece of the puzzle was about to be laid out on the table. But where was Elizabeth?

As if on cue, her niece's head suddenly appeared from behind a headrest in the backseat. Amazing that a child could even squeeze into that tiny space—the Mercedes was built only for two. Left to fend for herself, Elizabeth struggled to move the passenger seat forward, but couldn't quite reach the lever. She pushed herself up and vaulted over the right rear wheel, landing awkwardly on both feet. Nora could not look away. Elizabeth was not a little girl anymore, but an ungainly adolescent, shoulders already beginning to slump with attitude. She had her mother's coloration, and Nora knew that, up close, the child's face would be lightly freckled like her own.

Elizabeth opened the trunk and pulled out a backpack. As she set her pack on the ground, a wavy curtain of copper hair fell across her face. Both hands came up, automatically pushing the thick tangle behind her ears. Nora tightened her grip on the camera lens. Where had that gesture come from? Elizabeth couldn't possibly remember Tríona doing that. And yet there it was, an identical reflexive gesture, a distinct echo of her mother that was completely natural, completely unconscious.

Instead of following her father and Miranda into the house, Elizabeth ventured onto the terrace that overlooked the ravine and the steep riverbank beyond. She let her hand trail over the rough stone wall, stopping at the front steps at a shallow stone basin that held a mound of river rocks. Elizabeth picked up one of the stones and began to examine it. Eventually she set it back in the bowl and moved on. As far as Nora knew, no one had ever really explained to Elizabeth what had happened to her mother. How do you begin to explain such things to a six-year-old? A few days after the funeral, Nora had taken her aside, to ask whether she understood what it meant when someone died. Elizabeth had thought for a moment, and then asked if it was like the bird they'd once found on the sidewalk. A tiny fledgling, still and cold, pushed too soon from the nest. *Yes,* she had answered. *It is like that.* And she had held Elizabeth tight, feeling the child's rapid heartbeat right through her skin and bones. *So fragile,* she had thought. *We are such soft, fragile creatures.*

What had Elizabeth believed all these years since the murder? She was just now reaching the age of awareness, starting to see things beyond a child's perspective. And she probably knew more than anyone wanted to admit.

Now Elizabeth placed her hands flat on the broad limestone wall and peered over the edge, perhaps trying to see the water through the trees. A curious expression crossed her features, as though she'd caught a scent that brought back a memory. She put one knee on the wall and climbed up to stand on it, tottering under the weight of her backpack. Nora's heart leapt.

Peter's voice carried through the trees: "Elizabeth! Get down from there!"

Teetering precariously once more, Elizabeth jumped down from the wall as her father strode across the terrace and pulled her roughly by the elbow. Nora had to hold her breath and strain to hear snatches of their conversation:

"What were you thinking?"

"I just wanted to see the river—"

"When are you going to learn to think things through? What have I told you?"

"I wasn't going to fall."

"Don't let me see you up there again, do you hear me?"

Peter's fingers tightened on the child's arm. When she tried to twist away, he held her fast, bringing his face down to her level and speaking very slowly, as if she might have trouble taking his meaning. "Inside—now."

Someone else, someone ignorant of the facts, might see in Peter Hallett only a concerned father, taking a dreamy child in hand. But Nora was not ignorant of the facts. She had seen the defiance in Elizabeth's eyes. And it wasn't safe to defy Peter Hallett.

9

After a quick stop at the apartment to change and remove the dirt and grime from Hidden Falls, Nora headed to Lowertown, the warehouse district east of Saint Paul's city center. She circled Mears Park on one-way streets until she came to the entrance of an underground parking garage. She drove past slowly, suddenly claustrophobic, unable to turn in at the entrance. When the driver behind her honked impatiently, she pulled ahead and parked at a meter on the next block. Returning on foot, she slipped past the ticket dispenser and started circling down the steeply graded concrete into the depths of a man-made cavern. At the lowest level, she crossed to the far corner and stood staring down at the floor at a large painted number, 114. This was the spot where Tríona had been discovered, three days after she disappeared. Where all hope and speculation had come to an end.

Four stories below street level the temperature was at least twenty degrees cooler than the air outside. The only illumination came from the glare of bare bulbs, and the concrete walls seemed to soak up their minimal light. Nora reached into her bag for a small flashlight, listening to the sounds that ricocheted off the unforgiving concrete and echoed in the shadows. Hardly the safest spot to explore alone, even at midday. But she had to stand once more in the place that had become Tríona's monument and tomb.

She shone the light on the number painted on the floor, and remembered wondering whether the number was significant to Tríona's killer, or whether any space would have done. There had been no useful evidence here, only a small amount of blood with the body in the car trunk; Tríona had clearly been attacked elsewhere and moved here. But why this place? If they could just figure that part out—if her death had been the result of a random carjacking, then why on earth would the killer have parked in a garage, when it made more sense just to leave the car somewhere along the street? If Tríona had been killed at Hidden Falls, why not just leave her and the car there?

Perhaps because of Natalie Russo. Because the killer needed to draw attention away from the river, and the other body—or bodies—buried there. Still, a parking garage meant people walking by, security cameras, a level of scrutiny even the most dim-witted criminal couldn't possibly overlook. But as they'd soon discovered, the cameras in this garage weren't functioning at the time of Tríona's death—the whole security network was down for several days while a new system was being installed—there was no video of anyone coming or going from this ramp from two days before the murder to two days after. What were the chances that the killer had just been lucky? It seemed far more likely that the person who had chosen this place had done so deliberately, to avoid being caught on tape, despite leaving the car in such a public place. It was almost as if he wanted to make sure the body was discovered quickly. Looking at it that way, the location came across as a provocation, a deliberate catch-me-if-you-can. Not only did that fit Peter Hallett's personality, it also suggested a chilling degree of premeditation.

But Nora had spent weeks digging for a connection between Peter and this parking garage—whether it was owned by any of his friends or acquaintances, located near any restaurant or business or gallery he frequented. There was no proof that he'd ever been here. Nothing. So how could he have known about the security system?

The flashlight beam bouncing off the walls caught his attention on the monitor. Truman Stark pulled his chair closer to the bank of screens to study the picture. He watched the female subject crouch down to examine the floor and felt an irresistible flicker of interest, the pulse-quickening of the first sighting. All sorts of possibilities. His work might be boring most of the time, sitting in this tiny security office and staring at monitors for hours on end, but he liked watching how people behaved when they thought no one could see them. He reached for the joystick that let him maneuver the camera and zoomed in on the subject. Not bad-looking. Looked like she could handle herself. What the hell was she doing down there?

Pushing back from the monitors, he felt for the reassuring weight of the holstered gun on his hip and left the booth, making sure to pull the door shut behind him. It wasn't exactly standard procedure, leaving the office for something like this, but he had seniority and figured he was entitled to bend the rules once in a while. His shift was nearly over anyway. The cashiers could get him on the walkie-talkie if they ran into any trouble.

He enjoyed ranging around the building, checking the stairwells, making sure all the doors that were supposed to be locked actually were. The starched shirt and heavy shoes, they were all part of it too. He liked the noise his brogans made on the concrete floors, especially in the echoing stairwells. It felt almost like walking a beat. Sometimes he almost forgot it wasn't real.

His whole life, all he ever wanted was to be a cop. The desire had lived inside him every single day since he was a kid, a dream that kept him safe, protected from real life. He'd practiced swearing the oath, imagined himself answering calls on the radio, in uniform. The physical stuff wasn't a problem. He'd practiced with nightstick and cuffs and genuine police-issue sidearm until he knew how to use them blindfolded. It was the other stuff that tripped him up, all the reading and writing. That was the part he hadn't expected. He'd tried cracking a few books that summer before community college. But the words got turned around like they always did, and trying to decipher them made his head hurt. He thought being a cop would be different, but it was all just more of the same bullshit. Books and studying and sitting in classes—it was all so flat, so foreign to him. And what good was any of that when you were out on the street?

He felt the elevator vibrate, imagined the cables and the hydraulics through the walls, riding in a box to the basement. The worst thing hadn't been washing out of school, but going back home again. His mother was okay, but the old man couldn't resist rubbing it in. Truman had been told so many times that he'd never make anything of himself, that he must be some kind of moron. He knew his father would make him wallow in his failure, force him to eat it every day for breakfast, lunch, and dinner. But it must be true that meanness could give you cancer, because it was right about that time that the old man got sick. Just shriveled up, got smaller and smaller and smaller until he died. Nobody felt sorry for him, not then and not now. Not even close. What they all felt was more like relief.

On the whole, things had been better since then, but lately Truman had been feeling a new restlessness in his blood, a dissatisfaction that hovered somewhere between an itch and an ache. It wouldn't go away. Something inside him had changed. He used to look up to cops, study the way their handcuffs and holsters fit on their belts, how the uniforms made them look bigger, bulkier than they really were. He couldn't recall the exact moment his attitude had begun to turn. He only noticed one day that he felt something new as he walked past a squad car on his way to work. He could feel the cops sizing him up, checking the security company patch on his shoulder, and exchanging a dismissive glance. Now, every time he passed a police car parked on the street outside the ramp, he was almost overcome with one desire: to reach in through the open window and haul them out, to wipe those smug looks from their faces.

He remembered how the bright beam had crossed the space number on the monitor upstairs, and then it struck him—114 was the same parking space where they'd found that girl, the redhead. He hadn't known her name until he saw her picture on the TV news. His job might have been in danger if he'd said anything to the police. But he could have told them plenty. How he'd seen her—three and four times a week, all through that spring and summer. He could have told them how he'd watched her, even followed her outside sometimes, admiring the way her long hair seemed to float around her when the breeze came up. How he'd imagined all that beautiful hair spilling over him when he looked at the pictures he'd taped to the sloped ceiling above his bed. But the police had no need to know any of that. There was no way they were going to find out. Because if they did, all those private moments would be destroyed, and he could never let that happen.

10

Leaving the garage and heading back to the car, Nora walked along the south side of Mears Park. The square itself was shady this late in the afternoon, but yellow sunlight still glinted from the windows above the trees. The pavement radiated heat, and the air felt sticky. She wasn't over the shock of returning home. All the wide streets, the broad-shouldered buildings still felt strange and unfamiliar.

Pedestrians crossed the square with their dogs, accompanied by classical music piping from speakers in the modern band shell. Suddenly the true purpose of the music dawned: it was not about offering pleasure to the masses, but about repelling young people. The whole proposition rested on a presumption that no self-respecting, rap-loving juvenile would be caught dead within earshot of Mozart. There was something a little sad about that.

Nora pictured the timeline tacked up on the wall in her apartment, with at least eight hours in Tríona's last, fateful day still unaccounted for. Every minute of every hour was made up of so many intricate layers and intersections, places where one stream flowed into another. What were the chances that she was walking by something vitally important right now?

Her ears became attuned to the sound of running water, which came from the stream that cut across the park. It wasn't a real stream, of course, but a fountain that tumbled through faux boulders and feathery native grasses. An artificial prairie creek in the heart of the city. She followed the water to the opposite side of the park and crossed the street, moving to sidestep a couple of teenage girls walking by a large plate glass window of an empty office space. As she passed them, one of the girls shouted, "Hey, Latrice, that was us on the TV!" She yanked at her friend's arm, and Nora had to swerve to avoid a collision.

"No way," Latrice said. But she stared through the glass where her friend was pointing. Nora couldn't help being drawn in. The whole window became a video collage: multiple fast-motion images shot from above turned pedestrians into ants, and slow-motion, street-level video was interspersed with still photos.

The friend insisted. "I know what I saw."

"You trippin'," Latrice said. "I don't see nothin'."

"I'm tellin' you, *it was us*," her friend said again, annoyed. "There!" She yelped and smacked Latrice's bare arm. "Right there! Told you I wasn't lyin'."

Latrice finally caught a glimpse of her larger-than-life self. "Aw man, that's wack!" She started trying out a few dance moves. "Here's Latrice, baby. For real. Come on, everybody, get a good look!"

As she preened and strutted for the camera, her friend backed away, doubled over and breathless with laughter. A few other people stopped to watch the show. It was almost impossible not to get caught up in their high spirits. But when the images changed again, the girls moved on, jostling one another and laughing, embarrassed now at the stir they'd caused. Nora turned back to the window and saw her own image through the glass. She moved one hand slowly up and down, and her oversized likeness followed suit. The main screen suddenly switched to a street-level shot of a crowd in slow motion, perspective oddly flattened by the camera's stationary single eye.

Nora felt her breath stop as a face in the crowd emerged, then disappeared for a long second, only to emerge again from behind a blurry figure in the foreground. The long, loose hair lifted and seemed to float for an instant in the slow-motion breeze. She had not been mistaken.

The face was Tríona's.

Nora watched her sister's graceful approach, caught in a web of memory. There was so much she had forgotten, and she felt the need to drink it all in, every detail. Even in slow motion, it was far too fast. Tríona overtook the camera and disappeared into the edge of the frame. Nora spun around and scanned the faces around her. It was impossible, she knew, yet the image had been so clear. She turned back and studied the picture, trying to fix the camera's location. The shot had come from in front of the building where she stood, that much was certain. But the image also caught the edge of a distinctive stone arch half a block down. Tríona had been walking past that arch. Nora began to run, excusing herself to the passersby she jostled in her haste. She thought of the photo she'd shoved hastily into her bag and dug it out on the fly. She was on the verge of holding it up, saying to the passersby: *You must have seen her—she was just here!* But all at once she saw herself reflected in the blank stares all around her. They already saw her as a crazy person. The hand holding Tríona's picture dropped slowly to her side, and in a few seconds, the foot traffic closed around her once more.

She had gone away three years ago, angry and frustrated, and thinking every possible avenue had already been explored, but it was clear from the few brief, chance encounters that had begun piling up today that she had been wrong. She walked back to watch the projection in the window again, and finally realized that not all of the pictures were live. Herself and the two girls, yes, but most of the footage was a video collage that could have been shot at any time—five years ago or more. She stood at the window long enough to see that the whole thing ran on a continuous loop. There was her sister's face again, exactly the same as before. Standing in front of the glass, Nora knew what she had seen was a shadow, an image captured and reassembled in a stream of ones and zeros. A digital specter.

But what it meant was that Tríona had been here, on this street, at least once, perhaps many times. Where was she going? Nora scanned the buildings ahead for a sign, anything that might have drawn her sister inside. A half block down, the dark silhouette of an animal caught her eye.

The Blue Coyote Café was in the corner space of the Sturgis Building, one of the few old warehouses in the neighborhood that had resisted gentrification, and still gloried in its original cast-iron and raw timber framework. When Nora pushed open the coffee-shop door, not one of the half-dozen people sitting at brightly painted, mismatched tables even raised a glance. As she approached the counter, the glum barista set down her half-eaten apple and her paperback copy of *Anna Karenina* and stood up, eyeing her prospective customer without a hint of curiosity or interest. The girl was about eighteen, with impossibly jet-black hair, dark green lips, and a heavily studded dog collar.

"I'm not here for coffee," Nora said. "I'm looking for anyone who might have been working here five years ago."

"You're not looking for me, then," the girl said. "I was only twelve. But I think Val was around. Just a sec—" The girl ducked into the back room and returned a few seconds later in the company of a woman with spiky gray hair who sported a bright white chef's apron over street clothes.

"I'm Valerie Marchant," the woman said, wiping soapy hands on her apron front. "What can I do for you?"

Nora handed over Tríona's photo. "I was wondering if you recognize her."

The reaction was immediate. "Tríona Gavin. She used to come in here a lot. Sorry, what did you say your name was?"

"I didn't say—Nora Gavin. Tríona was my sister."

Valerie Marchant's demeanor changed. "I'm so sorry. We were all shocked to hear what happened. And doubly shocked when that husband of hers was never charged, when he was so obviously guilty—"

Nora interrupted: "I'm sorry, you said Tríona used to come in here?"

Valerie Marchant looked surprised. "All the time. She did voice work at a studio upstairs, Nick Mosher's place. Nicky always had actor friends coming through. I knew Tríona a little from her acting days, before she got married—I used to be a theater director once, before this place took over."

Nora was trying to understand. "If you and this Nick Mosher knew my sister, why didn't you come forward at the time of the murder?"

"I was abroad, in Helsinki on a fellowship, didn't get back until the following January. And Nicky—" Valerie Marchant shook her head sadly. "Nick Mosher is dead. He fell down the elevator shaft here in the building. The police said it was an accident."

Nora felt as if she'd missed something. "I'm sorry, when was this?"

"It happened five years ago yesterday. We always have a sort of memorial here on the anniversary. Nick's old buddies come over, I close up shop, and we all sit around and get roaring drunk on red wine. I apologize if I'm a little bleary—we're still clearing away the empties."

"What sort of work did Nick do?"

"Sound engineer. Radio ads mostly, some audiobooks, and a bit of music. He still did theater work—that's where he got started. But the real money was in advertising."

"And you said he had actors going up to his studio all the time?"

"Nick kept his friends in steady work. The money was good, too. He was a lifesaver."

"How did the accident happen?"

Valerie shook her head. "Nobody knows. Nick was always so safety-conscious. I've always had my suspicions about whether it was really an accident."

"But you've never talked to the police about any of this?"

"I wasn't here at the time—didn't think I could offer any useful information."

"How did my sister seem when she came in here? Did you ever happen to see anyone speaking to her, following her?"

"Not that I can recall. She'd come in, get hot tea with lemon for herself, and a double cappuccino with an extra shot for Nick, then head upstairs." She tapped her temple. "It's amazing—some of that useless crap never goes away."

"Hey, Val, where do you want these?" The barista held up a slightly warped pair of dark glasses. Valerie pivoted and craned her neck to see.

"Oh, just set them on my desk, will you?" Turning back, she spotted Nora's curious gaze.

"One of the melancholy mementoes we drag out every year—Nick's glasses. I guess I forgot to mention that he was blind."

"You never saw my sister's husband around here?"

Valerie shook her head. "I'm sure somebody would have told me if he'd come prowling around. Not exactly the kind of guy who escapes notice easily, is he? Or who liked sharing the spotlight, from what I've heard. Your sister was so gifted—we were all disappointed when she gave up acting. When I started seeing her down here, I was hopeful; it seemed like she might be getting back into it. But she always seemed a little edgy. I'm pretty sure Nick was paying her in cash, but I don't think it was the tax man she was trying to avoid. I'm not sure your sister's husband knew about her work down here. From the few things Nick said, I got the distinct impression that something bad would happen if he ever found out."

Nora remembered Tríona's words: *I've lied and deceived everyone.* Was it the work she'd been doing behind Peter's back, or was it something much worse? She asked: "Does the name Natalie Russo mean anything to you?"

"I can't say it does. I'm sorry. But listen, I really wish you luck. We were all hoping the police would nail that sonofabitch."

Outside the coffee-shop window, Truman Stark stopped and pretended to look for something on the ground, stealing a glance at the brunette who stood at the corner of the pastry case inside, talking to the owner. The same one he'd just seen at the garage, he was sure of it. She was putting something back in her bag—a picture of the redhead. They were connected somehow. He knew he'd seen her before, nosing around in the lower level at the parking ramp, right after the body turned up. But she hadn't been back lately, not for a couple of years at least.

Truman pretended to look at the menu board, keeping an eye on his subject. Some people had hobbies, like woodworking or raising pigeons or growing tomatoes. What he did in his spare time was much more important than any of that stuff. More like a calling.

He had tailed the redhead into this building a few times. The very last time, he'd followed her across the square. When she stopped to sit on a bench, he'd fallen back, used the time to pick a handful of flowers from one of the beds along the stream. A wrinkled old broad on a nearby bench pulled a face at him, like the park was her personal garden or something. He didn't care. He'd watched the redhead take a note from her purse. She stared at it for a minute, then she stuffed it in her pocket and started walking toward the Sturgis Building again. He'd caught up to her as she was waiting for the light. He thought about leaving the flowers somewhere she would find them. She'd be surprised, maybe even touched by the gesture. That's the way she was; he'd seen it plenty of times. He wouldn't leave a note or anything—that would be too much. When she walked into the coffee shop he stopped outside to observe through the glass, watching how her lips moved silently as she chatted with the girl at the counter, how her body swayed slightly as she waited.

He was going to head up to the fourth floor—he knew from the last time that's where she was headed. He'd leave the flowers for her there. He thought he'd timed it just right, but the coffee-shop line was faster than he'd anticipated, and she stepped onto the elevator just before the doors closed. She saw that the fourth-floor button was lit up, so he punched number five, glowing with embarrassment, pretending he'd made a mistake. Then she'd glanced at the flowers, and briefly at him. His knees had begun to tremble. *Open your mouth,* said the voice in his ears. For some reason, the voice always sounded like his father. *She likes the flowers—just open your mouth and say something, dickweed.* But all at once he felt the elevator sway on its cables, and knew that if he opened his mouth, he would throw up. He couldn't make a sound.

And so she'd stepped off on the fourth floor, leaving him standing there like a douchebag with the stupid flowers. He'd watched her plant a kiss on a bearded guy in dark glasses who met her off the elevator. Then she handed over the coffee, guiding beardy's fingers to the cup like he was blind or something. All at once the realization dawned—the fucking guy was blind. So was that how it worked when they did it? Did she have to show him where to put his hands then?

When the elevator doors finally closed, he'd slumped against the wall, eaten alive with humiliation and jealousy, feeling sicker and more feverish as the box ascended to the fifth floor, where he got off and headed up to the roof to try and cool down. The next person getting on the elevator had found a heap of wilting flowers on the floor.

Now Truman glanced back through the coffee-shop window at the brunette, and knew it was beginning again, that same bad feeling he used to get when the old man would start in on him. Once that feeling overtook him, he couldn't hold it together much longer. Everything was about to fly apart again, and there was nothing he could do to stop it.

11

After leaving the Blue Coyote, Nora drove up the hill out of Lowertown, maneuvering through two-way traffic on Fourth Street, considering what she'd just learned about her sister. Tríona had gone back to work without telling anyone in the family. Was that what she meant when she said she'd lied and deceived people? The man Tríona worked for had fallen down an elevator shaft the very same day she was killed. Could it just be coincidence? What if it was Tríona and not Peter who had some connection to the parking garage?

Nora pulled into a parking spot in front of the Saint Paul Central Library. After plugging the meter, she crossed the plaza to the building's main entrance. She had always admired the building's classical design—the regular arched windows, white marble balustrades and terraces. The ancient Romans would have felt at home. But she was here because this place formed another inexplicable piece of the puzzle: when Tríona's car turned up, the police found a parking ticket in her glove compartment, a citation for an expired meter in front of the Central Library. The ticket was stamped with a date and time, which placed her here less than twelve hours before she was killed. The police had canvassed the library and the area around it, and found only one witness who would swear he'd seen Tríona at the library that day. His name was Harry Shaughnessy, and he belonged to that flock of gray men who made a daily, circular migration from the homeless camps along the river to the library, then to the Dorothy Day Center for a hot meal at noon, and then back to the library or on to Listening House or the Union Gospel Mission, where the bottomless cup of coffee came with a side order of Jesus Saves.

As she entered the library, Nora was aware of the gaunt, bearded man leaving by the opposite door. He was dressed in telltale layers of clothing, including a scruffy trench coat, despite the heat. Their eyes met briefly, and Nora tried not to stare. Not having seen Harry Shaughnessy for nearly five years, she couldn't be sure this was the same man. When the police questioned him, Shaughnessy had seemed remarkably lucid at first, explaining that he went to the Central Library every morning to read the *New York Times*. He had been adamant about seeing Tríona on the day in question, and positive about the date. He even remembered something he'd read in the paper that day, which checked out. Then he told Frank Cordova that it was the same day he'd seen the angel Gabriel driving a flaming chariot down Market Street. So Harry Shaughnessy couldn't be counted upon as a credible witness in court. But what if they had discounted everything he said because part of it was unreliable? What if Harry Shaughnessy's disconnection from reality was not complete, and he *had* seen Tríona that day?

As it was, even with the parking ticket, and even counting Harry's statement placing Tríona at the library, they had never discovered what she was doing there. The library computer system showed no books checked out on her card that day, no returns. But the timing of the visit was important. Why would Tríona have taken the trouble to visit the library in those last hours, when her life seemed to be spiraling out of control?

Nora climbed the stairs to the second-floor reference room, a lofty space at the heart of the building. The smell of a library was instantly recognizable and distinct. Glancing up at the arched windows and polychromed ceiling beams, she was transported back to the time when she and Tríona used to come here every summer afternoon, escaping the scorching heat outside, spending languorous days in bookish coolness.

Much had changed since then, of course. The library had been remodeled; banks of computer terminals had replaced the dark oak card catalogs. It was possible that Tríona had been searching for something in the stacks or online, but library policy had put up an unexpected roadblock—call slips and computer logs were routinely shredded by librarians concerned about government bootprints on the Bill of Rights. Nora understood why it had to be so. Still, she had felt incredibly frustrated when all the luck seemed to run in Peter Hallett's favor. If only she could figure out what Tríona had been searching for.

The occupant of the nearest computer station seemed on the verge of vacating, so Nora moved closer, waiting for an opportunity. When he was a proper distance away, she dropped her bag on the floor under the desk and slid into the still-warm chair. She stared at the anonymous screen, and it blinked back at her, asking for a name, keyword, subject, author's name, title. She let her fingers rest on the keyboard, waiting.

What were you looking for? she asked silently. *Why were you here?* No vibration stirred. She laid a hand on the table's wood surface, imagining beneath her fingers the faint tracery of a hundred different pens on paper. Why could she sense so much in the presence of the *cailín rua,* the red-haired stranger she had never known, and yet feel nothing here from her own flesh and blood?

She suddenly felt foolish, and pushed the chair back. Hunches and intuition were fine, as long as they led to concrete evidence that would stand up in court. Did she really imagine that she could find such evidence here? There was nothing of Tríona in this place.

From the reference room, Nora ventured through the atrium stairwell to the nonfiction reading section. She remembered the moment of childhood discovery, when she'd found that the library had hidden places, flights of stairs to rooms that didn't seem to exist from the outside. The nonfiction stacks occupied just such an invisible place, down a half flight of stairs from the reading room. This was where she and Tríona had actually spent most of their time. The floor was carpeted, the atmosphere still and studious, and while there were no windows in this limbo between floors, the books themselves offered glimpses into all sorts of strange places concealed within the real world.

While Nora had worked her way methodically through the natural history collection, Tríona had found her own place in these stacks—a far, quiet corner where she was surrounded by books about gods and monsters, elves and mermaids, a whole universe of shape-shifters. Nora remembered all the times she'd tried to needle her sister, wondering aloud how books about otherworldly creatures came to be shelved in nonfiction. Tríona's only reply was a tiny, knowing smile. When they left the library in the late afternoons, Tríona would turn the spine of her current favorite book inward, a trick that made it easier to find the next time.

Nora counted down the stacks and stopped at the place she had invariably found her sister, sometimes flopped down on her belly with knees bent and bare feet swaying gently, sometimes with legs propped against the wall, and hair spread in a coppery nimbus about her head, so far immersed in whatever world she had entered that day that it sometimes took three or four hails and a hand waved in front of her face to drag her back to reality.

Nora felt a wave of despair. What on earth was she doing, standing here, dreaming? She was supposed to be cold, rational, relentless, connecting the facts of the case. But before turning around, she stooped down to check the lower shelves, and there it was—a single volume turned the wrong way. Pulling the battered green volume from the shelf, she opened it to a color plate, a rich illustration of a young man in doublet and hose, standing at the edge of a dark pool, holding a raised sword above his head. In the water, half submerged, writhed a naked female, a water sprite of some kind, with pale arms spread. The words at the bottom of the plate sounded like the text of a ballad:

Out then he drew his shining blade,
Thinking to stick her where she stood,
But she was vanishd to a fish,
And swam far off, a fair mermaid.

"O Mother, Mother, braid my hair;
My lusty lady, make my bed;
O brother, take my sword and spear,
For I have seen the false mermaid."

She checked the spine. *Married to Magic: Fairy Brides and Bridegrooms.* The spidery call letters, handwritten in white ink, were like something from another time.

Five full years had passed since her sister could have been here. What were the odds that someone else had left a book turned backward here in Tríona's favorite section? The rational part of her had to consider the number of people who had been in the library since then, picking through the hundreds of thousands of volumes on these shelves. Sliding the book back on the shelf, Nora felt a slight resistance. She pulled it out again and peered through the opening, then reached in and pulled out a crumpled sheet of paper, a printout of a *Pioneer Press* article dated July 13, just over five years ago.

MISSING ROWER CASE STILL A MYSTERY

Police have checked hundreds of leads in the weeks since Natalie Russo vanished, but admit they know little more about her disappearance now than they knew on the first day of the investigation. The probe has been hampered by a lack of

> information about the twenty-two-year-old Saint Paul woman, who remains listed as a missing person, police said. Russo's crewmates from the Twin Cities Rowing Club said her disappearance was all the more puzzling, since she was taking part in rigorous training for upcoming Olympic trials. Russo is believed to have disappeared June 3 while out for her regular early-morning run.

The date of Natalie Russo's disappearance was circled in red. A footer at the bottom of the sheet said the article had been printed five years ago yesterday. The day Tríona had been at the library. The day she'd died.

Nora dropped the crumpled sheet and began pulling books from the shelf, not thinking about the mess she was making, but riffling through the pages, checking endpapers and margins for any scribbled notes. Nothing. Nora suddenly realized that Tríona's prints might still be on the paper that lay facedown on the carpet. She pulled a zipper bag from her backpack, gingerly lifting the crumpled printout by a corner and slipping it into the bag. She should take it directly to Frank Cordova, but knew she would not do it. Not just yet.

Why would Tríona be digging around in newspaper archives for information about Natalie Russo? Nora felt the fear that surrounded her down at the river begin to rise again. If Tríona knew about Natalie, and about Hidden Falls—*I've done things, too. You don't know—unspeakable things—*

The ugly fear that had gripped her at the river reared its head again. All these years spent resisting that insidious worm of doubt, insisting that everything Peter had said about Tríona was a lie. *Stop it,* said the voice in her head. *It's exactly what he wants you to believe. Don't believe it.* A single newspaper clipping meant nothing on its own. They still had no real proof that Tríona had been at Natalie Russo's grave. Even if she had been there, Peter could have tricked her into going to the river, or forced her somehow—*Isn't it shocking, what you'll do when you love someone?*

Stepping from the library entrance a few minutes later, Nora saw a parking enforcement vehicle pull away from her car. She quickly crossed the street, but it was too late. She slipped the ticket from beneath the wiper, feeling a twist of bitter irony. With each passing minute of this strange day, she found herself becoming more and more convinced that there was no such thing as coincidence.

A knock sounded on the glass beside her head, and she turned with a start to find the homeless man she'd seen leaving the library. Harry Shaughnessy—she was certain of it now. As he motioned for her to roll down the window, his raincoat gapped open, revealing a stained gray sweatshirt. How anyone could wear such heavy clothes in this heat—

"Excuse me, miss," he said. "You dropped this." He handed over Tríona's headshot. How on earth had it escaped from her bag?

As she glanced up, the white block letters on Harry's sweatshirt—the few she could see—spelled out the word "LIAR." The front of the shirt was also smeared with a rusty brown stain. Shaughnessy began to back away, raising one arm in a kind of salute, showing a few more letters, and Nora felt a surge of adrenaline. She opened the car door. "Mr. Shaughnessy—it is Mr. Shaughnessy, isn't it? I wonder if you'd let me buy you lunch?"

He began to sidle away from her, uneasy at being recognized. "I was just on my way over to Dorothy Day—"

"Please—I'd like to thank you somehow for returning the picture. We could sit right here in the park." She gestured to the hot-dog cart at Fifth and Market. Harry Shaughnessy scratched his head, and his eyes flickered to the corner, weighing the offer of immediate food against waiting in line for lunch at the shelter. "Well—I guess that would be all right."

Nora climbed out of her car, trying not to make any sudden moves, and walked alongside Harry Shaughnessy to the opposite corner of the park. She ordered two hot dogs, studying Shaughnessy's face as he watched the vendor at work. Impossible to tell how old he was—living rough made many men old before their time. But something in his manner, the upright, dignified way he held himself, reminded her of a certain generation of men born in the throes of the Great Depression.

After paying for their lunch, Nora found an unoccupied bench near the central fountain. How on earth was she going to broach the delicate subject of the stained sweatshirt? There was a very real danger that the man would bolt if she opened her mouth. She cast a few sideways glances, watching Shaughnessy—he ate slowly, almost daintily, savoring each bite, as though this were the most delectable meal he'd consumed in months. Perhaps it was. His nails were black with grime, and a few gray inches of waffled underwear peeped out between trouser leg and sock. His high-top sneakers were nearly worn through. But these were small details. The most notable thing about Harry Shaughnessy was that his body was in constant motion, his eyes on high alert. Like a wild animal, Nora thought. Maybe that was how he had survived so long on the street.

Just beyond him, at the edge of her field of vision, a group of preschool children were crossing the park, hands holding loops tied into a long cord. Their teacher led the little flock, pulling them along behind her like ducklings. Harry gazed at the children, holding out one hand as if to pet them, though he was twenty yards away.

"Yeah, she was a real nice lady," he said, continuing some unfinished conversation. "That gal in the picture. Used to see her at the library. It's a few years back now. Always asked how I was getting on. Sometimes she had the little one with her—such pretty red hair, just like her mama. Most people, they don't see you, but she was different. Even bought me a cup of coffee a few times." His eyes focused somewhere in the middle distance as he remembered. "Never wanted to kill anyone. Not like some—" The grimy nails dug into his palms. "That's just was the way it was. The fellas on the other side, they were all as green and scared as we were. You could see it in their eyes—"

"Mr. Shaughnessy?" Nora said. He looked up at her, barely a sliver of recognition in his rheumy eyes. "I hope you don't mind my asking—where did you get that sweatshirt?"

He looked confused. "What?"

"Your sweatshirt. It's from Galliard College, in Maine."

"Is it?" He opened his coat wider and she saw the full word, just as she had suspected. Harry Shaughnessy was walking around in a sweatshirt from the college where Marc Staunton and Peter Hallett had become friends, where the trajectory of her sister's life—all their lives—had been altered. Nora found it impossible to keep her eyes off the dark stain. Its color seemed unmistakable when exposed to bright daylight.

"You don't see many people with sweatshirts from Galliard around here. My fiancé went to school there." The tiny voice in her head made the necessary red-pencil correction. *Ex-fiancé.*

Harry Shaughnessy glanced at the hot dog sitting untouched on Nora's lap, and his face changed in an instant, befuddlement retreating behind a sudden, hard wave of paranoia and suspicion. He pulled his coat closer, despite the afternoon's oppressive heat. "What do you want?"

She had no choice but to tell the truth. "I need a better look at your sweatshirt. I can explain everything—please, it's very important." She put out her hand—a mistake. Shaughnessy was off like a shot, cutting in front of the pack of preschoolers, so that when Nora gave chase she got caught in the line and pulled several of the children to their knees, frightened and wailing.

She shouted after him: "Mr. Shaughnessy—wait, please!" Apologizing as she extracted herself from the preschoolers, she beat a path to the corner. But Harry Shaughnessy was already more than a block away. All she could do was watch as he rounded the corner and disappeared from view. She stopped to catch her breath, holding on to the arm of a bench.

"Might as well give up, girlie," said a strange voice beside her. Nora glanced up. The speaker was a rail-thin crone dressed in a billowing powder-blue evening gown with a satin sash embroidered in flowing metallic script: "Princess of the North Star—1974."

"Nope," the princess muttered, her mouth a wry twist. "Nobody can catch ol' Harry when he don't want to get caught."

"I just wanted to talk to him."

"Well, it sure looks like he don't want to talk to you." The beauty queen eyed her suspiciously. "You a cop? You don't look like a cop."

"No, I'm not. Do you know Harry Shaughnessy?"

"Sure. Who don't know Harry?"

"Do you know where I might find him?"

"I might. But I sure could use some smokes—they always help my concentration." She tapped a wizened finger against her temple, and Nora finally realized what the woman was asking. She dug in her pocket and brought out a twenty-dollar bill. "Please, just tell me where to find him."

"Hold your horses, hold your horses—" The princess made an elaborate production of slipping the twenty into a secret place within the folds of her sagging bosom. "He'll be at the camp down below the old power plant. Sooner or later. Same as me."

12

Cormac emerged into the corridor outside Casualty after his second meeting with the doctors. He sat down on one of the hard chairs along the hallway, and Roz came and sat beside him. "Any news?"

"They're keeping him sedated until the swelling subsides. We probably won't know anything until tomorrow at the earliest." It was nearly ten o'clock in the evening now, and they'd been at the hospital all day. Cormac was still in his rowing gear. Roz looked worn out. "You should go back to the house, try to get some sleep," he said. "I'll stay."

"I'm not leaving."

"All right then, tell me more about this Mary Heaney case. How did the locals take to having a selkie in their midst?"

"Well, at first they were a bit leery, naturally—but I suppose they got used to her, in a way. The stories began to take on a life of their own. There were reports of her going up to the headland above the village while Heaney was out fishing. She'd sit there for hours, just staring out to sea. I think I mentioned that people heard her singing in a strange language. Some said that seals swam up onto the rocks when they heard her voice."

"And all of that played into the rumors, I suppose."

"How could it not? People began to believe that Heaney had some sort of power over her." Roz paused for a moment, and looked at him. "You don't have to pretend, you know. To be interested, for my sake."

"I'm not pretending, Roz. I genuinely want to know. Where did the stories come from, do you suppose?"

"Where does any myth originate? Fairy brides are one of the major motifs in folklore. These are stories that have been with us forever, and in almost every culture. Most of the selkie tales weren't written down until the nineteenth century, and it's always interesting to me how they're filtered through the prism of contemporary values. Loads of Victorian gentlemen were amateur anthropologists. They were tireless collectors, and we owe them a lot for all the work they did. But their fascination with what they called 'primitive' cultures was coupled with an equally strong aversion. They were especially put off by the looseness of marriage bonds amongst the 'savage races.' The Victorians saw fairy brides as downright dangerous—wild, uncontrollable, impervious to reason and morality. They always found a way to break their marriage bonds; the Victorians especially disliked that uncomfortable twist in the stories."

"How does a selkie break her marriage bond?"

"She discovers what was taken from her, the magic object that's kept her in captivity. In her case, it's a sealskin, stolen and hidden from her. If she can regain it, the stories say, she's able to return to her true self, her true home in the sea. In other stories, the magic object is a red cap or a feather cloak. In others there's no physical covering, but the human spouse might break some taboo—sometimes he strikes his bride three 'causeless blows.' In others he dares to speak her name aloud, or reminds her of her animal origins."

"And what does all that mean?"

"In psychological terms, you can see these stories being about women who desire autonomy and equality within marriage, or male fantasies about subjugating the power of the feminine. You can also see them reflecting male anxiety about abandonment by females. Your choice."

"What do you think?"

"I think we've always tried to come up with ways to explain the fundamental differences, not just between men and women, but between all of us as human beings. We're all mysterious, indecipherable creatures. Unknowable, really. To me, the story is all about trying to come to grips with the detritus of a broken relationship. What's ironic is that it's usually the selkie's children who find her sealskin. She loves her children, but can't take them with her when she leaves. They're half human, and would drown if she were to bring them with her under the sea. So her choices are grim: stay and renounce her true nature, or return to the sea and leave the children behind. It's about impossible dualities—no matter which choice the selkie makes, she has to remain divided."

"What was it that made you think your Mary Heaney was murdered?"

"It was nothing explicit, really. What we have from the song '*An Mhaighdean Mhara*' is only a fragment, but I still thought it strange that she and the children are called by name, but there's no mention at all of her husband. I started to wonder if it was a subtle way of assigning responsibility. Pointing the finger precisely by not pointing it, if you see what I mean."

"But how do you prove a negative?"

Roz nodded. "Exactly. In the absence of a body, what could anyone do? The case was written up in the local newspaper, complete with references to 'local superstitions' and 'fairy romances' and the ignorance of the Irish peasantry. Remind me to show you the piece—I've got it back at the house."

"But surely that wasn't what tipped the scales for you on Heaney?"

"No, there were several other bits of circumstantial evidence as well."

"Such as?"

"Several people told me stories they'd heard from parents and grandparents, about a strange old man who followed Heaney around at the next fair day after his wife disappeared, asking, 'Was it you? Was it you killed the woman?' "

"And how did Heaney react?"

"He struck the old man in the face, knocked him down, and bloodied his head. The old fella had never been seen before, and no one ever saw him again after that day. A few weeks later, there was a piece in the newspaper about a dozen seals found bludgeoned to death on Rathlin O'Birne."

Cormac felt his curiosity quickening. He knew Rathlin O'Birne—he'd seen the island from the cliffs at Bunglas. "And how do you connect that to Mary Heaney?"

"All my informants claimed that P. J. Heaney was the culprit."

"Was there any proof?"

"No witness to the actual deed. I can offer only what people told me. Some of them were still a little nervous talking about it. Depending on the day's fishing, it wasn't unusual for Heaney to return home spattered with fish blood. But several people claimed hearing stories that he pulled his boat into harbor the night of the seal slaughter without a single fish. The front of his gansey was soaked with blood—and not watery fish blood either, but something darker and more substantial. After he'd gone, a few of the locals had a look at his boat."

"What were they looking for?" Cormac's imagination had already conjured three ruddy-faced figures crouching among sodden nets with glowing lanterns.

"I'm not even sure they knew," Roz said. "But what they found was a heavy fishing weight, still covered with blood and bits of fur."

Cormac could see the terrible thing before him, glistening red in the lamplight. He imagined a lone figure out on the island, caught up in a fury of violence, striking confusion and fear into a crowd of hapless, slow-moving animals. He heard cries of alarm, desperate splashing as they tried to escape into the sea, and he thought of the creatures he'd seen this morning, not far from Rathlin O'Birne. Perhaps Heaney couldn't bear what he saw in the dark pools of their eyes. "So what did they do?"

"What could they do? It wasn't against the law to kill seals—not at that time."

"But if people believed that Heaney had killed his wife—and it seems as though there was widespread suspicion—why wouldn't they come out and say so?"

"I think it had to do with the remnants of fairy belief. And you have to consider the social context of that time. The local people feared Heaney, but they were just as fearful of the police—the Royal Irish Constabulary were an extension of English rule. Nobody wanted to cooperate, no matter what they knew. Heaney might come after them if they talked, and if he did, how could they entrust their families' safety to the very same bailiffs who had no compunction about evicting people when they couldn't pay the rent? The song might have been an indirect way to tell what really happened. I've always suspected that at its root, the selkie stories had far more to do with female emancipation than otherworldly sea creatures. Once they escape their enchantment, shape-shifting females are in possession of their own identities, liberated from the bonds of marriage and social expectation. In spite of being torn, they're still able to leave their husbands, even their children. It's a deeply unsettling notion, that there's something pulling at women, far larger than any possible domestic concerns. Something as deep and mysterious and otherworldly as the sea. A whole separate realm."

Cormac couldn't help thinking of Nora, perhaps content to be her own person, apart from him. Roz was right—it was an unsettling notion. He tried to shake it off. "What made you decide to spend months digging all this up?"

"I came across the words of the song again, just by chance, and there's something so powerful about the way it captures the wintry feeling of a place—the darkness and the snow, the cold sea, the utter desolation. It's the mood of the piece, and the ambiguity of the selkie's situation—she may have escaped her captivity, but she's not really free. It's there from the opening line of the song: *Is cosúil gur mheath tú nó gur thréig tú an greann*—'It seems you've faded away and abandoned the love of life.' The woman is trapped and heartsick and exhausted, but she can't seem to leave that place where her two worlds met. She's divided, in body and in spirit; the love she feels for her children is as strong as the pull of the sea." Roz gazed out the window into the middle distance. "I know she's out there somewhere, Cormac. People might imagine that I study these things because I harbor some secret belief in mermaids. I don't, as it happens. But our need for them is real. And so is all the anger and fear, the fierce love and jealousy embedded in the stories about them—all the things that make us humans carry on as we do. Think of it—Mary Heaney disappeared more than a hundred years ago, and yet people who live down the road still know intimate details of her life. Why? Because her dilemma speaks to them. Her story expresses a duality that's deeply embedded in all of us. Folktales are really complex psychological ideas given form and flesh." Roz touched his arm. "Tell me, Cormac, have you had a good look around your father's house? Surely you've noticed all the photographs on the walls—and have you counted how many are seals? When I remarked on the pictures, your father showed me how all the drawers and cupboards in his room are literally filled with notebooks of selkie stories his aunt Julia had collected. And I got a very strange feeling at that moment, wondering how it was your father and I just happened to meet that evening at Port na Rón. Even if you don't believe in other realms, or fate, or serendipity—'all that auld shite,' as your father likes to call it—you still have to admit, there's something funny going on."

13

It was just after five when Nora arrived at her parents' back door. No one answered the bell, and perhaps it was just as well; she hadn't yet worked out what to say to them. How could she speak about the shattered skull at the morgue this morning, about her visit to the river, seeing Elizabeth? She still felt peculiar, thinking about that ghostly vision of Tríona through the glass wall in Lowertown, the book turned inward on the library shelf, the way she happened to catch a glimpse of Harry Shaughnessy's stained sweatshirt. Now, at the end of the day, it all seemed like the addled plotline of a dream. She had considered going to the homeless camp below the power station, but couldn't convince herself that it would be either useful or prudent. There were probably lots of possible explanations for how Shaughnessy had come into possession of that sweatshirt, how it came to have that rusty-looking stain.

She glanced at her watch. Too late to call Cormac—she'd missed her chance. Pressing the bell again, she heard the old-fashioned ringer echoing through empty rooms. Her parents were probably still at work. It wasn't exactly as if they were expecting her.

She fished for her jumble of keys, which still included one for this house. Being here brought back dim recollections of the day they'd moved in more than thirty years ago, including the creeping apprehension she'd felt about a new house, a whole new country. Curiosity had quickly supplanted fear as she began to explore all the secret, hidden places here—the cellar and the closets, even an attic—all so different from their home in Ireland, so wonderfully foreign. It seemed so long ago now.

Walking through the kitchen and dining room to the front porch, she could make out the constant, faint hum of the freeway; in the far distance, the river bluffs were just visible through the trees. She suddenly remembered another summer night. The family was out here on the porch, just home from a summer holiday in Donegal. The weather had been unusually fine, warm enough to go swimming among the small, rocky islands in the bay near their rented cottage. Tríona had gone out too far, paddling until she was only a small, bright head bobbing between the waves. Then she disappeared. Their father had panicked, diving in and racing out to the island, where he found Tríona, coughing and spluttering on the rocks. She claimed a seal had rescued her from drowning. Nora had remained unconvinced, choosing to believe that Tríona had made the whole thing up, that she'd only pretended to drown to get attention. She was always doing things like that. Why was it no one else had seen any seals about?

Back home again two days after the misadventure, Tríona lay spread-eagled on the ottoman, rolling her small island around the porch as she paddled her arms and legs. Nora particularly remembered how the hollow noise of the casters against the porch floor had grated on her nerves. "Tríona, would you ever stop making that noise? Mam, make her stop!"

Tríona steered the ottoman to the middle of the room. She said: "I was just wondering what it would be like to be a seal." She flopped over on her back, looking up, as if the reflections that played on the ceiling were the surface of the ocean above her.

Nora remembered how she had been poised to make some cutting remark, but their mother, busy at a crossword at the other end of the porch, murmured absently: "We can get you a book about seals at the library, Tríona, if you want to know about them—"

"I don't want to *know,* Mam—I just want to wonder. Did you know they look like they're flying underwater? I wonder what they see out there, under the sea . . ."

Nora remembered feeling another reality rise up before her in that moment: whales and jellyfish and giant tortoises, sea snakes, and water spouts. She could feel the profound silence beneath endless swells. And suddenly she knew that Tríona hadn't been lying about the seal at all. She didn't have to lie. The world overflowed with wonders. Just because something was extraordinary or inexplicable—that didn't mean it wasn't true. Though they were as far from any ocean as it was possible to be, she had been immersed, feeling the pull of salt water half a continent away.

Back in the present, Nora gave the ottoman a little shove with her foot, listening to the hollow noise it made on the floorboards. Tríona had probably never understood what a rare gift she had passed along that night—only the first of many.

From the porch, Nora returned to the front hall and took the stairs two at a time, feeling familiar creaks underfoot like strange music. Everywhere she looked were ghostly images: Tríona cross-legged on the landing, engrossed in dolls or a game of solitaire; her mother putting away folded towels and linens in the hall; the sound of her father slowly climbing the stairs after checking the locks each night—the tiny, random slices of their lives here, all the seemingly insignificant moments that added up to earthly existence.

Passing the bathroom door conjured up the ritual of taming Tríona's unruly hair. Why that task had fallen to her, she couldn't recall; all that remained was an imprint of their daily battle of wills. She slid open the top drawer and found a limp circle of elastic strung with faux pearls and glass beads. Tríona's favorite—there had been a time when she insisted upon wearing it every day.

Nora set the hair band back in the drawer, and went out into the hallway. At one end was her parents' room; at the other end were two smaller bedrooms, hers and Tríona's. The door to Tríona's room was closed. She opened it, not sure what to expect. The air had a distinctive closed-up smell, a sign that the door was kept shut, perhaps a vain attempt to trap any ghosts that might dwell here. The room was now, just as it had always been during Tríona's lifetime, in a state of chaos: stacks of books everywhere, theater scripts wedged at every conceivable angle into the bookcases. In stark contrast to her own room, with its orderly shelves full of field guides and plant presses and specimen jars, Tríona's room had always been a realm of make-believe. She remembered believing that her sister must have been adopted, since she clearly wasn't related to the rest of the family.

Opening the closet door, Nora recognized a sun-faded denim shirt their father had worn for gardening until Tríona appropriated it and started wearing the thing around the house. Whenever she put it on, she also assumed their father's voice and mannerisms—the seeds of her acting career. Each of Tríona's transformations was tied to some item of clothing, whether this chambray shirt or a character costume—as though the act of changing clothes could alter who you were.

Nora took the faded shirt from its hanger and slipped it on over her own clothes, catching the ghost of a musky scent. Though Tríona had worn this shirt for ages, their father's essence still seemed embedded in it as well. She caught a glimpse of herself in the dressing table mirror. The low glass cut her head off; without it, she might easily be mistaken for her sister. She turned away, the sun-blanched cotton on her shoulders heavy as another skin.

Nora checked her watch again. After six, and still no one home. She sat down at the edge of the bed and started flipping through Tríona's collection of old audiocassettes. Most were homemade, compilations of favorite songs. She opened the cassette player and found an unlabeled tape inside. Popping it back in the machine, she pressed Play, and after a few rustling noises, heard her own voice—noticeably younger and higher—spilling from the small speakers.

Then something extraordinary happened. A second voice joined with hers—close in character, but not identical—blending at first in unison, and then diverging in an eerie harmony through the strange words of the refrain. There was so much she had forgotten. Like the steamy August night more than twenty years ago, when she had crept down into the musty cellar, intent on making this tape to capture a song that had been plaguing her. The prospect was exciting and terrifying, but the need to pour her own voice into the mysterious shape of that melody had driven her past fear. When Tríona joined in from the darkness at the top of the stairs, she had been startled and a little angry at first—and then too intrigued to stop. She had come home from Ireland carrying that song in her head, daring to sing it aloud only in moments when she was certain to be quite alone. But Tríona must have been there all the time, secretly listening. When the song ended, she began again, and they had sung it over and over, invisible to each other, but closer in spirit than they had ever been. Watching the tiny reels of the cassette rotate slowly in tandem, she bowed her head and let the hot tears sting her eyes—for the lonely sea maid upon the waves, for Tríona, and for herself.

When the song finally came to an end, Nora lifted her head, and turned to see her father standing in the doorway, supporting himself on the door frame with both arms. His hair had gone completely white since she had last seen him, and his face, so much older than she remembered, seemed drained of blood. She had never seen him shed a tear, not even in the terrible days immediately following Tríona's death. He did not weep now, but she could read distress in the deep hollows of his eyes.

"I thought you were—" Suddenly the words seemed to choke him.

Nora looked down at the faded chambray shirt.

"Tríona," she murmured.

Her father flinched, and Nora felt a surge of regret. She hadn't meant to say the name aloud. He shook his head and looked away. "I thought you were lost to us as well."

"But now I'm found," she said quietly. "The prodigal, returned."

He offered a wan half smile, and Nora realized that this strange, sad welcome was more than she had hoped for, and probably far more than she deserved.

There was a noise from downstairs, the rustle of someone pushing through the back door. "That's your mother home," he said. "Shall we go down to her?"

14

Frank Cordova closed his trunk. He'd just wasted three fruitless hours at the courier service on West Seventh where Natalie Russo had worked, and another two at the nearby house she'd shared with some of her coworkers. The company had never contracted with Peter Hallett's architectural firm, and not one of the current crop of bike messengers had ever known Natalie. To these kids, five years ago might as well have been ancient history. No one knew whether any of Natalie's belongings remained at the house, a run-down side-by-side duplex that held an accumulation of many temporary lives.

He checked his watch as he left the messenger service. A quarter to seven, just enough time to make his meeting with the coach at the Twin Cities Rowing Club. Natalie's emergency contact. He dropped down to Shepard Road at Randolph and sailed along the bluffs beyond Crosby Farm Park. The boathouse was on a private road that hairpinned from the top of the bluff down to the river's edge. He parked along the service road and began to make his way down the steep incline. The road's surface was loose gravel, and his leather-soled shoes weren't suited to the terrain.

Nobody was around when he reached the boathouse, but the doors were open, and he scoped around inside. Some of the wall racks were empty; brightly colored sculls hung from others. Outside the open door stood matched pairs of fabric-and-metal slings, evidently waiting for the rowers to return. He heard a shout through a bullhorn, and turned to see a flotilla of long, narrow watercraft approaching from downriver. Some were rowed solo, some in pairs; one of the boats held a foursome stroking gracefully in unison. Oars lifted as the boats pulled in on both sides of the dock, and the rowers glanced at him as they lifted their lightweight sculls from the water and flipped them upside down onto the waiting stands. They began unscrewing the rigging hardware, swabbing the boats down with towels.

He approached the nearest sling. "I'm looking for Sarah Cates. She said I'd find her here after practice."

The woman glanced up only briefly, eyes flicking to the badge he'd clipped to his belt. "She'll be along in a minute. She was following in the launch."

After all the rowers were in, a woman he gauged to be in her late thirties steered a motorized rowboat to the dock and raised a hand, signaling that she'd seen him. Not that hard to spot him, really—the only shirt and tie amid all the spandex. Sarah Cates had a lean, muscular body, and bronze skin that hinted at mixed origins like his own. Sunstreaks in her curly dark hair were evidence of hours spent out on the water. She tied up the launch and made her way up the dock. Cordova walked down to meet her.

"Ms. Cates—thanks for seeing me on short notice."

"Sarah, please. No trouble at all. I'm here every day—when I'm not out rowing myself, I'm coaching the women's team. We don't have a coach at the moment, so we're taking turns. Come on up." Halfway to the boathouse, she turned and threw him a sideways glance. "You don't remember me, do you?"

Cordova felt uneasy. He hadn't been involved in the initial investigation of Natalie Russo's disappearance, but then again, his memory seemed to be playing tricks on him recently. He shook his head. "Sorry—"

"You interviewed me—it was about three years ago." Still didn't register; he felt a little bewildered. She continued: "I found a body in the river. It's okay. I know it's impossible to remember everyone you talk to. You know, I'd always imagined that being a detective might be interesting, but after that—I certainly don't envy you that part of the job. He was so tiny."

At last Frank felt his memory kick in. The baby's body had been discovered first; his mother turned up a mile downstream the next day. Witnesses said that she had cradled the newborn in her arms as she jumped from a bridge more than a hundred feet above the river. The memory of mother and child laid out side by side in the morgue had disturbed his dreams for a long time. "That was you?"

She nodded. "We meet again. And I'm guessing you're here about another death."

"I'm afraid so. How well did you know Natalie Russo?"

From her reaction, Sarah Cates had been expecting this visit. "That body at Hidden Falls—it was Natalie, wasn't it?" Frank nodded, and she rubbed her bare arms, as if suddenly chilled. "I'm not sure any of us knew her all that well. When we talked, it was mostly about rowing."

"How often was she down here at the boathouse?"

"Every day, morning and evening, rain or shine, whenever the water was open. She was a serious rower."

"Isn't everyone here pretty serious?"

Sarah Cates smiled. "Yeah—but some more than others."

"Natalie was wearing running clothes when she was found. Can you tell me anything about that?"

"She ran every day, in addition to rowing practice. Most of us do some sort of cross-training—it helps build endurance."

Frank said: "The people at her job and the house where she lived didn't seem to know a lot about her. I was wondering if we might check club records for anything that might shed some light on what was happening in her life around the time of the disappearance."

"Not sure what the club records might tell you. All we keep is contact information and membership stuff, speed and distance records, and the daily logs." She pointed to a book hanging from a hook near the open boathouse door. "Liability insurance requires them on club equipment and private boats. It's a safety thing; if somebody checks a boat out and doesn't check back in, we have to send out a search party. That's just this month. All the older logs are upstairs. You're welcome to have a look."

She pointed to an open stairway that led to a loft on the second floor. Cordova took note of signs at the foot of the stairs that pointed the way to men's and women's locker rooms as they passed. "Would Natalie have kept a locker here?"

"I'm afraid I can't tell you. Not being uncooperative, it's just that we're not too strict about lockers. They're not assigned; you just bring a padlock if you want to use one. We don't really keep track of them."

As they continued upward, Frank glanced at the row of photographs that followed the staircase. The more recent images appeared in color; the older ones were black-and-white.

"Team pictures," Sarah Cates confirmed. "All the way back to the twenties, when the club was men only. We're still not terribly organized, but at least we operate a little less like a frat house now."

"Would Natalie be in any of these pictures?"

"At least one, I think. They're in chronological order, so if we start at the bottom and count back—here she is."

The photo showed Natalie Russo in the front row. She was smaller, slighter than most of her teammates. Her fellow rowers, caught up in the spirit of camaraderie, had arms thrown around one another's shoulders. He let his gaze rest on the blonde standing directly behind Natalie. The face was partially obscured by someone's elbow, but he was almost certain he'd seen it somewhere before, in a different context. The feeling was vague, but insistent.

Sarah said: "You know, it's funny; even though they're taken at the start of each season, you can tell just by looking which teams are going to be the great ones—"

"And this bunch?" Cordova nodded to the photo before them.

"Our best women's team ever. We could have sent at least four people to Olympic trials that year, but—"

Cordova prompted: "But what?"

"Natalie disappeared just before they were supposed to go." Her lips pressed together in consternation. "Things sort of fell apart."

The upstairs office was a jumble of loose paper and lost-and-found clothing. "Please excuse the mess," Sarah Cates said. "The usual problem—no one's really in charge. The office is always in chaos." She hauled a stack of boxes out from under a table, and found the one that held logbooks for five years previous. Flipping through the pages, she said: "Like I said, Natalie was on the water pretty much every day, from the time the ice was out—she usually did morning and evening workouts, and lots of running in between." She turned the heavy ledger to face him.

Cordova peered at the handwritten pages of the log. Most names were illegible, except for all the repetitions of "N. Russo" in neat blue ballpoint. From June 3 onward, no "N. Russo" appeared in any column. Here one day, gone the next. *Like we'll all vanish some day,* he thought, *without so much as a ripple.* He raised his eyes from the book. "She must have been good."

"Only the best natural rower I've ever seen. Flawless mechanics. I remember something she said once, that winning a race was the best high. She told me she'd grown up sort of uncomfortable in her own skin. Rowing had turned her from this awkward, chubby kid into someone who actually knew what she was doing, what she wanted. The way she said it—just made me think she'd overcome some difficult things in her past, you know? Most people float along, but Natalie never did. She definitely had that fire in the belly, a competitive spirit, but not the kind that made her hard to live with. There's always a certain amount of backbiting in any place like this, ego and temper and all that goes along with competition, but Natalie seemed above all that. She'd go out of her way to cheer on teammates, try to lift everybody's game—unlike most of the lightweights I've known." She lowered her voice. "They have to be cutting weight all the time, so they're usually hungry. Makes 'em cranky."

"Did any of Natalie's teammates resent her ability?"

"Why should they? It wasn't like she went around rubbing people's faces in how great she was. We all like winning. And we had a much better chance of winning when she was with us."

"What about friends, anybody in particular she hung out with?"

"Not that I recall. She did things with the team, but nobody in particular stood out."

"You know that you were her emergency contact?"

"Yeah, they told me when she disappeared. I thought it was kind of sad. She didn't seem to have any family—no one she wanted to stay in touch with, anyway."

"What do you remember about the time she disappeared?"

"She didn't show up for practice. That was totally out of character, especially with the trials coming up. I called her cell phone, but there was no answer. So I tried the messenger service, but they said she hadn't been to work either."

"So you reported her missing—"

"I wasn't sure anybody else would do it. Then somebody spotted her bike behind the boathouse. I remember having such a bad feeling, right here." She pointed to a place just below her sternum. "I'm constantly reminding people—novices, especially—what a dangerous place the river can be." She gestured to the top of the bluffs. "It's still wild down here, not like the world up there. We're dealing with weird stuff all the time—currents, hypothermia, deadheads, floaters—and don't even get me started on the wackos who think it's funny to drop things from bridges. We have to be constantly on our guard. I was always telling Natalie not to run alone, but she said she didn't need a bodyguard just to go for a run. I totally got what she was saying—it's not fair. But whenever I run down here by myself, I always come home feeling like I've dodged a bullet." She eyed him curiously. "It must be strange, doing what you do every day. Getting to know people only after they're dead, I mean."

"Guess I never looked at it that way," Frank said. "It's like any other line of work; some days are better than others." His eyes suddenly focused on the delicate sprinkling of freckles across Sarah Cates's face. All the time they'd been talking, and he had never noticed that detail until this moment. And her eyes, such an unusual hue—pale green, the same color as the river in the bright sunlight. "I could wonder about what you do every day, too. Cold, currents, deadheads, dead bodies—that's enough to keep most people in bed. And yet you're out here on the water every day."

"I can't really explain." She looked away for a few seconds. "When the wind is calm, and your cadence is just right—it's hard to put into words. If you really want to understand, I could take you out for a beginner's lesson some evening—we do it all the time. No charge."

15

The reunion with her parents was going somewhat better than Nora had expected. There were no recriminations about not calling, no questions about her plans. As if they all realized that the elaborate *pas de trois* they had been engaged in for the past five years had become necessary.

Going about the everyday rituals of preparing a meal, Nora felt two discussions going on at once—on their lips the mundane details of the flight home, her work in Dublin, the small permutations of her parents' daily lives, while the larger questions lurked beneath the surface, unasked and unanswered. She had already imagined most of the conversation: her father's inquiries about her work at Trinity, her mother asking after people they had known in Dublin, even the occasional awkward silences. They never spoke Tríona's name. Still, as the three of them ranged around the kitchen, opening drawers and cupboards, Nora felt how good it was to have her bearings, to know precisely where everything was. But for some reason, she was filled with a distant ache as well.

She understood on a rational level her father's reluctance to condemn Peter Hallett—or anyone else, for that matter—without proof. Watching him wrestle the cork from a wine bottle, she tried to imagine the place he'd been reared, the wild, wind-whipped west coast of Clare, where bleak history and compounded misfortune had fed a general faith in forces beyond the known world. From an early age, he had rebelled against that upbringing, rejecting all the old beliefs, demanding a rational explanation for everything. After Tríona's death, Nora and her mother had watched him retreat deeper and deeper into his research, taking refuge in his orderly, microscopic universe. He delighted in the abstract beauty of individual cells, in cracking open their inner workings, unmasking invisible chemical changes. In her own work, she had followed her father a long distance down that path, but had come to see the fault in hewing too closely to scientific method. Where human behavior was involved, there was often no rational explanation.

The conversation that had flowed almost normally as they'd moved about the kitchen suddenly slowed once they sat down to the table. Nora sensed her mother trying to coax the conversation forward, but one gambit after another faltered and failed, and they finished their meal in silence.

"You haven't told us how long you'll be staying," her father said abruptly. "I hope you haven't left Trinity for good."

"They're expecting me back for fall term." That much was true, at least.

A few moments later, Tom Gavin rose from the table. "I'm sorry to leave you, but I've got an early presentation tomorrow, and I've a few things left to prepare. Forgive me." As he passed by the back of her chair, Nora felt her father's hand hover briefly above her shoulder. Five years after Tríona's death, and here they were, still in limbo.

When he had retreated into the study, Eleanor Gavin said: "There's no presentation tomorrow. He's just having a difficult time."

Nora began to speak, but her mother hushed her. "I know—the past five years haven't been easy for any of us. But your father's been waiting out on the porch almost every night since you phoned. Now that you're here, he doesn't know what to do. He's completely exhausted. I'm not saying any of this is your fault, love—please don't misunderstand. I'm just telling you what's going on. He did the very same thing before you were born. Couldn't eat, couldn't sleep, couldn't concentrate. And when you finally did arrive, he was a complete wreck. He's missed you terribly, Nora. We both have."

"Is he all right, Mam? He looks so pale—and I know doctors make rotten patients."

Eleanor let out a breath that at once signaled her frustration, and her relief in having someone to talk to. "He's been driving himself too hard—his way of coping."

Nora studied her mother's face, moved by the subtle changes she read there: the etching of fine worry lines was more pronounced, the eyes even more deep-set. Her mother's hair had gone completely white as well. Seeing the changes the past three years had wrought, and imagining her parents alone in this house, the silences between them growing by a few seconds each evening—it was almost more than she could bear. "If you'd like, I could have a word with him—"

Her mother shot her a wry look. "And you think that might help? You know how he dotes on you, sweetheart, but you have to admit you've never been the most calming influence. You're too much like him—it's that Gavin stubborn streak. No, you worry about yourself. I'll have your father in hand, even if I've got to grind up the beta-blockers and dissolve them in his tea."

Nora couldn't help smiling. "You've got some neck, calling other people stubborn. You look as if you've lost weight, Mam. Are you eating? Remember what Mrs. Makabo said—"

"'No man likes a skinny wife, Missus Doctor,'" Eleanor said, echoing the musical accent of one of her longtime patients. They both smiled faintly, remembering the saucy wink that had accompanied the remark, and the chorus of giggles that erupted from the other patients in the waiting room.

"How is Mrs. Makabo?"

"Thriving—fourteen grandchildren. Number fifteen coming along any day now."

"Will you tell her I was asking for her?"

"I will, of course. She and the other ladies still ask after you."

The patients at her mother's clinic were mostly immigrant mothers and children, and Nora had seen firsthand how they struggled with a strange new language, with poverty and bureaucracy and bigotry, with the bitter Midwestern cold. Many had survived so much worse, in home places ravaged by famine, genocide, endless war. She had always thought it no great mystery that her mother could imagine what had really happened to Tríona, while her father, insulated from human contact in his sterile, air-conditioned laboratory, could not. She watched her mother check the door to the hallway once more, and then steel herself, apparently to deliver bad news. "Nora, there's something I haven't told you—"

"If it's about Miranda, Mam, I already know."

"How did you find out?"

"Does it matter?" Her mother's bewildered expression forced a confession of sorts. "All right—I was here last night, outside. I overheard you and Daddy talking."

"Nora, why didn't you come in?"

"It was a shock, hearing about Miranda, and then to find out about their trip to Ireland—"

"I wanted to tell you, Nora. I meant to tell you."

"I know, Mam. Please don't worry."

"I don't understand, Nora. If you were here, where did you sleep last night?"

"I got a little apartment. I didn't want to put you and Daddy out—"

"Put us out?"

Nora could see the hurt in her mother's eyes. "We both know it's for the best, Mam."

"Maybe you're right. I don't know. Sometimes I feel as if I don't know anything anymore. There's something else—" Eleanor's voice dropped to a whisper. She glanced down the hallway again to make sure the door to the study was completely shut. "Will you come upstairs?"

Nora followed her mother up the back stairs from the kitchen, wondering what all the secrecy was about.

Once inside Tríona's room, Eleanor sank down on the bed, taking up the chambray shirt Nora had left there. She began absently smoothing the faded material. "My God, I'd nearly forgotten this poor old thing. Your father wouldn't get rid of it, even after it was threadbare. I was going to peg it out, but Tríona wouldn't let me—" She lifted the material to her cheek, pulled back through its subtle fusion of scents to intimate memories of husband and daughter—lost, just as Nora had been, in an intensely private past.

After a moment, Eleanor spoke: "This is the only place I can still see her. I come in here every few months, thinking it's time we started to clear away—I mean, really, how many jars of shells and stones does a person need? But when I touch anything, I think, 'Tríona must have seen something special in this; she picked it up and saved it for a reason.' And so I put it back. And everything stays just as it was."

She had never heard her mother speak like this before. Nora crossed to a trio of antique apothecary jars resting on the window ledge. The nearest was filled with shells, the other two with sea glass and stones—all collected during their summers in Ireland. Every year, Tríona had smuggled home additions to her odd collections. Nora lifted the first lid and took out a conical shell—a black-footed limpet—turning it over and admiring all the varicolored stripes. "I tried to explain to her once, about all the different types of limpets. And do you know what she said? 'I don't need facts about everything, Nora. I just like the shapes and the colors.' "

"You've always tried to make sense of the world—that's just the way you are, love. It's your nature. There's nothing wrong with that. I'm sure Tríona didn't mean what she said as criticism."

Nora returned the shell to the jar and crossed to sit beside her mother on the bed.

"I know you believe we treated you differently," Eleanor said. "And I suppose we did, in a way, because you *were* so different, you and Tríona. Not just from each other; from your father and me as well. Sometimes I couldn't fathom where either of you came from. What all mothers have to wonder, I suppose." She reached out to touch Nora's face. "Every time I look at you, even now, I see you the second after you were born—such a shock of dark hair! I see you at six, at eleven, at fourteen, twenty-five. And the curious thing is that this package, this outward form that is you—it changes; it actually never stops changing, but the essence—" She laid her hand upon Nora's breastbone. "The essence of who you are—that has never altered, not ever, from the time I carried you inside me. I'm not sure why I find that reassuring, but I do."

Nora ached to let it all go—to tell her mother about Cormac, about Frank Cordova and the postmortem this morning, about Natalie Russo and the riverbank and the image of Tríona she had seen in that Lowertown window. How wrenching it had been to see Elizabeth so grown up today, and how fearful, witnessing that less-than-benign fatherly hand upon her. *There are things you don't know, Nora.* She could not speak about any of that. Instead, she reached for the hand that rested on the faded chambray, feeling the bones beneath her mother's beautifully translucent skin. "Was that what you wanted to tell me, Mam?"

Eleanor shook her head. "I wanted to say that I know why you've come home—"

Nora closed her eyes. *Here it comes,* she thought, the whole list of reasons why she ought not to be dredging everything up all over again. She could almost hear her father's voice, trying to talk sense into her. Her mother continued: "What I mean to say, Nora, is that I understand why you've come back. And I want to help you—I *need* to help, whatever way I can. I can't carry on anymore as I have been, doing nothing, feeling nothing. There's only one thing I can do, and must do—and that is to find out what happened to my child—to both of my beautiful children."

"Oh, Mam—"

"Wait, let me finish. I have to know if there's anything you haven't told me. Anything you know about what happened, that you couldn't share with your father and me, anything you felt you had to spare us. You've got to tell me now—please."

There were so many things she had tried to spare them. Nora took a deep breath, and dived in: "Frank Cordova brought me along to an autopsy this morning. A young woman found three days ago at the river. Her name was Natalie Russo. Does that name mean anything to you?" Eleanor shook her head, and Nora continued. "She disappeared six weeks before Tríona died, and was buried all this time in a seepage swamp at Hidden Falls—" The rising dread in her mother's eyes made Nora feel dizzy.

"What's she got to do with Tríona? Tell me."

"Their injuries were identical. Her face was destroyed, just like Tríona's."

"What are you saying? You think Peter murdered her as well?"

As well. Proof that the last doubts about Peter Hallett's guilt had finally given way.

16

By the time the clock downstairs struck ten, Nora had told her mother everything. Every sordid detail. It came in a flood, all the knowledge she had held back so long. When she finished, her mother looked hollowed out.

"I knew there was much more than you were willing to tell," Eleanor said at last. "Oh Nora, how can you ever forgive us?"

"I don't blame you for not wanting to see what was happening, not wanting to believe. It's all too horrible."

"But you saw it, Nora. You believed. I just can't understand—if Tríona was in such desperate trouble, why didn't she come to us? Why wouldn't she let us help her?"

"Maybe fear of what Peter would do. And shame. From what she said on the phone, I think she was afraid that she'd somehow let us all down—you and Daddy, me, Elizabeth—all of us. God knows what he put into her mind."

"It doesn't seem possible, Nora. That we could have been so utterly deceived—"

"He knows exactly what he's doing, Mam. I'm convinced of it. That's what makes him so dangerous."

"But she loved him. I know she did. What is wrong with him, Nora? What's missing in that man to make him turn against her?"

"I don't know, Mam. How can we ever know? It's the one riddle we're probably never going to crack."

After considering this fact for a moment, Eleanor took a deep breath and set her shoulders, as if trying to shake off despair. "So what can we do, right now? Tell me, I'll do it."

"I've been thinking—our first priority is keeping Elizabeth safe. In order to do that, we've got to get her away from Peter."

"But she's staying with us, Nora. While Peter and Miranda are in Ireland. It's all worked out. We're supposed to collect her tomorrow evening."

"And are you prepared to take her away, Mam? Someplace far away, where he won't find her, where he won't even think to look? You have to be ready to do it right away, tomorrow. Can you do that?"

Eleanor put a hand on Tríona's faded chambray shirt. "I've been making inquiries. Anticipating, I suppose. There's an amazing network if you know the right people to ask."

"It could mean living on the run, for weeks or even months, hiding from the police. Are you sure you're prepared for all that, Mam?"

"I know you may not believe me, but it's all I've been thinking about for the past five years. If it comes down to a choice between losing all this and protecting Elizabeth, which do you think I'd choose?"

Back at her apartment, Nora crossed to the window and stood looking down through fluttering cottonwood leaves. One full day gone. And only three more days before Peter left the country, perhaps for good. He would be smart enough to know where he could escape extradition, to plan a route that wouldn't raise suspicion. At least he was leaving Elizabeth behind. Had he perhaps just been waiting for the right opportunity to wash his hands of her?

What had she really discovered today, that couldn't be put down to accident or coincidence? There was still no concrete connection to Peter Hallett in any of the day's revelations. Maybe proof would come soon, but she was too tired to fit any more pieces together tonight.

She swung her backpack off the desk and reached for the cassette she'd lifted at the last minute from Tríona's room. How could she have forgotten making this? Tríona had saved the original, and from the look of it, even taken the trouble to repair the thing when it had broken down. For some reason, that detail moved her to the verge of tears once more. She tipped the cassette into the clock radio beside the bed and turned the volume low, leaning back as the two voices surrounded her again—similar, but not identical, pulling against each other in the words of a deceptively simple song:

All you who are in love
Aye and cannot it remove
I pity all the pain that you endure
For experience lets me know
That your hearts are full of woe
A woe that no mortal can cure.

Tríona had been barely fourteen when this recording was made, and yet something in her voice captured that fatal collision of hope and heartbreak. Here was love as illness, as a terminal condition. How had she understood those things, when Peter Hallett wouldn't even enter her life for another seven years? Nora shut her eyes, remembering a moment, only a few days ago, when, crossing the bog at Loughnabrone and seeing Cormac before her, she had suddenly been taken over—but by what? Some force she couldn't even name. Five years ago, she had imagined herself in love with Marc Staunton, and it turned out to be an illusion. That flash of awareness she had experienced out on the bog with Cormac had felt entirely new. How could it be new when it also felt impossibly old, as if it existed independent of time, of circumstance, of reason? Especially of reason. Her entire life up to that moment had been spent resisting the chaos of unruly emotion, and now she was caught in it, that impossible, inextricable web of joy and misery and madness that was love. That exquisite, exultant ache for which there was no mortal cure.

That was the one thing Peter Hallett probably hadn't counted on or even understood. That once Tríona was bound to him by such a feeling, there was no such thing as severance. *Isn't it shocking, what you'll do when you love someone?* What had Tríona done, how far had she gone for love?

Nora reached into her pocket for Cormac's knot, turning it over and over, fingers now accustomed to its gaunt shape, as she leaned back on the pillow, listening to the voices, to the music of cottonwood leaves outside the window, rustling in the night air. The verses of the first song eventually gave way to another as she lay there, limbs growing steadily heavier, until there was no fighting it. *Jet lag.* In her half-conscious state, Nora couldn't be certain whether she had spoken the words aloud or only imagined them. She tried to raise her head, but could not. Across her field of vision, the shadows of fluttering leaves outside turned to random diamonds, fracturing and melding together on the shimmering surface.

Outside on the street, Truman Stark turned off his idling engine. He still hadn't managed to figure the connection between this dark-haired female and the redhead. But now that he knew where she lived, he could keep an eye on her. He could just show up whenever he felt like it. Any time at all.

17

It was after midnight when Frank Cordova arrived home. Inside the front door, he stooped to pick up the jumble of mail that had come through the slot, and tossed everything onto the mounting pile on the dining room table. Every day it was the same—nothing but junk mail. He wasn't sure why he didn't just pitch it all as it came in. No explanation, except that adding it to the heap at the center of the table had taken on the force of habit. Hard to break now.

He'd spent the better part of the evening going through the case files on Natalie Russo. He felt used up. It didn't help that his head was still thick from all the tequila last night. Sleep was inviting, but he also felt a familiar rasp of hunger. He opened the fridge and leaned in. The blast of cool air felt good.

A noise came from the darkened space beyond the kitchen, and he felt a jolt of alarm. Across the nearly empty living room, a shadowy figure seemed to float up from the couch. The faint glow from the kitchen caught Karin Bledsoe's short fair hair, the bottle of red wine and two glasses on the table beside her. Even in the dim light, he could see the bottle was nearly empty. She'd been here awhile. A handful of old LP sleeves lay scattered across the floor, and now he heard the click of the record changer, the reedy throb of accordions, and the faint, pleading voice of a *corrido* singer. He let out his breath and felt the adrenaline rush subside.

"What are you doing here, Karin? It's late."

She moved closer and pressed a wineglass into his hand, her body swaying slightly. "Wow, you really know how to make a girl feel welcome. Not 'How was your day, Karin?' or 'Good to see you, Karin'? Not even 'Hello.' Just 'What are you doing here?'" She kept her distance, as if trying to gauge his mood. "I thought you might need to unwind. You seemed a little tense this morning." She swirled the wine in her own glass, still studying him curiously. "I told Rolf we were on surveillance again. I figure it's only half a lie—I'm keeping an eye on you."

He set down the glass she'd handed him without taking a drink. It was the last thing he needed right now.

"Oh, come on, Frank, if you're not going to drink with me, you've at least gotta dance." She took his hand and wrapped it around her, but he felt paralyzed. It had always seemed to him that unhappiness had its own distinct scent, and suddenly that sour, stale smell crept into his nostrils. Or maybe it was just acid fumes from the wine and dust from old record sleeves. Karin often paired *corridos* with serious wine-drinking. He remembered her tearstained face from the last time. He'd always hated *corridos* for their nauseating, self-pitying tone, and had meant to pitch those records ages ago, but somehow he never got around to it. They'd probably get stacked back on the shelf again after Karin went home this time, too. That was how it went.

Everybody at headquarters knew about them. He didn't know why they even bothered sneaking around anymore—that part had never been easy, even if Rolf Bledsoe had it coming. That bastard had been playing around on Karin since the day they met—he never bothered to deny it. Why she ever married Bledsoe was a mystery—maybe something to do with the perverse pleasure they seemed to take in tormenting each other. Frank had always understood that he was just the current round of ammunition in Rolf and Karin's ongoing marital war. The whole thing was pretty sick. He tried not to think about it as he walked over and switched off the turntable.

Karin spoke behind him. "Aren't you going to ask how everything went in court today?"

"How did it go?"

"Swell. The defense is dredging up the broken home, the abusive father, all the playground bullies who damaged his client's sensitive soul, but you can see it on every face in that jury box—our boy is going down." Karin moved in close behind him. "I suppose I should be happy. Another miscreant off the street. How did everything go with Dr. Gavin?"

That was the real reason she was here. Frank winced suddenly and pressed two fingers just below his breastbone. His stomach was at him again—that same hot, stabbing sensation, just like this morning. Then, as quickly as the pain had started, it began to pass. "Look, Karin, it's late. And I don't feel much like talking right now."

She set down her glass and turned him around with one languid motion, reaching for his tie and slowly slipping the knot. As she leaned closer, he felt the warm gush of her breath in his ear: "Who the hell said anything about talking?"

Just after five, he awakened with a start. It was that same dream again, wandering a strange house, hearing cries and words muttered over and over, like prayers or incantations. He always woke from it feeling anxious and unsettled, and usually couldn't get back to sleep. Sometimes, as he was waking or drifting off to sleep, he would see an old man, dressed all in white, crushing leaves, or brushing a kind of broom over someone lying facedown on a bed. *Susto, susto,* the old man kept whispering to himself. *Es muy importante*. Had he actually seen these things, or just dreamed them? He had often wondered who was on the bed, what power was in those leaves. Something else floated to the surface as well, a word he didn't know: *curandero*.

He sensed the warmth of someone beside him, and turned to find Karin's fair head on the pillow. Disappointment seeped through him—not exactly noble, but undeniably true. What he regretted most about this affair with Karin was that there was no real kindness between them. They'd fallen into bed the first time almost by default, and had stayed together—if you could even call it that—for pretty much the same reason. At least neither of them harbored any false illusions. He told himself that was a good thing. Karin stirred, sleepily propping herself up on one elbow. "What time is it? Did they page you?"

"It's only a little after five," he said. "You can go back to sleep." She slipped back into her dreams, and Frank lay back on the bed, crossing his arms beneath his head.

Natalie Russo's ravaged remains tugged at him. She might well have encountered Peter Hallett along the running paths at the river. The trick would be establishing a connection with witnesses, dates, documentation. Hallett was probably too smart for that; he would have made certain there was no trace of him in Natalie Russo's life. And if they had only met down at the river, she might never have known his name. Frank closed his eyes, trying to reconcile the smooth, dark hair in Natalie Russo's file photo with the weathered strands they had pulled from the riverbank.

He'd had a suspicion Nora would head down to the crime scene as soon as he dropped her at the apartment. She would try to figure out what her sister was doing out in the woods the night she was killed, maybe somewhere near a clandestine burial. There was still no proof that Tríona had been at Hidden Falls. Assuming they could prove it, there were three distinct possibilities. The least likely explanation was that Tríona had stumbled onto the burial site by accident. Or she might have suspected her husband of murdering Natalie Russo, and she was out there looking for proof.

There was at least one other scenario—one he couldn't even mention to Nora, who had never seen her sister as anything but a blameless victim. Experience had taught him that very few human souls were completely free of fault. He had to consider every possible explanation, even the remote chance that Tríona had known where Natalie Russo was buried because she had somehow been involved in the murder. Or possibly just the cover-up. He didn't like imagining that explanation, unlikely as it probably was, but someone had to. Nothing was ever as simple as it seemed.

Every once in a while, he could still feel the urgency he'd once felt on the job. He would have been glad to think he helped to spare or improve the life of even one innocent person. But the truth was that he couldn't protect anyone. Even if he wore himself ragged every day, he was destined to fail; they were all destined to fail. It had taken him almost nine years to comprehend that unpleasant reality. People like him didn't actually stop bad things from happening; their real function was to clean up after the fact, to write a report and file it away. His job was to maintain the illusion of order where it didn't exist.

Book Three

We then passed to the more important subject of the taboo. The taboo, strictly speaking, only appears where the peltry is absent. Several of its forms correspond with rules of antique etiquette. Others recall special points connected with savage life, such as the dislike of iron and steel, and the prejudice against the mention of a personal name. Other prohibitions are against reproaching the wife with her origin, against reminding her of her former condition, or against questioning her conduct or crossing her will.

But whether the taboo be present or absent, the loss of the wife is equally inevitable, equally foreseen from the beginning. It is the doom of the connection between a simple man and a superhuman female. Even where the feather-robe is absent the taboo is not always found. Among savages the marriage-bond is often very loose: notably in the more backward races. And among these the superhuman wife's excuse for flight is simpler; and sometimes it is only an arbitrary exercise of will.

—*The Science of Fairy Tales: An Inquiry into Fairy Mythology,*
by Edwin Sidney Hartland, 1916

1

Nora awakened to the click-click-click of a cassette stuck in the player beside her head. She batted at it, but the tape continued to tick away in the machine, unable to advance. Groggy, she struggled to raise herself and checked the time—7:26—then pressed the button on the radio, trying to turn the machine off.

She flopped back down on the mattress, and heard Tríona's voice through the speaker, anxious and urgent: "I haven't got much time—"

Nora sat up, suddenly awake, her whole body on high alert.

"If anything should happen to me—an accident, anything—I want to make sure you know—" Her voice dropped to a whisper, and Nora had to strain to hear. "My God, I can't believe I'm saying this. It's like some horrible dream. I thought I knew him. Then a part of me pulls back, says how can you even think such things? He's the father of your child. But I don't know who he is, Nora. I don't know how this all happened. There are so many things I don't remember. Hours—whole days sometimes. I feel like I'm losing my mind. And I'm afraid it won't matter what I say, because no one will believe me. But I'm not making anything up—I swear I'm not. I want you to go to the hiding place. You know the one I mean. Take what you find there to the police. I want Elizabeth to know I didn't just leave her, that I had to do this, I had to find the truth. If I turn up missing, I want you to go and look at Hidden Falls. I couldn't say anything on the phone just now, because I knew you'd come after me, and I can't let you do that. I've got to go now, it's almost time—"

There was no more, only the crackling of a microphone, then silence.

Almost time for what? Nora picked up the tape recorder and shook it. The small wheels kept turning, but there was nothing more. How could she have missed this for so long? Tríona had obviously thought she'd listen to this tape before now.

This was what they needed—proof that Tríona had been at Hidden Falls. And that she'd known something about Peter, something she was afraid to tell anyone, afraid even to think. What else?

I want you to go to the hiding place. You know the one I mean.

Nora scrambled to her feet, nearly knocking the lamp over in her haste to extract the tape. Fifteen minutes later, she was at her parents' house again, up in Tríona's bedroom, dragging the heavy cast-iron bed away from the wall. Behind the bed was a small paneled door, complete with miniature antique knob. When she turned it, the door creaked open, inviting a dusty, hot breath from the attic. Like the entrance to a secret world, she remembered thinking as a child. The opening was just large enough to crawl through.

Down on her hands and knees, Nora poked her head into the attic, feeling a little light-headed in the airless heat. As she ventured inward, her left shoulder pressed against the hardened ooze of plaster and lath, she tested for loose beams, while trying to avoid exposed nails that threatened to catch her from the right. Definitely a child's hiding place, an unfriendly environment for grown-ups. Nora had found this attic space herself, the day they moved into the house. The small breach behind the chimney would have been perfect for passing secret messages between their rooms, but it had never happened. By the time her sister was old enough for secret messages, Nora herself had outgrown them. The story of their lives, really—always slightly out of synch.

She felt blindly around the back side of the rough brickwork, trying not to imagine all the many-legged creatures and silken egg sacs she must be disturbing. Lifting out a battered wooden cigar box, she crawled back out into the dimly lit room, trailing spiderwebs. The contents of the box still gave off a faint, brackish whiff when she opened the lid. A sign in her own childish handwriting pronounced it NORA'S SECRET HIDING PLACE. Every object in it was something she had squirreled away so many years ago: three buffalo nickels, six Irish ha'pennies, and even a worn shilling; the tarnished bronze medal on a tattered ribbon she'd found in the dirt under the front porch; a rather toothsomely grisly squirrel skull; some interesting fossils excavated from the river bluffs. The box also held bits of green and bluish sea glass, a vial of bonelike coral from Connemara, two brilliant Kerry diamonds from Inch Strand outside of Dingle, and a softened shard of blue-and-cream delft she'd scavenged along the shore in Donegal. Everything was familiar; there was nothing new. She lifted the box to scan the underside. Nothing taped on, nothing extra written on it. Maybe Tríona hadn't left anything here after all.

Setting the cigar box aside, she crawled back into the attic space, reaching again into the gap behind the chimney. This time her fingertips brushed against something. Whatever it was, it had fallen down between the chimney and the eaves. She managed to work the object closer until at last she was able to pull it out. It was a blue nylon duffel bag, hoary with cobwebs and plaster dust. She crawled backward out of the attic and set the bag on the floor of Tríona's room. Inside, she found a small black datebook and a sheaf of papers—more newspaper articles about Natalie Russo. All printed out, just like the article she'd found at the library, on the last day of Tríona's life. She flipped open the datebook, and saw various dates marked with large red Xs, sometimes one per week, sometimes more. There was an envelope tucked inside the back cover, addressed to Peter Hallett, with an unsigned, hand-printed note inside:

> You're gonna pay. For what you did.

Nora checked the postmark—the letter had been sent from Portland, Maine, two weeks before Tríona died. How was all this connected? Finally, at the bottom of the duffel, she found a crumpled brown paper bag with something soft inside. It turned out to be several items of clothing: a pair of shorts; a T-shirt that she'd given Tríona, with a University of Minnesota Medical School logo; and a pair of lacy underwear with matching bra.

All were stiff with what seemed to be dried blood.

Nora felt a hollow flutter under her breastbone. She remembered giving Tríona this shirt. Last night she had offered her mother all kinds of reassurances, but still had to push her own fear back into the dark place it dwelt deep inside her. Tríona had told her to take what she found here to the police. All of this had to start making sense sometime, but so many pieces of the puzzle were still missing. So why did she feel that a new threshold had been crossed?

2

Cormac paced up and down the hospital corridor, stopping briefly in front of the window to the room where his father remained motionless, still in a drug-induced coma. Roz Byrne sat in a chair beside the bed, holding the old man's hand.

When Roz came out of the room, Cormac said: "I don't know if I can stay here any longer. There's nothing to do but walk the floor and wait. I've got to get out for a while."

"Why don't you head back to the house?"

"I'm guessing you could use a break, too. Why don't we go somewhere?"

"Where do you suggest?"

"I don't know—let's just drive. The doctors have my mobile if there's any news."

As they headed west out of Killybegs, neither of them spoke. Roz had the wheel. The land grew progressively wilder and more rocky as they traveled westward, through Kilcar and Carrick. Finally, Cormac said: "I've been thinking about Mary Heaney. If her body was never found, how do you know she didn't just walk away?"

"I hope she did. I hope she escaped, and lived to be a very old woman. I just don't think that's what happened."

"If things between her and Heaney were as bad as all that, what kept her from leaving? Why stay with him?"

"What keeps any woman in a bad relationship? It's one of those age-old mysteries. Unsolvable." Roz considered for a moment. "This wouldn't be anything to do with your person over in the States, would it?"

Cormac didn't seem able to respond. Part of him longed to retreat, sorry he'd ever opened that door.

Roz said quietly: "You don't have to tell me."

It suddenly occurred to him what Roz might surmise—that it was Nora who was trying to get away. "It's not what you think." Roz kept her eyes on the road, which seemed to make it easier to begin. "Nora's sister was murdered, five years ago. The sister's husband is the main suspect, always has been, but they've got no evidence against him. He's never been charged, never even arrested. Nora's gone back to see if she can't dig up some new evidence, and I was going over to see if I could help—"

"I am sorry, Cormac. I didn't realize."

"It goes against all reason, staying with someone who actually takes pleasure from hurting you. And yet people stay. How do you account for it if you don't believe in enchantment?"

"What do you know about the murder?"

"Not a lot. Nora hasn't actually told me much about it. I think she feels guilty for not seeing things earlier, not doing more to help. The husband was some sort of a brute, apparently. What really tears Nora up is the idea that her sister still loved him, in spite of everything."

"Is that so difficult to believe? We're complex creatures, with complicated motivations and desires, divisions even within ourselves."

They were approaching a crossroads. Roz pulled up and glanced over at him. "Will you bear with me a little while? There's something I'd like to show you."

He nodded his assent, and she turned from the main coast road and headed back up into the hills. Ten minutes later, they were rattling over a narrow road atop a heathery mountain. "Do you know where we are? Your father's house is just the other side of this headland," Roz said. As the car came over the mountain's crest, the sun disappeared behind clouds, and a slight mist began to blow against the windscreen. The road wound down along a mountain stream, and finally ended in a sort of rough patch of gravel where a footbridge crossed the flowing water to a rude path on the other side. Cormac climbed out of the car and surveyed the handful of ruins perched on the slope above a rocky beach and a disused pier. Stone walls cut the hilly outcrop into smaller fields, which were even further reduced by wire fencing. A few houses with corrugated metal roofs were apparently still in use as sheep sheds. There was no sign of life anywhere at the moment, even of the ovine variety, despite ample evidence of their recent presence underfoot. Cormac could hear the surf rolling on the beach—a distinct, hollow rattling of stone on stone. "What is this place?" he asked Roz.

"It's called Port na Rón."

Seal Harbor, in English. But *port* was one of those words that held a double meaning. In addition to "harbor," it also meant "tune." The music of the seals.

Roz continued: "The caves at the far side of the harbor are a rookery for gray seals. It's out of the way, but this used to be quite a busy place—a haven for smugglers and pirates, people tell me. It's been abandoned for years, but that house"—she pointed to a dilapidated cottage on the far side of the stream—"that's where Mary Heaney lived. I just tracked down the landowner and got permission to have a look around inside."

They crossed the bridge and climbed the rutted path to the Heaney cottage, four stone walls topped with crumbling thatch, home now to birds' nests and sprouting weeds. Nettles grew waist-high around the back and sides of the house, a typical Donegal fisherman's cottage, low to the ground, with small windows and a piggyback roof. No overhang—the wind here didn't need much foothold.

Cormac bent over to pick up a grapefruit-sized stone, measuring its weight in his hand. A dozen more lay scattered along the cottage walls. Tied together with rope and tossed over the top, they would have been all that kept the thatch from blowing away in a gale. He dropped the stone back on the path. "It's amazing this place wasn't pulled down ages ago."

"No one will go near it; the locals say there's an unlucky air about the place. Even more bad luck to him who pulls it down."

"Whatever happened to Heaney and his children?"

"Did I not tell you? Six years after his wife disappeared, Heaney himself vanished. His boat was found adrift out in the bay, but no body ever turned up. The children were shipped off to some cousins near Buncrana. I found records of a Patrick Heaney from Buncrana killed at Gallipoli in 1916, but I haven't been able to verify that it was the same one from Port na Rón."

"And the daughter?" Cormac couldn't help thinking of Nora's niece, only a child when her mother was killed.

"The 1911 census had no record of her, in Buncrana or anywhere in Donegal. She might have married or emigrated by that time—she would have been about the right age. I haven't had a chance to follow up on all that. Come and have a look inside. I've been here a couple of times, but haven't touched anything. You'll see why people still call it 'the selkie cottage.'"

Cormac followed Roz through the open entrance, and the first thing his eye fell upon was the half-door, torn from its hinges and lying in the middle of the kitchen. He let his gaze wander across the room. The once-whitewashed walls were peeling and had gone black and green from seeping damp. The pine dresser against the wall still held a few cracked pieces of blue-and-white delft. A traditional box bed was built into the far corner of the room, an iron-framed cot stood in the other. Under a window on the far wall, a cupboard held a washbasin, and empty tins and sacks spilled out from the shelves beneath. There was plentiful evidence that animals had lived here, taking advantage of abandoned food stores. Layers of dust covered everything: the rude table, the child-sized rush-seated chairs, the iron kettle that still hung from a hook over the hearth. Cormac could see a half-finished piece of knitting someone had set aside, the contours of a clay pipe under the dust in the hob beside the fireplace. Everything spoke of lives suddenly and rudely interrupted.

"What do you see?" Roz asked.

"Hard work. Long winter nights." He could actually imagine a family moving about this room, the woman tending the fire, the man mending nets in the flickering light, the children's muted breathing from the cot. He tried to conjure Mary and P. J. Heaney before him. What exactly had passed between them? How little was left here to illuminate how, and in what spirit, those two human beings had occupied this space. Nothing to capture the fleeting evidence of a glance, a touch, a word. There was nothing to encapsulate the longing or the revulsion—or perhaps both, in endless close succession—that had flowed through them every day. Did she mind his touch, or had she invited it? Was she a willing participant, a kidnap victim, an amnesiac? To say that she stayed with him for years was no measure. People stayed for all sorts of reasons: inertia, the hope that things would change, fear of the unknown, poverty, a dread that things could actually get much worse. Physical objects might offer some glimpses into a life, but how could they get down to the real texture of everyday existence? How infinitely subtle were the traces of happiness and despair?

Nora had become so much a part of him that he could not imagine living without her, and yet anyone digging through his possessions would find no physical evidence of her at all. Not a single trace. They had exchanged nothing but a look, a touch, a few words—and not even written words, only fleeting conversations and marks on a screen that evaporated into the ether. The one concrete thing he'd given her—the hazel knot—felt like a meager, temporary token.

Roz's voice startled him out of his thoughts. "I was hoping to get some pictures, to start documenting what's here."

As Roz went around the room snapping photos, Cormac sketched a quick floor plan of the house. He found marks on the floor, where a heavy object had been dragged through the dust. Someone had stacked up dozens of conical limpet shells to form narrow, teetering towers on the shelves where delft once stood.

He said to Roz: "I thought you told me no one would come near this place—"

She looked up at the piles of shells. "That's what people said. But it does seem as if someone's been here, doesn't it?"

Cormac noted the shells on his drawing, and left them undisturbed. Crossing to the iron-frame cot, he lifted the rotting straw mattress and heard something fall to the floor. Pulling the bed away from the wall, he found a threadbare muslin doll. The shape was not recognizably human, more like an animal—a seal. Someone had sewn on black metal buttons for eyes, but one had come loose. A mute witness to whatever had taken place here. Beneath the bed he found a short piece of a plank with holes in it, and two tiny sandbags that fit in the palm of his hand. The board was cracked and stained, but he brushed the dust away from its face, and saw that the plank had been brightly painted at one time. The only faint glimmer of happiness that this room had so far possessed. "Roz, look at this."

She came closer and snapped several photos. "Some sort of game?"

Cormac set the board aside and peered under the bed again, this time finding several long, fair hairs twisted around one of the springs. Had they been caught here during a harmless game of hide-and-seek, or something more ominous? He thought of all the things he had noticed from an early age, the gestures and conversations he'd witnessed between his parents and other adults when they believed he was elsewhere, or not paying attention. A child was capable of sensing things, of taking in and interpreting unspoken emotions, as well as any lesser creature. And what of the person who had hidden here—a girl, presumably—what memories, what images had she carried, only to have them triggered later by a certain sound or scent, or the angle of light at a certain time of day? The gleaming hair between his fingers suddenly seemed sturdy as wire. What if everyone had ignored the most important witness in Tríona Hallett's murder? It was perfectly natural, trying to protect a child, but if no one had ever spoken to Elizabeth about her mother's death—

He continued pulling out the jumble of objects hidden under the cot—a collection of small, rounded stones, no doubt robbed from the beach. More limpet shells, dozens of them. The last item was a woman's old-fashioned, high-button shoe.

He called Roz over and held up the shoe. "It was here, under the cot," he said. "Isn't it strange, though? Who leaves home wearing only one shoe?"

3

Nora sat in her car outside police headquarters in Saint Paul. Beside her on the seat were the things Tríona had hidden away in the attic. She had rushed over here, not stopping to change out of the clothes she had slept in. And now she was remembering how it had all happened last time. Her emotional dissolution had taken place slowly, imperceptibly at first, just like this. She'd find something that could be a lead, and would bring it in to Frank as she had brought these things this morning—just out of bed, hair uncombed. The last time she'd come here before leaving for Ireland, she'd brought a bag of old clothes she'd watched Peter Hallett dump in the Goodwill collection bin on University Avenue. When she had arrived here at headquarters, she'd been left in a chair at the front desk to wait for Frank. It was only after fifteen minutes or so that she had looked down and realized that she'd driven to the police station in her pajamas. She had felt conspicuous, sitting in that waiting area, with cops coming and going, glancing at her and looking away with dismissive expressions. They had her pegged. A crazy. A kook. But she couldn't leave until she'd handed over the clothing. And it had turned out to be useless.

That's when she knew Peter was tormenting her, trying to put her off balance. That was his specialty. He'd put that bag of old clothes in the Goodwill bin knowing that she was watching him—knowing it would prove worthless as evidence.

And what about the evidence she had just found? What if these things only served to incriminate Tríona? He could have planned it that way. She reached for the datebook and scanned the marked pages. What did the Xs mean? There seemed to be no pattern, no regular rhythm to their placement. Several one week, none the next. No other notations. Nothing even to say the Xs had been drawn by Tríona's hand. But if they were, what was she keeping track of, something that happened so randomly? Nora turned to the date of the museum opening. A large red X marked the day. She turned the page and found another on June 3, the day Natalie Russo disappeared. Maybe there was a pattern after all. Nora gathered up the evidence that could potentially paint her sister as a killer, and went to see Frank Cordova.

Ten minutes later, they were in the detective division's interview room. Frank was still upset about yesterday. He looked as if he hadn't slept. As she studied him, Nora became gradually aware of the other eyes outside the conference room window, the studiously averted gazes that said the whole detective division was watching them.

"Do you think we could close these blinds?" she asked.

Frank stood to pull the cords to shut off the glances from the cubicles outside.

Nora began to pace as she talked. "I know we always assumed it was Peter who had the connection to the parking garage in Lowertown, but maybe it was Tríona, and Peter somehow knew about it. Maybe he followed her. I found out yesterday that she'd been doing studio work for a guy called Nick Mosher, advertising spots and voice-overs for radio. I think she was trying to make some money and stashing it away, getting ready to walk out."

"Why didn't this Mosher come forward?"

"He couldn't. He was killed in a fall at the Sturgis Building."

Cordova grimaced. "Great."

"Do you know what's really odd? The accident happened the same day Tríona died."

"So who told you about the connection?"

"A woman named Valerie Marchant, who runs a coffee shop in the building. She knew Nick Mosher, and Tríona, too, from theater work. But Valerie Marchant was out of the country at the time of the murder and Nick Mosher's accident, and figured she didn't have any useful information when she got back six months later."

Frank's eyes narrowed. "How did you even know to talk to this woman?"

She couldn't tell him about seeing her sister's ghost in the plate-glass window, or the book turned backward at the library. Harry Shaughnessy, too, was off limits until she could be more certain of what she'd witnessed. "I went to the parking garage showing her picture around. Just got lucky. Right after you dropped me yesterday, I went down to Hidden Falls—I think I saw the fisherman there, the guy who found Natalie Russo."

"Asian guy, late thirties?"

"Yes—what do you know about him?"

"Keeps to himself. Lives with a cousin's family in Frogtown, works at their restaurant—a Cambodian place called Phnom Penh up on University. Told us he's been fishing that spot at Hidden Falls since he came to Saint Paul almost eight years ago. His English isn't great—and he wasn't all that excited to report the body."

"But he did, Frank, when he could have just run away. Do you think we could talk to him?"

"We might need to line up an interpreter. Like I said, his English isn't so hot. Don't forget, until we crack this, he's still a suspect." He met her questioning gaze. "What can I say? Hazard of the business."

Nora reached into the duffel and pulled out Tríona's tape. "I found this at my parents' house last night. I didn't listen to the second side until this morning. I want you to listen to it all the way through before you say anything." She played the tape for Frank, watching for a reaction. He pulled at his lip, frowning.

"I did what she said. I went to the hiding place. Here's what I found." Nora reached into the blue bag again and pulled out the datebook with its cryptic markings, the anonymous note addressed to Peter, the sheaf of clippings about Natalie Russo's disappearance, and, finally, the bloodstained clothes. He took a pen and lifted the corner of the shirt.

"They're Tríona's clothes, Frank. I gave her that shirt."

"I guess the next step is figuring out whose blood this is—"

"I have a feeling it might be Natalie's. I think Tríona was terrified of what she might have done. She kept saying she had to know the truth. I've been trying to work it out." Nora reached for the calendar. "Look at all these marked days, including the third of June, the day Natalie went missing. Put that together with what Tríona says on the tape, about the days she doesn't remember, all that liquid ecstasy you found in her purse, around the house. You know what I think, what I've thought all along—that it wasn't Tríona's stash, that Peter was feeding her the stuff. It's all beginning to fit."

"What exactly is beginning to fit?"

"For whatever reason, Peter doesn't want to be married anymore. He starts doping Tríona so she can't remember things, so he can do what he likes. Then he murders Natalie—I'll admit, I still haven't worked out how or why—and he tries to make Tríona believe that she's the killer. She wakes up on the third of June covered in blood, with no memory of what happened. It takes a while, but she finally figures out that she can go to the library, and scour the newspapers for an attack, a murder on that day. That's when she finds out about Natalie's disappearance—"

"But how does she know about Hidden Falls? That part doesn't connect—"

"Unless Hidden Falls was where she woke up that morning."

"You know, it's a great theory. I'm not saying it couldn't have happened that way, but all these things on their own—they don't add up to anything we could use in court."

"If Tríona was afraid that she'd done something terrible, why hang on to incriminating evidence? Why not just destroy it? And why dig up all those old newspaper articles about Natalie? At least we finally know what she was doing at the library that day. If she was getting ready to leave Peter, maybe she was also getting ready to tell someone what she knew, how she knew it."

"And what about this anonymous note?" He checked the envelope. "It's postmarked Maine. Any idea what Hallett did, why he's being accused?"

"No—I told you, I haven't got it all worked out."

Frank took up and flipped through the sheaf of newspaper articles. "Look at this." He showed her a page not from the *Pioneer Press,* but from the *Press Herald* in Portland, Maine.

CONFESSED KILLER OF OGUNQUIT COUPLE
TAKES OWN LIFE

Jesse Benoit, who confessed to the brutal murder of an Ogunquit couple, was found dead in his room at the Augusta Mental Health Institute on Tuesday, an apparent suicide. Hospital officials did not issue a statement, but scheduled a press conference for this afternoon. Constance and Harris Nash were found bludgeoned to death aboard their boat, anchored in Ogunquit Harbor. The small, tightly knit resort community reacted in disbelief when Benoit, a childhood friend of the victims' son, confessed to the brutal slaying, and was committed to state care at Augusta after being declared incompetent to stand trial.

"Where did this come from?" Frank asked.

"I don't know—I didn't notice it before."

"Do you recognize any of those names—Jesse Benoit, Constance and Harris Nash?"

"No. But I know Peter went to college in Maine. Let me work on this, Frank. You've got too much to follow up as it is. This is something I can do."

He was staring at her right hand resting on his sleeve. She had touched him without thinking. Nora pulled her hand away.

4

Elizabeth stayed in her room all morning with a pillow over her head. She could hear her father and Miranda talking and dragging suitcases up and down the hall. She was supposed to be packing, too, but her insides still felt upside down. Those awful words on the computer screen kept washing over and over her until she felt as if her head would burst. *Hallett slaying. The victim's husband. Primary suspect.* If everyone was so sure her dad had done those horrible things, why wasn't he in jail? They said her mother's body had been identified by distinguishing marks. What exactly was a distinguishing mark? Elizabeth raised the pillow a quarter-inch to look down at her arms and legs. Nothing but freckles and chewed fingernails, the dark scab on her knee. That couldn't be what it meant, she was sure.

She flung her pillow to the floor. They were talking about making her go with them on their stupid trip to Ireland. It was Miranda's idea. Her dad was arguing against it; he said she should stay here in Saint Paul with her grandparents. Miranda was trying to convince him what a great time they could all have together.

Elizabeth knew what to do. She would go away, someplace they couldn't find her. Wait until they were gone, and then go stay with her grandparents. How hard could it be, looking somebody up in the phone book? But first things first—she had to get out of the house.

She gathered up a few items of clothing and shoved them into her backpack, trying not to make any noise. She took her school ID from Seattle, and the book about the seal woman she'd stolen from the Seattle library. Almost as an afterthought, she stuffed in the worn and faded remnant of the baby blanket she still slept with at night. Finally, she tucked nearly two hundred dollars she'd saved from her allowance into a zippered compartment in the side of her shoe. She had a feeling her dad and Miranda would be glad to get rid of her. They might not even look very hard.

Peering out the door of her bedroom, Elizabeth made sure the coast was clear, and then scurried down the hallway to the front door. She cut through the leafy yard down to the road in front of the house. There were lots of other people on the path—running, biking, walking their dogs. It was so different from Seattle here. It wasn't just the trees and plants; there weren't so many people around when you lived on the edge of an island. She realized that she didn't know where she was going—and staying on the main roads meant that her dad might be able to find her just by driving around. But the riverbank was steep here. She had to walk until she could find a quiet spot, someplace out of the way, where she could sit and think about what to do.

The river was a long way down through the trees. On the other side of the road from the path were houses and big apartment buildings. The backpack began to feel heavy, pulling at her shoulders. Everything had changed since she'd read those words on the Internet. The whole world felt strange now, and not just because she was in a different city and the places she knew were far away. Something inside her had changed as well. To think that she had imagined her mother living happily somewhere else, with a new family. Stupid, stupid, stupid. Her stomach felt strange—maybe just hunger. But somehow the thought of food just made it worse.

A huge factory loomed across the road from the path, and Elizabeth could see smokestacks through the high fence. The road before her began to curve and slope downhill. There were no houses here, and fewer people along the path. All at once she came upon a wooden sign with carved letters that said HIDDEN FALLS PARK. Maybe this could be her quiet place to think. She set off down the steep drive, feeling the weight of her pack and the prickling of sweat making the back of her shirt damp. She hadn't expected Minnesota to be so hot. At the bottom of the hill the road ended in several parking lots. A guy in a pickup sat watching as she made her way toward the river. Elizabeth felt his eyes on her, but forgot about him as soon as she got down to the water. She'd been right about one thing—a river was not the same as Useless Bay. The water was a cloudy green color—it looked dirty. She stood on the bank and gazed across to the sandbar on the opposite side, at some boys throwing sticks for their dogs to fetch. The animals' sleek heads poking up out of the water reminded Elizabeth of her own spotted seal back at Useless Bay. She felt a pang of homesickness for her own beach, for a time when she knew nothing.

The ground beneath her feet was covered in small round pebbles of different colors that made a grinding, gravelly sound as she walked. She decided to venture farther up the beach, walking until she found a tree whose gnarled roots lay exposed at the river's edge. There she slipped out of her backpack and set it on the ground. The tightness in her stomach had grown worse. She pulled the pack onto her lap and wedged herself into the roots of the tree, trying to shrink as small as possible, and wondered how long it would take before her dad noticed she was gone. He might think she was still in her room—he probably wouldn't even check.

Those awful computer-screen words floated before her eyes again. She had never seen her mother's body. So why did she see the same pictures every time she closed her eyes—a still, white hand, red hair against a pale neck? It was getting so hard to breathe. The backpack pressed down on her, cutting off her air. She flung it away, and all at once there were sounds coming out of her that she couldn't seem to control. Her lungs felt as if they would burst.

"Hey!" said a voice from across the water. "Hey, Red—you all right?"

Elizabeth raised her head. She felt grit in her teeth, and smelled the sweet, rotting scent of dead fish. A curly-haired boy and his dog stared at her across the river. They started into the water, as though they might swim across. Elizabeth scrambled to her feet and picked up the backpack, plunging into the woods, running with no direction, just trying to get away. She could hear the boy's faint, disappointed voice behind her. "Jeez, I wasn't going to hurt you—just wondered if you were okay."

She kept running, but the dirt and tears in her eyes made it hard to see where she was going. Branches scratched her hands and face, and she felt a sharp pricking as the plants brushed against her bare skin. She ran until she saw a yellow tape strung between the trees, people in white coveralls. Another voice, a grown-up this time: "Jesus—stop her! Somebody grab that kid!"

Elizabeth put on a spurt, and heard several sets of footfalls pounding the earth behind her. Hands reached out. She tried to twist away, but a solid figure, with heavy shoes and a wide belt hung with flashlight and handcuffs and a big black gun, seemed to materialize directly in front of her. She looked up into a policeman's smooth, pink face just as he reached down and put his hands on her shoulders. "Hey—slow down there, kiddo. What's your hurry?"

A woman's breathless voice came from behind. "Thanks, Mike. I'll take her back to the squad." She kept one arm around Elizabeth's shoulder as they walked, steering her up a path that led to the parking lot, and straight to one of the police cars. The policewoman opened the door and motioned for Elizabeth to sit in the backseat, then scrunched down beside her. The woman had square shoulders and short blondish hair. Elizabeth thought she looked pretty tough.

"That backpack looks kind of heavy," the policewoman said. "You can set it down if you want. I'm not going to take it."

Elizabeth hugged the pack closer, guilty about the stolen book inside. She didn't want the police to know she was running away.

"Can you tell me your name?"

Elizabeth shook her head. She couldn't look into the officer's questioning eyes.

"Were you supposed to meet somebody here? It's okay—you can tell me."

Elizabeth heard kindness in the woman's voice, but maybe it was all just an act. They wanted her to say something, but she couldn't tell them about her mother, about why she was running away. Telling the police anything would just make her dad angry.

When another cop approached, the policewoman stood up suddenly and spoke under her breath: "Christ, will you look at her? The kids they're pulling get younger all the time. Bastards."

What were they talking about? Nobody had pulled her anywhere. The other officer was talking into his radio, but Elizabeth couldn't understand what he was saying. It was like they all spoke a foreign language. She looked over and saw the guy from the pickup sitting in the back of another squad car. Finally, the policewoman returned and crouched down beside the open door again.

"You're a very lucky girl, Elizabeth—that's your name, isn't it? Your mom and dad were pretty worried about you. They're on their way down here right now to pick you up."

As the policewoman spoke, one thought kept circling through Elizabeth's brain: *She's not my mother. She's not my mother. I don't care what anybody says. That witch Miranda Staunton will never be my mother.*

5

After arriving back from their expedition to Port na Rón, Cormac was alone in the sitting room of his father's house. Roz had gone upstairs to shower, and the house was quiet but for a steady wash of water down the exterior drain. The single high-button shoe at the house still plagued him. If Mary Heaney ran away, as her husband suggested, why would she have gone without one of her shoes? Women in her circumstances weren't likely to have had more than one pair; they probably counted themselves lucky to have shoes at all. On the other hand, if she had regained her sealskin and returned to the sea, as the local legend allowed, the whole subject of footwear was academic . . . And why was he wasting time trying to reason it through?

Remembering what Roz had told him, he roused himself from the fireside chair and began to peruse the photographs hanging on the walls. His great-aunt Julia must have been a schoolteacher at one time; one picture showed her with a gaggle of pupils—all bare knees, freckles, and ears—outside Carrick National School. The pupils were in focus, but Julia Maguire appeared as a hazy specter in a dotted dress, as if she'd set the camera and not made it to her place in time for the shutter. It was the only image Cormac had ever seen of her. Another photo was a study of gaunt, dark men in long overcoats standing outside a church door, looking for all the world like a murder of crows. The photograph was labeled in pencil at one corner of the image, *Father's Funeral, 1956.*

Cormac began to inspect the photos that hung on the opposite wall: crisp black-and-white images of standing stones up the Glen, the cliffs at Bunglas, modest homes of fishermen in Teelin. There were several of Donegal fiddle players—John Doherty, whom Cormac recognized from television, and a pair of middle-aged men, one dark, one with a shock of white hair and thick glasses. They were both playing fiddles, standing back to back. *Francie Dearg and Mici Bán,* read the caption. There were also, as Roz had noticed, many close-up shots exploring the wet, curious faces of seals. Each of the seal pictures was captioned as the others had been, at the lower right corner, and in the same old-fashioned script as the letter he'd received from his great-aunt. So she had been something of an amateur photographer as well as a schoolteacher. Suddenly Cormac understood all the brown glass bottles in the windowless garden shed built onto the back of the house—her darkroom.

He ventured into his father's bedroom. A chest of drawers stood before him—large, heavy, and dark, like all the furniture in this house, a legacy of the generations of Maguires who had been born and died here. It occurred to him that when his father died, he would become a part of that legacy as well. Scraps of shadowy lives a generation or two back, a few random details, that was all most people could reasonably manage. The rest faded into obscurity. Opening the drawers felt vaguely wrong, but he told himself that it was important to find out more about the old man in order to communicate with him. He was rationalizing, of course, unable to admit the curiosity that had consumed him for the past three years, growing in strength and intensity ever since Julia Maguire's letter had arrived in the mail.

The drawer slid open easily. He wasn't sure what he expected to find there, but was surprised to see stacks of neatly pressed handkerchiefs, some plain, some monogrammed with the initials ERM. A gold watch, a tray of loose coins—the old money—and a pair of wire-rimmed glasses. It looked as if nothing in the drawer had been touched since his great-grandfather's death fifty years ago. For some reason, he had no trouble imagining hotheaded young Joseph Maguire turning his back on this, on all worldly goods. But in the end, even he could not divest himself entirely of the legacy of his ancestors. You could deny who you were, where you were from, for a time—but eventually it laid claim to you, and would not be denied. Again Cormac detected in his own thoughts a creeping acknowledgment of mortality. Perhaps the gene that controlled the onset of old age also triggered a need to hear the stories of those who had come before. Perhaps his own devotion to archaeology was just an errant expression of that need.

He shut the handkerchief drawer and crossed to the bedside table, checking the drawer for anything he ought to bring along to the hospital. As he lifted the reading glasses from the book on the table, he saw the crinkled edge of a small black-and-white photograph peeping from between the pages. He cracked open the book and found the snapshot of a young dark-haired woman, standing somewhere overlooking the sea cliffs, head scarf untied and held aloft like a sail in a gesture of joyous abandon. His own mother. Could this have been taken in some oddly temperate stretch of days before he was born? He studied the smooth pliability of the flesh on her uplifted arms, trying to imagine his parents both young, flush with life and promise. The unique complexity of two individual lives became even more profoundly intricate with the addition of another life, a child. He had always wondered exactly what his arrival signified to his father, other than an unnecessary complication.

He slid the photo into his pocket for safekeeping and shut the book. *The Fairy-Faith in Celtic Countries* by W. Y. Evans-Wentz. He set it back, noting the title of the volume underneath: *On the Radical Nature of Love: From Plato to John Coltrane*. Perhaps his father was one of those people who found it impossible to apply abstract principles of philosophy to his own life. Cormac considered the title, remembering some of the freethinkers he'd met briefly at university, the ones who loved to rail against the plight of the downtrodden worker all night in pubs, oblivious to wives and girlfriends they themselves had left at home and up to their oxters in soiled nappies. Quare auld world.

He leaned over and pulled a pair of heavy brogues from under the nightstand. The same sort he wore on excavations. On a sudden whim, he set the shoes down on the floor and slipped his own feet into them. A perfect fit. He leaned forward, elbows on knees, staring down at the shoes, studying the cracks and creases in the leather, the places where the width of his father's foot had strained the cobbler's stitchery, the splatters of shiny red paint that matched the front door of this house. Apart from the shoes, he hadn't found any of his father's clothing. Rising from the bed, he crossed to the wardrobe that stood opposite. Inside, among print dresses and cardigans, and a pair of ancient worsted suits, he found a meager wardrobe of worn khakis and threadbare denim shirts, and a handknit jumper of undyed wool. Was it possible that this was all that Joseph Maguire had brought back with him from thirty years abroad? What was the old man doing here? Why had he come home? And as soon as the thought struck him, he quashed it. No point in worrying the question if he would never have an answer.

On the top shelf of the wardrobe he found a fiddle case. He took it down, and opened the case to find a stringless fiddle resting under a square of green velvet. Strange—he'd never known that anyone in his family had played music. Returning the fiddle case to the shelf, he found a dusty old 78 rpm record. He carried the disc out to the sitting room, where the gramophone occupied a corner near the fireplace. The record was labeled in the same hand as the photos. "*Fiddle Duet. Glencolumbkille Hotel, June 8, 1950.*" Cormac nearly dropped the disc when he saw the names of the players below: *Joseph and Julia Maguire*. His father would have been about sixteen years old.

Heading back to the sitting room, Cormac slipped the record from its sleeve and placed it gently on the turntable, wound up the old-fashioned crank on the side, and set the needle in the groove. Two fiddles sang out in unison—a wild, hectic reel—and it was as if a puzzle box was opening itself before his eyes, each note a key to an unfathomed existence. He could hear the two instruments growling together on the low notes and wondered: Was it his father bearing down more fiercely on the bow or his great-aunt? They leapt together from the end of one tune straight into another, the angular movement of the bows evident in their tone, and Cormac felt the heart swell in his chest at the sound. Although he loved the Clare music that had surrounded him as a child, he had also felt the pull of the wild, distinctive voice of Donegal. He had never really understood why.

He closed his eyes and tried to conjure the dining room of the Glencolumbkille Hotel on that day, the starched white linens, the gleaming glassware and cutlery, all vibrating in sympathy, tuned to the sound of the fiddles. From somewhere in the back of his head, the notion began to take hold—that this music might stir the old man from slumber. He couldn't have forgotten, not completely. The notes must remain somewhere within his subconscious, even if they had lain buried there for fifty years.

The B side was "Lord Mayo," a slow air played by one fiddle, both a lament for a past time and an anthem to carrying on.

At a turn halfway through the tune, Roz Byrne's voice carried over his shoulder: "What's that you're listening to?"

Cormac didn't answer, but lifted the record from the turntable and handed it to her, marking her surprise as the names on the label registered.

"And you'd no idea at all?"

"I've seen my father exactly three times since I was nine years old, Roz. Somehow, the subject of music never came up."

Roz shook her head. "I suppose he gave it up when he went off to university. Donegal music was all but banned from the radio in those days. Too foreign-sounding, the RTÉ people said. Ridiculous."

"It makes me wonder about all the other things I don't know," Cormac said.

Roz looked at him thoughtfully. "Did you have a look around at the pictures?"

He nodded. "The seals—they're almost like character portraits."

"I thought so, too. I wondered why there were so many, and your father told me a story, about his father—so that would be your grandfather and Julia's brother. A melancholy, lonely man. He was away for years, studying medicine in France. When his father died, he came home and set up a practice here. After a few months, he took a fishing trip to Tory Island, and to the astonishment of everyone in the Glen, he came home with a wife. Being from Tory, she spoke an Irish that was different to the people around here. They called her 'The Foreigner.' She stayed on for a while, until Joe was born—"

"And then?"

"She ran off. Your father was still an infant at the time. He said his aunt Julia was the only mother he ever knew."

Cormac felt thunderstruck. "Why did she leave?"

"No one ever knew. There was never any further communication; if she ever did get in touch with your grandfather, he never told anyone. He'd go and sit on the headland up at Port na Rón for hours, staring out to sea. It must have had a profound effect on Joe. He said when you came along, he wasn't prepared to be a father. He had no idea what it actually meant. The responsibility terrified him."

"We're talking about the same man who traveled halfway around the globe to face down a military junta—and you're saying a mewling infant terrified him?"

"I didn't say it was plausible, only that it's true."

6

Nora spent the morning at the library, keeping an eye out for Harry Shaughnessy, and digging through newspaper databases for information on the murders of the Maine couple, Constance and Harris Nash. She found more than two dozen articles on the Nash case, beginning with the discovery of the grisly crime scene on the victims' boat. The evidence trail implicated Jesse Benoit, a friend of the victims' son. There was an underlying class element to the story that the newspapers touched on briefly but didn't explore fully: Jesse Benoit's mother cleaned house for the Nash family, which was how the two boys had become friends as children. Tripp Nash went away to boarding school, while Jesse Benoit attended local public schools.

She printed out each story as she read, trying to piece together the facts from the sketchy details provided. Benoit told police he had paddled his canoe out to the victims' sailboat anchored in the harbor, and had gone on board intending to kill the couple as they slept. They'd been bludgeoned to death, Nash first, and then his wife, their faces completely destroyed. The murder happened while their son was away for the weekend, visiting a girlfriend in another part of the state. The murder weapon had never been recovered, but the police had found Jesse Benoit's bloody fingerprints at the scene. Traces of the victims' blood turned up in his canoe, and on clothing found stuffed in the back of his closet. A classic open-and-shut case. According to the newspaper reports, even though he confessed, Jesse Benoit had never offered any motive for the murders. After a psychiatric evaluation, he was found incompetent to stand trial and sent to the Augusta Mental Health Institute. After only a few weeks at Augusta, Jesse Benoit had taken his own life.

So far the only connection to Peter was the anonymous note addressed to him. What had he done? What was his connection to Constance and Harris Nash? From the physical evidence, there was never any doubt that Jesse Benoit had committed the murders.

After Tríona's death, the police had searched for Peter in all the national databases, looking for criminal history, family connections, known aliases, previous addresses, job history. The information they'd been able to find was limited: Peter's parents had been killed in a car accident when he was very young; his legal guardian was a widowed grandfather he barely knew. He had grown up mostly in boarding schools, then graduated from Galliard College in Maine and attended the Istituto Universitario di Architettura in Venice. After graduate school, he had spent several years in Europe. Nora had tried to envision him going around the streets and squares of Venice, sitting in cafés, speaking Italian. It was a side of him they had never really known. She couldn't imagine he'd ever gone long without female companionship—it was something he sought out, something he seemed to need. So why was there no prior history? No former girlfriends, no domestic assault charges. Of course there were many actions, many degrees of shocking behavior that didn't rise to the level of crime. But Peter paid his taxes, his professional licenses were up to date, he had a good credit history, sat on the boards of several respected charities, and gave generously to the arts and social causes. All part of the elaborate front he'd cultivated and presented to the world, Nora couldn't help thinking. Cover for the creature inside who got pleasure from hurting people.

Peter's only visible connection to the Nash murders was the fact that they had happened in Maine, where he went to boarding school and college. He would have been seventeen or eighteen at the time of the murder, about the same age as Jesse Benoit and the murdered couple's son. Could he have been at boarding school with Tripp Nash? Nora stared at the article on the screen before her now, the last piece about Jesse Benoit's suicide, the same one Frank had found in Tríona's stack. Gordon MacLeish, a detective from the Maine State Police, was quoted in some of the newspaper pieces. Maybe he'd be worth a call. But the Nash case was long closed. There was no practical connection to Tríona. She could spend days following crazy tangents, as she'd been doing all morning here, getting distracted from the real thread. And meanwhile, Peter Hallett was preparing to leave the country, maybe never to return. It was time to move on to the next lead, to find Harry Shaughnessy, or the Cambodian fisherman from the river.

Before leaving the nonfiction room, she took a quick detour down into the stacks once more, just to check on the book that had led her to the article about Natalie Russo. She counted down the row of bookcases again, and turned in at the same spot, but the back-to-front book—Tríona's book—was not there. There was a gap on the shelf. Maybe it had been checked out. She found an empty computer terminal, and quickly typed the title into a catalog search.

No matches found; nearby TITLES are:
Married to a Stranger
**** *Married to Magic: Fairy Brides and Bridegrooms* would be here ****
Married Woman Blues
The Marrow of a Bone

Impossible. That tattered green cloth cover, the spidery white lettering on the spine—she had seen it, held it in her hand. The blue-green hues of the watercolor plate stood out in her memory. Doubt began to pull at her. But maybe it didn't matter—after all, Frank had the paper she'd found here, perhaps with Tríona's fingerprints on it. They had the things from the hiding place. Nobody could doubt those—they were solid forensic evidence, concrete clues.

When his dark-haired subject finally came out the library's front entrance, Truman Stark, waiting in his truck, watched her unlock her car and get in. She'd been in there for ages—what could she possibly be doing for so long? He'd checked the car last night, out in front of her house. Clean—like it was brand-new, or maybe a rental. That was when the notion had struck him—she could be a private eye, or a reporter, digging up stuff for a story on one of those true-crime things on TV. He had to admit, that last idea had sent a small shiver of excitement through him. He liked those shows, seeing how the people who did the crimes were stupid enough to get caught. They hadn't spent time figuring out all the angles. Not like he had.

But the grinding feeling in his gut said the brunette was onto something. The way she'd gone straight from the garage to the coffee shop, she knew something was up, he was sure of it. Hadn't spotted him, though. And she wouldn't. He had been honing his surveillance technique for years. He'd gotten very good at it.

Remembering back to five years ago, he considered how the redhead always parked down on the lower level of the garage. Like she was hiding from somebody. That was how he'd first noticed her. He remembered studying the tilt of her head on the TV monitor as she waited for the elevator, the glances over her shoulder, in case someone might be tailing her. But she didn't know he was watching her. She couldn't have known.

7

Frank felt like he'd spent the whole day running back and forth between the crime lab and his office. The fingerprints lifted from the papers Nora had brought in were headed over to the state crime lab for analysis. The substance on the clothes was definitely blood, but now he'd have to wait for DNA results to find out if the blood matched anyone in their small circle of victims and suspects, or whether they'd have to start looking further afield. He had just retrieved the file on Nick Mosher's accident—probably just coincidence that he'd died the same day as Tríona Hallett, but everything was on the table now. They were quickly running out of time. He'd just returned to his desk with the file when his phone began to vibrate.

"Detective Cordova, it's Sarah Cates—from the rowing club. When you were here yesterday, you asked about the lockers, so I took a closer look. Some of them seemed abandoned, so I cut the locks. Thought you might want to see what I found."

It was after five when he arrived at the road above the Twin Cities Rowing Club. For the second time in two days, he parked at the top of the river bluff and skidded down the steep road to the boathouse. This time Sarah Cates met him at the huge sliding door.

"I haven't touched anything except the lock. I saved that in case you needed it—I wasn't sure." She handed him a clear plastic bag with the cut padlock inside. At the door of the women's locker room, she paused to shout inside: "Everybody decent? I'm bringing somebody in." A chorus of voices shouted an all-clear, and they advanced into the steamy locker room. "It's right over here. I put my own lock on until you arrived." She quickly dialed the combination and removed the temporary padlock, then stepped out of the way.

Cordova pulled on a pair of gloves and swung the locker open to find a series of snapshots stuck inside the door—Natalie Russo with various teammates, all grinning triumphantly at the camera. In one of the photos, there was a large silver cup blurred at the edge of the frame—a victory?

"That was the Winnipeg regatta," Sarah Cates said, watching his reaction. "Natalie broke all the club and event records that day. That's when we knew she was Olympic material."

"I'm going to take this all back to the shop. See what we can shake loose."

"So I did right to call you?"

"Yeah—you did."

Just then, an athletic-looking blonde rounded the corner, apparently not anticipating a man in the locker room. She seemed confused, and turned back to check the sign on the door. "This still the women's locker room?"

Sarah Cates stepped in: "We'll be out of your hair in just a minute." The blonde gave a shrug of indifference, and Frank knew it was the same face he'd seen in Natalie Russo's team photo. He was finally able to place her.

Miranda Staunton.

He'd interviewed her at the time of Tríona's death. But if his face rang any bells for her, it didn't show. She ducked past them without another glance. He turned to Sarah Cates.

"You wouldn't happen to have a spare box or a bag—something I could use to carry all this?"

She nodded. "Be right back."

While Sarah was gone, Cordova stayed put and took the opportunity to observe Miranda Staunton. She must have known Natalie Russo—they were on the same rowing team. He watched her, one foot up on the bench, tying a strange-looking shoe. Must attach somehow to the boats they used. Unaware that he was watching her, she slipped a wad of gum from her mouth and pressed it to the undersurface of the bench. Frank had always wondered what sort of person did a thing like that. Now he knew. He averted his gaze as Miranda stood up and headed out the locker room door.

When he was finished clearing out the locker, Sarah Cates walked him out to the driveway. He gestured over at Miranda, preparing a solo scull for practice. "Know her?"

"Miranda Staunton? Sure. Joined the club out of college. I heard she was living out in Seattle, but she just moved back and rejoined a couple of weeks ago."

"Good rower?"

"Great—"

Cordova sensed hesitation. "But?"

Sarah leaned forward slightly. "You know those cranky lightweights I mentioned the other day?"

The phone on his belt began to vibrate, and Sarah Cates signaled a silent good-bye as she backed down the driveway to the boathouse.

He expected to hear Karin Bledsoe's voice when he answered, but it was his sister Veronica, upset and out of breath. "Oh Frank, he just stopped breathing. I didn't know what to do—"

There was no reason to ask; he knew Veronica was talking about Chago. Frank and his brother had been born only minutes apart, but they were nothing alike. Twisted in his own umbilical cord, Chago had grown misshapen in the womb. His mind remained that of a child, ever joyful despite a halting gait and withered arm, his lopsided face perpetually split by a broad smile. Veronica, the eldest of his three sisters, had always been like a mother to them, looking after them ever since Frank could remember.

"Luis called the ambulance, and they took him away, to Regions Emergency. They said we should call the priest—" She broke off and began to sob.

"Go now. I'll meet you there," he told Veronica. "Get Luis to drive you."

Frank's tires sent gravel flying as he peeled out of the parking area above the boathouse.

8

Eleanor Gavin stood at her bedroom window, watching her husband deadhead flowers in the backyard. He'd been at it since they'd finished their supper this evening in awkward silence. Ever since her conversation with Nora, she'd debated telling him everything. But she wasn't at all sure he could take the news. He already felt like a failure as a father—not that he'd ever admitted as much, even to her—but she could see it, in his posture as he stooped over the rosebushes, in every word and every gesture for the past five years. She watched him bend and snip, bend and snip, dropping each spent bloom into a canvas sack he wore slung around him like a sower of seeds.

And suddenly she felt a flash of affection so fierce it took her breath away. All the years of their history together cascaded over her, including the very first time she'd laid eyes on him, a hurling game with his pals on the lawn at Belfield. His ease with the hurley was the first thing she noticed, along with his physical beauty, the pleasing proportions of his frame. Good bones. There were no questions at all, really, about the choices you made then. Things happened, and you went along with them. That's how she'd ended up here, in America, more than three decades gone, staring out the window at the man she loved and respected more than any other in the world, and making plans to deceive him.

She had to remind herself that he didn't have all the facts, all that she had come to know only last night. If he did have those facts, perhaps he wouldn't be out there, calmly snipping dead blossoms. He knew about Peter's impending marriage, of course. The whole world seemed to know about it, and for the first time, Eleanor wondered exactly how that coupling came to be. In some ways, Peter's choice hadn't surprised her. Miranda Staunton had been on the periphery of all their lives, for as long as Nora had known Marc—always there, inserting herself next to Peter at every opportunity. He'd always seemed rather indifferent. But Miranda happened to get a job in Seattle only a month after Peter went there, starting fresh with his million-dollar insurance settlement. As if she hadn't given a thought to Peter Hallett's guilt or innocence. Did she have any idea what she was letting herself in for?

Eleanor left the window and sat on the edge of the bed that she and Tom had shared for forty years. She picked up the telephone receiver and dialed, plunging in when she heard the answer at the other end: "Hello, Peter, it's Eleanor . . . Yes, we're fine. How is Miranda? And how are you finding everything at the house?" She heard the strange, false notes in her own voice, as she stared down at Tom working in the garden, watching deadheads as they fell, one by one, into his sack. "And how is Elizabeth? We're both so anxious and excited to see her. That's what I'm calling about."

9

A few minutes before eight, the lights began to blink off inside the Phnom Penh restaurant on University Avenue. Dinner business must be slow. Nora studied the sign on the brightly painted red and yellow storefront, top half in English, the bottom half in curling Khmer script. The fisherman she'd seen down at the river was the last one out, slipping through the side door just before the man with the keys locked up and closed the extra security gate. The men scattered silently, and the fisherman bent to unlock a bicycle chained to the fence.

The place he headed to was not far, a typical old Frogtown clapboard house, clad in terrible redwood siding, with an exterior staircase to the second floor. The fisherman locked his bike to the metal stair rail and had just placed his foot on the first step when Nora ventured to speak: "Excuse me—"

She was about ten feet away from him. He turned, braced for something, and glanced quickly up and down the street—what was he expecting? Better talk fast. She said: "I wonder if I could talk to you for a second?" His avoidance of Janelle Joyner and her cameraman down at the river gave her an idea. "I'm not a reporter, not with the police."

He started to back up the stairs, and Nora felt a stab of panic. "Wait, don't go. Please." She began rummaging in her bag, conscious of the troupe of neighborhood kids down the block who'd started to notice her presence. They were about fifty yards away, pulling a beat-up red wagon along the sidewalk. She didn't want to make trouble for the fisherman, but need drove her forward. She held up Tríona's picture. "The person you found at the river. My sister."

She felt guilty for lying, but couldn't take the time to explain. Natalie Russo could have been someone's sister. Frank had mentioned an interpreter. Maybe this man had no idea what she was saying. Her heart leapt when he said: "Your sister?"

"Yes—my sister. The person you found." She reached back into the bag again and pulled out Peter Hallett's picture. "What about this man? Did you ever see this man at the river?"

Too much—the fisherman started backing away again, glancing sidelong at the approaching gang of children. One of the older kids called out to him in a language she couldn't understand. From the tone, it was not a friendly hail.

He spoke under his breath, clearly anxious to get away. "This place—not good. You go now. I fish river, same place every day—very early. Big tree." His hands suggested a sloping trunk. "You find me there."

He was up the stairs and gone before she could even react. She tucked Tríona's photo inside her bag, and turned to find the children swarming around her. She looked down at smudged faces. In the wagon were four squirming puppies, panting from the heat.

"Hey lady," one of the kids sang out. "Wanna buy a dog? Only five"—a swift kick from one of his compatriots changed his tune—"I mean, ten dollars. Cheap."

She looked down at the dog he held up, a mixed breed somewhere between a golden retriever and a husky.

"He's beautiful, but I can't—"

"Tony's dad is going to drown them. He said so."

"Can you keep them until tomorrow?" They looked at one another, shrugging. "Do you know the clinic around the corner? If you bring them over there in the morning, I know some people who might be interested. I'm sorry—I have to go now."

She climbed into her car, suddenly surrounded by a group of older boys on bicycles, their figures throwing long shadows in the fierce horizontal light of the setting sun. They balanced on their bikes, holding on to the car's frame so that she couldn't ease out of her parking spot without fear of doing one of them injury. Wannabe gangsters, too young for the real thing, not much older than the kids hawking the puppies. As if responding to some silent signal, the boys began to pound on the car with the palms of their hands, slowly at first, then building to a thundering crescendo as Nora sat locked inside, debating whether to call 911, imagining the operator's voice. *What is the nature of your emergency?*

A hoarse yell pierced the air, and the pounding suddenly stopped. The crowd of teenagers lifted away on their bicycles like a flock of birds. In the rearview mirror Nora could see a uniformed figure climbing out of the dark pickup behind her, backlit by the sun. He was carrying a baseball bat. When he approached the driver's side window and leaned down to peer in, she saw that he wasn't a cop, but a security guard. The word "Centurion" was stitched above the breast pocket of his shirt; there were two holes in the fabric where his name badge had been removed. She decided against rolling down the window.

"You all right there, ma'am?" He rested his right hand on the car roof, and the fingers of his left played against the handle of the bat, which was now balanced on the ground.

"Yes, I'm okay—thanks for your help."

"You're better off not spending too much time in this neighborhood."

"I'm on my way." The security guard stepped aside. As she pulled away from the curb, Nora glanced up to see the fisherman silhouetted in an upstairs window, and wondered whether she would actually see him down by the river at dawn.

10

Time seemed to have ground to a halt as Frank sat with his sister and brother-in-law in the waiting area outside the ER. He hadn't even seen his brother; the doctors had said they would do everything they could, but they didn't want to sugarcoat things. Chago was in serious trouble. There was a dangerous buildup of fluid in his tissues, not uncommon in cases of advanced heart failure.

Just after eight, one of the doctors came out and led them back into the ER, to a curtained alcove where Chago lay on a gurney. "We did all we could," she said softly. "His lungs were just too full of fluid—I'm very sorry. The priest is with him now."

Veronica began to sob, and Luis had to help her to a chair.

Inside the alcove, Frank watched a black-clad figure whispering over Chago, anointing his forehead with oil in the sign of the cross. Then the priest drew the sheet up over Chago's face, and Frank felt the world tilt. This wasn't the way it was supposed to happen. He had driven as fast as he could. Chago had seemed fine only a couple of days ago, joking about getting together for a cookout, to play a little baseball.

"Soon," he had promised. "I'm on a big case right now, but just as soon as I get a break—"

Frank left Veronica's side and walked over to the gurney. He drew back the sheet, taking in his brother's broad brown face, the slack mouth, and closed eyes. His other half. The good half, pure of heart and mind.

Images began to fly past at alarming speed: the old man in white, waving a fan of feathers, whispering, "*Susto, susto.*" The sound of a rattle, and smoke stinging his eyes. He and Chago, cramped together under the bed, afraid to come out, afraid the dusty cowboy boots might come and find them. The sound of voices and blows, and stars bursting in a black sky like fireworks.

Frank stood at his brother's side, clutching the edge of the sheet. A dark wave seemed to stretch a great distance above him, trembling with a dreadful anticipation, until it finally came crashing down upon him with a deafening roar.

11

At eight-twenty, Nora pulled up in front of Peter Hallett's house for the second time in two days. This time, the house was lit up by the sunset, a blaze of light that punched through the trees. She reached for her camera and focused in on the living room. She could see Peter surveying the space. He shoved the sofa two inches closer to the fireplace, and turned to shift an antique Asian shield five degrees toward the center of the room. *He has to have everything a certain way,* Tríona once said.

Nora adjusted the camera lens, studying the perfect musculature of his face, the slightly cleft chin, the broad shoulders and graceful hands. What strange power had this man held over Tríona, and perhaps others as well? What happened when he focused his charms on someone? Peter lifted his head and gazed in her direction. It wasn't possible that he knew she was out here, but the expression on his face nearly made her drop the camera.

A red Volvo sedan passed by on the river road and turned in at the driveway. Nora focused on the bright windows, and once again, the glass house afforded a view of the story being played out, as if on a stage. She watched her mother embrace Peter at the front door. A convincing performance. After a minute or so, Elizabeth appeared, and Peter stood behind her, his right hand on the back of her neck. When it was time to go, and her father bent down to kiss her good-bye, the child twisted away, shrugging off his touch. Why was she was so anxious to get away? When her mother got Elizabeth settled in the car and drove away at last, Nora felt an enormous weight lift from her. One major worry out of the way.

She set the camera down and glanced through the windshield, startled to see Miranda Staunton standing not twenty yards in front of the car, apparently loosening up for a run. This might be her only chance to speak to Miranda. It was now or never.

After jogging in place for a few seconds, Miranda checked her watch and took off. Nora got out of the car and followed on foot, staying about fifty yards behind, and relieved that she happened to be wearing decent shoes. They traveled through the light and shadow of the streetlamps, under the graffiti-covered bridge at Ford Parkway. Miranda's pace wasn't killer, but it never slowed. She finally turned in at the north entrance to Hidden Falls. At the bottom of the ravine, she cut across the parking areas, headed toward the path that traced the river's edge south of the boat landing. It was time to seize the moment.

Nora put on a spurt and called out: "Miranda—wait!"

Miranda stopped and whirled around. There was a brief pause as she put together the voice, the face of the person who issued the hail. "Nora? What are you doing here?"

"I need to talk to you."

Miranda eyed her suspiciously. "What about?"

"Just to say—" Nora was out of breath, panting. She watched Miranda's expression harden. "To tell you it's not too late. You can still back out—"

Miranda cut her off. "You know, Peter warned me. He said you'd come around one day, making crazy accusations—"

"They're not crazy, Miranda. Look at what happened to Tríona when she tried to leave. When she found out what he was. Please, listen—"

Miranda was trembling. "How dare you? Flinging around those sorry old lies. Peter had nothing to do with your sister's death. Why can't you get that through your head?"

Nora lowered her voice, hoping to find another way in. "Maybe you don't know yet what I'm talking about. Maybe he's been good to you. He was that way with Tríona as well, at first. I can't just stand by and let you—"

Miranda's voice turned cold. "You can't *let* me? Just who the hell do you think you are?" She held up her left hand, flashing a large diamond and thick gold band. "And just for the record—we're already married. We went to the courthouse before we left Seattle."

"Miranda, you don't know what he's done—"

"I know exactly what he's done. Nothing. You know, Nora, I pity you. You're a bitter, mixed-up person who can't stand anybody else getting something you can't have. I don't blame my brother for walking away. Your whole family is so screwed up. You know nothing about Peter. You have no right coming here, twisting the facts, trying to ruin everything. You need to stay away from us."

Nora swallowed hard. "Please, Miranda—please think about what I've said." She fumbled in her pocket for a card. "Here's my number—"

Miranda batted the card away and it fluttered to the ground. She stamped on it, grinding it into the blacktop with the heel of her running shoe. "Now get the hell away from me—before I call the police."

Nora held up both hands and backed away slowly. But the confrontation had evidently put Miranda off her evening run; she turned and headed back up to the river road.

Nora had plenty of time to berate herself as she walked back to where she'd left the car. What a disaster. A whole-scale, head-on debacle. Why had she imagined that Miranda would listen to her? Everything she said and did managed to make her look completely off balance. If Miranda had been experiencing any second thoughts, she had managed to quash them completely, coming on like some addled, street-corner prophet. *Stop it,* said the voice in her head. *Stop it. You had to take the chance.* Two days gone now. Miranda and Peter would soon be on the plane to Dublin. The one consolation was that Elizabeth was safely away from her father.

Nora opened her car door, realizing with a flash of annoyance that she'd left it unlocked. Fortunately, nothing seemed disturbed—not even the camera she'd inadvertently left on the passenger seat. She headed south along the river road, ticking through the day's events. No word from Frank on the results from Tríona's bloodstained clothing. Maybe she ought to try finding Harry Shaughnessy. She hoped the fisherman would have something useful for her in the morning. If he had recognized Peter from the picture, and could say that he'd spotted him at the river—

Caught up in her thoughts, Nora sailed along the river road. She tapped on the brake as she approached a curve, and wondered why it was so slow to respond—the bloody car was brand new, for God's sake. And in a flash, she knew. It wasn't a slow response; the pedal was stuck. She had no brakes at all.

Time seemed to slow as the car rocketed forward and left the road. The last thing Nora perceived was leafy branches whipping against the windshield as the car plummeted through underbrush, and finally came to rest, battered and steaming, against two trees at the bottom of the ravine.

Book Four

He wooed her so earnestly and lovingly, that she put on some woman's clothing which he brought her from his cottage, followed him home, and became his wife. Some years later, when their home was enlivened by the presence of two children, the husband awaking one night, heard voices in conversation from the kitchen. Stealing softly to the room door, he heard his wife talking in a low tone with someone outside the window. The interview was just at an end, and he had only time to ensconce himself in bed, when his wife was stealing across the room. He was greatly disturbed, but determined to do or say nothing till he should acquire further knowledge.

Next evening, as he was returning home by the strand, he spied a male and female *phoca* sprawling on a rock a few yards out at sea. The rougher animal, raising himself on his tail and fins, thus addressed the astonished man in the dialect spoken in these islands:—"You deprived me of her whom I was to make my companion; and it was only yesternight that I discovered her outer garment, the loss of which obliged her to be your wife. I bear no malice, as you were kind to her in your own fashion; besides, my heart is too full of joy to hold any malice. Look on your wife for the last time."

The other seal glanced at him with all the shyness and sorrow she could force into her now uncouth features; but when the bereaved husband rushed toward the rock to secure his lost treasure, she and her companion were in the water on the other side of it in a moment, and the poor fisherman was obliged to return sadly to his motherless children and desolate home.

—*Legendary Fictions of the Irish Celts,* by Patrick Kennedy, 1891

1

Karin Bledsoe pulled a cigarette from the crumpled pack she kept stashed in her purse and lit it, taking a long drag. She never smoked in bed when Rolf was home, but he was out at a trade show in Las Vegas. Or so he said. She took another drag. To hell with him. Bastard.

The phone on the bedside table began to vibrate, and the glowing number on the screen registered as somebody on the exchange at headquarters. It was the patrol supervisor from Central Division. Don Padgett's voice sounded apologetic. "Sorry to call you at home, Karin. We've got a disturbance in the ER at Regions—"

"That's your patch, Don. Since when doesn't patrol handle a riot in the ER?"

"Since the person causing it is a detective. Your partner."

"Frank?"

"His brother came in on a 911. I guess they did what they could, but—"

"Are you telling me Frank's brother is dead?"

"That's what I was told. That's when he lost it."

"I didn't even know he had a brother."

"Me neither. Anyway, I thought you might want to get down there. Things are up in the air—and he's still got his weapon on him. Maybe you could talk to him."

Karin Bledsoe flashed her badge at the ER desk, and followed the noise to the last curtained bay. Frank's sister stood outside, weeping, comforted by her husband. Four uniformed cops were crouched close to the floor, trying to talk Frank out of the corner where he'd retreated. He sat on the floor, holding his brother's body close, keeping one hand clamped tightly over the slack mouth. One of the uniforms, a sergeant, spoke into his radio: "Yeah, we've got a situation here. We're going to need additional backup." He saw Karin and came over to her side, never turning his back on Frank. "You're his partner? Thanks for coming. I'm assuming Don filled you in—we need that weapon."

She glanced in and saw the waffled grip of Frank's service piece peeping from the fold in his jacket. It didn't seem like he was going to use the gun, but it was an obstacle. Nobody could think straight with a loaded Glock as part of this equation. It could take them all down a road nobody wanted to travel.

Karin said: "Let me talk to him." She edged into the curtained space, aware of anxious faces all around her. "Hey, Frank? It's Karin."

His eyes were open but he didn't seem to see anything. He was somewhere else. So she hadn't just been imagining things—he had been acting strange these past few days. She'd put that down to the return of Nora Gavin, but maybe there was more to it. "Frank, we need you to hand over your piece. I know you don't want to put anybody in danger. As soon as you hand me the gun, we can talk this over, all right?"

He was like a frightened animal, kept trying to cover his brother's mouth, turning his head as if he could hear things no one else around him could hear. His lips moved, repeating the same words over and over, in what seemed like a prayer. She edged closer, thinking she might be able to reach for the gun and slip it from the holster. *Take it slow,* she told herself. *Tell him what you're doing every step of the way.*

"I'm going to come closer, and then I'm going to reach into your jacket for the gun. Is that all right, Frank?" All she could think was: *This whole thing is seriously, seriously messed up.*

"*Santa María, Madre de Díos . . .*" he droned in a dull whisper.

When she was within inches, he suddenly lashed out with both legs, knocking her over, and bringing all four uniforms down upon himself in the process. There was a wild scramble as they struggled to restrain him, one limb at a time. Karin had seen plenty of suspects fight, but Frank—even in this diminished state—was strong and difficult to subdue.

"I have it—I have the weapon," the patrol sergeant said.

Karin scrambled to her feet as a couple of the uniforms sat on Frank and applied the cuffs. The other two lifted his brother's crumpled body and gently set it on the gurney. Frank's face was pressed hard into the floor. His tears streamed onto the shiny linoleum.

2

Nora awakened to a throbbing pain in her head. She lay back for a moment, and then began checking her limbs—everything moved, nothing broken, but she could feel nascent bruises on her chest and arms and knees. All her joints felt as if someone had tried to jolt them loose. She searched for the bump of a cell phone in her left pocket, then managed to work the thing out and flipped it open. No service—must be a dead spot, down here below the bluffs. Her head hurt like hell, but as long as nothing was fractured, it was time to make a move.

She released her seat belt and cracked open the car door, setting one foot tentatively on the steep ground outside. Moving slowly, she managed to slide from the car and stand, holding onto saplings and the rough ledges that protruded from the limestone. The noise of birdsong seemed to come from a great distance, and her head felt like a chiming clock tower.

The car was wedged between the trunks of two stout trees, evidently slowed in its wild ride by the undergrowth. She was lucky to have gone over at the point where she did, and not at some sheer drop-off over the water. Lucky as well, to have plowed between two trees, and not head on into one of them.

She dug into her right pocket, feeling for Cormac's love knot—it was gone. Her memory flashed on the moment last night, as she scrabbled for the card to give Miranda. It must have fallen to the ground then. A cold panic clutched at her. She had to find the spot where she'd spoken to Miranda, and get it back. Then she remembered having to do something, to be somewhere, first thing in the morning. To meet the fisherman at the big tree that leaned out over the water, early. What time was it, anyway? How long had she been out? She looked toward the river, where a thick haze hung over the water's surface. She couldn't see more than ten feet in either direction through the mist. Was that the edge of a path up ahead?

A hand suddenly clamped across her mouth from behind. She could hear rustling deeper in the woods, and heard strange voices arguing in the woods above her.

"Skeeter, what the fuck, man—"

"I just went for a piss. I had to go."

"I told you to stay there and not touch anything. Now she's gone. Grab the stuff, and let's get out of here."

The person who held her was not large, but strong and wiry. At last the voices receded and the hand slid from her mouth. She turned to face the Cambodian fisherman. He spoke in a whisper. "You okay? Need doctor?" He pointed to her head.

"I have to find my love knot. I can't lose it." Feeling as though she was going to pass out again, Nora reached for the fisherman's sleeve. "Please help me."

3

At the Emergency Room, Nora opened her eyes to find an unfamiliar figure sitting in the chair beside her. She must be dreaming—this couldn't be real. Hanging above her, she saw an IV dripping clear liquid. All right, so maybe it wasn't a dream.

Fragments of the previous night started coming back to her. Talking to Miranda at the river, the crash. After that, everything was a little hazy. They must have given her something. She struggled to prop herself up.

The figure in the chair sat forward. The fisherman held a small plastic tackle box on his lap. "You okay?"

"Why did you want me to meet you at the river? You were going to tell me about my sister—I'm sorry, I don't have her picture anymore."

He pushed his tackle box toward her. "You look."

Nora took the box and opened the lid. Inside were all the same sorts of useless treasures she had saved as a child: an orange plastic keychain in the shape of a crab, a rusty ball-bearing, a brass key gone to green, assorted marbles and coins. Collected like this, they seemed not like useless junk, but amulets or jujus, objects that carried a powerful spiritual charge. What was it he wanted her to look for? She pulled out a weathered scrap of paper with block letters in blue ballpoint: *I know what you did. Hidden Falls 11 pm tonite.* A smudge of something that looked like blood marked the corner of the paper. She set the note aside and kept searching. At the bottom of the box, her fingers crossed a rubbery surface. She parted the jumble to find a Nokia cell phone, the same model as Tríona's missing mobile. No wonder they hadn't found it in the crime scene evidence. All at once, she saw Tríona running for her life through the underbrush, trying to call for help, dropping the phone as she fled. She imagined herself in the hotel lobby that night, calling and calling, while this phone lay useless amid dead leaves.

She reached out for the fisherman, seizing his shirtsleeve. "Where did you get this? I mean, where *exactly* did it come from—do you remember?"

He backed away, alarmed. "At river. All from river."

Nora let go of his sleeve. "I'm sorry, I didn't mean to—" Her gaze caught on a faded color photo taped inside the tackle box lid. A father, mother, children. "Is this your family?"

He nodded. "In Cambodia—before."

Nora struggled to focus on their faces: the bespectacled father, mother in a white blouse and dark skirt, and four boys, lined up eldest to youngest, mugging for the camera. All apparently unaware of the terrible wave that was about to catch them. "Which is you?"

He pointed to the youngest boy, with the biggest ears and the widest grin. She peered closer and noticed the stethoscope slung around the father's neck. "Your father was a doctor?"

She looked up, recognizing the guarded, hollow look in his eyes. He must have been only a child when the Khmer Rouge came to power. When the killing started. "I'm sorry—" She struggled to think what else to say. "You've been so kind, and I don't even know your name."

"Sotharith."

Nora threw off her blanket and sat up at the edge of the gurney. Sotharith looked alarmed. "I can't stay here," she said. "I've got to go. Do you know what happened to my cell phone?"

He handed over a bag evidently containing her personal items. Nora dug for her phone and quickly checked for messages. Still nothing from Frank.

A nurse pulled back the curtain and strode over to the bed, checking the IV and monitor in a single glance. "So—how are we doing here?" When Nora didn't respond, she spoke sotto voce to Sotharith. "I'm sorry, sir, you'll have to go back to the waiting area now." She pointed to the large double doors outside in the hall. "We'll let you know when your friend is ready to be discharged."

Sotharith backed out of the room with the tackle box pressed to his chest. When the nurse's back was turned, Nora managed to tuck the note and the two phones under her pillow. She spoke to Sotharith over the nurse's shoulder. "Don't leave, please. I'll come out to you as soon as I can—" The door swung open, and he was gone.

The nurse spoke again, nodding toward someone standing outside the curtain. "The police are here to take your statement, Dr. Gavin."

Nora looked up to see whether they'd sent a patrol officer or a detective to take her statement. The one person she didn't expect was Frank's partner, Karin Bledsoe.

"Hello, Dr. Gavin. The ER docs said you kept telling them the crash wasn't an accident."

Nora tried to keep her voice calm. "It wasn't. Somebody jammed the brakes in my car."

"And who would have any reason to do that?"

"The same man who murdered my sister—Peter Hallett."

She walked Karin Bledsoe through the events of the previous night, from the time she arrived at Peter's house to the time she woke up in the ER this morning. There were a few gaps, of course.

Karin Bledsoe listened, and jotted down a few notes. "Do you mind telling me what you were doing parked outside Mr. Hallett's residence?" she asked.

Nora took that question—and the skeptical look that accompanied it—to mean that Karin Bledsoe had run her name through the computer and come up with the restraining order Peter had filed against her four years ago. Once again, she was coming across as the lunatic stalker, and Peter Hallett as long-suffering victim. "If you just look at my car, you'll see that somebody jammed the brakes—"

"We checked the vehicle. There was a water bottle rolling around on the driver's side floor. Is it possible that your own bottle accidentally got stuck under the pedal?"

"It was in the cup holder."

"And you didn't notice it missing when you returned to the car?"

"I can't remember—I wasn't thinking about water bottles. I was thinking about the person who murdered my sister. What about all those runners and dog walkers along the river road? One of them could have seen something—"

"We've got officers working on that. We'll let you know."

"And in the meantime, Peter Hallett is about to leave the country tomorrow. I really need to speak to Frank. He doesn't answer his phone. Could you let him know that I need to talk to him? Please—it's important."

"I can pass along a message—but I can't promise that he'll get back to you right away."

"Why—what's happened to him? Where is he?"

"Detective Cordova is on leave. That's really all I can say . . . Thanks for your statement, Dr. Gavin. Here's my number—" She handed Nora a card. "Call me if you think of anything else, or if you need anything. We'll be in touch again soon."

When Karin Bledsoe closed her notebook and stepped away, Nora knew she was on her own. Did the woman seriously think she would drive off an embankment and crash a car, just to implicate Peter Hallett? How could she be sure that Karin Bledsoe would send someone to Peter's house, check on his movements last night?

Just then, a familiar voice cut through the chaotic noise of the ER. "She's here, Tom." Eleanor Gavin pushed back the curtain, taking in the bandage on Nora's head, the bruises, the IV drip. "Oh, Nora—we've been trying to find you all night. We didn't know where you were."

Her father stood at the foot of the bed, lack of sleep evident in the dark circles beneath his eyes. "What's happened, Nora?"

She couldn't tell them the car wreck wasn't an accident. "It was stupid—I took a curve too fast, went off the road. I'm all right, really. Nothing broken—just a few bruises. Why were you trying to find me?"

Eleanor Gavin broke down. "Oh, Nora—"

"What is it, Mam? What's wrong?"

"She's gone, Nora. Elizabeth's gone. Peter's taken her. We were going to go away, the three of us—"

"What happened, Mam?"

Her father said: "Let me, Eleanor. It's all right, Nora. I know everything. Your mother had just brought Elizabeth back to our house. It was just after nine. We were loading our bags into the car when Peter and Miranda drove up in a limousine, saying they'd talked it over, and decided that Elizabeth was coming along with them after all. They were on their way to the airport."

Nora looked at her parents in turn. "No—no! They weren't supposed to leave until Saturday."

Eleanor seized her hand. "We had to let her go, Nora—what else could we do? What could we have told the police? And Peter saw our bags; he knew what was happening, I'm sure of it. Oh, Nora, I'm so afraid we'll never see her again."

4

Cormac watched his father's eyelids flutter. Surely that was a good sign. Dreaming—if that's what it was—meant brain activity, at least. The afternoon crawled by as they waited for a sign—any evidence to indicate how much damage the stroke had done. At this point there were no external symptoms—no drooping face, no apparent weakness in his limbs, but the brain controlled all other functions as well: language, sensation, personality. Damage to any of those mysterious bundles of cells could wreak swift havoc.

Roz dozed in the chair beside the window. She was putting a good face on it, but he knew she was confounded. Bollixed before she ever had a chance. They were a strange trio. Anyone looking in might jump to completely erroneous conclusions. Several of the nurses had already taken himself and Roz for a married couple, and he hadn't the heart to correct them.

He'd been reading up on some of the materials the doctor had provided on stroke rehabilitation, and was alternately encouraged and depressed. At this point they still had no idea who would come out of the coma. Would the man who woke up here be some reduced version of Joseph Maguire? There was risk of a still-vital mind trapped in a nonfunctioning body. Cormac suddenly realized he wouldn't have much longer to wait and wonder. Joseph's eyes began to flutter again, more rapidly this time. Then they opened wide, just as he took a deep lungful of air. It was almost as if he'd been underwater, holding his breath. Cormac watched his father blink several times, apparently unable to focus. Probably all he could see was the dust-clogged grate in the ceiling. Did that shape mean anything to him? Did he even know what it was?

The old man's lips began to move; he was struggling to make a sound, but managed only a low moan. His hand reached out, and Cormac took it and held on. "Raahhh. Raaaahhh," the old man croaked, and Cormac moved closer, unsure whether to speak. "Da?" he said at last. The shape of the word felt foreign on his tongue. It was as if they were both infants again, reduced to single syllables.

"Unnhhh. Raaaahhh," the old man said again. Was he trying to say "Roz"?

"I'm right here. Roz and I are both here."

Tears began to trickle from the corners of the old man's eyes, but whether they were brought on by emotion, or merely the effort of trying to speak, Cormac could not tell. He only knew he was overwhelmed by the notion of having a second chance, an opportunity to forge something new from ruins destroyed long ago. How many received that gift?

Roz stirred in her chair. "What's happening—what did I miss?"

"Nothing," Cormac said. "He's just now opened his eyes." The old man's hand felt warm, leathery. The words might be absent, but Cormac looked into his father's eyes and saw something burning in the depths of those dark pools, a light of recognition. "I think he knows me, Roz." His father's warm, dry fingers closed around his hand. "That's it. Do you know who I am?" Another small compression—but Cormac felt it as a semaphore, a signal between far-distant sentries.

"Do you know my name?" Again the slight pressure. "My God, you're there, aren't you?"

Roz approached the bedside, her eyes shining. "How are you, Joe? We've missed you."

The old man's gaze turned to her, and with a sinking feeling, Cormac watched the small light of recognition sputter and flicker out. "It's Roz," he said. "You know Roz—"

But it was no good. And Roz could see it as well. She had been erased from Joe's memory by the recent brain storm. Every tender feeling the old man held for her had been wiped away. It made sense that the memories last formed were the least solid, while the older memories—of people, places, events—were cemented into place like a building's foundation, the last thing left standing in the event of calamity.

Roz tried not to show how much she felt the slight. "Why don't I just wait out in the—" She waved a hand and left the room. Cormac found her a few minutes later at the far end of the corridor, her face flushed and wet with tears.

"Roz, listen to me. You can't expect everything just to be there as if nothing had happened. He'll come back. Everything will come back, eventually. You have to be patient."

"I'm not there at all, Cormac. It's as if I never existed."

5

When their plane touched town at Dublin Airport, Elizabeth managed to fall a few steps behind her father and Miranda after they made their way through customs and passport control. She fell a little farther behind as they headed toward the airport exit, and her heart rose into her throat as she slipped into a shop filled with whiskey bottles and perfume and all kinds of gleaming jewelry. DUTY FREE, said the sign above the door. She hung back beside a wall of crystal bowls and glasses and clocks, watching passersby through the glass, their faces and limbs distorted and shattered into hundreds of facets edged with rainbows, thinking about how those two words together—DUTY FREE—seemed like a contradiction. She watched her dad and Miranda move out of sight without even noticing she was gone.

Her plan was to look up Nora's address in the phone book, and get a taxi to take her there. She approached the shop counter and addressed the woman who stood behind it: "Excuse me—would you happen to have a phone book?"

The woman looked like somebody's grandmother, with her soft brown sweater set and glasses that perched on the end of her nose. She squinted down through them. "Sorry, love, what was it you needed?"

"I was wondering if you had a phone book I could use?"

"Phone book? Oh—the telephone directory, is it? What would you be needing with that? Sure, no one uses those old printed books anymore, not when you can just ring directory enquiries on your mobile—" She glanced down, sensing Elizabeth's disappointment. "Do you know, I'm sure we must have a directory here somewhere. The oh-one for Dublin, is it?" The woman began to search under the counter.

Elizabeth glanced over her shoulder to make sure her dad and Miranda had not come back. "I'm not sure. I just need to look something up."

The woman continued rooting around in the boxes under the counter, finally producing a fat telephone book. "There you are, now. You're not lost, are you, love?"

Elizabeth shook her head, and started flipping through the book, startled at all the pages and pages of Lynches, Kennedys, Kavanaghs—until at last she came to a page full of Gavins. There must be hundreds of them. She traced her finger down the column, looking for one in particular, and there it was: "Gavin, N., Whitefriar Street, Dublin 8." The woman behind the counter was staring at her.

"Um—you wouldn't have a pen?"

"Would a biro suit?"

Elizabeth wasn't sure how to reply. Would a Byro Suit what?

The woman smiled and handed her a ballpoint pen. She quickly scribbled Nora's address and phone number on the inside of her wrist, yanking her sleeve down to cover it.

The woman leaned down and spoke quietly. "First time in Ireland? You're not in trouble, are you, love?"

"Oh no—nothing like that. I just wanted to surprise someone." Elizabeth turned to see a well-dressed couple passing the store entrance. "There's my mom and dad now—they're looking for me. Thanks for your help."

Outside the airport's front entrance, she climbed into the first taxi in line. "I need to go to Whitefriar Street," Elizabeth said to the driver, and waited for a reaction. She hoped he wouldn't guess that she didn't have money to pay the fare. Not the right kind of money, anyway. Elizabeth tried not to look nervous when he glanced back at her in the rearview mirror. What if he'd seen her checking the address on her arm?

"No luggage, miss?" he asked.

"No. I have to get to Whitefriar Street—where my aunt lives. It's a family emergency." That made it sound serious enough. The driver glanced at her again in the rearview mirror, then edged his cab out into the flow of traffic.

6

On the way out of the Emergency Room with her mother, Nora saw the fisherman, Sotharith. He was still there, waiting for her. She pulled on Eleanor's arm.

"Mam, wait—there's someone I have to see."

Sotharith looked up as they approached. He stood, clearly uncomfortable in this place. But he had stayed. "You—okay?" he asked.

"Yes, they're letting me go. This is my mother, Eleanor Gavin. Mam, this is Sotharith—I'm sorry, I don't know your family name."

"Seng," he said. "Seng Sotharith."

"My Good Samaritan," Nora said to her mother. "He flagged someone down after the accident, and got me here."

Eleanor pressed her palms together close to her face and bowed deeply. "*Choum reap suor,*" she said.

Sotharith would not meet Eleanor's gaze. "*Choum reap suor,*" he murmured, mirroring her bow but bending even lower. "You speak Khmer?"

"Very little," Eleanor said. "A few words picked up from my patients."

A new light sparked in Sotharith's averted eyes. "You a doctor?" he asked.

Eleanor nodded. "I run the community clinic in Frogtown."

"Sotharith's father was a doctor," Nora explained. "Before the war." She could see her mother grasp what had become of this man's doctor-father, and perhaps the rest of his family as well.

Eleanor turned to him. "Lok Sotharith, you've been very good to us. I would like to repay your kindness somehow." She handed him a card. "Will you come and see me at the clinic when you can?" He took the card and nodded, bowing low to her mother once more.

Nora couldn't bear the thought of leaving her rescuer. She needed to speak to him, to find out more about what he knew about the phone and the note he'd found in the woods. "My father is bringing the car around—can we take you home, or offer you a meal—something?" He shook his head, and she realized that he had spent nearly a whole day looking after her. He might have put his job at the restaurant in jeopardy.

"*Choum reap suor,*" he said, bowing again. Nora joined her mother this time, pressing her palms together and repeating after him as her mother did: "*Choum reap suor.*"

When Tom Gavin pulled the car up in front of the Emergency Room entrance, he said: "We're taking you home with us, Nora. No arguments."

"None offered."

As they turned onto John Ireland Boulevard near the Capitol, Nora's phone began to chirp. She hoped it was Frank, but the voice on the phone was female, and worried.

"Nora, it's Saoirse Donovan. I'm not quite sure how to tell you this—I've got a child here who says she's your niece."

"Hang on, Saoirse—" Nora pressed the phone to her shoulder and spoke to her parents. "It's a friend from Dublin. She says Elizabeth is there with her. I'll find out what's going on." Lifting the phone to her ear again, she said: "Saoirse, tell me what happened."

"Well, Jack and I were getting ready for a short holiday up at our summer place in Skerries. And as we were loading up the car, who should appear but this beautiful child, asking if you lived at this address. When I told her that you did, but you'd gone home to the States, she was very upset. She hasn't said much more, only that she's your niece, and needs to see you—it's very important. And that's all we've been able to get out of her. She wouldn't even give her name."

"How did she know where to find me?"

"I don't know. She arrived in a taxi from the airport, had the address written on her arm. The thing is, Nora"—Saoirse seemed uneasy, and lowered her voice—"the thing is, the taxi man is still here as well. Says he's got kids of his own, and he's not about to leave a child with strangers unless he can be given assurances that she's going to be all right. We explained to him that you're a good friend, that we're happy to look after the child, but—maybe you could talk to him. He's quite adamant."

"Let me speak to him," Nora said.

A voice with a broad Dublin accent came on the phone. "Sean Meehan here. Who am I speakin' to?"

"Nora Gavin. If the child with you is my niece, then her name is

Elizabeth Hallett. You can ask her if you want to be sure." She could hear him put the question: "I have your auntie here, child. She asks if you'll tell us your name now?"

A young voice answered: "Elizabeth. Elizabeth Hallett." Nora's heart leapt.

"And your auntie's name, the one you're looking for?"

"Nora Gavin."

Meehan was still skeptical. "How do I know you're who you say you are? These people could have phoned anyone, told you what to say."

The question was valid, Nora thought. How could she prove who she was, from thousands of miles away, without benefit of photographs, fingerprints, DNA? She frowned, trying to scare up some tidbit of information that only she and Elizabeth might know. A password to a shared past. Then it came to her. "Ask Elizabeth if she remembers the song her mother used to sing to her when she was little—"

There were muffled sounds of the question being asked, and Meehan's voice came on again. "She says she's not sure."

"Could I just try something? Would you just hold up the phone so she can hear me?" Closing her eyes and placing the receiver close to her lips, Nora began to sing the mysterious words that echoed the language of the seals, hoping they would awaken something in Elizabeth, stir a memory that would reconnect them. When she finished, there was only silence at the other end. "Elizabeth, do you remember?"

Meehan spoke into the phone again, his voice husky with emotion. "Jaysus Christ, the poor little yoke. What happened to her mammy?"

"My sister was murdered, Mr. Meehan," Nora said. She could hear him curse softly. "Elizabeth was very young; she never really understood what happened, never knew her father was a suspect. There's never been enough evidence to charge him. That's why it's vital that you not take her to the Guards. Her father has probably gone to them already. And the way things stand, they'd be obliged to return her to him—do you understand why I can't let that happen?"

Meehan was still uneasy. "Christ—I pulled over at one point, tried to get her to go back to the airport. She said there was no way she was going back. Made me wonder if there wasn't something funny going on."

"I can catch the next flight over and be there tomorrow—if you'll leave her in care of the Donovans. Please. I can vouch for them, and they'll take good care of her until I can get there—"

"One question. Does the child's daddy have this address?"

Nora thought for a moment. "No—I mean, I'm not sure. Why?"

"Well, I was just thinking—if he does know where to look, you might want to consider keeping the little one somewhere else—far away from here, like."

"The Donovans were on their way up to their summer place in Skerries. Elizabeth would be safe there for the moment. Her father would have no idea where to look."

7

Harry Shaughnessy made his way down the stairs cut into the steep hill, wondering how he was going to get across Shepard Road. Cars streamed in both directions. He shouldn't have come this way, but it was the quickest way to get down to the camp. Everyone had used these stairs in the old days. It was a long time since then, the streetcar days. Nobody seemed to walk now; everybody drove. And all the places people used to walk were neglected and overgrown with weeds.

He was glad that he'd so far managed to avoid that young lady he'd met outside the library a couple of days ago. Saw her again yesterday. What did she want? Better if he didn't get close enough to find out. She'd start asking questions. That's what she really wanted, he could see it in her eyes. The thought of having to answer questions always triggered a panicky feeling inside him. A need to get away. Next she'd be wanting to have a look in his pack, and he wasn't about to give up any of that. Not without a fair trade—not on your life.

He sat down at the bottom of the steps to rest for just a minute, pressing at the stitch in his side, and looking down at the battered high-tops on his feet, water stains up the sides, a crack in the left sole, and it suddenly occurred to him—why not both soles? Didn't he take just as many steps with the right as the left? Whatever the answer to that puzzle, these shoes wouldn't be good much longer. Only a few more days' wear in them, really. In his situation, a man needed decent footwear.

Reaching into his pack, he brought out a crumpled paper bag, and unrolled it, taking out a pair of new-looking black sneakers. Had anyone ever seen such a pair of shoes? He held them up, admiring the electric blue stripes along the sides. Still like new—only a little blood on them. Beggars couldn't be choosers, as his mother used to say.

He still remembered the day they'd been given to him. That was how he thought of it, like a divine bestowal. Down on the riverbank one summer morning, washing his feet—he always felt more human when he had clean feet—so there he was, sitting on a rock, pants rolled up to his knees, rubbing cold water and sand between his toes, when a heavy bundle came hurtling down from above, and landed with a splash in the gravelly riverbed not three feet from where he sat. The water began to push against the bundle, and he had to move quickly to keep it from tumbling away. Once he had it, he looked up, trying to spot whoever had dropped the thing. Maybe they'd want it back—you never knew. No one visible above on the bridge. So he'd kept it, not even opening the bag until later that evening. That's when he'd found the shoes, the sweatshirt he was wearing, and a pair of pants, too. As if someone up there knew exactly what he needed. It got cold, sleeping on the ground, even in summer. The clothes fit him all right; the hell of it was that the shoes had not. Never would. He'd hung onto them anyway, thinking maybe he could trade them for a different pair. But these shoes were extra special, worth a lot in trade. Nobody had ever offered what they were worth. Years of wear left in them. He'd swap them for something that would last a long time, with all the walking he did. When he'd finished admiring the shoes, he carefully rewrapped them in the brown paper bag, and stowed them again in his pack. He reached into the front pouch pocket of his shirt and pulled out the handwritten note he'd found there when he'd first put the sweatshirt on. *I know what you did,* it said. *Hidden Falls 11 pm tonite.* How could anyone know what he did? He only did what was necessary, what he had to do. What they all had done.

Harry hefted the pack on his shoulder, and looked across the empty railroad tracks, and beyond them, at Shepard Road. He crossed the rail bed, watching where he put a foot in case he'd stumble and fall. There wasn't much danger. Trains came through only a couple of times a day now, and walking the tracks wasn't as perilous as it had once been. But beyond the tracks, the cars on Shepard Road flew along at ungodly speeds.

He waited patiently until the road was clear in both directions before picking his moment to cross. And when it came, he moved with the grace and agility of a much younger man, hardly conscious of the muscles in his legs and back, of all the bones and sinews that worked together so miraculously to propel him forward.

But the SUV that hit him was traveling nearly sixty miles an hour, and Harry Shaughnessy was suddenly and unceremoniously removed from the mortal world.

Book Five

In all three versions the bridegroom is forbidden to strike "three causeless blows." Of course he disobeys . . . Once the husband and wife were invited to a christening in the neighbourhood. The lady, however, seemed reluctant to go, making the feminine excuse that the distance was too far to walk. Her husband told her to fetch one of the horses from the field. "I will," said she, "if you will bring me my gloves, which I left in the house." He went, and, returning with the gloves, found that she had not gone for the horse, so he jocularly slapped her shoulder with one of the gloves, saying: "Go, go!" Whereupon she reminded him of the condition that he was not to strike her without a cause, and warned him to be more careful in future.

Another time, when they were together at a wedding, she burst out sobbing amid the joy and mirth of all around her. Her husband touched her on the shoulder and inquired the cause of her weeping. She replied: "Now people are entering into trouble; and your troubles are likely to commence, as you have the second time stricken me without a cause."

Finding how very wide an interpretation she put upon the "causeless blows," the unfortunate husband did his best to avoid anything which could give occasion for the third and last blow. But one day they were together at a funeral, where, in the midst of the grief, she appeared in the highest spirits and indulged in immoderate fits of laughter. Her husband was so shocked that he touched her, saying: "Hush, hush! Don't laugh!" She retorted that she laughed "because people, when they die, go out of trouble"; and, rising up, she left the house, exclaiming: "The last blow has been struck; our marriage contract is broken, and at an end! Farewell!"

—*The Science of Fairy Tales: An Inquiry into Fairy Mythology,* by Edwin Sidney Hartland, 1916

1

When Nora came through the sliding doors to the arrivals lounge at Dublin Airport, Sean Meehan was holding a hand-lettered sign: GAVIN. He'd promised to collect her, and was as good as his word. He was almost exactly what she expected: an ordinary working-class Dub, clean-shaven with short-cropped salt-and-pepper hair, gray hoodie under a black leather bomber jacket, black jeans. He was clearly sizing her up as well.

"Car's outside," he said. She had evidently passed muster.

"Look, Mr. Meehan, you really don't have to do this. You've already done more than enough. Jack Donovan said he'd be glad to collect me from the bus—"

"Ah no—we're going to Skerries, you and I, and you're off the clock. No arguments. And call me Sean."

He took her bag and they walked out to the car park. After paying at one of the automated kiosks, he turned to her. "I didn't want to do this inside—anybody could have been watching—but I figured you might like some proof that I am who I say. Before getting into a car with me, like. So here you go"—he handed each one over as he spoke—"driver's licence, passport, taxi licence, the wife's mobile number—you can ring her if you like."

Nora glanced at the cards, and pushed them back. "There's no need for all that—I believe you."

"Just want you to know—" He took the cards and the passport and stuffed them back into his pockets. "I've got to go up to Skerries. Wouldn't feel right, leaving the little one without seeing how she's getting on. I just keep thinking—what if she was me own kid?"

As Nora got into the car, she spied a snapshot tucked into the driver's side visor. Three boys and a girl, all between the ages of six and twelve, and all dark-haired and blue-eyed, like the man beside her. "Your kids?"

"Ah, yeah, but that's an old picture. The eldest, Damien, he's nearly sixteen. Jaysus, where does the time get to?"

From the airport, they drove on in silence out the M1, through the village of Swords. Sean Meehan pulled a pack of Majors from his pocket and lit one up. Then he spoke, as though he'd been thinking about it for a while: "It's not as if you can just make a child disappear. They're sure to be on the lookout for her. What'll you do?"

"I don't know. Try to find somewhere to lie low, I suppose. We're digging for new evidence on my brother-in-law at home, but whether it'll turn into anything—"

"Want some advice?"

Nora considered Sean Meehan's sensible idea from the day before, about getting Elizabeth out of Dublin. "What do you suggest?"

"Go as far away from Dublin as you can get. Somewhere in Cork or Kerry maybe, or Mayo—up the West, where there's not too many people. Someplace remote. Up the side of some boggy mountain, where no one would ever think to look. A safe house. That's where you want to be. Don't tell anyone where you're going. And make sure you have transport that can't be traced to you. I suppose stealing a car is totally out of the question?" Before she could respond, he cast a sidelong glance at her and grinned. "Only joking. Maybe the Donovans would give you the loan of theirs. Whatever you do—cash only, no credit cards." He handed her an envelope with banknotes in it. "There's about three hundred euro in there. I can get more if you need it. You'll need a mobile as well, one of them pay-as-you-go jobs. I can pick one up in the next village—that way it's traced only to me. And if you should need other transport—say, a boat, just for instance—give us a shout."

Nora studied his profile for a moment. "I hate to ask how you know all this."

"Let's just say I knew people who knew people, back when." He glanced over at her. "All water under the bridge now."

He took one last, long drag on his cigarette, and flicked the butt out the window. "Just read of a fella up in Ballina, done for smoking in his own fuckin' cab—two hundred fifty euro of a fine. Did you ever hear the bate of that? The youngest has been at me to give them up. I'm trying, but it's a devil of a thing to quit, you know? You never smoked, yourself?"

Nora shook her head. "Not in my line of work."

"Your friends were saying—you're a doctor?"

"Pathologist."

"What, like those fellas on *CSI?*"

"Not exactly. I teach anatomy. But what I see on the dissecting table—well, let's just say it's incentive enough to stay off the fags."

"Sweet Jaysus." Sean Meehan pulled the half-empty packet of Majors from his pocket and stared at it for a few seconds, then pitched the whole thing out the car window.

They arrived just before noon at the Donovans' place in Skerries. The house was part of a Victorian terrace that looked out over the Irish Sea. Gulls wheeled and cried overhead as they drove up the narrow street and parked outside. The house and the wall around the postage-stamp garden were painted in storybook colors, bright yellow and blue. The air was redolent of seaweed and fish, and the seawall opposite looked down over sand and rocks that would be covered with water at high tide, and were now furry with brown kelp.

Nora suddenly realized that Elizabeth had probably seen Ireland only in pictures. Would it seem foreign to her, or would she have some impossible memory of the place, a pentimento written in blood and bone? She thought of something Cormac had said to her once: *We're made out of the water, the earth, the air of the places that fed our ancestors, quenched their thirst, the basic elements of the places that gave them life. Is it really so strange if we feel the heave and pitch of those places, even centuries later, in the vibrations of our atoms?*

Saoirse Donovan met her at the door. "Oh, Nora, I'm so glad you're here. Sean—thanks for bringing her along. Won't you come in? Elizabeth is in the sitting room, Nora. I'll let you go in to her while I make tea."

Nora took her friend's arm. "Is she all right, Saoirse?"

"She won't speak to anyone but you, Nora. But I should warn you—" She hesitated, nervous.

"What is it, Saoirse? Tell me."

"Last night she took a scissors to all that lovely hair—cut it all off, right down to the scalp. I feel so terrible, Nora—I ought to have kept a closer watch. I thought you should know before you see her. So it wouldn't be such a shock."

Sean Meehan frowned and jerked a thumb over his shoulder. "I'll be here if you need anything."

Nora pushed through the door to the sitting room, her stomach heavy with dread. She found Elizabeth sitting cross-legged in the front window seat, a large book open across her knees. As Saoirse had warned, the child's long hair was gone, roughly chopped off. What was left stuck up in strange tufts and ridges. Her eyes, so like Tríona's, so large and luminous. Now, with her hair cut short, they were almost too large for her face. Nora watched her niece's gaze flick to the bandage on her head.

She felt an impulse to rush forward and fold Elizabeth in her arms. And yet for some reason she could not do it. Something in the child's questioning, wounded gaze stopped her. They stared at each other for a long moment, each wondering what to say, what to do next, how to bridge the chasm of the last five years.

Nora crossed to the far end of the window seat, keeping a space between them. "You wanted to see me," she said. "Here I am."

Elizabeth closed her book and began playing with the laces on her shoes, pulling the bows taut, winding herself tighter and tighter—waiting and wishing, Nora knew, for that bad feeling in the pit of her stomach to go away. Only it would not go away, not ever, not completely. It would seem to diminish for a while, and then, for no apparent reason, would blossom anew, reviving itself like a living thing.

Nora put out a hand to still the fidgeting fingers. "I've missed you, Lizzabet—"

Her head lifted. "Nobody calls me that—not anymore." The child was an injured animal, snapping at any hand that came near, even those offering aid. Although Elizabeth's instincts told her to resist, Nora was more than ready. She had been anticipating this moment; dreaming it and dreading it every day for five years. At last, she pulled Elizabeth close, wrapping her arms around the thin shoulders, feeling the force of the silent howl caught inside. Words were not enough. All she could offer right now was fierce steadfastness, a promise never to let go. There were no tears, from either of them. Plenty of time for those, Nora told herself. They would come. She stroked Elizabeth's hair, wondering how on earth they were going to get through this. There were practical decisions to be made, plans to be laid, as if their lives depended on it. Perhaps they did. She would not allow anyone to harm this child. And if that meant breaking the law, if it meant not seeing people she loved for a very long time, then she would do it.

But Sean Meehan was right. They had to go somewhere remote, a place no one would think to look. Then she remembered the way Cormac had described his father's house. A *very remote spot,* he had said. *I didn't know places like this still existed.*

She had resisted heaping her troubles on him; it didn't seem fair. And yet what choice did she have, when there was so much at stake? She tipped Elizabeth's head up and looked into her eyes. "Listen to me, Lizzabet. I think I know a place we can go."

2

Frank Cordova slid over the threshold of consciousness. A few random ghosts seemed to lurk at the edges of his perception: there was the sweep of a leaf fan, the oppressive heat and dust, and that odd, sudden, thick-thin sensation he had felt as a kid, and had never been able to explain. The room was dark, and for some reason he felt exhausted, even though he was just waking up. He opened his eyes, vaguely aware that he was gripping a woman's arm, but he couldn't seem to feel his fingers. His legs were heavy, and there was a continual, low-pitched buzz in the back of his head. His mouth felt chalky. "What's happening?"

"You're in Regions Hospital. You've been sedated for a bit. I'll call the doctor and let him know you're feeling better."

He raised his head slightly to look down at his legs. No cast. No bullet holes. So what was he doing in the hospital? He said to the nurse: "How long have I been here?"

She smiled. "You were admitted Thursday night—well, Friday morning, I guess, technically speaking. And today is Saturday—"

"Saturday? I have to get out of here."

"I really think you need to speak to the doctor first—"

He tried to sit up. "You don't understand. I'm working a case, and I haven't got time—" He stopped speaking as fragments of memory began to stir again: Veronica's teary face, the sound of ragged breathing, that horrible disinfectant smell, and an almost noiseless scuffle against a hard, cold floor. He knew then what he'd put off knowing in long hours of shadowy sleep. A spasm of anguish gripped him, and he knew that the strange dreams he'd been having were not dreams at all.

Chago.

There was nothing he could do to protect his brother. Not anymore. The room began to spin, and he lay back down on the bed, hot tears trickling into his ears. *Santa María, Madre de Díos, ruega por nosotros pecadores, ahora y en la hora de nuestra muerte*—Now and at the hour of our death.

"Rest for a while." The nurse began tucking the blanket around him again. "Sometimes it helps if you just try to concentrate on breathing."

He nodded, but as soon as she left the room, he tore the tape off his IV and removed the needle, applying pressure to stop any bleeding. He found his clothes in the cupboard, but his wallet, badge, gun, and cell phone were all gone—as were his car keys. He distinctly remembered driving to the ER after Veronica's call. Picking up the room phone, he dialed his partner, and cut straight to the chase. "Karin, I need a lift."

Her response was wary: "I take it you're feeling better?"

"Yeah." He couldn't tell from her voice whether she knew about everything that had happened—although it was probably safe to say she knew a lot more than he did. That thought made him uncomfortable. "I'm at Regions. I need you to pick me up, right away."

"Do you think that's wise, Frank?"

"I don't care if it's wise. If you won't pick me up, I'll take a cab."

"All right, all right—I'm down at the shop. See you in ten at the main entrance."

He slipped down the nearest stairwell and made his way to the ground floor. Karin was already waiting for him.

"You sure you're all right, Frank?" She was looking at his hand, still bearing the IV tape. "I had patrol bring your car back to headquarters the other night, but I can drive you straight home, if you'd rather—"

"I'll be okay." He turned to Karin. "It's Saturday. What are you doing at the shop?"

"With you out, we were a little shorthanded, and we got a couple of new cases. Your friend Dr. Gavin drove her car off a bluff down at Hidden Falls Thursday night."

Frank felt a sudden stab of fear. "Is she okay?"

"A little banged up—nothing serious. But she claimed it wasn't an accident—she says somebody jammed her brakes."

"And you don't believe her?"

"Hard to say. We've got the car up in the garage right now. It looks like a water bottle just got loose and rolled under her brake pedal. No prints on the bottle but hers. We can't prove a thing."

Frank took in this new information. Peter Hallett might as well have left a signature. Jigger the brakes so it looks like Nora might have done it herself. Then she looks extra crazy, trying to pin it on him. "What's the other case?"

"Hit-and-run yesterday. Homeless guy, maybe you knew him—Harry Shaughnessy?"

3

Nora drove northward and westward toward Donegal. She wasn't used to thinking like a fugitive—never spent time thinking about how to avoid being noticed, how to communicate without being tracked. She had told no one where she and Elizabeth were headed from Skerries, not even Sean Meehan or the Donovans, whose car she'd managed to cadge. Even so, she knew they were far from safe. The authorities were no doubt searching for Elizabeth, but she didn't dare turn on the news to find out. Peter would be just as adept at manipulating official opinion here as he had been at home. Donegal was at least far away from Dublin, but nowhere on the island felt secure.

She drove through the pastures of Meath and Cavan, sticking to secondary roads, winding through villages fluttering with county flags to support whatever team was headed to the next regional championship. As they wound around the small hills of Leitrim, carefully skirting the border—no need to invite official scrutiny by crossing into the North—the rain poured down, obscuring the view.

Elizabeth remained silent, eyes trained out the window. The child would have a terrible crick in her neck by the time they stopped. Occasionally, she would wipe the moisture from the glass, but the vapor from their breath only beaded up again.

What happened? Nora wanted to ask. *Did you remember something? Did you just figure it out on your own?* She tried to reconstruct her own consciousness at age six, about the time she and Tríona and her parents had come to America. When did a person begin to emerge from that fantastical sea of childhood onto the dry land of adult existence? Elizabeth, now at eleven, was standing at the edge of that ocean, heels still in the water, already missing the pull of the surf. It was easy to feel clumsy and ungainly in the new world of adulthood; breathable air must feel thin and insubstantial compared to childhood's all-enveloping sea.

Nora turned to her niece. "Shall we have some music?"

No response. Nora switched the radio on anyway, speeding past the stations blasting bright commercial patter, finally landing on some traditional music, Raidió na Gaeltachta, the Irish-language station. Just what she was looking for. Not a word of English. No chance that they'd hear urgent updates about a nationwide search for a missing child. At least not in any language Elizabeth would understand. The tune ended, and the presenter began chatting away about the selection they'd just heard. Elizabeth's head snapped around. She listened intently for a few seconds. "What is that?"

"It's Irish. The language people speak here."

Elizabeth considered for a moment. "I thought people here spoke English."

"Well, yes—they do. But some people speak mostly Irish, especially in places like where we're going."

Elizabeth listened to the radio presenter again. "It sounds"—she spent a few seconds trying to dredge up the right word—"soft."

Nora had to agree. Irish had always struck her as such an expressive, musical language, and she regretted not knowing more of it.

After four hours on the road, they were coming up on the outskirts of Donegal town. They stopped at a station shop and bought some anemic-looking sandwiches and crisps, apples and bananas, bottled water, and a few biscuits. Past Donegal town, the road wound down along the coast, and cut inland at Mountcharles. Elizabeth kept her face to the window. At Bruckless, it was time to take a break from driving. Nora turned off the main road, and headed down a quiet, wooded lane that led to a rocky beach. She parked the car at the edge of the wood.

"Come on," she said. "Let's take our sandwiches down to the shore."

Elizabeth looked skeptical, but followed her out onto a rocky peninsula that trailed out into Bruckless Bay. They sat on a pair of flat boulders and set out the sandwiches and drinks. The briny smell of seaweed filled the air—not the strong, rotting odor that sometimes came at low tide, but a cleaner, lighter scent. It was a mystery why some coasts were more malodorous than others. Nora pointed across the water to a house high up on the side of the hill. "See that house? It's very like a place we stayed one summer when I was your age. Your mama would have been about six or seven."

In fact, the more Nora studied the surrounding hills, the more she became convinced that this was the very place where the seal had rescued Tríona from drowning. It must have rained sometime during those summer weeks, yet Nora couldn't recall even a single cloudy day. She and Tríona had spent hours climbing among the rocks, searching for sea glass and other treasure. That shard of blue-and-white delft in her treasure box had come from somewhere along this coast. Visiting the grandparents in Clare every summer was never a holiday in the usual sense. There were eggs to be gathered, cows to be milked, garden patches to be weeded, honey to be collected from hives. Here in Donegal, there had been no responsibilities, only endless days of exploring and make-believe. She had dreamt of shipwrecks all summer long.

"Look!" Elizabeth's voice had an excited edge.

Nora shielded her eyes against the strong afternoon sun, and peered out over the water to see a dark head bobbing just above the calm surface. "I see it."

The seal swam closer, evidently curious about the pale creatures stretched out on the rocks. As it drew near, Nora could see that the left side of the animal's face was damaged. It regarded them with a single dark and glassy eye.

Elizabeth jumped to her feet and ventured as far out on the spit as she could go, feeling her way over the rocks, never taking her eyes from the sleek head in the water. Girl and seal studied each other with intense interest. The creature's nose and whiskers twitched as it huffed the air for clues about the human child, and Elizabeth's hand remained half-raised in a gesture of greeting. Then the seal began to spin, rising up out of the water in a joyful dance.

Nora watched, fascinated, thinking of all the instinctive, animal ways of knowing that humans had begun to forget as soon as they had words. After a few moments of silent communication, the seal's head slid beneath the surface and disappeared from view, leaving only a circling eddy where it had been. Elizabeth stood searching the water for a few more minutes before she turned around. Nora studied her face as she trudged back up to the flat rocks.

"Were you saying something to that seal?"

"No!" Elizabeth's newly exposed ears glowed bright red.

"It's all right, Lizzabet. Your mother used to talk to them. She said they didn't understand when she spoke English, but they seemed to have a bit of Irish." Elizabeth looked up, as if she had just confirmed something that had lurked in the murky realm of suspicion for a long time.

That was exactly what Tríona had said. Nora had completely forgotten until the words came out of her mouth. Strange, how revisiting a place could bring back memories in that way. The smell of the seaweed, the texture of the stone underfoot, the way the light hit the water at a certain angle—if she closed her eyes, she could see pale limbs underwater, hair floating upward, a pair of coal-black eyes looming close.

Back in the car, the radio sprang to life with the engine. As they reached Carrick, a tune began flowing from the speakers, and Nora knew she had heard it somewhere before. The fiddler slid his bow along the strings, expertly teasing great feeling from the notes, starting low and rising up in exhilarating waves.

It was the same tune Cormac had sent her in his e-mail the other night, she was certain.

When the music ended, the presenter began chatting in Irish, from which she could only pick out a few words—*go hailainn,* wonderful; *an fhidil,* the fiddle. The tune's title went by in a flash. Something *i Meiriceá*—in America. He had promised her the name of the tune the next time they met. It wouldn't be long now.

Outside Carrick, they hurtled by a handmade banner fluttering from a pair of stakes at the roadside. Nora registered what it said only after they'd gone past: FÁILTE FIDLEIRI!—WELCOME FIDDLERS! FIDDLE WEEK IN THE GLEN.

When they reached Glencolumbkille, the post office was closed, but the publican at the *ósta*n, the inn next door, knew the Maguire place.

"It's about three miles outside The Glen, just beyond a little place called Port na Rón," the man said. "The village itself mightn't be on your map. There's no one living in it for years now. But head out this road, anyway, until you come to a fork. Keep to the left there, and the Maguire place will be on your left as you go down that lane, kind of up under a hill. You can't miss it. And if you get all the way to Maghera, you'll know you've missed the turn entirely."

"Do you know Joseph Maguire?"

"Sure, wasn't I in school with him? Josie, we used to call him, in them days. His auntie Julia was our schoolteacher. She's the one left the house to him there about three years ago. We heard he was off in Bolivia or somewhere. Never thought he'd come back. But that's the thing about Donegal people, you see. They'll go off, for years sometimes. To America, Australia, Scotland, all sorts of foreign shores. But they always come back. Something about this place that draws them—something in the blood. You know, it's amazing. Maguire's after having a fierce rake of visitors lately. I was terrible sorry to hear about his trouble, taking ill like that—he's still in hospital beyond in Killybegs. I'm surprised you didn't know, being a friend of the family, like."

Nora saw the gossip hunger in the eyes that peered over the glasses at her, and she scrambled to make up a credible lie. "I have to confess—I don't actually know him. He's a third cousin to my husband, something like that. My daughter and I are up for the Fiddle Week—my husband is joining us at the weekend. We're staying with friends up in Ardara, but I was supposed to call in, if we were passing this way. Still in hospital, though—that's a pity."

"I'm sure he'll be up for visitors soon. But aren't you lucky to have friends in these parts? When you came in, I was afraid you might ask if we'd any rooms left. I would have hated to turn away such a lovely wee woman as yourself."

Down the road where the barman had directed them, the car climbed up past the church and out of the Glen. Houses were few and far between beyond the village, surrounded on all sides by treeless, mountainy bog. They passed shallow black cuttings, clamps of turf walled in by pallets held together with rope and netting to foil thieves, and thatched with rushes to fend off unforgiving wind and rain. Stone and wire fences hiked up over the hills, marking narrow fields for grazing sheep. The place looked barren, but Nora knew that—at least culturally speaking—nothing could be further from the truth. From the poorest places came the richest music—it had always been that way.

Suddenly she felt so tired that it was difficult to keep her hands on the steering wheel. She looked over at Elizabeth in the passenger seat. Was she doing the right thing, coming here, landing on Cormac without a word of warning? "Hang in there," she said to Elizabeth. "We're almost there."

As she spoke, Nora felt a wave of exhaustion verging on dizziness. She reached up and touched the bandage on her forehead. More than anything in the world, she longed to sleep, but a host of worries pressed down on her. Around the next curve, they came to a Y-junction. Turning to the left, Nora coaxed the car along a rough patch of road. There it was, ahead on the left, a hill with a house tucked under it, just as the barman had said. Nora had never been so glad to arrive anywhere. The long dusk was beginning to settle. There were two cars parked outside, and she could see a light through the windows. Cormac was home, then. She pulled in behind his Jeep and turned to Elizabeth.

"Let me go in first—" She saw trepidation in her niece's face. "Don't worry. I'll be right back, I promise."

Elizabeth didn't look up. She picked at the zipper on her backpack, and Nora noticed for the first time how the skin around her nails was chewed ragged. And the child never let go of that bloody pack—what on earth was she carrying around in there?

The door of the house was open as Nora rounded the corner, and the tinny noise of an old fiddle recording trickled out through the open door. She peered inside and saw the back of Cormac's head, and felt a breaker of homesickness so strong it threatened to knock her down. He was sitting on an old leather sofa in front of the fireplace. She was just about to call out when a mop of ginger hair lifted from the crook of his shoulder. "Please don't, Roz," she heard him say. "Don't cry. Everything's going to be all right."

The ground seemed to roil under her feet, and the music grew louder. She gripped the doorjamb, trying to remain upright, but felt her knees buckle. The floor came up abruptly to meet her.

Nora felt herself drifting in and out of consciousness for what seemed like a very long time. A damp cloth against her face, the sound of whispering voices. She had the same sensation as when she was a child, riding in the backseat when the adults thought she was asleep. The image of a car pricked her into alertness, and she sat up abruptly.

"Where's Elizabeth? I left her in the car—"

Cormac's voice was near, mingled notes of worry and relief: "Elizabeth is right here, Nora." The child's face loomed close as he continued. "You've only been out for a minute or two. We just got you inside the house." His fingers brushed her face. "Rest awhile."

Nora felt small, cold fingers press into her hand. No sign of the ginger-haired female. Maybe she was imagining things. She seemed to be drifting away again on the tide.

It must have been some time later when the chiming of a clock awakened her. Elizabeth was curled up at the other end of the sofa, draped in a blanket and fast asleep. Nora felt someone stir in the chair beside her. She looked up to find the ginger-haired woman, the one who'd been crying on Cormac's shoulder. She was dry-eyed now, and spoke in a whisper: "How are you feeling?"

"Better." Nora tried to sit up without disturbing Elizabeth. Her muscles were still stiff and sore from the impact of the crash. "How long was I asleep?"

"About an hour and a quarter," the woman said. "I'm Roz Byrne, by the way—colleague of Cormac's from UCD, and extraneous houseguest. He's just gone into the kitchen—I'll send him out to you, shall I?" She retreated through the sitting-room door, and Cormac emerged a second later.

"Nora—" He knelt on the floor and brought his face close. "How are you?"

"I'm all right. You must wonder what we're doing here."

"You've hardly had a chance to explain anything. Including that—" He gestured to the bandage on her head. "I was beginning to think you might have a concussion."

"No—it's just a scratch. Really." Nora glanced back at Elizabeth, still slumbering deeply. It was amazing how much younger children could look while they were asleep. "It's a very long story. Any chance of a cup of tea?"

Cormac helped her up, circling an arm around her waist as they moved across the room. Out in the hall, he stopped, pressing her against the wall with the length of his body, cradling the back of her head, kissing her with gently parted lips until she was floating, breathless with desire. He pressed his forehead against hers. "Sorry. But God, how I missed you, Nora. It seems like decades since you left."

She raised a hand to touch his face. "I know. Lifetimes."

4

Harry Shaughnessy's clothing was laid out on the table at the center of the crime lab. Frank Cordova stared at the bloodstains on the sweatshirt—that's what they seemed to be, here under the bright lights of the lab—heavy, fresh stains around the neckline, and several large, lighter areas under the white letters spelling out "Galliard." What was Harry Shaughnessy doing with a sweatshirt from Peter Hallett's alma mater? Frank reminded himself that the shirt hadn't necessarily belonged to Hallett—he could think of several other people in the Twin Cities who might belong to the same alumni association, including Marc Staunton. Harry might have picked the shirt up at the Goodwill, or the St. Vincent de Paul shop on West Seventh Street.

Jackie Smart, the forensic scientist, was going over the sweatshirt inch by inch with magnifier, tweezers, tape, and swabs, on the hunt for DNA. "Somebody said you knew this guy," she said.

"Everybody knew him." It was true. Generations of Saint Paul cops knew Harry Shaughnessy. He'd haunted Rice Park ever since he got back from Korea in 1953. Never the same after. And there were plenty like him—more after every war—sleeping under bridges, unable to cope with "normal" life, men who took to raving on street corners or quietly drinking themselves to death. Probably plenty of others, too—playing golf, puttering around in garages and basement wood shops—who were never the same either. Most of them just managed to hide it better than Harry Shaughnessy had. "Have you tested these spots that look like bloodstains?"

"The police lab did the presumptive—it's definitely blood. There wasn't much from the accident, the ME said. The vic's heart stopped pretty much on impact. To me, those stains under the letters look quite a bit older than the accident anyway. See how the surface here is all cracked, and completely flaked off in places? What do you make of that?" She pointed to a small scrap of paper next to the sweatshirt—a handwritten note, gray with grime, and worn tissue-thin. "I found it in the pocket."

Frank studied the faint block letters, written in blue ballpoint: *I know what you did. Hidden Falls 11 pm tonite.* It sounded like a threat. Hidden Falls tonight, or else. Or else what? I'll tell where you buried Natalie Russo? The note made nailing down the DNA evidence even more crucial.

He said: "Jackie, can you get wearer DNA on all these things?"

"Sure, I can try—we usually get pretty good samples under the arms, around the collar."

Frank picked up the nearly new pair of black running shoes, examined their slightly muddy soles. "What about these?"

"Again, the presumptive for blood comes up positive; we have to do more tests to see if it matches the blood on the shirt. It's kinda funny—the vic was wearing all these clothes, but not those shoes; they were stuffed in his backpack. He had on these lovely size twelves." She held up a battered pair of high-top sneakers. "The running shoes would have been way too small for him. But somebody wore them—I found white cotton threads inside when I was swabbing for DNA. There was quite a bit of dirt in the treads, too. When I'm done here, I'll send all this over to trace. You can have a look—"

She waved a thumb over her shoulder, and Frank leaned down to peer through the eyepiece of a microscope at varicolored crystals of soil particles, dull fragments of decaying leaves, and dozens of small, wrinkled spheres. They looked exactly like the seeds from Holly Blume's poster, the one with a picture of that rare plant she'd identified from Tríona Hallett's hair. *Plants are clever stowaways,* Holly had said. *They're all about survival.* All at once, he felt a thousand flashbulbs going off in his brain, and the usual sour feeling in his stomach was suddenly swallowed up in a surge of hope.

"Listen, Jackie, can you do me a favor, and run a DNA comparison on samples from these clothes against these two cases?" He scribbled names and case file numbers in his notebook, then tore out the sheet and handed it to her. "I promise, I'll fill out all the proper forms as soon as I can. And one more thing, too—can you take a sample of that dirt from the shoe treads and send it over to Holly Blume, the forensic botanist at the University?"

"And how soon do you need this done?"

"Yesterday. No, the day before—thanks, Jackie. I'll owe you one."

5

Garda Detective Garrett Devaney had just packed the last item in the boot of the car, his daughter Róisín's fiddle case, resting lightly on top of their other luggage. He was always amazed at the apparent weightlessness of an instrument that could bring forth so much. "You're sure that's everything now?" he asked Róisín.

"Yes, Daddy." She rolled her eyes, as if asking who should be more nervous about this trip—dear old dad, or the one who was actually going to be playing in competition. He'd tried to downplay it, his anxiety over this milestone, but it somehow seemed the measure of him, both as a teacher and as a father. He tried not to let it show, but Róisín understood exactly what her taking up the fiddle meant to him. She was determined not to let him down, and therein lay the danger.

His wife Nuala had tried to ease his mind a bit the previous night, slipping into bed beside him. "Just look at her face when she plays, Gar. She's going to bowl them over. I wish I'd had that kind of confidence at her age."

He hadn't said anything, but his thoughts were troubled. Certainly, by rights, Róisín should bowl them over. But what if she didn't? You were always at the mercy of adjudicators at these things—narrow-minded people, some of them, with their own parochial tastes. Róisín had talked about nothing but this Fiddle Week for months. She wanted to compete, and in the end, he couldn't refuse her. He often observed her, head tilted to one side over the fiddle's round belly, a picture of concentration. He had watched the secret notes seep into her ears, and then into her soul, and understood that what he was doing was only window dressing. What she needed to learn could never be taught, not directly. The music was a thing that could only be grown into, like a well-worn pair of britches or an oversized jumper.

Fortunately, Róisín had fallen in love with the sound of the fiddle, just as he had, with all its shades and feelings. No amount of technical ability could substitute for that. She had become a hunter of those quicksilver flashes of genius that entered the soul and came out the fingers—the enchantment, the *draíocht*. All he could do was to show her his own way of recognizing those rare moments, how to receive them when they came.

Traditional tunes were only simple auld music, some argued. Notes you could learn out of a book. But the people who made such claims were not standing beside him as he turned off the light in Róisín's room, as he looked back from the doorway, watching her fingers stretch to fourth position as she slept. You didn't get that from any fucking book.

He had worried and fretted for weeks about whether the competition was a good idea, but decided that in the end, for a child like Róisín, at least it couldn't do much damage. She had to develop confidence in her own ear, her own taste in music, from listening to others. She hadn't even heard many fiddle players, apart from himself, and it was time to start expanding her musical world. The idea that she might find someone whose style she admired more than his own had not occurred to him until this very moment. What would he do then, if she found someone else to look up to and emulate? Knowing the field, he decided to take his chances.

Róisín waggled a hand in front of his face. "Da," she said, "snap out of it, will you? We have to go." He focused, and saw her looking up at him with an expression that held both anticipation and a bit of mischief. Cheeky, as well as smart.

Nuala came out of the house to see them off, giving Róisín a squeeze and a kiss on top of the head. She wouldn't be able to do that much longer, the way the child was growing. Róisín was going to be twelve in a few months. How had that happened?

"I'll be rooting for you, sweetheart," Nuala said, speaking over Róisín's head straight at him. "I know you'll do your very best. I'm already so proud of you for that."

Devaney raised his hand out the window as they drove away. At moments like this, he usually felt as if he didn't deserve to be enjoying life so much. There had to be a stumbling block down the road. He could feel it waiting for him. And yet he carried on—did his job, lived his life. What other choice did he have?

Garrett and Róisín were hardly gone when the phone rang. Nuala Devaney picked up, thinking it might be her husband, having forgotten something. But the voice on the other end was unfamiliar. Not to mention female, and American. "Hello—I was trying to reach Detective Devaney?"

Something to do with work, then, Nuala thought. It wasn't purely American, the accent. Her ears had become finely tuned over the years to strange voices on the phone. Being married to a policeman forced you to act the detective, whether you wanted to or not. "Sorry, he's not available just at the minute—"

"I hate to trouble him at home, but he said to call anytime."

Of course he had. They'd argued about that endlessly—how he let people of every description ring their house at all hours. She had tried to make him understand the danger, and the calls had mostly stopped—until now. "If you'd like to leave your name, I could pass along a message."

"No, it's really—" The caller was trying to decide whether to ask for a mobile number, and eventually thought better of it. Just as well. There was no way she was giving out Garrett's unlisted mobile to a stranger. Could be some tout who wouldn't give a second thought to dragging him away from his Fiddle Week with Róisín. They'd been planning this trip for too long, and Róisín had worked much too hard for it all to be spoiled.

The caller must have sensed her resistance. "Why don't I just try again later? Thanks for your help."

After she set the phone down, Nuala's hand lingered on the receiver. What help? She'd put up roadblocks right and left. Now she had two choices: she could ring Garrett and see what he wanted to do, or she could do nothing at all.

There had been no message. Surely it couldn't be that important, could it?

6

Frank Cordova stared down at the items on his desk, just delivered by Tom and Eleanor Gavin. Along with the news that Nora was back in Ireland, they'd brought in three manila envelopes she'd prepared for him.

The first contained several items discovered at the river by the Cambodian fisherman, Seng Sotharith: a dirt-encrusted Nokia cell phone, and a handwritten note. *I know what you did. Hidden Falls 11 pm tonite.* The wording was the same as the note from Harry Shaughnessy's sweatshirt pocket; it even had the same block capitals in blue ballpoint. Was the extra just a backup copy—or had somebody sent the same note to two different people?

In the second envelope was Nora's account of her meeting with Harry Shaughnessy outside the library, a description of his bloodstained sweatshirt. She obviously didn't know what had happened to Harry; she was asking Frank to find him.

The third manila envelope held a sheaf of articles about the Nash murders in Maine. Nora had circled the name of the lead detective on the case, a Gordon MacLeish.

He had just ended a call to the Maine State Police when his phone rang again. It was Nora.

"Frank, thank God you're all right. I've been trying to reach you for days. Did Karin Bledsoe tell you I was trying to get in touch? She would only tell me that you were on leave."

"I got tied up—some family business." He couldn't bring himself to talk about Chago, about the events that had landed him in the hospital. He pushed it all away. "Everything's okay. Your parents were just here, dropping off your packages—they said you were back in Ireland."

"And did they explain why I had to come back? Elizabeth ran away, Frank. She ditched Peter and Miranda when they arrived in Dublin, and she came looking for me. I couldn't let them send her back to her father. I couldn't."

"So where are you now?"

She hesitated. "We're okay, Frank. We're safe."

"You haven't had any contact with Hallett?"

"No. I haven't heard anything at all. I don't even know whether he's contacted the police. If he suspects that I have Elizabeth, I can imagine what he's telling people—that I kidnapped her. But it's not true—and this time I have witnesses to prove it. I tried getting in touch with a detective I know over here—no luck so far. That's why I need your help, Frank. If you could talk to someone here, explain the situation, tell them Elizabeth is safe, that I'm not a danger to her—"

"Somebody here must have a contact in the Irish police. I'll get in touch with the FBI and Interpol too, see if we can't get some help tracking Hallett. You should have told me you were looking for Harry Shaughnessy—"

"I tried, but I couldn't reach you, Frank. You have to find him, and ask him—"

"I'm afraid we can't ask him anything. He was hit by a car, trying to cross Shepard Road. Killed instantly." He could hear an intake of breath on the other end.

Nora finally spoke. "He was running from me, Frank. He thought I wanted something from him—and I did. That sweatshirt he was wearing—"

"—from Galliard. We've got it in the lab right now. The sweatshirt and a pair of shoes he was carrying both tested positive for blood. We're checking against samples from Tríona and Natalie right now. It might be a break for us."

"I've been thinking about that, Frank, and it's too good to be true. I'm not trusting it, somehow. Even if the blood turns out to be a match to Tríona or Natalie, Peter is far too clever to leave such damning evidence. That sweatshirt can't be his."

"Let's wait for the DNA results. You have to admit we're doing a lot better than we were this time last week. If this is Tríona's phone you got from the fisherman, we'll finally have our first link to the primary crime scene. And even possible blood evidence. That note—"

"I think it may have been what sent Tríona down to the river that night. Maybe she thought the person who sent it could tell her what happened the night Natalie disappeared."

"I thought of that too. We found a second note in Harry's pocket, identical to that one—same words, same writing."

Nora hesitated. "Two notes? That doesn't make sense. Unless Tríona and the person who wore the sweatshirt both got one—"

"Which could mean a third party?"

"Maybe. Let's see what the DNA results say. What about the murder case from Maine? And that anonymous letter addressed to Peter—what do you suppose he could have done to be threatened like that? I can't figure out a connection."

"I've got a call in to the Maine State Police. If I hear anything, I'll keep you posted." He felt the stabbing pain in his stomach again, and doubled over, hoping he hadn't made any audible noise. But Nora must have heard something.

"Are you sure you're all right, Frank? When I couldn't reach you, I started to worry. You'd tell me, wouldn't you, if there was something wrong?"

He cut her off. "My brother was sick."

"Is he all right, Frank?"

He didn't answer her immediately, but there was no way to avoid it now. "No, he's not all right, Nora. He died."

"Oh, Frank, I'm so sorry—"

"You didn't know." He didn't expect her to understand. How could she? He'd never told her anything about his family. And now the subject was closed.

"I know all about your crash, Nora. About the bottle jamming the brake pedal. There were no prints on it but yours. But the crime scene investigators did find fingerprints on the car, above the driver's side window—"

Nora was silent for a moment. "That could have been the security guard."

"What security guard?"

"I went to the Cambodian place on University, and followed Seng Sotharith to where he lives in Frogtown, to see if I could talk to him. Some neighborhood hooligans were trying to spook me. A guy in a security uniform happened to be there, and he chased them off. He was driving a pickup—I didn't get a license number, but the patch on his shirt said 'Centurion.' The prints are probably his—Peter wouldn't be careless enough to leave prints, you know that."

"He tried to kill you, Nora. You know it, and I know it. If he finds out where you are, that you've got Elizabeth, he'll come after you again. He's not going to give up—"

"He won't find us. We're safe here."

Was it something in her voice? Frank suddenly knew where she was. With him—Mr. Serious. He felt gripped by a twisting jealousy. "Just tell me one thing. This friend of yours over there—he's not a cop, is he?"

Her voice was quiet. "Frank, please don't do this. I care about you. You were the one person who stuck with me through everything, who kept me from going under—the only one. But I wasn't thinking straight that night we were together—I wasn't thinking at all, to tell the truth. I don't want to lose everything we had because of one reckless night."

It was clear that she would never remember that night in the same way he had. Not ever. He couldn't think how to respond.

"Frank, say something. Please."

But there was nothing more to say. He pulled the phone from his ear and pressed the button to hang up.

Cormac had followed the sound of Nora's voice to the kitchen. It was late—almost one in the morning—but he could have sworn she was speaking to someone. As he approached, he heard a bit of her end of the conversation: *I don't want to lose everything we had because of one reckless night.* A pause. *Frank, say something. Please.*

He stood at the door, conflicted about whether to knock or to hold back, not wanting to make it so obvious that he'd overheard. There were clearly some things she was not telling him. How easily the seeds of doubt and jealousy were planted. He hesitated a moment longer and pushed through the kitchen door.

"You're up, too?" She gestured to the phone lying on the table. "I was just talking to Frank Cordova."

"Any news?"

"Everything comes in such small increments. We may have found Tríona's cell phone, which could help pinpoint the crime scene. They also have a bloodstained sweatshirt from Peter's college—they have to run DNA tests to see if the blood could be Tríona's."

"Well, that would be something, wouldn't it? I mean, all this time you've been looking for evidence—"

"Yes, but there's something not quite right about it. They don't know for sure that it's Peter's sweatshirt, and I just don't believe he would be that careless—about anything. He plans things, figures out every angle. Making a stupid mistake like that—it isn't like him. Trust me, I know from experience how he manages every last detail. I haven't told you the half of it."

"Will you tell me now?" He pointed to the bandage on her forehead. "I'd especially like to know how you got that."

"Only if you promise not to lecture me." He held up his hand as if to swear, and she continued: "My car went off the road. I think someone jammed a water bottle under the brake pedal—"

He couldn't help reacting. "Jesus Christ, Nora."

"You promised not to lecture. There's no proof, of course. No fingerprints but mine. Nothing to say the bottle didn't just roll under the pedal by accident. Or that I didn't put it there, trying to incriminate Peter."

Cormac glanced up the stairs where Elizabeth was asleep. "We have to talk about what to do if he shows up here. He could be headed in this direction right now."

"How would he know where to look?"

"Sooner or later he's going to be able to connect us, Nora—if he's half as clever as you say. At least a half-dozen people in Dublin knew I was coming up here." He drew back and looked at her. "How did you find this place?"

"I stopped at the *óstan* in Glencolumbkille—but I made up a story, about bringing my daughter up for Fiddle Week, about your father being a distant relation—"

He spoke quietly: "Still, you're an American, traveling with a child. I'm not criticizing, Nora. All I'm saying is that it won't be difficult to track you, if he's really intent upon it. We're only being prudent to realize that. We should have a plan, a rendezvous spot, in case we're separated. There's an abandoned fishing village called Port na Rón just the other side of the headland from here. Roz told me about some caves under the rocks on the far side of the bay. That might be a good place to meet, even stay for a while if we had to."

Nora looked at him curiously. "You've been thinking about this."

"No such thing as too careful." He reached for a bag under the table and pulled out a pair of walkie-talkies. "Mobile coverage can be spotty up here, so I thought we could try these—I use them on excavations. They're on the same frequency, good up to twenty-six miles. We could each carry one."

"You really think he'll come here?"

"I think we have to be prepared for it. Would he have reported Elizabeth missing?"

"Probably," Nora said. "He must have been surprised when she ran away, because he knew I was still in the States. But Elizabeth didn't. I imagine he'd go to the police—he's always had great luck with them so far." After a moment she added: "Most of them, anyway."

"If your picture's likely to show up on the television, it might be best to steer clear of civilization. Keep out of sight."

"I do have the offer of a boat—" She tried to force a smile, but couldn't. "Oh, Cormac, I never meant to put any of this on you—"

He leaned closer. "Will you stop? Your troubles are my troubles, Nora. We'll get through this—we just need to be vigilant. Let me show you how to find the caves at Port na Rón." He reached into his bag for a map and flipped to the area showing the cluster of houses and outbuildings where they sat, with long, narrow plots of bog and pastureland going up over the mountain. "Go over the headland to the south here, and you'll come to the village. You'll see a rocky beach. The caves I mentioned are here, around the south side of the harbor. I've got to go see on my father in hospital tomorrow morning; you and Elizabeth could go over and have a look at the caves while I'm away. I can stop on my way back and get some extra provisions to stash there if we need them." He drew back and looked at her. "Has Elizabeth told you why she ran away?" He was thinking of the long, fair hairs and the lone shoe he'd found under the cot at the selkie cottage. "Maybe she knows something she's not telling. Children notice a lot more than we realize."

Nora shook her head. "I've tried, but I can't seem to draw her out. Once in a while I get the impression she wants to talk, but feels as if she can't—maybe out of loyalty to her father. In spite of everything, he is still her father. That'll never change with wishing, unfortunately."

Cormac put his hand over Nora's, and let his glance stray to the hall that led to his father's empty room. "No, I don't suppose it will."

7

Elizabeth awakened to a room bathed in light. Heavy bedclothes pressed down the length of her body, and the air smelled strange—cold and musty, damp. Nothing had felt real since they arrived here. She had no recollection of getting to this room on her own—maybe someone had carried her. Opening her eyes a crack, she could make out the dark outlines of flower-patterned wallpaper, the bulk of a wardrobe at the foot of the bed. She sat up slowly and glanced around. From the small window she could see down a driveway, out to the road. Would they just stay here, never go back to America? If they were supposed to be hiding, this strange, bare place didn't seem like a very good spot. This house was odd; its windows were small and close to the floor, like something from a fairy story. Old black-and-white pictures crammed the walls, and there were bookcases everywhere, even up in this bedroom. She tilted her head sideways to read the titles of the books on the nearest shelf: *The Sea Folk. The Selkie in Folklore, Myth, and Legend.*

Yesterday already seemed like a dream, waking up to the sound of the sea outside at the Donovans' house, then the long drive to this place, and stopping at that spit of land where the one-eyed seal came swimming up to her. It was just as if they had never been apart. Her brain said it wasn't possible—her old friend from Useless Bay couldn't have followed her all the way to this place. Ireland must be at least halfway around the world from Seattle. But how many seals had such an identical star-shaped spot? And the way it had watched her, too—bobbing high out of the water, just like her friend back at Useless Bay. She wanted to call out to it in that strange, inhuman language she had sometimes heard it use, but she had not made a sound.

A dull pressure in her abdomen said it was time to find the bathroom. She slid out of bed and crept down the hall, holding her breath when her foot set off a loud creak from one of the floorboards. The bathroom door had a rippled glass window; inside was a deep bathtub with feet, and one of those high, old-fashioned toilets with a chain for a handle. She slipped inside and shut the door, imagining that everyone downstairs could hear her moving about. Each embarrassing noise—the click of the latch, the squeaking hinges, and especially the hollow splash as she emptied her bladder—seemed magnified in the echoing room.

While washing her hands, Elizabeth examined her newly shorn head in the mirror, pulling at the uneven tufts, remembering the weight of each handful of long hair as it was cut, how it looked at the bottom of that wastebasket. She had never held any desire to be part of the secret, grown-up world, and had focused all her energy the past few months on refusing to be dragged over that threshold. But the transformation was happening anyway, against her will. She didn't know the person who looked back at her from the mirror. At times it felt like there was someone else, something else inside her—a dangerous, wild creature who might come screeching out if she opened her mouth.

She opened the bathroom door and stood listening to a pair of voices from downstairs. One was Cormac—was he Nora's boyfriend? From the way he'd acted last night, she thought he might be. Elizabeth tiptoed to the top of the stairs and saw him in the hallway below talking to Roz, the woman they'd met last night. Cormac was speaking to her now in a low voice, as if he didn't want Nora to hear. "Please don't go, Roz. You don't have to leave."

"I do, Cormac. I can't stay here."

"He could come back to himself anytime."

Elizabeth wondered who they were talking about.

"Please, Cormac—we both know he won't. I'm not sure I can take that look in his eyes, day after day."

"What about your work here—do you not want to go back to the selkie cottage?"

"I've finished all the interviews I had planned. I'm never going to find Mary Heaney, Cormac. She just became an excuse to stay on—"

Roz began to cry, and Cormac put his arms around her. Elizabeth's stomach began to squeeze tight. Maybe he wasn't Nora's boyfriend after all. She went back to the bedroom, unsure whether she should go downstairs, and remembering another conversation she'd overheard three days ago. Her dad hadn't known she was on the landing, but she had heard every word they said.

"I can't believe you don't see what she's up to. All this acting out, trying to get your attention, just when we're supposed to be going away? It's her way of

getting Daddy all to herself again. That's what she's wanted from the beginning."

"She's only a kid, Miranda."

"You really don't see it, do you? I can't believe you're so blind—"

"That's enough. Something could have happened to her down at the river."

"Nothing happened."

"All right, maybe nothing did happen, but what was she doing, running off like that? Did you say something?"

"Oh, that's rich. The kid runs off, and naturally I'm to blame. Maybe it had nothing to do with me. Maybe she's more like her mother than you thought—"

Elizabeth hadn't actually seen the slap, but its sharp noise still seemed to reverberate in her ears. When her father spoke again, his voice was almost unrecognizable. *"Don't ever let me hear you talk like that again, do you hear me? Stay away from my daughter."*

Remembering that confrontation, Elizabeth began to feel queasy again. Miranda and her father had never argued like that before, at least not that she knew. It was all her fault, for running away. Why did she have to go and find all that stuff on the Internet and mess everything up? It was better not to know. She missed the empty space inside her that was now filled with doubts and questions. All she wanted was for everything to get back to normal.

She crawled back into the narrow bed, pulling the covers over her head. Maybe running away had been a mistake. She knew what they were all thinking, Nora and everyone else, that she was running away from her dad, but it wasn't true. He got angry sometimes, but he had reasons. She was always messing up, doing stupid things—like climbing up on that wall. He was trying to protect her. That's why he got mad when Miranda said those things. He couldn't have hurt Mama—if he had, he would be locked up, wouldn't he? You couldn't do things like that and not go to jail. She felt the questions crowding, pushing into one another inside her. Nora, her dad, Miranda, her grandparents—they all said something different, and it couldn't all be true. Somebody had to be lying.

She hadn't actually planned to run away at the airport until they were walking off the plane. What did Miranda mean—*maybe she's more like her mother than you thought*? Sometimes when she lay in bed at night, with darkness close around her, certain memories came back, mostly as she was drifting off to sleep, or just waking. Suddenly she felt a string of words rising up inside her, each a separate bubble, bursting as it hit the surface: *Lizzabet—Mama's tired.*

And then it all came back, like water under a door, rising around her ankles in a flood. All the days Mama was so tired she couldn't wake up. Elizabeth remembered wandering through the silent house—frightened by the noises from the icemaker, looking up at the sink piled high with dishes, hallways and bedrooms strewn with toys and clothes. Whole days playing alone in her room, eventually having to brave the rumbling refrigerator for something to eat. Then she would go back into the bedroom and try shaking Mama's shoulder again. Why wouldn't she wake up?

The damp air under the covers pressed down on her, until she had to throw off the blankets and take a breath of cool outside air. With it came the smell of toast and bacon, floating up from below, awakening something in her—a hollow, cavernous hunger she hadn't felt for days, and with it a sharp memory of her dad making toast on Sunday mornings, cut into triangles just the way she liked it, dripping with butter. Elizabeth wrapped her arms around her stomach, fighting the hunger inside. She missed her dad so much. Running away had been a mistake.

8

Truman Stark always took the back streets home from downtown. Ninth to Broadway to Grove Street, up past police headquarters on Olive, along the tracks at Phalen Boulevard to Clarence. From his bedroom window, he'd watched the workers put up the shiny new building on the corner. The Bureau of Criminal Apprehension, the BCA. Sort of like the state FBI. They thought they were so special, the people who worked there. He had watched them, talking, laughing, getting into cars at the end of their shifts. He even followed a few of them, once in a while. They were just regular people, like him. Nobody special at all. So why did they get to work at a place like that, while he was stuck in a parking ramp, staring at TV screens, marking time? The injustice of it all stuck in his craw, threatened to choke him every time he looked out his bedroom window.

He turned left on Clarence, knowing what would happen when he got home. What always happened: his mother would have some little chore for him, some stupid job like changing a lightbulb or running up to Walgreen's for her medicine. Or she'd want him to sit with her and watch one of her game shows, when he had more important things to do.

As long as he was out of the house, he could forget about all the stacks of junk mail and newspapers and the garbage bags full of old clothes, forget the reek of cat piss so strong from downstairs that it made his eyes water even all the way up in his room. His mother hadn't been like this when the old man was alive. It was like she'd lost a screw or something.

He saw the cops as soon as he turned the pickup into his own street. A man and a woman. Detectives. You could tell by the way they were dressed, the way they moved. The woman was smoking, but dropped the butt on the weedy boulevard when she saw his truck. That was when he remembered all the pictures tacked up on the wall in his room. He thought briefly about gunning the engine and making a run for it. But he didn't. For one thing, the street was a dead end, and besides, they'd already spotted him. He didn't have a hope of getting away. There was something else, too. Some part of him was itching to find out what they knew.

"We're looking for Elwyn T. Stark." Karin Bledsoe flashed her badge and ID. "Are you Elwyn?"

The young man squinted at her. "Nobody calls me that."

"What do they call you?

"Truman."

"All right, Truman. I'm Detective Bledsoe; this is Detective Cordova. Do you mind answering a few questions?"

"I don't mind." The kid practically grinned at her. Frank could see Karin's eyes flash, and heard her voice in his head: *You cocky little sonofabitch—who do you think you are?* They knew who he was. Stark worked for Centurion, the company that provided security at a dozen downtown parking ramps, including the one where Tríona Hallett's body had been found. They'd matched his fingerprints from the company database. Stark shifted his weight and avoided looking at the house, a posture that said he wasn't anxious to have them any closer.

"Just checking to see if you happen to know this woman." Frank held up Nora's photo, the image he'd pulled from DMV driver's license records.

Stark examined it. "Never met her."

Not quite a straight answer. "But you've seen her before?"

"Might have. I don't remember."

"You don't remember seeing her at your parking garage on Thursday afternoon? Your supervisor told us you got off at three that day."

Stark was starting to look alarmed. "What's this about?"

"Do you mind telling us where you went after work on Thursday?"

Stark looked away, uncomfortable. "I don't know. I was just driving."

"Did you stop anywhere, talk to anyone? Can anybody vouch for your whereabouts?"

"Probably not. I told you, I was just driving around."

Karin said: "We have a description of a pickup like yours at a disturbance in Frogtown just after eight that night. A security guard in a Centurion uniform chasing off a bunch of neighborhood kids with a baseball bat. Was Frogtown one of the places you just happened to be driving around?"

"Might have been. Like I said—I don't really remember. I went lots of places that night." He crossed his arms in front of him.

"You asked what this was about," Karin said. "We got your prints off the car that was involved in the Frogtown incident. The same car that crashed into a ravine at Hidden Falls a little while later that night."

"What about this person—do you ever remember seeing her?" Frank held up a photograph of Tríona Hallett, and watched Stark's face go pale. "Maybe I can refresh your memory. Her body turned up five years ago at the parking garage where you work. Ring any bells?"

Stark licked his lips nervously. "I kinda remember something like that, all right—"

Frank held up Nora's photo again. "But you're telling us you didn't follow this woman after she left your parking garage Thursday afternoon? Maybe you'd better look again."

Karin said, "I guess you thought things had died down after the murder. Maybe you didn't appreciate somebody poking around, stirring everything up again. You wanted to make sure she wasn't going to make trouble for you."

"That's bullshit. I never touched those brakes—" He stopped, too late to snatch the words back.

Frank rubbed his chin, letting Stark twist for a long couple of seconds. "Tell me, Mr. Stark, why would you jump to the conclusion that brakes had anything to do with why we're here?"

"No reason." The young man's whole body suddenly shut down.

"I'm sure I didn't mention it," Karin said. "And I don't think you did either, Detective Cordova. Looks like we'll have to go over a few details with Mr. Stark back at headquarters."

A tiny, gray-haired woman came to the screen door of the house and peered out at them. "Truman—what's going on? What do they want?"

"Nothing, Ma. Go back in the house."

The woman's voice climbed into a higher register. "Why are you people bothering my son? He's a good boy. Truman?"

Stark tucked his head to one side and barked: "Jesus Christ, Ma, just go inside and shut the fucking door!"

Standing nearly three feet away, Frank almost felt the heat of the young man's shame. Without warning, all the emotion that had been building inside him burst out: "Why try to pin it on me? Can I help it if you're not doing your job, protecting people? Where were the cops when those punks broke in here and stole my ma's TV, huh? Look at her—that stinkin' television is the only thing she's got. But when she asked about getting it back, the cops just laughed in her face. Like she was some kind of moron for wanting her own goddamn TV back. You people make me sick." He spat the last word at them. "Go ahead, drag me down to the station, give me the third degree if you want. I never did nothing to that redhead, or the other one either. You'll never prove I did."

Once they got Truman Stark down to Grove Street, it took another couple of hours to get a search warrant, but Frank eventually pushed his way past the garbage bags full of clothes and stacks of old newspapers and climbed the stairs to Stark's third-floor attic bedroom, with Karin right behind him. In contrast to the lower floors, the attic was neat and orderly, but despite air fresheners placed strategically throughout the room, the smell of cat urine still permeated. On a bookcase and table at the top of the stairs were a police scanner, a latent fingerprint kit, several types of batons, cans of pepper spray and several pairs of handcuffs, and a pair of night-vision goggles.

Karin said: "Holy shit, Frank, will you look at this stuff? I knew there was something up with the little weasel, and whaddya know—we've got us a serious cop wannabe."

"There's a good chunk of change in all this gear." Frank opened the closet door to find a crisply pressed wardrobe of official-looking blue uniform shirts, along with an ironing board and iron, and half a dozen cans of spray starch.

The double bed tucked into an alcove would have passed any boot camp quarter test. Frank had to crane his neck back to see the pictures plastered all over the sloping ceiling above it. A series of grainy black-and-white images of a woman, looking over her shoulder. Even without color there was no mistaking all that beautiful long hair, those eyes, those cheekbones, the curve of the throat.

Karin, crouched beside him, squinting up at the pictures as well. After a moment, she said, "Hey, wait a minute, isn't that—"

"Tríona Hallett," Frank said softly. "Yeah, it is."

9

Cormac sat in the chair beside his father's bed. The old man had been breathing well on his own since yesterday, the doctors said. But he still hovered in that otherworld between life and death. Cormac thought about telling his father that Roz was gone, but what good would it do, if he had no memory of her? Instead he leaned forward and said: "I might have to go away for a bit. If it happens, I wouldn't be able to visit for a few days. Just thought I should let you know. In case you can hear me. It's Cormac, by the way." No reply, just breath in, breath out. "All right—see you later, then."

When he got back to Glencolumbkille, the village seemed completely overrun with fiddle players. A flapping banner emblazoned with musical notes and spirals stretched between the shops above the street, and there was an excitement in the air that hadn't been present on his earlier trip through the village: teenagers toting instrument cases dashed across the road; knots of people gathered on street corners; shop signs advertised spare rooms turned into festival lodging, most with NO VACANCY posted over the top.

Cormac headed into the shop to stock up on tinned goods that would do in case of emergency. After finishing that part of his shopping, he turned to the hardware section, perusing the selection of heavy deadbolts and window locks, trying to remember what sort of security his aunt Julia thought necessary at Ardcrinn. Beside the deadbolts hung a few tin whistles—and a great selection of violin strings. Only in this part of the country, where fiddle players grew so thick on the ground, were violin strings among the daily staples you might find in any corner shop. He'd picked up a couple of sets, thinking he might restring that fiddle he'd found in the wardrobe in his father's room. It wasn't as if the old man was going to be able to take up the fiddle and play. But there was also nothing like music to lure a man back from the gate of the grave.

As Cormac was paying for his purchases, a dark-haired girl passed by on the path outside the shop window, deep in conversation with a man sporting a distinctive head of silver-white curls. The man's face was turned away, but there was something familiar about his bearing.

The pair appeared again as Cormac was loading his box of provisions into the back of the Jeep. This time they were headed into the pub, and he decided to follow, just out of curiosity. The pub's interior was dim after the bright day outside, but thanks to the smoking ban, at least it wasn't filled with a noxious haze of cigarette smoke. Cormac ordered a glass of ale and turned to survey the room. The silver-haired man and his young companion had found a place at the back. They'd begun to take out their instruments when Cormac's attention was pulled away by a pair of middle-aged men who stood to the bar at his elbow. The first wore a plain flat cap, the other a narrow-brimmed tweed fedora—and a broken expression.

"Never mind now, Denis, never mind," said the cap, trying to cheer his friend. "There's always next year. Your young one will catch up next year." West Kerry, Cormac surmised, from the broad accent.

But Denis the Hat was having none of it. He made a disgusted gesture. "I wouldn't mind, but that little one is only after taking up the fiddle a twelvemonth ago. Playing like that after a twelvemonth—doesn't it bate all?" He shook his head sadly and downed the shot of brandy his friend had ordered, then started in on his pint, downing nearly half of it before coming up for air. "I'll tell you one thing, Michael—" He wiped the foam from his lips with the back of a hand, pausing for dramatic effect. "When I get home, that fuckin' television is goin' straight out the window!"

Cormac turned back to the fiddle players in the corner. It was no wonder the silver-haired man was familiar; now that his eyes were used to the pub atmosphere, Cormac could see that the man in question was Garrett Devaney—the policeman he and Nora had met down in Galway. What class of coincidence was at work here? As he was often reminded, very few things were completely random. Even what humans perceived as chaos had patterns.

Devaney must be here for the Fiddle Week. That was something of a surprise. He hadn't seemed like the type who went in for music competitions. From the look of her, the girl was his daughter; maybe that was explanation enough. Cormac watched as the pair tightened their bows with an almost identical flick of the wrist, and launched into "The Pigeon on the Gate" in G minor. Cormac found himself struck by the looks that passed between them as the tune whirled along, the obvious delight they took in the music, a conversation expressed in the secret language of notes. The girl was definitely the policeman's daughter, and clearly his pupil as well. Cormac thought of his own father, lying in the bed back at the hospital, feeling again the full measure of what he had missed. Too late now. Sometimes the resentment still flared inside him, imagining what they might have had. If only. Then he thought of the story Roz had told him about his own grandparents, and the sound of those two fiddles on the old 78 recording. It was Aunt Julia who had played with his father all those years ago. Perhaps the detail was insignificant. But perhaps it was part of the complex story, the reasons why Joseph Maguire had never learned to be a father.

Cormac stood listening to the sound of two fiddles in tight unison, going note for note, and felt something inside him breaking up, cracking apart, ice on a frozen river. The winter he had held so long inside him would soon be past. His anger, once a means of protection, didn't seem to serve much purpose anymore.

Looking up as the tune finished, Devaney recognized Cormac, and raised his pint in greeting. He set down the fiddle, handing the bow to his daughter for safekeeping, and made his way through the bar patrons to Cormac's side. His face glowed a healthy pink. "Maguire, by Jaysus, how are you getting on? You're not here for the competition?"

"I'm not, no. Just visiting—relations nearby." *My father.* He still couldn't say those words in sequence. Still had trouble even thinking them.

"Is Dr. Gavin about?"

Cormac suddenly felt ears all around him, listening in. "She went home to the States for a bit." He changed the subject. "You seem to be celebrating. Good result today?"

Devaney gave his characteristic tight-lipped smile. "Ah, Róisín did well enough. But that's not why we're celebrating. No, one day into it, and she's made up her mind that competitions are a load of bollocks. I couldn't be more fuckin' delighted. You haven't the machine on you?" he asked, looking around Cormac's person for a flute case. He tipped his head in the direction of the corner. "Nice spot for a tune, that."

"Sorry, can't stay—I just came into town for a few things, and I've got to be getting back."

"Right. Well, sure—" Devaney reached for a beer mat and produced a biro to scribble down a phone number. "We're here for the week, anyway, hoping for a few tunes and a bit of *craic*. That's my mobile. Give us a shout, and we'll have a bit of music next time you're about."

Cormac looked down to the corner where Róisín sat waiting for her father to return, fingering the next tune on the neck of her fiddle. "You've taught her well."

Devaney tried to downplay the compliment. "Ah, she's coming along. You know as well as I do, teaching's got very little to do with it."

Cormac tapped the edge of the beer mat in a parting salute, then tucked it into his pocket as he headed for the door.

10

Karin Bledsoe sat on the edge of the table and addressed Truman Stark. "Okay, let's go over it once more. We've got your prints on a car that crashed because someone jammed the brakes. And you're telling us you don't know anything about it?"

"That's right."

"Come on, Truman, just tell us what happened. We can't work with you if you won't work with us."

They'd been talking to Stark for three hours. So far all he'd done was deny everything. Frank looked down at a sketch he'd made in his notebook, an oval filled with interlocking hexagons. Karin had been batting the kid around like a puma playing with a turtle. And Truman Stark did what any creature would do in that situation—he withdrew. His eyes had that watchful look of a person who'd been struck too often to trust anyone. But if he knew somebody had tampered with Nora's brakes, why wouldn't he tell them? Who was he trying to protect?

"We found the pictures, Truman—the ones of Tríona Hallett up in your bedroom. Did you enjoy making up little scenarios for the two of you to play out? What happened—did things not go quite the way you'd planned?"

Truman sat, hands in his pockets, staring at the tabletop. He hadn't asked for a lawyer , and Frank couldn't shake the notion that he wanted to give them something—but what?

Karin tried again. "What do you do with all that gear we found in your room?"

"Nothing."

"Don't give me that. I think you go out on patrol. Almost like a real cop. You think you're Superman and Batman and Spiderman all rolled into one, don't you? With your radio and your handcuffs, and your big nightstick. What happened—did you wash out of law enforcement at community college? Maybe you never made it that far."

Stark's breathing grew shallower, more agitated. "You don't know anything."

"I know it's illegal, impersonating an officer."

"I never told anybody I was a cop."

"No, just went out on patrol every night in your spiffy uniform and your shiny fake badge. That wouldn't be anything like impersonation, hell no."

"Somebody's got to—"

Karin set her face only inches from Stark's. When she spoke, her voice was deadly quiet. "What? What were you going to say? 'Somebody's got to do it?' Don't make me laugh. If we have to let you go, and I find out down the road that you've just been jerking us around, that you really did smash those women's faces in, you are going to need serious reconstructive surgery yourself, my friend. Do you get me?"

At that moment, Stark's defiance seemed to mask something else—was it shock? For a split second, Frank imagined that Truman Stark had never known exactly how Tríona Hallett died—or that she wasn't the only victim. Unless he was mistaken, Karin's tiny slip was the exact moment Truman Stark had found out. But they were still getting nowhere. He cut in: "Detective Bledsoe, can I talk to you for a minute?"

They stepped out into the corridor, and Frank kept his voice low. "Karin, this isn't working. He's not going to give us anything at this rate."

"Are you dissing my interview technique?"

"No—I just think we need to switch gears, try a different approach."

"Be my guest. You haven't exactly been keeping up in there so far—"

"Look, if you're upset with me for some reason—"

"What reason could I possibly have for being upset with you, Frank? Let's see—ignoring my phone calls? No, couldn't be that. Going off on your own, checking leads on cases we're supposed to be working together—that's not really it. Oh yeah—maybe it's the fact that your brother died, and I had to find out you even *had* a brother from Don Padgett in patrol. We're supposed to be *partners,* Frank. Does that mean anything to you? You've cut me off. You've been dancing around, trying like hell to avoid me ever since you got that fucking phone call from Dublin. You know it's true."

It was true. But he suddenly felt so weary of it all—of Karin, Nora, everything. "Look, do we have to talk about this right now? We're in the middle of something here—"

"No—*you're* in the middle of something, Frank. And I'm out in left field. I'm fucking miles away." She studied him for a few seconds. "Okay—you deal with Stark. Be my guest. I'm going upstairs to start filling out paperwork for a transfer."

"Karin—" He could hear the note of resignation in his own voice, which meant she could hear it too.

"Cheer up, Frank. I know it's a relief for you. And let's face it: I've never exactly been the sentimental type. We've both seen this coming for a while." She turned on her heel and walked away.

Frank waited a few seconds before going back in. He sat across the table from Truman Stark, and opened a file he'd been carrying with him. He read a flash of panic in the kid's eyes, but went about his business calmly, methodically.

He set a photo of Nora on the table in front of Stark. "We know this woman was in your parking garage the other day. Looking at the place they found her sister's body." A quick glance up said Truman Stark hadn't been in possession of that fact. "Yeah, sisters. Bet you wondered why she was so interested in that space. What did you think—that she was a reporter, maybe a private eye?" No eye contact. "You chased those kids away in Frogtown, kept her from getting roughed up. So I'm wondering, why you would do that if you were just going to try to harm her later? Doesn't make much sense."

"I didn't do anything."

"I'm not saying you did. But you saw something, didn't you?"

Frank had imagined a gloved hand, Peter Hallett's hand, slipping that water bottle under the brake pedal, hoping to be rid of Nora Gavin once and for all. He was so close to nailing that bastard right now, he could taste it. And at this moment, Truman Stark was all that stood in his way. Hard not to pressure the kid, but he knew that would be exactly the wrong move.

Instead he slid a glossy headshot of Tríona Hallett across the table. Stark tried not to look, but in the end, he couldn't resist.

Frank said: "Beautiful, isn't she? I could understand somebody just wanting to watch her. To admire her." No reaction. Frank continued: "Used to see her around Lowertown, didn't you? Don't worry, I'm not trying to pin anything on you. I just need information."

After a long pause, Stark mumbled: "She used to park at the garage. I'd see her on the cameras. Not every day, but pretty often."

Frank studied the young man's miserable expression. "Did you ever speak to her—at the garage or anywhere else?"

Stark shook his head wordlessly.

"But you copied her picture off the video at work. You followed her."

"It wasn't like that—"

"What was it like? Tell me." Frank waited. Silence—the interrogator's best friend. He watched the kid's eyes dart back and forth, his lips twisting with indecision. "We talked to everyone who worked in the parking garage. But you're the only one who definitely saw Tríona Hallett in the neighborhood, and lied about it. You told us at the time of the murder that you'd never seen her before, and it turns out you've got pictures of her plastered all over your bedroom. You do see my problem, don't you?"

Stark said nothing.

"What happened, Truman? Did you follow her, try to talk to her? Maybe you didn't mean to hurt her. Accidents happen—we get that. The thing is, you lied to us—and I have to tell you, that part doesn't look good at all."

"I never touched her, I swear. You said you weren't trying to pin anything on me—" His voice was becoming a reedy whine.

"And you said you were at home on the night she was killed. Your mother backed you up, but you weren't home that night, were you, Truman? You were out on patrol, just like you were on Thursday night, like you are every night. I've been inside your house. I know why you can't stay there."

"If I told the truth you wouldn't believe me. You've got it all backwards—"

Frank heard something new in the kid's voice. "What have we got backwards?"

"You just don't get it. I would never hurt her—I was trying to protect her."

"And why did she need protecting?"

"She was always looking over her shoulder, like somebody was after her."

"Did you ever see anyone following her?"

"Once. Maybe."

"Was it this man?" He fished a picture of Peter Hallett out of his folder, and slid it in front of Stark.

"No, not him."

Frank felt hope sputter and fizzle out. Truman Stark looked him directly in the eye for the first time. "Wasn't a guy at all—it was a woman. Blonde. Kinda stuck-up looking. I saw her again at the river on Thursday night. With her—" He pointed to the picture of Nora. "They were arguing about something."

11

The road that passed in front of the house at Ardcrinn was empty for miles, but Nora still couldn't help looking back over her shoulder as she and Elizabeth made their way over the headland to the fishing village of Port na Rón. She had slipped one of Cormac's walkie-talkies into her jacket pocket before leaving the house—just in case. He must have taken the other one into town. She glanced over at Elizabeth, trudging across the treeless upland, staring at what must seem like nothing but windswept desolation. The blanket bogs here in Donegal were completely different from the high bogs of the midlands. Here the peat was only four or five sods deep—a thin brown mantle stretched over unforgiving stone. This place, like all bogland, only appeared barren and empty; it was actually teeming with life: foxes and pheasants, hares and birds and insects and strange plants, a huge variety of miniature and microscopic worlds.

They found the ruined village as deserted as the road. But the view from the headland was spectacular. A beach of round stones stretched in a crescent shape from the foot of the cliff around the mouth of the bay. The waves were wild today, rumbling like thunder on the way in, hissing and tumbling the pebbles as they withdrew. A silent white waterfall cut into the green cliff around the side of the small bay. A dozen mottled black-and-white sheep grazed in the pasture above the rocky strand, their shaggy flanks splotched with bright azure dye. From the height, Nora could also see several craggy islands, and the dark shapes of seabirds clinging to their precarious nesting places. The caves Cormac had mentioned must be over below the falls somewhere. The wind was relentless as ever, but the salt air it carried was warm and damp under heavy clouds. Nora plucked at her jersey front. They'd not even begun the climb down the beach, and she was already starting to sweat.

She had told no one of the tiny, unsettling detail she had observed yesterday on the cross-country journey. Elizabeth had left everything behind in her luggage at Dublin Airport, so they stopped at Dunnes Stores on the outskirts of Sligo to pick up toiletries and a few items of clothing. Passing by the curtained fitting room, Nora had caught a fleeting sideways glimpse of Elizabeth in her white cotton briefs—and something else as well. A piece of sheeting, or something like it, wrapped tight around her child's slender torso, fixed in place with a safety pin. The image actually took a moment to register. Nora's immediate thought was of the old ballads about girls who bound their chests and dressed in sailors' clothes to go off to sea. What was Elizabeth's reason for disguising her developing shape? All sorts of disturbing possibilities loomed, and now Nora teetered once more upon the point where she had remained suspended for nearly two days now: broach the subject, or keep silent and wait?

In the end, there was no guarantee that waiting would bring about a result. She said: "Lizzabet, I want you to know that I'm ready, whenever you want to talk." No response. Nora felt as though she was treading on dangerous ground. She pushed on: "I remember being your age, not wanting to grow up, and wishing everything could just stay the same—"

Elizabeth stared at the ground below her feet, newly exposed ears glowing with mortification, and Nora knew she'd gone too far. "Never mind. We don't have to talk about it right now."

Nora's probing words had left Elizabeth slightly unsettled, but standing here above the rocky beach, she turned toward the sea and felt her spirits lift. This place was the closest thing yet to her own Useless Bay. Following Nora down the embankment to the beach, she felt her attention drawn to tufts of wet grass that grew between the rocks, fascinated to find perfect spiderwebs sagging with tiny beads of dew, the curling fiddleheads of ferns, black-and-white-striped snails leaving shiny trails on the undersides of every prickly thistle leaf. As they reached the stony beach, she stopped to lift the drooping head of a delicate purple flower.

"A harebell," Nora said from beside her. "I didn't know you were interested in plants."

Elizabeth shrugged. "I don't know the names—I just like looking at them." She bent to pick up a smooth oval stone, examining its tumbled, whitened surface. "I like collecting things."

"What sorts of things?"

"Rocks and shells, mostly—I had to leave them in Seattle. My dad said there was no point in carting worthless crap halfway across the country." She set the first stone back, and picked up another. "I kept the sea glass, though. It's kind of hard to find."

Nora turned away abruptly, and Elizabeth stood for a moment, wondering if she'd said something wrong. "Is it all right if I look around?"

Nora nodded without turning back. Elizabeth stepped away gingerly, following the line left by the high tide, eyes zeroing in on the ridgy cups of limpet shells, the blue glint of mussels with their bright pearly insides. She stooped to pick up a small scallop shell and glanced back at Nora—who was still standing, arms crossed, like she was stuck in that spot.

Elizabeth picked her way across the rounded stones that looked as if they had tumbled out of the sea. She was hunting treasure, but finding mostly trash instead—fishnets and nylon rope and yogurt cups, their bright colors standing out against the stones. She glanced up at Nora, who was hanging back and watching her. She thought about what Nora had said, about not wanting to grow up. It was hard to know what to tell, and what was better kept to herself.

She thought of the book she'd stolen from the library, and began to imagine its story played out on this beach. She could almost see the strange seal woman being rowed to shore by the fisherman, helping him to pull up the boat, going home with him and becoming his wife. She tried to summon an image of how exactly someone changed from seal to human. Did it hurt to slip from your sealskin? Was it as simple as taking off clothes, or was it messier and more complicated—like that film she'd seen once on television, of a calf being born? All that icky wetness had made her feel strange. She tried to picture a woman oozing from a sealskin, strange and slippery, her new skin underneath as pale and tender as a newborn baby's. If you got your old skin again, like the boy's mother did in the story, how exactly would you go about putting it back on? What if it didn't fit? The book hadn't bothered to explain any of that.

The weather was warm here, not at all what she'd imagined. She sat down on a flat rock and removed her shoes and socks, then stood at the water's edge and closed her eyes, putting her hands to her face and tasting the salt and seaweed on her fingers. There was no mistaking it now. This beach was just like the ones in her dreams. The ones where she walked with the red-haired stranger out into the water, out past the rocks and down through swaying seaweed to where the sea people carried on, safe in their secret, hidden world. She had seen it all in her dreams.

Nora shielded her eyes to watch two huge brown sea eagles flapping and fighting over something at the edge of the precipice. She had been watching Elizabeth explore, but her attention had been pulled away for a moment by the birds. When she looked back to where she'd last spied the child, all that remained was a pair of empty shoes and socks. Elizabeth was walking out into the water. Waves were breaking at her chest, now over her shoulders, and all at once, her head disappeared behind a rising swell.

Nora stripped off her pack and began to run, the round stones slowing her progress. It felt as if she were moving through some awful dream. Finally she splashed into the shallows, and flung herself into the waves, head down and arms churning, until she felt the wake of Elizabeth's flailing limbs. "Put your arms around my neck," she shouted. She felt the child's sharp elbow deliver a solid blow to her cheekbone. Somehow she managed to hang on through an exploding field of stars. "It's all right—I've got you. Just hold tight."

With one arm, she clasped the child to her side and took long, even strokes with the other until they finally reached a spot shallow enough to stand up. She seized Elizabeth by the arms. "What the hell were you doing out there? Do you not know how dangerous it is—"

She watched the child's huge eyes fill with tears. "Please don't be frightened, Lizzabet. I'm not angry with you, love, I promise. I was just scared, that's all. If anything were to happen to you—" She felt Elizabeth begin to shiver. "Promise me you won't wander off like that again. Will you promise?"

Elizabeth nodded. Nora looked around, spotting a ruined cottage just above the beach. "Come on, let's get out of the wind."

They made their way up the steep bank to an abandoned house. A fisherman's cottage, Nora thought, as they crossed the threshold. Decaying nets hung from the roof beams. There was a washbasin beside the back door, and a rude sideboard with bits of broken crockery and piles of limpet shells stacked where cups and saucers had been. The little light that pierced the room came from a gaping hole in the roof at the far corner of the house, and the relentless wind that came through shattered windows had reduced the curtains to gray tatters, airy as cobwebs.

She settled Elizabeth on a low chair beside the hearth. The child still shivered violently. As her eyes grew accustomed to the light inside, Nora could see that the abandoned house was strangely intact—furniture, candles, bedclothes, even a pipe on the mantel. The effect of everything left in place was quite eerie, as if the occupants had simply walked away.

She spied a basket beside the hearth and opened the lid. "There's a little turf in here. I'm going to try building a fire." Gathering a few handfuls of straw from a ruined mattress and a candle stub for a firelighter, she dug in her pack for a couple of strike-anywhere matches and managed to get a small blaze going, astonished that the ancient peat was still dry enough to burn. She beckoned to Elizabeth to come closer. They sat in small chairs pulled up to the fire, and Nora alternated rubbing Elizabeth's arms with blowing on the meager flame.

"D-does s-s-somebody live here?" Elizabeth asked through chattering teeth.

"Not anymore. Cormac said this whole village was abandoned—" She stopped as her gaze fell upon a primitive muslin doll in Elizabeth's left hand. It had one small black button eye on one side of a long nose; a bit of stuffing escaped from a frayed seam. "Where did you get that?" she asked.

"Over there." Elizabeth indicated the cot pushed up against the wall.

"May I see it?" Nora asked. The single button eye stared blankly. The arms were flat and stubby, like flippers, the lower half all of a piece. A seal. She finally handed the doll back, and Elizabeth cradled it on her lap.

Nora took a deep breath. "You know we'll have to talk about it, sooner or later, Lizzabet. About why you ran away. I think I can guess part of it. You found out, didn't you—about what happened to your mama?"

Elizabeth stared wordlessly at the floor. After a few seconds, she wiped away a tear, and Nora felt as if her heart would burst. "Oh, Lizzabet, I wish we could have explained, but you were so little. It was so hard to know what to say—" She reached out a hand, but Elizabeth pulled away.

"Does everybody think my dad is a murderer?"

"Elizabeth—"

"He didn't do anything, I know he didn't. He couldn't have."

"There's still so much we don't know—"

"I don't want to know! I'm not going to listen." Elizabeth covered her head with both arms and began to weep. Nora felt helpless. What could she say to this child? What reassurances could she possibly offer?

She said nothing, but pulled the child to her side. Elizabeth tried to fight, but in the end clung on just as she had out in the water, frightened and overwhelmed. *This is it,* Nora thought. *This is where it begins.*

At last, warmed by the tiny fire, and no doubt worn out by jet lag and tears, Elizabeth's limbs began to grow heavy. Nora cradled her, afraid to move, knowing how desperately she needed even the temporary respite of sleep. By the time either of them stirred, twenty minutes later, Nora's whole right side had gone numb.

Elizabeth opened her eyes and pulled away, evidently surprised to be in the cottage still. "I had a dream about this place," she said. She seemed dazed, unsettled, perhaps still half in the dream. "There were people living here. Somebody was singing." Elizabeth found the muslin doll on her lap, and began to fiddle with its ragged tail.

"Do you know, even with your hair cut short, you're very like your mother?"

Elizabeth didn't want to let on how interested she was in this information. "Really?"

"The same hair, the same freckles, even the same scabby knees. Tríona was always falling off her bike."

"Is that true?"

"It is." She reached up to smooth a ragged lock over Elizabeth's forehead. "Do you remember much about her?"

Elizabeth stared at the floor again, thinking. "I remember how she smelled—like lemony soap." A slight hesitation, a rubbing of the eyes. "Sometimes she let me climb up in the bed with her. She said she would read to me, but usually she just fell asleep. She slept a lot. That was okay. I knew how to make my own breakfast."

Climbing back over the headland again a short while later, Nora felt something heavy and damp strike against her shoulder and fall to the ground. She looked up to find a sea eagle, probably one of the pair she'd spied earlier, flapping and calling out in dismay. She bent to pick up the object the bird had dropped. It was a black woolen stocking. Quite fine, if slightly moth-eaten in places, and the heel was thickened with darning. Strange thing for a bird to be carrying in a place like this. She was about to drop the stocking on the ground, but reconsidered and hastily stuffed it into her pocket. She could have a closer look at it back at the house.

12

Truman Stark seemed tired; it was nearly four in the morning, and he'd been answering questions since late afternoon. And yet he didn't seem anxious to go home. Frank couldn't shake the feeling that there was some extra piece of information the kid wanted to give up—but he didn't know how.

Frank tapped the pen against his notepad. "Okay, let's go over it one more time. You admit to following Dr. Gavin from the parking garage on Wednesday afternoon—"

"I knew she had something to do with the murder, the way she was looking at that parking stall—the one where they found the body."

"So you thought you'd do a little investigation on your own?"

"No law against it, is there? People do stuff like that all the time—when the police fall down on the job—"

"Let's leave the department out of it for now. So you followed Dr. Gavin home on Wednesday night, and tailed her all the next day. You must have. How else would you know where she was going to be that evening?" Stark didn't respond, and Frank took it as an admission. "You chased away those kids in Frogtown." Still no answer. "Then you followed her to the river road, watched her talking to this mystery blonde down at Hidden Falls. They got into an argument, and then what happened?"

"The blonde headed back up to the road. Walked right by me—she was pissed."

"But you stuck to Dr. Gavin?"

"Yeah. She went back to her car, headed south on the river road."

"And—?"

"And nothing. I went home."

"But you knew somebody had fiddled with her brakes."

"I didn't know. I just—"

"You just what, Truman?"

"Assumed."

"You saw what happened. How she started taking the curves a little too fast. You knew she didn't have any brakes. And then she went over. Why didn't you do something?"

"I panicked, all right? I knew you'd think I had something to do with the crash, and I didn't."

"If you were so concerned about her, why didn't you stop to see if she was injured? You didn't even call 911, Truman."

"She didn't land very hard. There were lots of small trees—I thought I could see her moving around, and there was no fire or anything—it looked like she was going to walk away. I couldn't afford to get mixed up in it, okay? My mother depends on me for everything. I got back in the truck and went home."

"But you were already mixed up in it, Truman—I guess you forgot about leaving your fingerprints on the car. It was just lucky for you that she was okay."

Stark stared at the table with a miserable expression.

"Okay, let's go back. You said you saw this blonde—the same one who was arguing with Dr. Gavin—following Tríona Hallett in Lowertown a few days before her murder."

"Yeah. I've told you that, like a hundred times."

"How can you be sure it was the same person?"

"'Cause I knew her. I saw her at work."

Frank sat forward. "Tell me."

"I never got her name. She was putting on some big charity thing at the building across the street—"

"The Great Northern Trust?"

"Whatever—I don't know what it's called. The boss brought her around on a tour. She was going on and on about VIP security—she had a couple of movie stars and some big football player coming in for the party. They were going to use our ramp for valet parking, and she wanted to make sure everything was cool on our end. The boss started bragging to her about our new state-of-the-art system, how it was going in the next week. She asked a lot of questions."

Frank felt as if someone had pulled all the air from his lungs. Stark looked up, wounded and defiant. "Yeah. All this time, and you never knew about her. I could have told you—"

"So why didn't you?"

"Because nobody ever asked. That was your job. To talk to me like I wasn't just some piece of shit from the bottom of your shoe. But nobody ever did."

Book Six

The Irish peasant, hungry albeit he may be, is very particular as regards the description of animal food in which he allows himself to indulge. For instance, I have heard a fisherman object to skate as having a "wild taste," and have endeavoured without success to convince them that whale's flesh is an excellent substitute for beef . . .

I found it far more easy to sympathize with their prejudice against eating the flesh of seals. They have a superstition, a poetical one in my opinion, that the souls of the hapless beings who were drowned in the deluge, entered into the bodies of seals and dwelt there. The plaintive expression which in the eyes of these amphibious creatures is noticeable, lends itself to this fanciful idea . . .

They are evidently fond of music, and will follow a boat for long distances when the whistle or song of one of the crew attracts their attention. I was once the unfortunate witness of a successful shot which killed a nursing mother as its child, a tiny creature, lay placidly on the parent's damp and comfortless-looking back. The piteous look of the bereaved one, as it floated past me, was more than human in the intensity of its reproachful despair.

—"Net Fishing in the Killary Bay," by M. C. Houstoun, from *London Society: A Monthly Magazine of Light and Amusing Literature for the Hours of Relaxation*, Vol. LVIII, July to December 1890

1

While Nora was showering after their dip in the sea, Elizabeth crept downstairs to the kitchen, glad to have all that itchy salt off her skin. In her left hand was the seal doll she had stolen from the cottage, tucked under her shirt when Nora wasn't looking. The black button eye stared back at her, unblinking. She wasn't even sure why she'd taken it, except that the poor thing seemed to need looking after. She pushed the springy wool back into the open seam at the side of its head, feeling a little uneasy about her conversation with Nora at the cottage. Should she have said all those things about her mother? Her dad said it wasn't a good idea to talk about the naps mama used to take. He said talking about it could get them all into trouble.

Cormac came in through the back door with a heavy box of provisions. Elizabeth drew back into a corner of the kitchen, dropping whatever it was she'd been holding. He stooped to pick it up—and recognized the seal poppet from the selkie cottage. He studied the creature for a minute before handing it back. "Is everything all right, Elizabeth? Where's Nora?"

"Upstairs—taking a shower."

"I've got a surprise," Cormac said, hoping to put her at ease. "Something I hope you'll find interesting." Fishing in his box of groceries, he pulled out a flat brown paper bag. "Here's the first thing we need," he said. "And here's the second." Ducking into his father's room, he brought out the fiddle case he'd found there earlier. He lifted the instrument from the case and set it on the table. "Can you see our trouble?"

Elizabeth looked closer. "No strings."

"And that's what we're going to remedy, right now." Elizabeth sat at the table, keeping the seal hidden on her lap as he took out his flute case as well.

"Did you and Nora get up to anything interesting while I was out?"

"We went to a beach. It had all these round stones—"

"Ah—I know the place you mean. It's called Port na Rón. *Rón* is the Irish word for seal—like your friend there. 'Port na Rón' means 'Seal Harbor.' People say it used to be a great spot for smugglers and pirates."

"Pirates?"

"I swear. Those round stones are called *duirlings*. Do you have any Irish?" Elizabeth shook her head. "Would you like to learn a bit?" Her answer was a noncommittal shrug. "All right, say somebody wanted to ask your name. They'd say: '*Cad is ainm duit?*'"

"*Cahd iss AH-nim ditch.*"

"Good. And you would answer, '*Is mise Éilis*'—'I'm Elizabeth.' Can you say that?"

"*Iss missha AY-lish.*"

"Excellent. Elizabeth was my mother's name, too. But she always went by Éilis."

Nora came through the door, with her hair still damp from the shower, and evidently surprised to see the instruments on the table between them. "Whose fiddle?"

Cormac looked up. "I found it in the wardrobe, and thought I'd try restringing it—with the help of my able assistant of course." Elizabeth colored slightly, but kept twisting the fiddle string around her peg. "You're just in time. We're about to tune up and give it a go."

"You don't even play the fiddle—do you?"

"No—but you learn a few things, hanging around fiddle players." He took up the flute and blew an A, and looked to Elizabeth to pluck the A string. He showed her how to use the fine tuners to match the note. When the strings were within range, Cormac picked up the fiddle and bowed each pair to check the intonation and handed the instrument to Elizabeth. "All right, your turn now. Let the neck rest in your hand, and tuck the chin rest just under here, like that." He set the bow between her fingers. "You don't have to hold it tight. Just relax, keep the wrist loose. Off you go."

Elizabeth pulled the bow, and the top string made a deep groan.

"Good! Keep going. Just play with it." He slid down the bench to join Nora, raising a hand to shield his voice from Elizabeth. "You'll never guess who I met in the village just now—Garrett Devaney."

Her eyes widened. "You're joking."

"He was in the pub. Here for the Fiddle Week with his daughter."

"That's strange. I tried to ring him on the way up here, but whoever answered—his wife, probably—said he wasn't available. Now I know why. Did you speak to him?"

"Briefly. He invited me for a tune sometime. His daughter is about Elizabeth's age—a nice player. He asked after you, by the way, but I told him you were gone home to the States. I wasn't sure what else to say—the walls might have ears."

"Do you think we could ask them for a tune here—right away, this evening? Frank Cordova—the detective back in Saint Paul—said he'd get in touch with the Guards, to see if he couldn't get some help tracking Peter. We could ask Devaney to keep his ear to the ground, let us know if he hears anything."

Cormac reached into his pocket and pulled out a beer mat with a mobile number scrawled in the margin. "Shall I say half-past six?"

Elizabeth was still tentatively trying out different notes on the fiddle. Her plaintive chords summoned up the singing of the seals he'd heard out rowing. Cormac looked down into Nora's anxious face and offered a hopeful half smile. "What do you know about that? She might just take to it."

2

In the end, after hours of interviews, Frank had to spring Truman Stark. The kid still wasn't telling the whole truth, but there wasn't enough to hold him—on any charge. And Frank wanted to start checking into Miranda Staunton. He had spent what was left of the night going back into the files for interview records. At the time, they'd seen only Miranda's glancing connection with Tríona Hallett; her brother was engaged to Tríona's sister. Miranda had been interviewed twice, and had made all the right noises, provided additional background. She hadn't even been on their radar as a suspect. With Stark's statement, all that had changed.

Miranda never mentioned that she was working at the Great Northern Trust Building at the time of Tríona Hallett's murder. The actual event wasn't until several months later, but she had been out doing the advance prep work in July. Nobody would have looked askance at her being in the neighborhood. But if she happened to see Tríona, or was actually following her, as Truman Stark claimed . . .

At ten past seven in the morning, Frank's phone began to buzz. He dug through the blizzard of papers on his desk to find it. "Cordova here."

"Holly Blume here, Detective. I think I have something you should see."

Twenty minutes later, Frank was at the Herbarium, looking through the eyepiece of a microscope at the same shriveled shapes he'd seen at the crime lab.

"That's the first of the two samples you brought me," Holly said. "From the separate crime scenes. You wanted to know if we could say from the plant evidence whether any of the seeds or leaves in the two samples were from the same site—"

"And?"

"They are. I don't know if you recognize those seeds—do you remember the plant Nora and I were talking about the last time you were here?"

"False mermaid—the seeds you identified from Tríona Hallett's hair."

"That's right. *Floerkea proserpinacoides*. Both of the samples you brought me that day happened to contain *Floerkea* seeds. So did the third sample, the one you had sent over yesterday from the crime lab. *Floerkea* has some interesting and unusual properties. Part of the reason the species is so endangered here is that it produces very few seeds, usually only about four to twelve per stem. They're quite large and heavy, for such a small plant, and they have no wings or hooks, or other features that help them disperse. In population terms, those things can pose a real problem. And to compound that, insects usually reject the seeds, because they contain toxic flavonol glycosides—in other words, they taste awful. What I'm trying to say is that *Floerkea* seeds don't usually travel very far from their parent plant, not without help. I'm telling you all this as a prelude to the DNA results. I went down to the crime scene, collected additional samples for testing. To do the sort of test you needed, I first had to establish allele frequencies, which alleles are most common within the species, and which are more rare. Does that make sense so far?"

"I think so—go on."

"I got some good data from a colleague who's studied *Floerkea* in detail. The upshot is that the seeds from all three of your samples did come from the same parent plant. The DNA profiles are identical."

Frank had to step back and think for a minute. This new evidence meant they could place Tríona Hallett, and the person who wore Harry Shaughnessy's shoes, at Natalie Russo's grave. It still didn't tell them who'd killed Natalie, or Tríona, but it was a definite connection. Something to build upon, at long last.

"There was something else as well," Holly said. "I don't know if they showed you this at the crime lab." She waved him over to an adjacent bench. "On this first scope, we've got Sample A—from the first crime scene sample you brought me."

"The material combed from Tríona Hallett's hair."

"Next is Sample B, collected from your Hidden Falls crime scene. The third, C, is the most recent sample from the state crime lab, from the shoe treads. Take a look, and tell me what you see."

Frank peered through each lens in turn. "They all look like the same sort of seed."

"Yes—they're all false mermaid. What else do you notice?"

"Samples A and C seem to be a slightly different color."

"Very good. Some of the *Floerkea* seeds from your samples looked like they were coated in a foreign substance. I sent a few back to the crime lab, asked them to check. They just called back. That's the second bit of information I have for you. The foreign substance turned out to be dried blood—"

"Which means the blood was fresh when the seeds were picked up. So whoever wore Harry Shaughnessy's spare shoes could be a witness—or a killer."

"You're getting there, Detective—congratulations."

"Thanks, Holly. I owe you for this. Big time."

"Just doing my job. I'll write up my results and get them over to you ASAP."

Frank paused on his way out the door. "Can you hear that?"

Holly peered at him curiously. "Sorry—I don't hear anything."

"Listen carefully. It's the sound of a cold case cracking wide open."

3

Nora felt a moment of panic when the bell rang at half-past six. Cormac opened the door to Garrett Devaney, who proffered a bottle of red wine with an apologetic aside. "Only what was on offer at the pub, I'm afraid."

"It'll do nicely. Come in." Cormac ushered Devaney and his daughter into the sitting room. The policeman's face registered mild surprise when he saw Nora.

"Dr. Gavin," he said. "Heard you were over in the States."

"I just got back—and it's Nora, please. This is my niece—"

"Éilis," said Elizabeth. "Is mise Éilis."

Nora had to mask her own surprise. She checked Devaney's reaction. If he had heard anything official about a missing red-headed eleven-year-old, the policeman showed no sign of it, though he might have looked slightly askance at Elizabeth's strange haircut.

"My daughter, Róisín," he said.

Nora watched the two girls eye each other warily. How quickly children learned to take the measure of another person, she thought. Elizabeth seemed especially intrigued by the fact that Róisín carried her own fiddle case.

As they sat down to the table, Nora couldn't help noticing the deference Garrett Devaney showed his daughter, in tiny, gentle ways—turning the spoon as he passed the potatoes, putting a word in her ear about which cut of the roast chicken might suit. Nora saw that Elizabeth couldn't help noticing either.

After supper, they took advantage of the long summer daylight to walk over to Port na Rón, stopping at the top of the headland to enjoy the view. The evening was fine, and the rattle of the pebbles on the beach nearly drowned out the faint bluster of the wind. The two girls wandered off, leaving the adults at the top of the headland.

"I'm afraid we had an ulterior motive in asking you for dinner," Nora said to Devaney. "I'll just tell you straight out. The police may be looking for us—Elizabeth and me. She ran away from her father and stepmother when they arrived in Dublin on Friday—"

"Gave them the slip at the airport," Cormac said. "Took a taxi straight to Nora's apartment."

"Only I wasn't there; I'd gone back to the States last week. Fortunately, I have kind neighbors, who were able to look after her until I could fly over the next day."

Devaney frowned. "Why did the child run away?"

Nora glanced at Cormac. "I think she found out about her mother. My sister Tríona was murdered—it happened five years ago. Elizabeth was too young to understand."

"We think she may have discovered that her father is still the main suspect," Cormac added.

Nora said: "He's never been charged. Unfortunately, whenever we get a promising lead, it seems to evaporate. The point is that Elizabeth came to me for help, for protection. I can't just let her go back—"

Cormac said: "There's another possible wrinkle as well. Her father might claim that Nora abducted her. You see our predicament—"

Devaney rubbed his chin. "You haven't spoken to anyone in the police over here?"

"I wasn't sure what to do," Nora said. "The detective working the case at home said he would contact Garda headquarters and Interpol, let them know he had a murder suspect on the loose over here. My brother-in-law's name is Hallett, by the way—Peter Hallett."

"And so far as you know, nobody's got him under obso?"

"No—not as far as we know. As I said, he arrived in Dublin on Friday, so he could be anywhere in the country by now."

"And you don't know if he's filed a missing persons report?"

Nora shook her head. "I'm afraid we're completely in the dark. We obviously couldn't just phone up and ask. Frank Cordova, the detective back in the States, has been working on some new leads. A few things have just turned up in the past few days, but—"

"Still not enough to file charges?"

"I'm afraid not."

Devaney pondered for a minute. "Well now, it seems to me your only choice is to dig in for a bit, at least until your detective can scare up more on those leads. He should get in touch with me directly, and I can shuttle him to the right person in the Serious Crimes Unit. In the meantime, I'll work a few contacts, see what I can find out."

"I'd be so grateful for any help. I should warn you—Peter Hallett is dangerous. He has a way of twisting things, turning everything around so that he looks like the victim, and anyone who dares to question him seems seriously disturbed. He made my sister seem completely mad—and he's been trying to back me into that same corner for five years."

The two girls had climbed to the top of the opposite promontory overlooking the harbor. Nora shaded her eyes to peer over at them.

Devaney's voice was thoughtful. "Could Elizabeth know enough about her mother's death to be in danger?"

"I don't know. She was only six, and she was out of town with my parents at the time of Tríona's murder."

"Still, children see and hear things nobody else does. Especially true in domestic cases. But kids don't want to be grassing on the other parent. Has she ever been interviewed by a social worker or counselor?"

"Her father wouldn't allow it. He moved away after my sister's death, so I've had no contact with Elizabeth for the past four years. Even now, I can't get her to talk to me. I tried to ask this afternoon why she ran away, and do you know what she asked me? If everyone believed her dad was a murderer. She flatly denies that he had anything to do with my sister's death."

"Not uncommon, unfortunately. Sometimes it takes them a long time to figure things out. But she did come to you—that's a good sign."

Nora was remembering how Elizabeth fidgeted when pressed. "I'm afraid I don't have much experience with children."

Devaney offered a sympathetic wince. "My wife tells me to stop worrying and start listening—I think it's very good advice." He turned to Cormac. "Ready for that tune now?"

Back at the house after the excursion, Nora watched the musicians getting ready to play, Róisín taking a half-sized fiddle from her case while her father slid an amber cake of rosin up and down his bow, the rounded belly of his fiddle still dusty from the last application. When all was ready, the two fiddlers sat cradling their instruments, plucking absently at their strings, bows at the ready on the table. "Why don't you and Róisín play something together to start us off?" Cormac suggested to Devaney. "Maybe the tune you were playing down at the pub this afternoon—'The Pigeon on the Gate.' That was a nice setting."

Father and daughter exchanged a quick glance and launched into the tune, not too fast, not too slow, triplets slipping up and over the head of the melody like tiny snares, the low notes a throaty growl. Elizabeth seemed secretly impressed that someone her own age could just sit down and start playing an instrument. She couldn't take her eyes off Róisín's dancing fingers. When the two fiddles slipped easily into a second set of reels and Cormac picked up his flute to join in, Elizabeth's eyes grew wider.

Nora thought about something a teetotaling friend had said to her once, as they were crushed in the crowded back room of a pub. *I don't drink myself,* this friend had shouted in her ear over the din. *But I like being where it is.* That was what being near this music felt like, she thought. The tunes belonged to another realm, a separate world of which she was not really a part. She did not speak the language, and yet hearing these tunes was somehow essential, almost like nourishment. Elizabeth's eyes were still on Róisín's fiddle. Some people were susceptible to this music, and some were not. Elizabeth looked to be smitten.

"Shall we try a few Donegal tunes?" Cormac asked. "What about 'The Gravel Walks'?" He began to play, leading them into a thicket of angular reels. There was definitely something different about the music in a place like this. Donegal had a reputation as a "gentle" place, where the veil between worlds was thin. Otherworldliness was simply fact here, like hearing music on the wind, or swimming with the souls of the drowned.

The evening passed quickly, but after a feast of excellent tunes, Róisín looked as if she might be tiring. Nora knew the evening was drawing to a close when she felt Cormac's eyes upon her.

"Nora, would you ever give us a song?"

"I'm not in great form—"

He touched her hand. "Please, Nora."

How was it possible to refuse? She closed her eyes and began:

Is cosúil gur mheath tú nó gur thréig tú an greann
Tá an sneachta go frasach fá bhéal na trá
Do chúl buí daite is do bhéilín sámh
Siúd chugaibh Mary hÉighnigh is í i ndiaidh an Éirne a shnámh.

There was a sudden commotion, and Nora opened her eyes to find that Elizabeth had risen from her chair and darted from the room.

"Excuse me," Nora said to the others at the table. By the time she reached the upstairs bedroom, Elizabeth had managed to wedge herself in between the wardrobe and the wall, and was pressing her face into the cupboard as if wishing she might crawl behind it. Was it something in the song that set her off? She couldn't possibly know the meaning of the words.

Nora crouched against the wardrobe. "Elizabeth, please tell me what's troubling you."

"Go—away—" Dry sobs came like short, involuntary howls. Cormac's head appeared at the door, but Nora signaled him that she was all right, for the moment, and he retreated.

"Lizzabet, please don't push me away."

"You don't understand anything."

"Will you let me try?"

"You think—I ran away—because my dad—" Her voice slid up almost an octave. "He didn't do anything. He's my dad—I miss him."

Nora felt yet again as if her heart would crack. "Why, then, Lizzabet? Why did you come to me?"

There was no answer for a moment but ragged sobs. When Elizabeth finally spoke, her voice sounded small and faraway. "Because of Miranda. She said she knew what I was up to. But I don't know what she's talking about—I'm not up to anything."

"No, of course you're not."

"She said I was looking for attention. And maybe I was more like my mother than anybody knew. What was she talking about? Why does she have to be so mean?"

"Oh, Lizzabet. I don't know." Nora had inched close enough to reach into the gap between the wall and cupboard to stroke Elizabeth's back. "I do know one true thing: your mama loved you more than anyone or anything else in the world. She has her arms around you right now, love. And she's never letting go."

4

It was after ten when Elizabeth finally drifted off. Nora returned to the kitchen to find Garrett Devaney and his daughter gone. The only illumination came from candles on the table and on the wide windowsills as Cormac finished the washing up. He set the last wineglass in the cupboard and brought out a package he'd evidently placed there earlier. He handed it to Nora, slightly embarrassed when she looked inside to find several extra heavy-duty door chains. "I thought it might be a good idea, but didn't want to set off any alarm bells this afternoon." He produced a screwdriver, and began marking the doorframe. "That song you started to sing tonight, *'An Mhaighdean Mhara'*—where did you get it?"

"I heard someone sing it at a competition once," Nora said. She could still see the face of the young woman, whose name she couldn't recall, standing alone before a restless crowd in a drafty school gymnasium. Little by little the crowd hushed as each person was drawn in. When the song finished, the girl calmly returned to her chair while the silence in the room gave way to shouts and crushing waves of applause.

"You know it's a famous Donegal song."

"No, I didn't know."

"What made you sing it tonight?"

"I don't know. Maybe because Tríona and I used to sing it together. That was a long time ago—I don't think Elizabeth ever heard us."

"You think it was the song that upset her?"

Nora crossed her arms and sighed. "I don't know. I don't seem to know anything."

Cormac set down the door chain and came closer. "Nora, what's wrong? What did Elizabeth say?"

"It's everything that's happened—yesterday, and this morning while you were away. We went over to Port na Rón to check out the caves, like you suggested. We never made it that far. We got as far as the beach. I got distracted for a moment, and when I turned around, Elizabeth was walking straight out into the water, like she was headed somewhere. I had to go in after her—"

"You don't think she was trying to harm herself?"

"I don't know, Cormac. I'm baffled. I just can't seem to get through to her. I feel so unprepared for this, so inadequate."

"You're doing your best."

"Elizabeth is having second thoughts about running away. Do you know what she told me upstairs? That it wasn't her father she was running from—it was Miranda." Cormac tried to step closer, but she put up a hand to keep him away. "What am I doing here? I shouldn't be here." She began to pace.

"Nora, what are you talking about?"

"All this time I've spent over here, these last three years, digging in bogs—it wasn't what I should have been doing at all. I should have been at home. All the things we stumbled upon this week back in Saint Paul, they were there all along—"

"Nora, what's got into you? This isn't like you—"

"How do you know? Maybe this is the real me. And now—" She held up the door chain. "Now I've brought it all down on you, on Frank. His brother died, Cormac, but he's still over there, working the case, because he doesn't want to let me down. I'm the one who let everyone down. I keep thinking, 'This time, we'll get the evidence, we're finally going to get down to the truth. This time, it's going to work. It's got to work.' Well, what if it doesn't? What if Peter gets Elizabeth back, and he manages to make everyone believe that I took her? It could happen—and if it does, it won't just be a restraining order for me this time—I could actually go to jail for kidnapping."

"Nora, let me help—"

"How? How can you help me? There are so many things I haven't told you—"

"Tell me now."

Nora had the feeling she was standing at the edge of a precipice. She was about to close her eyes and fall forward, and there was no parachute. She let Cormac settle her in a chair, and let out a long breath. "Nobody had any idea what was really going on. After Tríona was killed, all kinds of strange details started to surface, bit by bit. Most of it still doesn't make any sense." She paused, trying to gather her thoughts. "The first bizarre piece of evidence was a bottle of eyedrops found in Tríona's purse.

When the police analyzed the stuff in the bottle, they found it wasn't eyedrops at all. It was a drug called GHB—"

Cormac shook his head. "I'm sorry, I don't know what that is."

"It has all sorts of names—Grievous Bodily Harm, liquid ecstasy. One of the club drugs. I don't know what they call it here. It was developed years ago as a presurgery anesthetic, until someone discovered how it could affect a person's sexual appetite. Lots of people started to use it recreationally. When the police searched Tríona's house, they found a dozen similar bottles stashed all over the place—all with her fingerprints on them."

"You think she was using the stuff?"

"That's what everyone assumed, but Tríona didn't do drugs, Cormac. She wouldn't. The thing is, GHB also induces amnesia—one capful, and you don't remember a thing. It's easy to slip into drinks, and gets metabolized very quickly—the cops will tell you, that's what makes it the trickiest of the date rape drugs. I think Peter was giving it to her. I found a tape when I was home, a message Tríona left for me, about what to do if something happened to her. She says on the tape that there were hours, whole days, that she couldn't remember. She didn't know what was happening to her."

"If she was being drugged, there must be some way to prove it."

"The effects of GHB wear off as soon as it's out of your system. There's no way to prove she wasn't taking it on her own. And the more I find out about what he did, the worse it gets." Nora struggled to maintain control. "At first, Peter seemed horrified about the drugs. He told the police he was mystified, that their marriage was rock solid. He couldn't imagine who had a motive to kill Tríona. But when they kept questioning him—"

"Let me try to help you, Nora. Please."

"After several interviews, Peter broke down, and started telling stories about coming home from work and finding Tríona asleep, Elizabeth still in her pajamas. He told them that since the prior summer, Tríona had been going out at all hours, coming home with leaves in her hair, strange bruises, and no memory of where she'd been or what happened. He said for months he'd been at his wit's end, wondering every night whether she'd come home at all. It was lies, Cormac, it had to be. That wasn't Tríona—it just wasn't. But he was so convincing—and there was no way to prove it hadn't happened just as he described. When the police searched the house, they found not just the GHB, but the clothes as well—" She shut her eyes, trying to keep it together. "Tríona's clothes, all torn and stained with dirt and—"

"What? Nora, tell me."

She couldn't speak above a whisper. "Biological substances—blood and semen. From multiple unknown donors, as the crime lab so delicately put it. Peter managed to make it look as if my sister had been neglecting her child, that she'd been going out and getting high, and screwing everything in sight—"

"So a murder could be down to her own risky behavior, and he looks perfectly innocent—"

"Not just innocent—saintly. You have no idea how devious he is. Destroying Tríona's reputation wasn't enough. He stole everything from her. She began to doubt who she was. She didn't even know herself anymore. In her message on the tape, Tríona pointed me to some things she'd hidden away—a datebook, with certain days marked. I thought maybe those were the days she knew she'd been drugged. There were also some bloody clothes, and a whole raft of newspaper articles about a woman who'd gone missing a few weeks before. I think Peter murdered the other woman, and tried to make Tríona believe that she had done it. I think she woke up one morning covered in blood, with no idea what had happened. I think he set it all up, to make her believe she'd done something terrible. And some part of her believed it. She must have felt like she was losing her mind. But she didn't get rid of the bloody clothes. She hung onto them, hid them away, told me where to find them. She'd been working, saving up money, and she sent Elizabeth away that weekend she was killed. I know she was walking out, Cormac, she was this close—"

"What stopped her?"

"I don't know. All I know is what she said to me on the phone that night—"

"What did she say, Nora?"

"What I told you once before, that Peter seemed to get some strange pleasure from hurting her. I thought he was hitting her, but it turned out to be far worse than that. And—"

Cormac took her face between his hands. "Tell me, Nora, please."

"She said that she had done things, too, unspeakable things—that she had lied and deceived everyone. That she had to find out the truth.

The last thing she said was: 'Isn't it shocking, what you'll do when you love someone?'"

"Oh, Nora—"

"She doubted herself more than she doubted him. That's what drove her to the woods that night. It wasn't the truth about Peter she was looking for, it was the truth about herself. She truly loved him, and he used that to destroy her. He goes on destroying her, in the eyes of her child, the eyes of the world. I can't let him do it any longer. I won't."

"You've been carrying this alone, all these years?"

"Only one other person in the world ever knew as much as I've just told you."

"Frank Cordova."

"He was the only person who took me seriously—do you have any idea what it's like, to be undermined and disbelieved for so many years? What it means to have one person stand by you? I didn't mean for it to happen, that night with Frank. It was before I met you, Cormac. I just couldn't go on—"

Cormac moved closer, but she pushed him away again. "Do you understand? I can't—what we've had these past few months—I don't deserve it, any of it. I should have listened to Tríona, I should have seen—"

But he moved in again, slowly, gently, folding her body into his. After a few moments, she stopped resisting and her head dropped forward, finally coming to rest against his chest.

Out beyond the harbor at Port na Rón, Ferghal O'Gara hit the switch to reel his nets in for the night. Another pitiful catch. He'd have to give it up, if things didn't improve. But what would he do? Fishing was all he knew—the tides and banks, maneuvering a boat through rough seas, running the nets, negotiating a price for his catch—but it was all going by the wayside, with the corporate crowd taking everything over.

Ferghal didn't allow himself to trust anything that operated on such a colossal scale. It was madness. Because when disasters came—for they had always come and always would—those disasters were on a colossal scale as well. All he wanted was to bring home enough to feed the children. Was that so much to ask? And maybe enough for the odd pint once in a while.

Once the nets were in, and the catch (what little there was) safely stowed, he started up the diesel engine and began motoring back to port.

The moon was high and bright, and as he passed by the harbor at Port na Rón, he could see a disturbance in the water. Seals, dozens of them, calling out and splashing in the bay. What could have set them off? He'd never heard of killer whales hunting at night.

Ferghal cut his engine and stepped out onto the foredeck, listening to the eerie wailing, and remembering a story his grandfather had told him, about a group of men, a hundred years ago or more, out hunting seals in the caves below Port na Rón. One of the men had raised up his club to strike a pup when he heard the mother cry out in Irish: *Mo pháistín, mo pháistín!* My child, my child!

Ferghal himself was well used to the creatures—he'd practically been reared with them, always swimming around the boat looking for any fish that might escape his nets. He had to admit there was something about them, the way they looked up at you from the water, that expression in their eyes saying they knew and shared your deepest sorrows.

All at once, the sound of a single voice rose above the others.

Oro, mo pháistín! Oroo!

It carried like the voices of the old women he'd once heard at a wake, with their strange prayers and incantations. There was no more. He strained to listen, but the noise of the water and the wind in his ears made it impossible to tell if what he had heard was true, or only his imagination.

The boat heeled suddenly, as the broad back of a killer whale breached the water on his starboard side. Ferghal grasped the gunwale and scrambled to keep from falling back against the wheelhouse. As the huge predator glided by, he almost felt that if he could only reach out far enough, his fingers might brush against the creature's high dorsal fin. But the whale moved on, and as it dived and disappeared, the white underside of its tail glowed briefly in the moonlight. The seals had fallen silent.

Ferghal shivered and switched the diesel engine back on. He'd have a mug of strong tea when he got home tonight, maybe a drop of something stronger. Then he'd go to bed, have a tumble with the wife, if he were lucky and she were willing. And he would never, ever tell anyone what he had seen and heard out here tonight, in case they would say he was mad.

5

Frank Cordova sat at his desk, trying to piece together all he knew about Miranda Staunton. She'd been spotted following Tríona Hallett around Lowertown, and if Truman Stark was telling the truth, she knew about the parking ramp security system. All the work they'd done to try to nail Peter Hallett, and now everything was beginning to point away from him and toward Miranda.

Frank glanced at his watch. Already after four, and he had to be down at the funeral home by six for a private family viewing before his brother's wake. The phone at his elbow rang, and he picked up. "Cordova here."

"Okay, here's the lowdown on all those clothes you asked me to check." Frank could heard Jackie Smart sorting through papers as she spoke. "The blood on the U of M tee shirt and shorts matched your vic from Hidden Falls, Natalie Russo. I got some wearer DNA from the inside as well, but the sample was pretty cross-contaminated—"

"Which means?"

"Just that more than one person seems to have worn them. At least one male, one female. Don't ask me why. Still working on those profiles."

So even though Tríona had possession of clothes worn by the person who likely killed Natalie Russo, they couldn't prove she had worn them. They also couldn't prove that she hadn't. What mystery man would have worn Tríona Hallett's clothes?

Jackie continued: "The DNA on your hit-and-run was pretty interesting, too. The newer bloodstains on the Galliard sweatshirt were a match to the accident victim, Harry Shaughnessy—no surprise there. The older stains were pretty degraded, but with amplification I was able to get a match to your cold-case vic—Tríona Hallett."

Frank felt a flare of emotion. "That's great, Jackie. I appreciate you turning everything around so fast—"

"I haven't even come to the interesting part yet—the third DNA profile from *inside* the sweatshirt." She shifted more papers. "I got Harry Shaughnessy's DNA from the collar and cuffs—probably the only areas that ever made contact with his skin. But I got additional wearer DNA from inside the shirt. No hits against any forensic profiles or convicted offenders in the system. All I can say for sure at this point is that the other person who wore the clothes was female."

"Female?"

"Yup. The fancy running shoes were the same; blood on the outside was a match to the same cold-case vic, Tríona Hallett. And inside, the same unknown female who wore the shirt."

Cordova sank down into his chair. Peter Hallett was slipping away from them—again. "You're absolutely positive it's a female?"

"As positive as any forensic scientist will admit to being. Sorry if it's not what you wanted to hear. Since we got no hits in the database, it's going to be tough to find out who our mystery woman is—unless you have some idea."

"I might."

"We'd need a known sample to run a comparison."

"I'll see what I can do."

He hung up the phone. Another round of evidence pointing to Miranda Staunton. There was also her direct link with Natalie Russo, through the rowing club. A strong rower like Miranda must have good upper body strength—enough to render a human face unrecognizable? And where was he going to get a known sample from Miranda Staunton? Frank let his memory travel back to the last time he'd seen her—in the rowing club locker room. He picked up the phone.

When Sarah Cates met him at the door of the boathouse thirty minutes later, she was dressed not in workout gear, as he'd expected, but in a dark blue-green suit that set off the color of her eyes. "Welcome back, Detective. What can I do for you this time?"

"I need to get into the women's locker room again."

Sarah Cates led the way, again making sure the coast was clear before bringing Frank inside the locker room. He made a beeline for the bench where he'd seen Miranda lacing up those odd-looking shoes. Sliding an evidence envelope from his pocket, he opened his penknife and crouched down beside the bench. There it was, the wad of chewing gum Miranda had stuck on the underside of the plank two days ago. He prized the gum loose and let it drop into the envelope.

Sarah Cates spoke behind him. "I have a question, when you're finished there."

"Done," Frank said, climbing to his feet. "What's your question?"

"You asked me before if anyone might have resented Natalie's ability—"

"You said you couldn't think of anyone."

"But the question got me thinking. The finals were screwy at one of our big races that year. There was some controversy about handicapping. I don't even remember what the disagreement was about; I just know the person who took second thought she should have won. The judges' decision was final. She was pretty steamed—"

"Who are we talking about?"

"You asked me if I knew her last time you were here—Miranda Staunton."

"You mentioned that she joined the club right after college."

"And we were lucky to have her. Galliard had a great rowing program—really top class."

6

At six-thirty, Frank Cordova stood looking down into the casket at his brother's face. Composed, expressionless—completely unlike the way it had been when he was alive. Frank touched Chago's cheek, knowing it would be cold, but he was surprised nonetheless. Like a wax figure, a puppet. Not the real Chago. He knew Veronica and Luis were worried that he might lose it again, but he knew that wouldn't happen. Chago was beyond anyone's help now. He wished he could believe what Veronica said, that Chago was with their mother in heaven now, that there was a reward for those who had suffered, but he could not believe it. He had tried.

Frank turned away and sat down in the back row of chairs, watching his sister greet the mourners at the door. She saw him sitting, and came to rest her feet beside him. As a boy, he had thought her the most beautiful of his sisters, and she still was. A little extra bulk around the middle now proclaimed her age, but Veronica's hands and feet had always been small and delicate, and her face remained as lovely as ever. He could see the worry in her eyes.

"I'm all right, Noni. I won't make any trouble."

"You know that's not what I'm worried about, Paco." She put an arm around him and squeezed his hand. "We never knew it was so bad for you and Chago, I swear. We never would have left, Mila and Luisa and I, but we needed those jobs at the luggage factory up here. We didn't know how bad things were back home. Mami always wanted to bring you here, you and Chago, to have a better life, I know she did, but she couldn't leave Papi. She knew he had the spirit sickness. She even brought in the healer, the *curandero*—"

"The old man in white? I thought he came for Chago."

"No, for Papi. You were too young to understand, Paco. We didn't know how much you would remember, how much of it you or Chago would even understand. He didn't know what he was doing, Paco, it was the sickness inside him, the spirit sickness. He never would have hurt

Mami like that, I know." She laid a hand on his chest. "You may look like him, Paco, but you are not Papi. Do you hear me? You must never worry about that."

He looked up at Chago's composed face in the casket, and a kind of effervescence began to rise up inside him. Everything in his life up to now had been part of a confusing dream. Now that Chago was gone, he could begin to wash off the dust, to unwind the jagged wire that had lashed them together all these years. Veronica's voice broke in beside him. "Paco, your phone is buzzing."

He pulled it out, and stared at the unfamiliar number. "I'm sorry, Noni. I have to take this—"

"Go," she said. "Chago knows you love him. Go."

Frank stepped out onto the veranda. As he closed the door behind him, he thought he glimpsed a figure in a blue-green suit at the front door of the funeral home. He pressed the phone to his ear. "Frank Cordova."

"Detective Cordova? Gordon MacLeish, Maine State Police—retired. I heard you were looking for information about an old case of mine."

"That's right. The Nash murders."

"How much do you know about the case?"

"Not a lot, just what was in the papers—that the Nashes were killed on board their boat, and the son's friend confessed to it—"

"That's right—Jesse Benoit. All the physical evidence pointed to him—"

Frank sensed a hesitation. "But?"

"Well, Jesse never gave any reason for the murders. After he was sent down to Augusta—that's our state mental hospital—his mother came to me and claimed he couldn't have planned and carried out a double murder, not on his own. She said he was her son and she loved him, but he was easily led. She thought Tripp Nash put him up to it, planned the whole thing."

"How did she figure?"

"After he went down to Augusta, Jesse told his mother why he'd killed the Nashes. He said it was for Tripp. Years before, Harris Nash had discovered the two of them fooling around with makeup, trying on Connie Nash's clothes. And according to Jesse, Nash threatened Tripp if the boy didn't perform certain . . . services for him. Jesse claimed Connie knew, and did nothing, just kept herself medicated with booze and tried not to think about it. Jesse's mother said her kid couldn't stand seeing his friend used like that any longer."

"Why hadn't he said anything earlier?"

"He said Tripp begged him not to tell anyone about their little dress-up adventures. Jesse's mother claimed that he had never lied. She said he might hear voices, or think he was a bird sometimes, but that didn't mean he wasn't telling the truth. I believed her, but before I could arrange to talk to Jesse, he'd managed to hang himself from one of the windows in his room. I went back to the Nash kid. He swore up and down there'd never been any cross-dressing or sexual abuse, that Jesse must have made the whole thing up."

"And nobody but himself left to argue."

"Exactly. It smelled rotten, but we didn't have a scrap of physical evidence to tie Tripp Nash to the murders. I kept at him, tried to wear him down, see if he wouldn't slip somewhere. After about six months, he said he felt like he could trust me." Frank could hear MacLeish shaking his head, remembering.

"What did he tell you?"

"That he and Jesse had been best friends since they were kids, but in the past year, Jesse had started to 'act strange.' That was the way he put it. When I asked for examples, he said Jesse got jealous if he talked about any of the girls he'd met at boarding school. That made him uncomfortable, so he'd tried to ease things off, but that just made the situation worse."

"How?"

"He said Jesse got upset, started to make threats against him and his family. All my years in law enforcement, and I swear I've never met such a convincing liar. He knew exactly how to play it, how far to push—the kid was only seventeen, but he'd figured all the angles. He knew I couldn't touch him, and he was right."

"So you think it was murder by proxy?"

"I'd stake my life on it. I never told anybody this, but I used to drive down to his college, park at the edge of campus and just sit in the car—out in the open, where he could see me, wondering if he had the nerve to try something right under my nose. He never did—way too smart for that. I lost track of him after he left college. But you know what it's like—there's always one case that gets stuck in your head. I'm retired eight years now, but I still flip through my notes on the Nash case every once in a while, just in case something might pop. And I have to tell you, I've kind of been expecting this call. The last time I talked to Jesse's mother—

must be at least five years ago now—she told me she'd finally found Tripp Nash. After all this time. But before I could get the details, she died."

"What happened?"

"Heart attack. I tried to find out what she knew, but she was living in a halfway house in Portland by then. They'd pitched her stuff by the time I got the news that she was dead. I'm curious—what's any of this got to do with your case?"

"I'm not really sure. We found an article about the Nash case in with a bunch of newspaper clips about one of our victims, Natalie Russo. Does that name ring a bell?"

"Not really."

"There was a note in with the clips as well. Addressed to our suspect. Unsigned. 'You're gonna pay. For what you did.' Postmarked in Portland, Maine."

"And what's your suspect's name?"

"Hallett. Peter Hallett."

MacLeish cursed on the other end of the phone—softly, but vehemently. "Connie Nash was Tripp's aunt—his father's sister. The kid's maternal grandfather became his legal guardian after the parents were killed in a car crash, but the old man never paid much attention to him, so Connie and her husband took the boy in. He went by Nash when he lived with them, but there was never any legal adoption process. And Tripp was just a nickname. The kid's real name was—"

"Don't tell me," Frank said. "Peter Hallett." Now it was his turn to swear. He filled MacLeish in on Tríona's murder, the discovery of Natalie Russo's body at the river, how they hadn't been able to establish a connection between Hallett and the first victim. "We're convinced he was involved, but all the physical evidence so far points to the killer in both cases being female."

"That doesn't surprise me. You know what does? That he had no handy scapegoat waiting in the wings for his wife's murder, nobody conveniently lined up to take the fall. Tripp Nash, Peter Hallett, call him whatever you like, he doesn't do anything for himself. Doesn't have to. You want my advice? Look around. Your killer's got to be someone close to him, somebody like Jesse Benoit—prone to jealousy, easily led. Somebody who believes Hallett's been ill-treated, abused." MacLeish was silent for a moment. "He's just going to keep at it, isn't he? Until somebody stops him."

7

The following morning, while Cormac was on his daily visit to the hospital, Nora and Elizabeth set out again for the caves at Port na Rón. The clouds from the previous day had given way to clear blue overhead, but beneath the open vault of sky, a thick mist rolled in on the sea's glassy surface. The mist had the strange effect of altering distance, of making the small islands in the cove seem to loom close, and then recede. At times it was only a thin veil, and other times it appeared amazingly solid, looking for all the world like a footbridge upon which a person might walk straight out to the rocky crags in the harbor.

They bypassed the beach this time, and crossed over to the far side of the bay beyond the fisherman's cottage. The caves were more easily accessible from water than from land. Nora led the way as they climbed down between the rocks. As they drew closer, the smell of salt and seaweed mingled with a distinctive animal scent. These caves were a rookery, Cormac had said—a birthing place for seals, where they came for rest and respite during their most vulnerable time. Nora moved forward into the cave, imagining the floor carpeted with warm bodies, white pups nursing at their mothers' breasts. Cormac had assured her that seal breeding season wasn't until the autumn, a few weeks away, and that they could stay here if need be without interfering with the annual migration.

While Elizabeth's back was turned, Nora removed a bundle of candles, batteries, and food from her pack, and stashed it in a cleft in the rocks. She turned to see Elizabeth crouched and staring at the floor of the cave.

"Look," Elizabeth said, as Nora approached, pointing to a shallow indentation in the rocks at her feet. "What do you think it is?"

The dishlike depression was splashed with deep crimson. Blood—it had to be. Some creature had been injured here.

Nora heard the soft sound of breathing, and looked up to find herself and Elizabeth observed from the cave's opening by a spotted gray seal. One of the animal's eyes was damaged; the side of its head bore a star-shaped scar. It was very like the creature they'd seen down the road at Bruckless. Not completely inconceivable—seals migrated long distances, looking for food. Still, it was odd.

"Lizzabet," Nora said. She kept her voice calm, hoping not to startle the animal. "Here's your friend again."

Elizabeth turned slowly, her eyes widening at the sight of the unexpected intruder. The seal's fleshy body was draped across the threshold of the cave, and its single dark eye glinted as it looked to each of them in turn. Nora realized she had never been so close to a wild creature, at least never one so large as this seal. She studied the fine white eyebrow whiskers that lent it a look of perpetual wonder. There was a gash in the seal's fleshy neck—perhaps that's where the blood had come from. The creature made a soft snuffling sound, and then opened its mouth, exposing teeth and tongue, and let out a bawl that sounded unnaturally loud inside the cave.

"What do you suppose it wants?" Nora asked.

As if in answer to her question, the seal began to shuffle in reverse. Once outside the cave, the animal heaved its bulk to one side, casting a glance back at them with its good right eye.

"She wants us to follow her," Elizabeth said.

The seal led them down to the water's edge and along the edge of the beach, turning to check every few seconds, as if to make sure they were still in pursuit. At the end of the rocky alcove, the seal galloped out into the rippling waves and dived, immediately transformed from lumbering beast to sleek bullet—the webbed flippers, useless on land, now marvelously graceful in that watery world. Then it was gone, leaving only widening circles in its wake.

Elizabeth stood staring out at the water, perhaps hoping for a glimpse of a glossy head, while Nora's attention was pulled to a gleaming cabin cruiser tied up at the near side of the concrete pier. She hadn't heard a boat approaching, but the thick mist and the sound of the rolling stones might have been enough to mask any engine noise. Or it might have been there all along. Small waves rocked the white hull gently from side to side. No one seemed to be aboard.

Nora felt a cold chill down her arms. She climbed the hill where the pier was attached to the harbor side, and Elizabeth followed. Before venturing out onto the narrow concrete jetty, she turned. "Stay right there, Lizzabet. Don't move."

The boat was twenty-five feet at least, with a cabin belowdecks and a powerful inboard motor that wouldn't have made a lot of noise coming in. Why had someone just abandoned it here? She glanced back at Elizabeth and reached for the walkie-talkie, hoping she remembered Cormac's instructions on how to work it.

"Cormac—come in. Are you there?" She crept closer to the boat, expecting a head to emerge any moment from below.

His voice came crackling through the speaker. "What's happening, Nora? Where are you?"

"At Port na Rón. There's a boat tied up at the pier, but I can't see anyone around. You haven't heard from Devaney?"

"No. Maybe you should head back to the house—"

"I'm going to see if anyone's below."

"Nora, don't—"

His voice cut out as she clipped the walkie-talkie to her belt, and started down the ladder at the side of the pier. "Stay there," she called to Elizabeth. "I'll be right back."

Down on the level with the boat, she vaulted onto the deck over the gunwale. A pair of sunglasses lay on the ledge above the wheel, but there were no other obvious signs of occupancy. No keys in the ignition. She called down into the cabin through the open hatch door. "Hello—anyone here?" No answer. She unclipped the walkie-talkie and pressed the button to speak. "Cormac, are you still there?"

"What's happening? Is everything all right?"

"There's no one on the boat. Nobody around at all. It's odd."

"Listen, I'm coming up to Kilcar, and I'm calling Devaney right now. Will you please get out of there? Let me know as soon as you get back to the house."

"I will—I promise."

She clipped the walkie-talkie to her belt again and climbed up the ladder, stopping short at the sight that greeted her. Elizabeth stood at the far end of the pier, arms pinned behind her back. The person who held her was Miranda Staunton—the new Mrs. Hallett.

8

Miranda offered a chilly smile. "What's the matter, Nora—not the person you expected? Take a step closer, and I'll break her arms. Don't tempt me." Elizabeth caught a sharp breath as Miranda tugged at her elbows.

Nora raised her right hand, signaling her niece to keep still, while her left hand inched closer to the walkie-talkie at her waist. Miranda's icy voice stopped her: "No, you don't—drop it."

There was no choice. Nora slid her thumb across the "talk" button as she lifted the walkie-talkie from her belt, and Cormac's voice sounded through hissing static. "Nora? Nora—are you there?"

Miranda shook her head. "Too bad you can't answer. Now kick that thing into the water. Do it!"

Nora tried nudging the walkie-talkie with her foot, hoping she could get it to land on the lower pier, but the rubber casing that rendered the bloody thing indestructible also made it bounce. The walkie-talkie landed in the water with a loud plop.

Miranda began to edge up the side of the ridge above the pier, keeping her eyes on Nora, and Elizabeth in front of her. Nora's mind raced. If she could just buy some time—

"How on earth did you find us?"

Miranda fumbled for Elizabeth's backpack and held up a small disk attached to the zipper. "The wonders of modern technology—a GPS kid tracker. Turn-by-turn directions at the touch of a BlackBerry."

"And you think Peter will be grateful when you bring Elizabeth back, is that it?"

Miranda's voice was steel: "I didn't come here to bring her back." She continued: "Whose idea do you think it was to drag her along in the first place? Her father was going to leave her in Saint Paul. Of course the original plan didn't include you, but now that we're all here, I'm thinking this might actually work out for the best. The tragedy will just be compounded. Elizabeth will have an unfortunate accident, trying to escape from her kidnapper—that's you—and then, in a fit of remorse, you'll throw yourself onto the rocks. Or maybe you'll just lose your footing—I haven't decided. Sometimes it's better to let things develop naturally." She continued climbing backward up the hill, pulling Elizabeth along. The ground beneath their feet grew steeper with every step.

Nora knew she had to keep Miranda talking if they were to have any chance at all. "How can you think you'll get away with this?"

Miranda stopped and beamed with malicious satisfaction. "You mean, besides the fact that I've gotten away with everything so far? Including your precious sister—"

Nora watched Elizabeth's lips move soundlessly: *Mama*.

"You're telling me Peter had nothing to do with Tríona's death?"

"When are you going to get it through your thick skull, Nora? Peter couldn't hurt a fly—that's always been his problem. Fortunately, it's a fault I'm willing to overlook."

"You put that bottle under my brake pedal."

"Someone had to make sure you didn't ruin everything. For Chrissake, Nora, you left the car unlocked. It was practically an invitation."

"And Natalie Russo? What about her?"

Miranda's eyes narrowed. "You think you're so clever, don't you? I knew there'd be trouble when somebody found poor Natalie. It was bound to happen. I just hoped I'd be far away by then. Thought she could knock me out of the trials—"

Miranda was approaching the top of the crag. She stood for a moment, slightly winded, still pinning Elizabeth's arms behind her back.

"I don't know how Tríona found out about Natalie, but she did. And she was going to make me pay. You have this idea that she was so perfect, but you don't know what she was up to—the drugs, going down to the river, screwing her brains out every night. Did you know she threatened to accuse Peter of child abuse if she didn't get what she wanted? She was planning to take him to the cleaners in the divorce. You have no idea what she was capable of."

"You sent the note—to get her to meet you out in the woods that night."

"What do you mean? She was the one who sent me a note about meeting at Hidden Falls."

"What did you do with it?"

"With what?"

"The note, Miranda—what did you do with the note?"

"I stuck it in my pocket. What does it matter?"

Nora's thoughts raced. The Galliard sweatshirt—it never belonged to Peter, it was Miranda's. She'd dumped it after killing Tríona. But there were two notes, one in Harry Shaughnessy's sweatshirt pocket and one Sotharith the fisherman picked up in the woods. Miranda thought Tríona had sent her the note, trying to blackmail her about Natalie—but Tríona had received an identical note, telling her to go to Hidden Falls, the place where she believed that *she* had killed Natalie—all at once, the horror of it began to crystallize.

Miranda was just a murder weapon, the blunt instrument Peter Hallett had wielded from a distance. The deviousness, the cunning of his plan almost took her breath away. But she had to speak. "I know how long you've loved him, Miranda. Since the beginning, long before he ever met Tríona. Peter knew it, too. He's been taking advantage of you, using you this whole time. Did you never wonder why he changed? Why, after so many years of indifference, he suddenly took an interest in you? Because you were useful. You could solve a problem for him. I suppose he broke down a few times about Tríona, all the suffering she'd put him through. He depended on you—if only she were out of the way, he'd finally belong to you. But what's going to happen when *you* become the problem, Miranda? Because sooner or later, you will. And you'll disappear, just like my sister. You think he hasn't got it all worked out? He's way ahead of you, Miranda. He's been ahead of us all for years."

"Be quiet."

"He lied about Tríona. Nothing he told you about her was true. He made up all kinds of outrageous stories to egg you on. Somehow he knew about Natalie—maybe he was out running when he saw you attack her at the river. That was when he knew he could use you. He took the clothes you dumped that morning and put Natalie's blood all over Tríona. Convinced her that she had something to do with Natalie's murder. He sent her a note that said, I know what you did. The same as the note he sent you. All he had to do then was to sit back and watch. Tríona went to the river that night because she was terrified that *she* had killed Natalie. Because he'd taken away her self-respect. He made her believe it. Peter has been watching you, and using you for years, Miranda. Can't you see that?"

Miranda's voice was cold. "I told you to stop talking." She pulled a flare gun from her waistband and pointed it at Elizabeth's head. "Not another word."

They continued to edge upward, and Miranda's foothold on the small ridges grew increasingly precarious. Nora stayed silent. She forced herself to keep from focusing on the muzzle pressed to Elizabeth's temple, and looked instead into the child's frightened eyes. *Don't speak, Lizzabet,* she urged silently. *Keep still—*

Without warning, Miranda's right foot went from under her. This was their only chance.

Seizing Elizabeth by the hand, Nora pushed the child ahead of her, shouting: "Keep going up! Don't look down, just keep going. Go!" She followed, feeling for footholds, struggling to keep from slipping down the steep incline. As a cloud of mist began to envelop the headland, Nora knew that Miranda was close behind, but the only sounds she could hear were her own ragged breathing and the pulse of the surf below.

After a few seconds, she felt Miranda's fingers grasp at her ankle. "Keep going," she urged Elizabeth. "Don't stop!" Giving a sharp thrust downward, Nora heard a cry as her foot made contact with some part of Miranda's body. "Not much farther," she shouted upward again. "Keep going. Can you see the top?"

Through the mist she saw a pair of legs cantilever out for a few seconds, and then disappear from view. "Run back to the house, Elizabeth. Find Cormac."

Reaching the top a few seconds later, Nora heaved herself up over the edge and staggered to her feet, scrabbling up the gravel wash where Elizabeth had fled. She hadn't gone more than ten yards when Miranda tackled her from behind. They rolled down the steep incline, until Nora's head and arms dangled over the edge. The wind had come up, and now waves below churned violently.

9

Nora was pinned, with Miranda astride her, holding a stone in both hands above her head. She grabbed for Miranda's wrists, trying to keep the deadly weapon at arm's length. They struggled, and finally, with a sharp twist, Nora pushed Miranda aside and scrambled to her feet. She raced for the top of the hill, but again Miranda came from behind and lunged at her, sending them both sprawling down the rocky bed of scree. They struggled to their feet, hanging on to one another, banged up and breathing heavily, like grapplers in a ring. A voice sounded above them: "Miranda—what are you doing?"

They both looked up to see Peter at the top of the ridge. He came skidding down the loose stones, nearly losing his balance. "What's going on?"

Nora knew she only had one more chance. She took Miranda by the shoulders. "Tell me—do you ever wake up and not remember what happened?"

Peter cut in: "Miranda, don't listen to that—"

But Nora could see that her question had struck home, and she kept talking. "How many times has it happened? Once, twice—more? That's GHB—liquid ecstasy—you can't remember anything. He's already turned on you, Miranda. Just like he turned on Tríona."

"That's a lie, Miranda. You know how she twists everything—" Peter began to inch forward, but Miranda raised a hand to warn him off.

"Shut up—just shut up, both of you!"

No one spoke. Nora's left foot, bracing against the rim of the precipice, began to tremble. She glanced down as a few small pebbles tumbled off the edge and disappeared.

Miranda spoke: "That stuff—how does it make you feel?"

"Ready to fuck anything. And then it makes you sleep—"

Peter had begun to edge closer. Nora looked into his eyes and saw the same expression she'd seen there the morning after Tríona's murder. He was perfectly calm. A person might even imagine that he was enjoying himself. And why shouldn't he, when his two biggest troubles were about to take care of each other? He didn't have to lift a finger, and he was about to triumph yet again.

Nora suddenly stopped struggling. She felt so outrageously tired. "Go ahead," she said to Miranda. "Push me. See what happens. He'll tell the police he tried to stop you. You'll go down for murder, and he'll be rid of us both. That's what he really wants." She started to pull Miranda closer to the edge. "It would be even more convenient if we went down together." Miranda's feet were skidding along the gravel bed as Nora pulled her along.

"Peter—help me! She's trying to kill me!"

But Peter kept his distance, as Nora knew he would. "Miranda, don't try anything foolish."

Nora could see the fear in Miranda's eyes. "He *wants* you to try something foolish, don't you see? That's exactly what he wants. Whatever happens here, he's sitting pretty, rid of us both—just like that."

All at once, something happened that Nora had not anticipated. Elizabeth slid down the gravel wash, shouting, "Stop it, stop it—all of you!" She began to flail with both fists against Miranda's back. "Leave her alone! Leave Nora alone!"

Before anyone could stop her, Miranda reacted. She whirled around and gave a savage kick, and Elizabeth's arms and legs seemed to windmill in slow motion as she sailed off the edge of the precipice. All Nora could see were the luminous eyes, so like Tríona's, wide with terror. Then she was gone.

Miranda gave a short, mirthless laugh. And in that moment, a transformation came over Peter. His face, so relaxed and calm only a moment ago, was suddenly drained of color. He took two steps forward, seized Miranda savagely by the throat, and pushed her to the ground. His left hand searched blindly in the gravel for a stone heavy enough to crush her skull. His voice was quiet, toneless, as if he were berating a disobedient dog. "You crazy, stupid bitch—I told you to stay away from her. I told you she was only a kid—"

By the time Nora spotted the orange flare gun, it was too late to react. All she could do was watch as Miranda lifted the muzzle to Peter's face and pulled the trigger.

There was a flash as the flare exploded, and Nora fell back, watching in horror as he half rose and staggered back a step, dazed and disoriented, head engulfed in flames, his right hand still gripping the stone. The flare cartridge, lodged in his right eye, released a coruscating hail of sparks.

Miranda threw herself at him and began to shriek: "I didn't mean to—look what you made me do!" He roared in pain, and tried to fight her off, but she clung fiercely. They thrashed about, engulfed in a terrible rain of fire, before tumbling together into the sea.

Nora scrambled to the rim, but all she could see was a small spot of flame, glowing red under the water at the bottom of the cliff.

Cormac's voice came from the top of the ridge. "Nora!" He scrambled down the gravel wash. "What's happened here? Where's Elizabeth?"

She pointed wordlessly, and Cormac craned his neck over the edge. "I don't see her. She's not there."

"But I saw it—I watched her fall."

"Come on," he said. He pulled her to her feet, and they both scrambled down the steep slope to the rocky beach.

Standing at the water's edge, Nora spotted something floating on the surface a short distance away—what seemed like a human form, strangely buoyant. It was not possible. She closed her eyes and opened them again. It was.

Elizabeth floated, face up in the shallow surf, tangled in a raft of seaweed. Nora waded out and ran her hands over the child's slack limbs, feeling for fractures. There seemed to be none. A few scratches and scrapes, but no other outward signs of injury. How could that be? A faint snuffling noise made her turn, just in time to catch sight of a gray seal retreating into the waves. The animal turned to face her, one good eye clearly visible. It let out a single, plaintive bark before plunging into the surf.

Nora sank to her knees in the lapping water, cradling Elizabeth and smoothing her still-ragged hair. Suddenly Cormac was beside her, sinking down to catch the two of them in his arms, murmuring: "Ah no, please—"

Nora looked down at the smooth, insensible face of the child in her arms, then reached up to touch his face. "No, Cormac—she's alive. She lives."

Book Seven

Ireland and Brittany remain especially the regions in which fairy beliefs widely prevail; and the attachment of the people there to religion may have something to do with the continuance of the belief in fairies . . .

There is a queer imagination about this. When fairies want to take a person away from this world into fairy-land, the Irish say that they make the person melancholy, tired of life. If you are melancholy and do not care whether you live or die, the fairies get power to take you away. You die and your soul becomes a fairy . . . Mysterious disappearances of peasant women are sometimes thus accounted for in Ireland. Very possibly the woman has been killed, or lost in a bog.

—*Life and Literature,* by Lafcadio Hearn, from a series of lectures delivered at the University of Tokyo between 1896 and 1902, selected and edited with an introduction by John Erskine, Ph.D., Professor of English at Columbia University, 1917

1

Frank Cordova held the phone receiver to his ear, unsure that he had heard correctly. He felt as if he'd taken a hard punch to the sternum. It didn't seem possible that Peter Hallett was dead. Five long years and it was all over, just like that.

Miranda Staunton had confessed to killing Tríona, but everything he had suspected since that conversation with Gordon MacLeish was true. Peter Hallett had murdered his wife as surely as if he had crushed her skull himself. Just as he had murdered his aunt and uncle all those years ago in Maine. But when Nora told him how it all went down, Frank hadn't felt vindicated at all—he felt robbed, cheated out of his chance to look that bastard in the face inside a courtroom, to present the evidence and hear the word pronounced from the bench: *Guilty*.

Did Nora feel as betrayed as he did, the whole focus of her life for the past five years suddenly snatched away? Maybe she'd found something else to replace it already. The pain in his chest wouldn't seem to go away.

"Frank—are you still there?" Her voice sounded distant. "There's so much we haven't talked about—"

He felt her presence at the other end of the connection and wondered if things had been different between them, if they had met in other circumstances—

But things had been as they were. Nothing to be done about it now. He cleared his throat. "I should let you get back to Elizabeth. Thanks for calling—"

After a pause, she said: "Look after yourself, Frank." He closed his eyes and felt her hand brush against his face as it had that one brief, haunting night. "Promise me."

"You too." He felt the door of possibility about to close again, this time forever. "Good-bye, Nora."

He hung up the phone. Looking at the piles on his desk, thinking about all the misdirected, messed-up lives they represented, he felt an immense, cavernous emptiness. It was as if all his insides had been removed, and the open space left behind had been scoured clean. And yet there was one thing, one tiny detail that tugged at him: how Elizabeth Hallett had not only survived a fall that had killed her father and Miranda, but was apparently uninjured. Sometimes the innocents survived. The only way to describe it was miraculous.

Milagroso! The word fluttered up from somewhere inside him, and with it he felt the breath of the *curandero*'s fan.

2

After washing up on the beach at Port na Rón, Elizabeth slept. She was not in a coma, the doctors said, but in a state of hypersomnia, long hours of deep slumber from which she could be roused only with great difficulty. Her eyes would open occasionally, but the wakefulness didn't last. The larger mystery, from a medical standpoint, was how she hadn't sustained any major physical injuries—either internal or external—in her fall from the cliff. No one could explain it.

Nora barely left Elizabeth's bedside at the hospital. She spent the night in a chair. Now she stood looking down at her niece, and noticed the child's eyes moving almost imperceptibly under their lids in the dim half light. What did Elizabeth dream about, in that mysterious, overpowering sleep? Given all that had happened, no one could blame her for not wanting to wake to the world again. Seized by a sudden stab of fear, Nora leaned forward and spoke softly into Elizabeth's ear: "Come back to us, Lizzabet—you're not finished here."

Elizabeth stirred and drew a deep breath as though finally surfacing. She pushed herself up from the pillow and opened her eyes, though she didn't seem completely conscious. Nora reached out to rouse Cormac, who was dozing in the chair in the corner.

"I'll get the nurse," he said, and quickly headed off down the hall.

"I'm thirsty," Elizabeth murmured.

Nora poured a glass of water and pressed it into her niece's hand. "How are you feeling?"

"Where's my dad? I have to see my dad."

Nora moved closer. "What about something to eat?"

Elizabeth shook her head and gave a great yawn as she sank back on the pillow again. "No, I just want to see my dad. Where is he?"

"He's—not here, Lizzabet."

"What do you mean? Where is he?" She seemed to understand that something was not right, and sat up in the bed, regarding Nora with alarm, as if she suspected some conspiracy. "Why won't you tell me where he is?"

"Oh, Lizzabet. He fell, out at the harbor—there was a struggle, and he and Miranda fell—" She couldn't say any more.

Elizabeth drew herself up against the headboard. Her voice was a whisper: "He's dead, isn't he? My daddy is dead?"

Nora could only nod. She reached out, but Elizabeth pushed her hand away, and began to thrash under the bedclothes as the memories began to return. "I heard, all that stuff you said about him to Miranda. It's not true—it can't be. You're a liar!" She struck out, landing a few hard slaps before Nora could fend her off. "Why would you say those things? You're nothing but a stinking liar!"

Nora tried to move closer, to calm her. "Lizzabet, please listen, please—"

But Elizabeth kept thrashing. "Get out! You don't know anything. I don't want you here. Get out!"

Nora backed away and retreated into the corridor, the angry slaps still smarting. What did she think would happen, how had she imagined a child might respond to such news? That was the trouble—she hadn't imagined anything. She had never let herself get that far. It was always about nailing down evidence, convicting Peter, not about the consequences that would follow. She had let herself imagine that everything would be resolved, if only justice prevailed, if only she could convince the world of Peter Hallett's guilt. But she had so far failed to convince the one person whose belief mattered most.

Her parents would be arriving tomorrow, and what would she say to them? After everything, there was still no concrete proof against Peter. He was ultimately responsible for the deaths of at least five people, maybe more, but it was possible that there never would be any proof. It had come down to her word against his, yet again.

Nora leaned forward and pressed her aching head against the cold tiles of the corridor. She felt so weary. It was clear from everything Miranda told her out on the headland, everything she'd learned from Frank, that they'd only begun to scratch the surface. But who would continue digging, now that Tríona's killers were dead? She couldn't rely on Frank any longer—the case would be officially closed. He had other leads to follow, other responsibilities. They might speak on the phone, but Nora knew with perfect certainty that she would never lay eyes on Frank Cordova again. This was not the way things were supposed to happen. Peter Hallett would continue to dog her for the rest of her life.

Nora felt someone standing behind her. Cormac touched her shoulder. "Elizabeth is all right," he said. "The nurse is with her now. She's still in shock, Nora."

"He turned her against me—he's still turning her against me, even after he's dead. She's never going to believe anything I say."

"Elizabeth has to protect herself right now, Nora. Just to survive. It's going to take some time for her to see what's true and what isn't."

"She heard everything, Cormac. What he did to Tríona, what he was doing to Miranda. How can she not believe it?"

"She's a child, Nora. All the family she's had for the past five years is suddenly ripped away, and she doesn't know where to turn. She's suddenly thrust into the adult world, not at all sure that's where she wants to be. You can't blame her for wanting to retreat back into the past, the time when she still believed her father a decent man. We all want to believe our fathers are decent men. Even if they're not." He turned her around. "Will you come with me? There's someone I want you to meet."

"I can't, Cormac—"

"You can—come." He took her arm, and they walked down the corridor to the stroke unit, with patients behind glass windows. Cormac stopped and let her look in at a white-haired man, asleep with his mouth open, insensible to the world around him.

"I haven't introduced you to my father," Cormac said. "You may never have a chance to know him as he was. I've barely had that chance myself. Whatever brief time we had may be over. But being here with him these last few days has taught me something, Nora. I need to understand who he is, where I've come from—just as Elizabeth will need to understand, one day." He turned her face to him, stroked her cheek. "Please believe me, Nora. She will come back to you—if you give her time."

Nora gazed through the glass at Joseph Maguire, tears streaming down her face.

3

Nora stared out the car window through a light rain. The sky couldn't decide whether it was stormy or fair; showers were mixed with bouts of sunshine. They were on their way back to the house, and had just come through a festival-clogged Glencolumbkille when Cormac's mobile rang.

After a brief conversation, he snapped the phone shut and turned to her. "Garrett Devaney," he said. "Are you up for a quick detour? Devaney says he has information on the case that he'd rather convey in person. He's at a bar called Cassidy's. On this road, he says, up near the crossroads at Largybrack. I gather there's a sort of hideaway session going on there. Are you up to it?"

"To tell you the truth, I could use a drink."

Cassidy's was an old stone building at the side of a crossroads near the mouth of a glen. Cormac ordered up a pair of large whiskeys, and brought them back to where Nora sat in the mostly empty lounge. She glanced over at the small group of players in the back corner of the bar, and saw that Garrett Devaney had spotted them as well. After the next reel set finished, he put down the fiddle and made his way over.

"And how's Elizabeth?"

Nora didn't seem able to answer. Cormac jumped in: "A little better—she's awake. But she hasn't had a chance to process everything. She knows her father was killed, but—"

Devaney grimaced. "Still denies he did anything wrong?"

"She blames me," Nora said. "For everything."

Devaney shook his head. "Now listen, you can't be thinking like that. It's rough, I know, but you can't." He glanced around at the pub packed with patrons, and lowered his voice. "I've been checking with a few contacts. I've a mate over at the Serious Crimes Unit, the crowd that are handling the investigation. Here's something he told me—searching through Hallett's bags, they found his BlackBerry, with a link to a tracking device planted inside Miranda's mobile."

Cormac asked, "What does that mean, exactly?"

Nora said: "That makes sense. Peter knew where Miranda was all along, just as they both knew where Elizabeth was. Peter didn't leave anything to chance. He must have known what she was up to—that she was coming after us. He was using her to get to me."

"That's not all," Devaney said. "The scene-of-crime squad also found a small bottle of eyedrops—"

"But it wasn't eyedrops at all. I can tell you what it was. GHB—liquid ecstasy. He told everyone that my sister was addicted to the stuff, out of control, but he was feeding it to her. Out there on the headland, I asked Miranda if she ever had blackouts—from her reaction, I think Peter had done the same thing to her. There's probably no way to prove it."

"But finding the stuff in his possession proves that he knew where to get it," Cormac offered. "That's something."

Devaney pursed his lips and looked slightly uncomfortable. "I'm not sure how to tell you this last bit, except to say it straight out—your man Hallett was evidently into wearing women's clothes. The state pathologist found lacy underpants on him at postmortem, under his regular clothes. I can't say what it means—I'll leave that to the psychologists. But I thought you ought to know about it, in case something should leak out in the press."

Nora could hear Cormac ask a question, but her thoughts were far away, back in the cardboard evidence boxes at Saint Paul police headquarters. All those items of unwashed lingerie the crime scene investigators had found stuffed into the backs of drawers and under Tríona's bed, all marked with her DNA, and Peter's, along with unknown donors, male and female. They had always assumed Peter's DNA was present because he and Tríona were married—and it was a logical assumption—but now there was another possible explanation altogether.

The river was where people went to become someone else. To shed all the strictures, the guises they maintained above, in the real world.

There are things you don't know, Nora. About Peter, about me—

"For I have seen the false mermaid—" she whispered.

Devaney exchanged a quick look with Cormac. "Well, I'll leave you. That's all the news I've got for now. I'd better get back to Róisín before she's completely corrupted by all these Donegal tunes. Give us a shout if you need anything, right?"

After Devaney left them, Nora was silent a long time, staring down at her empty whiskey glass. "Why didn't she come to me, Cormac? Why wouldn't she trust me? I could have done something to help her—"

Suddenly the musicians hushed, and all ears in the pub tuned to the sound of an old woman singing. Only a few words of Irish came through; the other sounds seemed nonsensical, a series of long, plaintive vowels. But the leathery voice was so full of experience and grief that all who heard it were mesmerized, unable to move until the last note faded away. Nora swiped at her eyes.

"Who was that singing?" Cormac asked the barman, who'd come to collect their empty glasses.

"Ah, that's Kitty Sean Cunningham. From Cappagh, just above Teelin. Seventy-eight last Monday week, but she can still wind a good song." He leaned forward and lowered his voice. "They say she used to sing, out collecting seaweed, and the seals would come up onto the rocks and listen. Not everyone can call them. But Kitty has the power, they say, because her grandmother was one of 'em."

"And people still believe that?" Cormac asked.

The barman smiled. "Ah, sure, no one believes the old stories anymore. But like my granny used to say, that doesn't mean they aren't true. Can I get you another drink?"

"No thanks," Cormac said. "We're finished here."

As they left the bar, Nora still felt stunned. Devaney's report dredged up all sorts of dreadful possibilities about what Tríona had gone through in those last few weeks. Each new realization brought fresh pain. Cormac followed her outside, apparently unsure what he should say. What could he say?

At the car, she turned to him. "Do you realize what this means? All this time, I thought Peter was just possessive and jealous. That he killed Tríona—had her killed—because he couldn't bear to let her go. But it wasn't that kind of jealousy at all. It was a different kind. He was taking her clothes, Cormac, wearing them down to the river. He didn't just want to possess Tríona, he wanted to *be* her—I never understood until now."

"Nora, what are you saying?"

"All those awful things he accused her of—the drugs and the late nights, the sex with random strangers—Tríona didn't have any memory of doing those things, because she never did them. *He did.* And she must have found out somehow. That's what she was trying to tell me, when she talked about letting things go too far. But she gave him the benefit of the doubt. Right up until the very end. Even after she knew he was deliberately tormenting her, she still wouldn't believe it. My God—it's all so twisted." Though the night was warm, Nora couldn't keep from shivering. "And it just keeps getting worse. How could he have fooled us for so long—how could we not see what he was? He must have realized that Tríona would try to leave him sooner or later, that eventually she'd begin to figure it out."

"But just as he was getting desperate enough to act, Miranda came onto the scene, mad jealous of Natalie Russo," Cormac said. "She played right into his hand."

"Oh, Cormac—how can I ever tell Elizabeth any of this? It's all so insane."

"Don't think about it, not tonight. Let me take you home."

4

The next morning, Cormac awakened to find Nora beside him in bed, the fingers of her right hand laced through his. They'd managed to make it through the night, but neither of them had slept well. He could see that the revelations of the previous evening had not loosed their grip on Nora. She looked pale, exhausted. And her parents were due to arrive in less than six hours. That meant everything would be gone over again, in detail, including Elizabeth's accusations, and he could not save her from any of it.

Nora's eyes were closed, but she was awake. He touched her face. "I meant to ask, where's your hazel knot—the one I made you out at Loughnabrone?"

Her hand slipped from his. "It must have fallen out of my pocket the night of the crash. I kept it with me, Cormac, I swear. Right here in my pocket—" She leaned down to pick up her jeans from the floor, showing him where she'd kept it.

A crinkled bit of fabric peeped from the pocket, and he pulled it out, surprised to find an old-fashioned woolen stocking. "What's this?"

"I'd almost forgotten about that," she said. "I think an eagle dropped it on me, over at Port na Rón."

Cormac held the stocking up to the light. Fine black wool—and the heel was neatly darned. He felt a vibration, the same frequency as when he'd first laid eyes on the high-button shoe from the abandoned cottage.

Nora continued: "I'm not sure why I kept it. An odd thing to find at a beach, I guess."

"Could you show me exactly where you found it?"

"What is it, Cormac? What's wrong?"

"I'll explain when we get there."

At the deserted village, they climbed down the rocky escarpment. Cormac glanced up at the craggy rocks, and at the steep bank that fell away above the beach. The enormous heap of pale stones had washed out of the boggy earth above them.

"Tell me what you saw that day," he said to Nora.

"When we first arrived at the beach, I was standing here," she said. "Elizabeth was on the rocks over there—" She pointed out a trio of flat stones at the north edge of the bay. "I was watching her, but something—a movement up there—distracted me. It was a pair of sea eagles. I've never seen two of them together like that. They were fighting over something." She cast her eyes about for the exact spot. "Look, there's one of them now—"

She set off climbing up the rocks, and Cormac followed. By the time they reached the top of the eroding bank, the eagle was long gone. But as they drew near, Cormac could see where the giant bird had been perched. The stony ground was covered in a blanket of peat that stretched to the edge of the escarpment. He crouched down for a closer look. The edge was unstable; one false move, and you might do a header right down onto the beach below—unless you had wings, of course. Two pairs of talons had made a series of gashes in the soft ground where the two birds had been wrestling. Cormac edged closer to the brink to push aside the drying edge of peat, and drew back in surprise.

"What is it?" Nora asked.

"I'll let you see for yourself." He grasped Nora's hand as she leaned forward. What they were looking at was a human foot, mostly stripped of flesh, the toe delicately pointed seaward. Beside it, the toe of an old-fashioned shoe had begun to surface from under the peat.

"She's here," Cormac murmured. "She was right here under their noses all along."

"What are you talking about?" Nora demanded.

He moved to where the woman's head should be if this was a normal supine burial, and pulled out his pocketknife, cutting through the grass carpet and peeling it back to expose the wet peat underneath. As he dug with bare hands, he wondered: What would the face of a sea maid look like? Would she still have her beauty after years under the peat, like the *cailín rua*? His mind conjured the curious faces, the mournful eyes of the seals who surrounded him while he was out rowing. At last his fingers felt something—the roundness of a cranium vault. But as he worked to remove the peat, in the place where he expected to find a forehead, a brow ridge, a nose, there was nothing but a shallow depression and a fistful of splintered bones. Whoever this woman was, her face had been battered in, her identity effectively erased.

Nora knelt beside him. She said: "You know who she is, don't you?"

"I haven't had a chance to tell you about this place," he said. "Remember the other night, when you sang *'An Mhaighdean Mhara,'* and I asked why you chose that song? There's a local connection. This is where she lived—"

"Who?"

"The woman from the song—Mary Heaney."

Nora drew back. "It's only a story, Cormac. It's not real."

"I don't blame you for being skeptical. I was, too—" He climbed to his feet and reached for her hand. "Come with me."

Inside the selkie cottage, he dug through the stones and shells under the cot until he found the high-button shoe. He handed it to Nora. "It's been bothering me for days, ever since I first came here. Why would anyone leave home with only one shoe? Two shoes makes sense, or none—but one shoe doesn't make any sense at all."

Nora sat in one of the low chairs to examine the shoe. It was rimed with dust and white mildew, but the cutwork around the ankle was distinctive. This was unmistakably the mate of the one they'd just seen peeping from the turf.

Cormac sank into the opposite chair. "The woman they called Mary Heaney, the woman who lived in this house, was a foreigner. She showed up one day in 1889 on a small boat with a local fisherman, P. J. Heaney. The woman spoke no Irish, no English. But she stayed on and lived with Heaney as his wife, had two children by him. People began to believe she was a selkie, like the Mary Heaney in the song. She would sit alone on the headland; Roz had reports of her singing in a strange language. She has all this documented—Roz has—census records, interviews, newspaper reports. When Mary Heaney disappeared six years later, people said she had discovered the sealskin Heaney had stolen from her, and returned to the sea. Everyone bought into it—all her neighbors here at Port na Rón, the newspapers, even the police. Everyone wanted to believe the myth of the seal wife when it wasn't what actually happened."

"But that song is quite old, isn't it? How could the person who lived here be Mary Heaney if the song has been around for hundreds of years?"

"They did share the same name. And people wanted to believe—Roz thinks it was a convenient way to absolve themselves of responsibility, since it was likely everyone in the village knew she was being ill-treated.

Her husband encouraged the selkie stories. If everyone believed she'd gone back to the sea, it would stop them having to search for her."

"And was the husband never a suspect?"

"He was, of course, but because there was no body, and therefore no proof of murder, Heaney was never charged. Never even arrested. He disappeared from his boat a few years later—presumed drowned."

"And the children?"

"Shipped off to relations near Buncrana; Roz thinks the boy may have been killed in the First World War. She still hasn't traced the daughter."

Nora turned to stare out the cottage door at the tumbling surf. They sat in silence for a long time, listening to the hiss of the tide, the rattling stones. At last she stood up.

"Let's go back," Nora said. "We ought to at least cover her face."

5

Frank Cordova spent the day after Nora Gavin's phone call putting away the murder book on her sister. Evidence would keep drifting in for a few more weeks, but it was over. At five, he got a call from Jackie Smart in the crime lab.

"Hey, remember that chewing gum you brought in the other day? We got a positive match to the unknown female from Harry Shaughnessy's sweatshirt and shoes. Hope that helps."

"It does, Jackie—thanks."

With the DNA and the false mermaid seeds from the crime scenes, they would have had more than enough physical evidence to convict Miranda Staunton of two murders—if she had lived.

What they didn't have was definitive proof that she'd actually been set up, that killing Tríona hadn't been her own idea. But how did you prove Peter Hallett's subtle brand of manipulation? In all likelihood, he would be remembered—by most people who knew him, at least—as a victim, an innocent bystander done in by the excesses of people around him.

The story of any crime left out most of the details, the tiny minutiae that he dealt with every day. So much of what they discovered about people—the victims and the perpetrators—stayed buried in the files: the secret lives, all the missed or hidden connections that were either too complex or too sordid for the public to comprehend. Heroes and villains, that's what the public wanted, so they could shake their heads and cluck over their newspapers in the morning. The truth never really lined up with the facts.

The Nick Mosher connection had been bothering him ever since Nora brought it up, a dull presence lodged in the side of his head. How could it be just coincidence that Tríona and the friend she was working for both ended up dead on the same day? One thing was certain: Truman Stark knew more than he was telling.

Frank opened a drawer and dug out the file he'd retrieved on Nick

Mosher's accident. His body had been found at the bottom of an elevator shaft; cause of death was a broken neck, compounded by blunt force trauma to the head and face, injuries consistent with a fall.

Closing his eyes, Frank saw the shape of a body sprawled four stories below. He saw a pair of dark glasses, lying facedown next to the elevator, one of the lenses cracked. The investigating officers had ruled out suicide. If Nick Mosher had simply stepped into thin air, why were his glasses still up on the fourth floor, and not at the bottom of the elevator shaft? Were they already broken when he fell?

There was another strange detail in the file as well: a bunch of wilted flowers in the elevator. Nothing fancy, just a handful of garden-variety blooms—picked, not cut, according to the lab. Not that a thing like that made much difference in a case like this. The weird thing was that the flowers had been crushed before they hit the elevator floor and wilted there. So what did mangled flowers conjure up—a jilted suitor, maybe? No way to know if the flowers were connected. Only one elevator in the building; everyone used it.

Truman Stark had admitted following Nora from the parking garage to the Sturgis Building, maybe afraid that she knew something, or that she'd discover something. Stark claimed he'd been watching Tríona in order to protect her, but she'd still ended up dead. If Stark was supposed to be protecting her, where had he been that night? What was he doing when Tríona was attacked? Maybe the kid felt like he'd failed, fallen down as a guardian angel. What would make him think that? Frank's brain circled back to something Stark had said during his recent interview: *If I told the truth you wouldn't believe me.*

Frank slid the file back in his drawer, the image of Nick Mosher's broken glasses, and those flowers in the elevator still lingering. He picked up his phone and scrolled through the recent calls until he found the number he was looking for. Sarah Cates answered on the first ring.

"It's Frank Cordova. I wanted to thank you for coming to the visitation the other night. I saw you come in as I was leaving. Sorry I couldn't stay."

"That's okay—I happened to see the notice in the paper. Thought I'd pay my respects. I'm sorry—"

"Thanks." Frank felt his chest constrict, and braced himself for the stabbing pain, but it never came. "Does that offer of a free rowing lesson still stand?" He closed his eyes and pictured the two of them out on the water, pulling in the same direction, her turning to him with those eyes the color of the river in sunlight.

"Anytime. If you wanted to drop by after practice tomorrow—"

"I'll be there."

"You might not believe this, but when you called, I had just picked up the phone to call you. I'm organizing a kind of a memorial for Natalie. She wasn't religious—neither am I, really—but I thought a few of us could meet down at the river some evening next week, maybe go out on the water for a while. A sort of remembrance. I can tell you more about it tomorrow."

"That sounds good. See you then."

As Frank passed through the station's front lobby a few minutes later, the duty sergeant waved him over, indicating a figure slumped in one of the plastic chairs beside the front door. Truman Stark sat with his hands clasped before him, staring at the floor between his feet, both legs jigging to some internal rhythm.

"Somebody to see you, Detective. Wouldn't give a name. Says he's got information for you on an accidental death."

In the interview room, Truman Stark once again avoided eye contact. And once again, Frank waited. The kid asked to see him. Maybe his hunch had been right; maybe Stark hadn't spilled everything. A bit of a childhood prayer ran through Frank's head: *Ruega por nosotros pecadores*. Pray for us sinners. *Ahora y en la hora de nuestra muerte*—now and at the hour of our death.

He leaned back in his chair, trying to put the kid at ease. "When you were here before, you said if you told the truth, I wouldn't believe. Why don't you try me?"

It was clear that Truman Stark had made up his mind to tell what he knew. He just had no idea how to begin.

"The duty officer said you mentioned an accidental death—" Frank prompted.

Stark nodded. "Five years ago, in the Sturgis Building."

"Didn't happen to be a guy named Nick Mosher—the guy who fell down the elevator shaft?"

"I was there—" The kid looked as if he might choke.

"Relax, Truman. We're in no hurry here."

Stark nodded, and settled his shoulders. "I followed the redhead to the Sturgis Building that day. She met up with this guy on the fourth floor. He was wearing dark glasses."

"Nick Mosher."

"That was the last time I saw her, I swear."

"Did she seem happy to see Mosher?"

The memory clearly pained him. "She kissed him."

"Just a friendly kiss, or something more?"

"I don't know—why are you asking me? She kissed him, and handed over a coffee she'd brought him from downstairs."

"And then?"

"I hit the elevator button. I wasn't going to stick around. I had to get back to work."

An image began to form in the back of Frank's brain. The flowers, the jilted lover. He kept quiet—the kid might clam up. "So you don't know what Tríona Hallett was doing on the fourth floor of the Sturgis Building that day?"

Stark shook his head.

"But you had some idea?"

"I knew she was married. I thought maybe she was fooling around."

"And you wanted to get your feet wet as a private eye, was that it?"

"No—no. I just wanted to find out why she was always looking over her shoulder. I saw the blonde following her a couple of days before. I thought maybe the blonde was a private eye the husband sent to check up on things."

"You didn't know who the redhead's husband was?"

"Not then, no. I saw his picture in the paper, after—"

"Let's get back to that day. You go back to work, you put in your shift, until what time?"

"Nine. I might have left the ramp around nine-fifteen."

"And then—"

"I went back to the Sturgis Building."

"Why?"

"I don't know—"

"To see if the redhead was still there?"

"I told you, I don't know why." Stark was getting agitated. "I got in the elevator—it was the old-fashioned kind, with the gate that comes down—"

"A freight elevator."

"I didn't see anybody around, so I opened the gate on the fourth floor and got off. Then somebody upstairs must have called the elevator, 'cause it took off."

"With the gate still open?"

"Yeah. Some of these old buildings—I had my flashlight, so I took a look down into the shaft, to see what I could see. And then I hear this voice behind me—'Careful. It's a long way to the bottom.' It was the blind guy I saw earlier. I wondered how he knew the elevator wasn't there. He says to me, 'You were on that elevator, weren't you? This afternoon.' And I'm thinking—how the fuck does he know that? He's blind. So I asked him, and he says—" Truman's voice had dropped to a whisper. Shame rolled off him in waves. "He says, 'Because you still smell of those flowers you were holding.' Next thing I know, he's behind me—" Frank stopped breathing. "And he—puts his hands on me. What did he have to go and do that for? I'm not a fucking queer. I had to get him off me, and it just—happened."

Unburdened at last, Truman Stark laid his head on the table and sobbed like a child.

6

All night, Nora had tried to sleep and failed. It was something of a reversal; Cormac was the usual insomniac. She lay beside him in the gray morning light, listening to the pulse of the surf outside, reading a musty old volume she'd pulled from a bookcase behind the door—*Ortha na nGael: Hymns and Incantations*—a compilation of verses collected in western Donegal in the late nineteenth century. Most were dressed up as Christian prayers, invoking the trinity or the Virgin or Saint Brigid, but retained their old shapes from the time before trinities had anything to do with Christ. The verses had been translated from the Irish, no doubt filtered through the transcriber's Victorian sensibility, but much of the beauty and plainness of the original language remained. Even written on the page, their repetitive rhythms still held the power of incantations.

In addition to the prayers, there were stories of shape-changers, and eerie lullabies; charms for all sorts of bodily afflictions, for fire smooring and night shielding; invocations addressing the moon and sun, for rituals of birth and death, and blessings for all sorts of animals, and not only cattle and sheep, but the wild beasts that figured in the local mythology as well: the salmon and the swan, the bull, the horse, the otter and the limpet, the seal. Rare glimpses into the rhythm of daily life in a place that had been for centuries the last outpost of the known world.

Nora closed her eyes, hearing the music of the words, seeing the images they brought forth, of darkness and light, of work and harvest, the damp breath of animals. The words carried a palpable sense of wonder from the people who had composed and repeated them so many generations before. Nora looked back at the book on her lap, fallen open to a charm against drowning. The words of the last stanza seemed to float up off the page:

A part of thee on grey stones,
A part of thee on steep mountains,
A part of thee on swift streams,

A part of thee on gleaming clouds,
A part of thee on ocean-whales,
A part of thee on meadow-beasts,
A part of thee on fenny swamps,
A part of thee on cotton-grass moors,
A part of thee on the great surging sea—
She herself has best means to carry
The great surging sea.
She herself has best means to carry.

She closed the book and set it aside. How did someone even attempt to carry the great surging sea?

Nearly two weeks had passed since her parents had arrived to take Elizabeth home with them to Saint Paul. Two weeks since the return of her hazel knot, discovered along a river path by Seng Sotharith, and two weeks since she learned that her parents had taken her protector in, that he would be staying in her old room and embarking on studies that would eventually transform him into a physician's assistant.

It was also exactly two weeks to the day since she and Cormac had helped to recover the preserved body of a young woman from the blanket bog above the rocky beach at Port na Rón. When she went into the bog, the young woman had been wearing two long black woolen stockings and one high-button shoe, a long skirt and petticoat, along with a shirtwaist and short jacket, in the fashion of the time. Her clothing had been preserved as if she'd dressed in it only a few days before, and not over a hundred years ago. There was still no definitive proof that the body in the grave was Mary Heaney, but Roz Byrne was now on a mission to trace the female line, to see if any link could be established through mitochondrial DNA between Mary Heaney's descendants and the faceless female from the bog.

Nora turned to observe Cormac, breathing softly, his chest moving up and down in a steady rhythm. How many times had she lain like this beside him, trying to comprehend the lightning storm of thoughts and dreams that crisscrossed his brain in sleep? She put out a hand, feeling the warmth of his breath against her palm, hearing in the back of her head the notes of the melody he'd sent her that first night in Saint Paul. He still hadn't spoken its name.

Maybe Cormac was right, and Elizabeth would come around. Maybe someday she would want to know the truth about her parents. But what was the truth? Nora knew she had to brace herself for the possibility that Elizabeth might travel the rest of her life on a razor's edge, on the one hand loathing the creature responsible for her mother's death, and on the other, feeling affection for the decent human being her father had appeared to be.

The universe had turned out to be a much stranger and more fluid place than she had ever imagined. All the boundaries and borders she had once believed in now seemed to be shifting and disappearing. Nothing was cut and dried. If anything, she felt much closer now to the view she had held as a child, where any eventuality—wondrous or hair-raising—was equally possible. The image of Tríona walking along that street in Lowertown, the book turned backward in the library stacks, how Harry Shaughnessy just happened to be the person who picked up Tríona's photo on the library plaza. The seal who had delivered Elizabeth from harm. These things could not be real, and yet they were—as real and true as any events in the history of the world.

Nora was beginning to realize that she had clung desperately to her own version of Tríona, much like one of the faithful might adhere to the legend of a saint—though everyone knew that saints' legends contained only fragments of truth, along with large portions of exaggeration, even falsehood. In some ways, keeping Tríona preserved like a saint under glass was almost as much a diminution as the calumnies Peter Hallett had engineered. Surely the truest remembrance would not reduce her, not make her any less in death than she had been in life. What about the hidden, contradictory sides of Tríona Gavin? They had existed, and might still be discovered—maybe it wasn't too late.

Rising from the bed, Nora tiptoed downstairs, past the door of Joseph Maguire's darkened room. He was still in hospital, and would remain there for another few days. He had awakened from forced slumber a changed creature, not himself even to himself, but submerged in a sea of strangeness, speaking in a language no human could understand. Cormac hadn't yet faced the prospect of what would happen when his father was ready to come home.

As she passed through the hallway, Nora perused a series of silver prints that hung on the wall. Photographs of seals—portraits, really—taken by Cormac's great-aunt Julia. Perhaps it was the combination of the gray dawn and the waning moonlight, but each image took on the aspect of a ghostly negative: the seals' eyes glowed white, their formerly white whiskers now looked dark against pale muzzles. She had often wondered what it was that triggered Tríona's fascination with these creatures. Was it the wordless, soulful eyes—the soft, motherly bodies? Or perhaps the amazing way they could move and hold their breath underwater? Nora herself had always judged seals a little too strange and ungainly, but Tríona had been extraordinarily drawn to them. Evidently the connection had been passed down to Elizabeth.

Nora leaned forward to read the lightly penciled caption beneath the last portrait: *A still dawn at Port na Rón—July 1947.* More than sixty years ago. The last and most haunting of the pictures showed an animal with a star-shaped mark around its one good eye.

Seized with a sudden desire to greet the dawn at Port na Rón, Nora threw on her jacket and shoes and slipped out of the house. As she pulled the door closed, the latch fell into place with a loud click. She stood still for several seconds, making sure Cormac had not been disturbed.

The sun was not quite up as she made her way over the headland. A thick mist drifted over the harbor ahead, and through it she caught occasional glimpses of the sea, as calm and glassy as it must have been that morning in 1947, with only a few ripples stirring against the pebbled beach. She stood at the top of the ridge, drinking in the fishy scent, while out in the harbor, a sleek form twisted up from the water and landed with a splash, the sign of a creature reveling in its own strength and speed, the sheer joy of sensation.

Nora climbed down to the beach and kept walking, not stopping to remove shoes or clothes, but striding straight out into waves until she was up to her hips, and within ten yards of the seal. It swam closer, only an arm's length now, its whiskered face raised out of the water. She could see how the features on one side of its face were scarred from some ancient injury. The same face as in the portrait, she was sure of it. How could that be? She reached out a hand to touch its fur, and the creature allowed her. It felt sleek, warm beneath the wetness. She remembered the words of the charm:

A part of thee on ocean-whales,
A part of thee on meadow-beasts,
A part of thee on fenny swamps,
A part of thee on cotton-grass moors,

A part of thee on the great surging sea—
She herself has best means to carry
The great surging sea.

The seal regarded her for a few seconds with an air of infinite compassion, before opening its mouth to offer a single rounded vowel of a bark. Was it a greeting or a valediction? As if in answer, the animal twisted away with a flourish of its tail, and sank once more into the sea. Nora took a deep breath, and plunged straight down. She felt compelled to follow. What was it Tríona had seen that day she had been rescued from drowning?

Nora swam forward, eyes wide open, when all at once someone or something caught her by the waist and lifted her clear of the water. Setting her upright in the shallows, Cormac took her face between his hands. "I can't let you do it, Nora—"

All at once it occurred to her what he must have imagined, following her, watching her walk out into the sea. "Oh, Cormac, I wasn't trying to—"

"Weren't you?"

"No—I don't know what I was doing. But it wasn't that, truly—I swear."

"You walked straight into the water, with all your clothes on—"

She looked him up and down. "So did you."

"But I was only going after you—" He stopped and sighed, resting his forehead against hers. "Why are we doing this to ourselves? You've been running from me for nearly two years, Nora. Why do you keep running?"

"I don't know, Cormac. I can't—"

"Can't what? Do you really believe Tríona would want you to suffer as you have? I know you could go on punishing yourself forever—but when will it ever be enough? You wanted to know the name of the tune I sent—I'll tell you. It's 'My Love Is in America.' Do you understand? Can you not see that I love you? Stop running, Nora. Stay with me. Be with me."

She looked into his eyes, and felt deep within them—and deep within herself—an immense, eternal pulse, calling up the words of that ancient, mysterious charm: *She herself has best means to carry.* When she offered Cormac her answer, it did not come in words.

As daylight broke over the headland, the mist slowly disappeared, and the surf began to churn around them with the incoming tide. The rising sun threw golden shafts on gulls and choughs as they took wing, and on the wet, curious faces of three young seals cavorting in the waves beyond the harbor rocks. High above the headland, almost out of sight, a lone sea eagle soared aloft.

ACKNOWLEDGMENTS

I am indebted to a number of people who helped with research for this book: Dónal and Libby Ward, for their hospitality, for sharing their knowledge of the history, folklore, and music of their home county, and for introducing me to some of the wonderful, hidden corners of southwest Donegal; Jill Cooper of the Minneapolis Rowing Club; Hannah Texler of the Minnesota Department of Natural Resources, Tim Whitfeld and Anita Cholewa of the Bell Museum/University of Minnesota Herbarium, Doug Mensing of the Minnesota Native Plant Society, Jennifer Doubt of the Canadian Museum of Nature / Musée canadien de la nature, and Dr. Carol C. Baskin of the Department of Biology at the University of Kentucky, for details on *Floerkea proserpinacoides* (false mermaid); Kathleen J. Craft, Ph.D., for information on population genetics and its application to the world of forensic botany; Ann Marie Gross of the DNA Section at the Minnesota Bureau of Criminal Apprehension, for information on DNA analysis and BCA procedure; Sergeant Mary Nash and Detective Jane Laurence of the Saint Paul Police Department for help with police procedure and background (and to fellow writers Kent Krueger and Lori Lake for sharing law enforcement contacts); Patrick J. Cleary of the Garda Síochána (retired), for assistance with Irish police procedure; flute player and physician Dr. Frank Claudy, and Jean Cleary, RN, for help with information on PTSD, emergency room procedure, and hospital admissions; fiddle player Randall Bays for background on Useless Bay in Washington State. I am indebted to my friend, artist Virginia McBride, for her creative support, and to her son and fellow artist, Owen Platt, who created the wonderful map of my fictional location Port na Rón. And I am grateful to Dáithí Sproule for his invaluable help with Irish language translation, and to singer Mairéad Ní Mhaonaigh of Altan, whose beautiful rendition of "*An Mhaighdean Mhara*" helped inspire this story. The help of all these individuals undoubtedly prevented many errors; they are not responsible for the literary license

I have taken, and any faults that remain are mine alone. Thanks also to my wonderful editors, Susanne Kirk and Samantha Martin at Scribner, and my peerless agent, Sally Wofford-Girand. And to the countless people who offered encouragement—not to mention a bit of gentle nudging—fans, neighbors, and friends (especially Lisa McDaniel, Karen Mueller, Lori Hindbjorgen, Elizabeth Childs, Pat McMorrow, and all the Widening Gyre writers); my beloved family; and my incredible, inspiring husband, Paddy—*go raibh mile maith agaibh.*

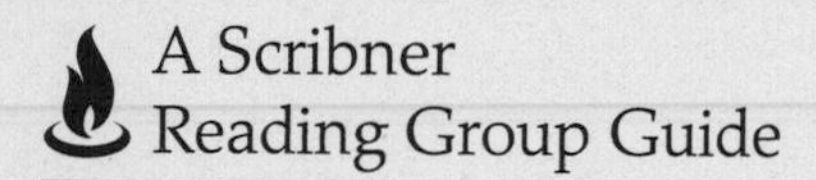

FALSE MERMAID

ERIN HART

This reading group guide for *False Mermaid* by Erin Hart includes discussion questions for your book club. The suggested questions are intended to help your reading group find new and interesting angles and topics for your discussion. We hope that these ideas will enrich your conversation and increase your enjoyment of the book.

Discussion Questions

1. *False Mermaid* opens with a newspaper article about the disappearance of a young Irish woman believed by some to have been a selkie (a seal temporarily transformed into a human). What ideas and images did this newspaper article bring to mind? How did the piece set up or color your impressions about how the novel would take shape?

2. What parallels do you see between the murder of Nora's sister in Saint Paul and the hundred-year-old disappearance of Mary Heaney, the young Donegal woman who was rumored to be a selkie? How relevant is the selkie story to the tale of Mary Heaney, or to Tríona Hallett's death?

3. Nora believes that her brother-in-law, Peter Hallett, had some sort of power over her sister, Tríona. Do you agree? Discuss Peter and his relations with the women in his life, including Tríona, Miranda, and Elizabeth.

4. Nora remembers what Tríona said, that Peter's behavior seemed harmless at first, but that she "let things go too far." What do you think Tríona meant by this? Do you think it's possible that she still loved her husband?

5. What sorts of experiences and connections do Elizabeth, Tríona, and Nora have with seals in the novel? If the one-eyed seal is a symbol, who or what do you think it represents? What does Cormac discover about his own previously unknown connections with seals and selkies?

6. Many characters in the novel are conflicted, torn between loyalties or emotions or places. How does internal conflict affect their external actions? Can you think of instances when it is a positive force or a negative one?

7. Shape-shifting and transformation are among the major themes in *False Mermaid*. Several characters are shown changing shape, wearing disguises, or assuming a different identity. Can you think of instances where this sort of change is depicted or suggested?

8. Ireland has long been a place where belief in the otherworld remains strong. Does the American portion of *False Mermaid* also contain otherworldly elements? Which characters, scenes, or images in the Saint Paul–based chapters help to underscore the novel's otherworldly atmosphere?

9. Each section of *False Mermaid* begins with a quotation from a Victorian folklorist or naturalist. What did you learn about the prevailing Victorian attitudes toward the subjects these men were writing about—the relationships between humans and animals and between civilized societies and so-called "primitive cultures" (which included most of Irish rural culture at the time), and unsettling, ancient notions of female emancipation represented by the selkie stories?

10. Both Nora and Tríona fear that they've lost the ability to distinguish truth from falsehood. Why? Think about the different meanings of the words "true" and "false." How do these different meanings come into play in *False Mermaid*?

11. The title *False Mermaid* is an obvious reference to the botanical clue that eventually solves Tríona's murder, but it could also refer to other aspects of the novel. What are they? How is this sort of layering, of providing multiple meanings or ways of looking at something, central to the novel?

12. What recurring themes or symbols did you see in the novel? Consider, for example, the role of water in critical events, or the importance of music to the characters. What other elements stood out to you?

13. The novel ends with Elizabeth unable to believe her father culpable in her mother's terrible murder. How did you react to this ending? Why do you think the author chose to leave Elizabeth Hallett's feelings for her father unresolved?

14. Which were the most memorable scenes in *False Mermaid*? What ideas or images stayed in your mind after reading the book, and what were the most interesting bits of insight or information you gained?

15. How does Erin Hart's work fit into the tradition of mystery/crime writing? Are there any authors—past or present—that you would consider similar in style or tone?

Many thanks to Wendy Webb, Marlyn Beebe, Marlys Johnson, and Linda White for their excellent ideas and suggestions.
Go raibh mile maith agaibh!

An Essay from Erin Hart

How to Grow a Book

One question I'm always asked at book chats is: "Do you know how the story ends when you begin writing?"

And my answer is a resounding: "Never."

It's not that I haven't a clue, mind you; I do have theories about whodunit, and why, but I'm wrong more often than I am right. How can that be? you ask . . . Aren't you, as the writer, the creator of your own story, the manipulator of character, the inserter of clues? Well, yes, but . . .

All I can say is that I don't *have* to know how the story ends before I can start. And that's because I write to find things out. For me, the process of writing is similar to what my characters—an archaeologist and a pathologist—go through when they are engaged in an excavation or an autopsy. Writing is an investigation, and I sometimes think it's better if I'm finding things out along with my characters, rather than directing them about what to find, even what to look for.

So what do I need to know in order to begin?

Most of my stories have begun with some actual piece of history: *Haunted Ground* grew from a true story about two farmers cutting turf who came upon the perfectly preserved, severed head of a beautiful red-haired girl. *Lake of Sorrows* sprang from many visits to Ireland's National Museum, perusing displays of mysterious votive offerings—gold jewelry, weapons, and human beings—found in bogs. *False Mermaid* is a bit of a departure, because it digs into the main character's backstory: pathologist Nora Gavin finally returns to Minnesota to tackle her sister's unsolved murder.

I usually also have an idea for setting before I begin. For *Haunted Ground,* I envisioned a seventeenth-century manor with an adjoining ruin of a tower house at the edge of a lake. I wanted to set *Lake of Sorrows* in a place that not many tourists would have seen, the barren-looking industrial bogs of the Irish midlands. It helped that my husband, Paddy, used to work on those very bogs and was full of fascinating details about peat storms and bloodred sunsets that would help color my tale. (It also helped that Paddy's cousin discovered a 2,300-year-old corpse while digging a drain in a bog, just as I was finishing up research for the book. I really couldn't make this stuff up.)

For *False Mermaid,* I knew that the Mississippi River would play a role in the story, because of the themes I wanted to explore.

At the risk of sounding like a major geek, I have to say that theme—the central idea behind the story—is really at the root of what I do. It's the single most important factor driving the plots of my novels. And once again, the writing becomes an investigation of my characters' thoughts and feelings around that central idea.

Haunted Ground grew out of a look back at Irish history, at all the various waves of invasion over the centuries and seeing that the lives of the conquerors and the lives of the people they conquered were far more intertwined than one might at first imagine. Archaeology has been a wonderful metaphor for me. I'm fascinated by the layers of the past that remain directly underfoot, how pieces of the past are constantly intruding into the present.

As William Faulkner once pointed out, "The past isn't dead. Hell, it isn't even past." *Lake of Sorrows* was about pagan sacrifice and exploring the notion that humans have been repeating the same patterns—the same beliefs and behaviors—for thousands of years. How all of us are connected to the past in so many ways we don't even perceive.

So what's the theme in *False Mermaid*? One of the few details I had settled upon in the murder of Nora's sister was that she was killed by several savage blows to the face. In psychological terms, it meant that the killer somehow wanted to destroy her identity. At the time that I decided upon that detail, I wasn't even sure where it might lead. My other strong desire was to somehow connect the murder of Nora's sister with something that lies deep inside us, and that is a strong belief in the otherworld. I'm fascinated by folklore about fairies, mermaids, and selkies, because those stories tell us so much about our fear of changelings, of people who can slip from one personality into another.

I wanted to play with the multiple meanings of the words "true" and "false." There's an awful lot of gray area between what is fact and what is fiction. And when the words "true" and "false" are used about a person, as they are in old traditional songs about true and false lovers, those words take on implications about faithfulness and loyalty. As Nora is exploring her sister's final days, I wanted her to face the possibility that she didn't really know Tríona at all, that the person she discovers at last might be a complex, hybrid creature from mythology, half animal and half human, wild and even dangerous, a disturbing embodiment of the duality that exists in all of us. Even though Nora has suspected her brother-in-law all along, I wanted her to begin to doubt her own convictions about him as well.

And because I'm not satisfied with a single mystery, part of the story is set back in Ireland with Nora's sweetheart, Cormac Maguire. I gave him a historical murder case, the disappearance of a woman many people believed to be a selkie, a seal that could shed its skin and become human. In the folktales, the selkie only retains its human form if someone captures its sealskin; once the skin is returned, the selkie must return to the sea. Cormac comes to believe that the woman who disappeared was not a selkie who returned to the sea, as local stories maintained, but that she may have been murdered by her husband. It's a puzzle that seems unsolvable, since her remains have never been found.

As I write, I find that each of my characters embodies some aspect of the theme, and as the characters themselves develop, their thoughts and actions drive the plot. So that's why I don't know the ending before I arrive there, along with my detectives. As I said, I might have a few pet theories along the way, but I can't really know what will happen until I get to know each of the characters and discover what they might do.

Growing a novel is such an intuitive, organic process for me, every single time.

Fishing for Invitations on *False Mermaid*

An Open Call to Book Clubs from Author Erin Hart

Reading and talking about books has always been one of my favorite pursuits. And as I was thinking of ways to give something back and really engage with readers, it occurred to me that one of the best ways might be to become an even more active participant in book clubs.

Since my first novel (*Haunted Ground* came out in 2003), I've visited dozens of local book clubs—and made contact with even more book club readers across the country with the help of a speaker phone!

It's always a great experience, so with the publication of this trade paperback edition of *False Mermaid,* I wanted to extend a hand to book clubs everywhere. Invite me to your book club and I'll be delighted to join in your discussion. Really.

Monday through Friday, from 7 to 11 p.m. CST, I'll be available to join your book club by phone anywhere in the United States or Canada. (Book clubs should have at least ten members and a speaker phone or a Skype connection.)

Just contact me directly at: mail@erinhart.com

Looking for some suggested discussion questions? Check the back of this book, or look in the Books section of my website (www.erinhart.com), or under the Book Club Resources tab for this title at the Simon & Schuster website (www.simonandschuster.com).

Of course, the published discussion questions are only suggestions—you may have your own. We can also talk about how the novels came about, the landscape and culture of Ireland (especially the bogs and all the riches found there), the road to publication, and lots more.

Looking forward to our chat!

Erin Hart

About the Author

Erin Hart is a Minnesota theater critic and former administrator at the Minnesota State Arts Board. A lifelong interest in Irish traditional music led her to cofound Minnesota's Irish Music and Dance Association. A theater major from St. Olaf College, she has an M.A. in English and Creative Writing from the University of Minnesota, Minneapolis. She and her husband, musician Paddy O'Brien, live in Saint Paul and frequently visit Ireland. Erin Hart was nominated for Agatha and Anthony awards for her debut novel *Haunted Ground,* which won the Friends of American Writers Award in 2004. Her second novel, *Lake of Sorrows,* was a 2004 Minnesota Book Award finalist. Visit her website at www.erinhart.com.